PRAISE FOR
JUST ONE LOOK

"Harlan Coben remains one of the best in the game. . . . It's one of those books in which the main character—and readers—has no real idea what's going on until the very last pages. This is both highly satisfying and enjoyably frustrating, especially when the plot twists are being carefully doled out by a pro like Coben."   —*San Francisco Chronicle*

"It's only when the last page turns that the reader has a chance to breathe, say 'Wow!' and marvel at the impressively interconnected structure."
—*The Miami Herald*

"Coben proves his nimble, knowing grasp of plot and pace, juggling as many as seven plotlines while still imparting a healthy backstory to cameo characters. You'll read it in a day, maybe two; it's fresh fast food in a cup-of-ramen world."   —*Entertainment Weekly*

"Interesting and intricate . . . a gripping tale . . . not for the faint of heart."
—*Pittsburgh Post-Gazette*

"Just as Alfred Hitchcock carved out a niche with films about a seemingly innocent person caught in machinations beyond comprehension, Harlan Coben is earning a reputation for creating the literary equivalent . . . imaginative. . . . *Just One Look* takes an unpredictable route as the author leads the reader on a merry chase . . . delivers more than its share of thrills and keeps us engrossed by the strong characters and the fast-clipped plot. . . . Hitchcock would be envious."   —*South Florida Sun-Sentinel*

continued . . .

"A heck of a ride. . . . Grace enters a world of menace made gripping by Coben's ability to write audaciously terrifying action scenes."
—*New York Daily News*

"Provocative."
—*Seattle Post-Intelligencer*

"Drops a suburban mother into a terrifying hunt through her husband's past."
—*The Washington Post Book World*

"A nifty suspense premise. . . . [Coben] does a good job of riveting the reader."
—*The New York Times*

"There was no way I was going to put this book down until I found out everything. Harlan Coben will do that to you."
—*St. Petersburg Times*

"[Coben has a] diabolical ingenuity for seemingly endless plot twists."
—*Houston Chronicle*

"Well-written and compelling . . . a terrific mystery . . . *Just One Look* opens up—over many pages—like an elegantly constructed puzzle box."
—*San Jose Mercury News*

"A yarn so bizarre that you're willing to shelve your sleep for one weekend . . . wild."
—*Rockford Register Star* (Rockford, IL)

"With each thriller, Coben just gets better and better. His latest is terrifying on several levels, offering so many questions with intricate and complex answers. The pages fly until the last piece of the puzzle falls neatly into place. Just one look, and you will be hooked."
—*Library Journal*

HARLAN COBEN

JUST ONE LOOK

NEW AMERICAN LIBRARY

NEW AMERICAN LIBRARY
Published by New American Library,
a division of Penguin Group (USA) Inc.,
375 Hudson Street, New York, New York 10014, USA
Penguin Group (Canada), 90 Eglinton Avenue East, Suite 700, Toronto,
Ontario M4P 2Y3, Canada (a division of Pearson Penguin Canada Inc.)
Penguin Books Ltd., 80 Strand, London WC2R 0RL, England
Penguin Ireland, 25 St. Stephen's Green, Dublin 2,
Ireland (a division of Penguin Books Ltd.)
Penguin Group (Australia), 250 Camberwell Road, Camberwell,
Victoria 3124, Australia (a division of Pearson Australia Group Pty. Ltd.)
Penguin Books India Pvt. Ltd., 11 Community Centre,
Panchsheel Park, New Delhi - 110 017, India
Penguin Group (NZ), 67 Apollo Drive, Rosedale, Auckland 0632,
New Zealand (a division of Pearson New Zealand Ltd.)
Penguin Books (South Africa) (Pty.) Ltd., 24 Sturdee Avenue,
Rosebank, Johannesburg 2196, South Africa

Penguin Books Ltd., Registered Offices:
80 Strand, London WC2R 0RL, England

Published by New American Library, a division of Penguin Group (USA) Inc. Previously
published in a Dutton hardcover edition and a Signet mass market edition.

First New American Library Printing, September 2011
1   3   5   7   9   10   8   6   4   2

This book is for Jack Armstrong,
because he's one of the good guys.

ACKNOWLEDGMENTS

The author wishes to thank the following for their technical expertise: Mitchell F. Reiter, MD, Chief, Division of Spine Surgery, UMDNJ (aka "Cuz"); David A. Gold, MD; Christopher J. Christie, United States attorney for the state of New Jersey; Captain Keith Killion of the Ridgewood Police Department; Steven Miller, MD, Director of Pediatric Emergency Medicine, Children's Hospital of New York Presbyterian; John Elias; Anthony Dellapelle (the nonfictional one); Jennifer van Dam; Linda Fairstein; and Craig Coben (aka "Bro"). As always, if there are errors, technical or otherwise, the fault is with these people. I'm tired of being the fall guy.

A nod of gratitude to Carole Baron, Mitch Hoffman, Lisa Johnson, and all at Dutton and Penguin Group USA; Jon Woods, Malcolm Edwards, Susan Lamb, Juliet Ewers, Nicky Jeanes, Emma Noble and the gang at Orion; Aaron Priest, Lisa Erbach Vance, Bryant and Hil (for helping me over that first hump), Mike and Taylor (for helping me over the second one), and Maggie Griffin.

Characters in this book may share a name with people I know, but they are still completely fictional. In fact, this entire novel is a work of fiction. That means I make stuff up.

A special thanks to Charlotte Coben for Emma's poems. All rights reserved, as they say.

"Babe, give me your best memory,
But it don't equal pale ink."

———

—*Chinese proverb adapted for lyrics in the song*
"Pale Ink" by the Jimmy X Band

JUST ONE LOOK

cott Duncan sat across from the killer.

The windowless room of thundercloud gray was awkward and still, stuck in that lull when the music first starts and neither stranger is sure how to begin the dance. Scott tried a noncommittal nod. The killer, decked out in prison-issue orange, simply stared. Scott folded his hands and put them on the metal table. The killer—his file said he was Monte Scanlon, but there was no way that was his real name—might have done likewise had his hands not been cuffed.

Why, Scott wondered yet again, am I here?

His specialty was prosecuting corrupt politicians—something of a vigorous cottage industry in his home state of New Jersey—but three hours ago, Monte Scanlon, a mass executioner by any standards, had finally broken his silence to make a demand.

That demand?

A private meeting with Assistant U.S. Attorney Scott Duncan.

This was strange for a large variety of reasons, but here were two: one, a killer should not be in a position to make demands; two, Scott had never met or even heard of Monte Scanlon.

Scott broke the silence. "You asked to see me?"

"Yes."

2 · HARLAN COBEN

Scott nodded, waited for him to say more. He didn't. "So what can I do for you?"

Monte Scanlon maintained the stare. "Do you know why I'm here?"

Scott glanced around the room. Besides Scanlon and himself, four people were present. Linda Morgan, the United States attorney, leaned against the back wall trying to give off the ease of Sinatra against a lamppost. Standing behind the prisoner were two beefy, nearly identical prison guards with tree-stump arms and chests like antique armoires. Scott had met the two cocky agents before, had seen them go about their tasks with the sereneness of yoga instructors. But today, with this well-shackled prisoner, even these guys were on edge. Scanlon's lawyer, a ferret reeking of checkout-counter cologne, rounded out the group. All eyes were on Scott.

"You killed people," Scott answered. "Lots of them."

"I was what is commonly called a hit man. I was"—Scanlon paused—"an assassin for hire."

"On cases that don't involve me."

"True."

Scott's morning had started off normal enough. He'd been drafting a subpoena on a waste-disposal executive who was paying off a small-town mayor. Routine matter. Everyday graft in the Garden State of New Jersey. That had been, what, an hour, an hour and a half ago? Now he sat across the bolted-down table from a man who had murdered—according to Linda Morgan's rough estimate—one hundred people.

"So why did you ask for me?"

Scanlon looked like an aging playboy who might have squired a Gabor sister in the fifties. He was small, wizened even. His graying hair was slicked back, his teeth cigarette yellow, his skin leathery from midday sun and too many long nights in too many dark clubs. No one in the room knew his real name. When captured, his passport read Monte Scanlon, an Argentinean national, age fifty-one. The age seemed about right, but that would be about it. His fingerprints had not popped up in the NCIC computer banks. Facial recognition software had come up with a big goose egg.

"We need to speak alone."

"This is not my case," Scott said again. "There's a U.S. attorney assigned to you."

"This has nothing to do with her."

"And it does with me?"

Scanlon leaned forward. "What I'm about to tell you," he said, "will change your entire life."

Part of Scott wanted to wiggle his fingers in Scanlon's face and say, "Ooooo." He was used to the captured criminal mind-set—their serpentine maneuverings, their quest for an edge, their search for a way out, their overblown sense of importance. Linda Morgan, perhaps sensing his thoughts, shot a warning glare across his bow. Monte Scanlon, she'd told him, had worked for various connected families for the better part of thirty years. RICO hungered for his cooperation in a starving-man-near-a-buffet way. Since his capture, Scanlon had refused to talk. Until this morning.

So here Scott was.

"Your boss," Scanlon said, gesturing with his chin at Linda Morgan, "she hopes for my cooperation."

"You're going to get the needle," Morgan responded, still trying to give off the scent of nonchalance. "Nothing you say or do will change that."

Scanlon smiled. "Please. You fear losing what I have to say much greater than I fear death."

"Right. Another tough guy who doesn't fear death." She peeled herself off the wall. "Know what, Monte? The tough guys are always the ones who soil their pants when we strap them to the gurney."

Again Scott fought off the desire to wiggle his fingers, this time at his boss. Scanlon kept smiling. His eyes never left Scott's. Scott didn't like what he saw. Scanlon's eyes were, as one would expect, black and shiny and cruel. But—and Scott might have been imagining things—maybe he saw something else there. Something beyond the standard vacancy. There seemed to be a pleading in the eyes; Scott couldn't turn away from them. There was regret there maybe.

Remorse even.

Scott looked up at Linda and nodded. She frowned, but Scanlon had called her bluff. She touched one of the beefy guards on the shoulder and gestured for them to leave. Rising from his seat, Scanlon's lawyer spoke for the first time. "Anything he says is off the record."

"Stay with them," Scanlon ordered. "I want you to make sure that they don't listen in."

The lawyer picked up his briefcase and followed Linda Morgan to the door. Soon Scott and Scanlon were alone. In the movies, killers are omnipotent. In real life, they are not. They don't escape from handcuffs in the middle of a high-security federal penitentiary. The Beef Brothers, Scott knew, would be behind the one-way glass. The intercom, per Scanlon's instructions, would be off. But they'd all be watching.

Scott shrugged a *well?* at him.

"I am not your typical assassin for hire."

"Uh-huh."

"I have rules."

Scott waited.

"For example, I only kill men."

"Wow," Scott said. "You're a prince."

Scanlon ignored the sarcasm. "That is my first rule. I kill only men. No women."

"Right. Tell me, does rule two have anything to do with not putting out until the third date?"

"You think I'm a monster?"

Scott shrugged as if the answer was obvious.

"You don't respect my rules?"

"What rules? You kill people. You make up these so-called rules because you need the illusion of being human."

Scanlon seemed to consider that. "Perhaps," he allowed, "but the men I've killed were scum. I was hired by scum to kill scum. I am no more than a weapon."

"A weapon?" Scott repeated.

"Yes."

"A weapon doesn't care who it kills, Monte. Men, women, grannies, little kids. A weapon doesn't differentiate."

Scanlon smiled. "Touché."

Scott rubbed his palms on his pant legs. "You didn't call me here for an ethics class. What do you want?"

"You're divorced, aren't you, Scott?"

He said nothing.

"No children, amicable split, still friendly with the ex."

"What do you want?"

"To explain."

"To explain what?"

He lowered his eyes but only for a moment. "What I did to you."

"I don't even know you."

"But I know you. I've known you for a long time."

Scott let the silence in. He glanced at the mirror. Linda Morgan would be behind the glass, wondering what they were talking about. She wanted information. He wondered if they had the room bugged. Probably. Either way, it would pay to keep Scanlon talking.

"You are Scott Duncan. Thirty-nine years old. You graduated from Columbia Law School. You could be making a great deal more money in private practice, but that bores you. You've been with the U.S. attorney's office six months. Your mother and father moved to Miami last year. You had a sister, but she died in college."

Scott shifted in his seat. Scanlon studied him.

"You finished?"

"Do you know how my business operates?"

Change of subject. Scott waited a beat. Scanlon was playing a head game, trying to keep him off-balance or some such nonsense. Scott was not about to fall for it. Nothing he had "revealed" about Scott's family was surprising. A person could pick up most of that info with a few well-placed keystrokes and phone calls.

"Why don't you tell me?" Scott said.

"Let's pretend," Scanlon began, "that you wanted someone dead."

"Okay."

"You would contact a friend, who knows a friend, who knows a friend, who can reach me."

"And only that last friend would know you?"

"Something like that. I had only one go-between man, but I was careful even with him. We never met face-to-face. We used code names. The payments always went to offshore accounts. I would open a new account for every, shall we say, transaction, and I closed it as soon as the transaction was completed. You still with me?"

"It's not that complicated," Scott said.

"No, I guess not. But you see, nowadays we communicate by e-mail. I'll set up a temporary e-mail account with Hotmail or Yahoo! or whatever, with fake names. Nothing that can be traced back. But even if it could, even if you could find out who sent it, where would it lead you? All e-mails were sent and read at libraries or public places. We were totally covered."

Scott was about to mention that this total coverage had eventually landed Scanlon's ass in jail, but he decided to save it. "What does this have to do with me?"

"I'm getting to that." Scott could see that Scanlon was warming up to his own tale. "In the old days—when I say old days, I mean, eight, ten years ago—we did it mostly with pay phones. I'd never see the name written. The guy would just tell me over the phone."

Scanlon stopped and made sure that he had Scott's full attention.

His tone softened a bit, became less matter-of-fact. "That's the key, Scott. It was by phone. I'd only hear the name on the phone, not see it."

He looked at Scott expectantly. Scott had no idea what he was trying to say, so he went, "Uh-huh."

"Do you understand why I'm stressing that it was done by phone?"

"No."

"Because a person like me, a person with rules, could make a mistake with the phone."

Scott thought about that. "I still don't get it."

"I never kill women. That was rule number one."

"So you said."

"So if you wanted to put a hit on someone named Billy Smith, I'd figure Billy was a man. You know, with a *y*. I'd never think Billy would be a woman. With an *ie* at the end. You understand?"

Scott went very still. Scanlon saw it. He dropped the smile. His voice was very soft.

"We talked before about your sister, didn't we, Scott?"

Scott did not respond.

"Her name was Geri—am I right?"

Silence.

"You see the problem, Scott? Geri is one of those names. If you heard it on the phone, you'd assume it would be with a *j* in the front and a *y* at the end. So fifteen years ago, I got a phone call. From that go-between man I told you about. . . ."

Scott shook his head.

"I was given an address. I was told exactly what time 'Jerry' "— Scanlon made quote marks with his fingers—"would be home."

Scott's own voice seemed to come from very far away. "It was ruled an accident."

"Most arsons are, if you know what you're doing."

"I don't believe you."

But Scott looked at the eyes again and felt his world teeter. The images flooded in: Geri's contagious smile, the unruly hair, the braces, the way she stuck her tongue out at him during family gatherings. He remembered her first real boyfriend (a dork named Brad), her not getting a date to the junior prom, the gung-ho speech she made when she ran for student council treasurer, her first rock band (they were awful), her college acceptance letter.

Scott felt his eyes well up. "She was only twenty-one."

No response.

"Why?"

"I don't get into the whys, Scott. I'm just a hired hand—"

"No, not that." Scott looked up. "Why are you telling me this now?"

Scanlon studied his reflection in the mirror. His voice was very quiet. "Maybe you were right."

"Right about what?"

"What you said before." He turned back toward Scott. "Maybe after all is said and done, I need the illusion of being human."

THREE MONTHS LATER

CHAPTER 1

There are sudden rips. There are tears in your life, deep knife wounds that slash through your flesh. Your life is one thing; then it is shredded into another. It comes apart as though gutted in a belly slit. And then there are those moments when your life simply unravels. A loose thread pulled. A seam gives way. The change is slow at first, nearly imperceptible.

For Grace Lawson, the unraveling began at the Fotomat.

She was about to enter the photo-developing shop when she heard a somewhat familiar voice. "Why don't you get a digital camera, Grace?"

Grace turned toward the woman. "I'm not good with that techno stuff."

"Oh, come now. Digital technology is a snap." The woman raised her hand and actually snapped, just in case Grace didn't know what the word meant. "And digital cameras are sooo much more convenient than conventional cameras. You just erase the photos you don't want. Like computer files. For our Christmas card? Barry, well, he must have taken a zillion pictures of the kids, you know, snapping away because Blake blinked or Kyle was looking the wrong way, whatever, but when you shoot that many, well, like Barry says, you're going to get one that's pretty decent—am I right?"

Grace nodded. She was trying to unearth the woman's name, but it wouldn't surface. The woman's daughter—Blake, was it?—was in Grace's son's class in first grade. Or maybe it was last year in kindergarten. Hard to keep track. Grace kept the smile frozen to her face. The woman was nice enough, but she blended in with the others. Grace wondered, not for the first time, if she was blending in too, if her once great individuality had joined the unpleasant swirl of suburban uniformity.

The thought was not a comforting one.

The woman kept describing the wonders of the digital age. Grace's frozen smile began to ache. She glanced at her watch, hoping Tech Mom would pick up the hint. Two forty-five. Almost time to pick up Max at school. Emma had swim team practice, but another mom was driving the car pool today. A car *pool* to the *pool*, as the too-jolly mother had reminded Grace with a little tee-hee. Yeah, funny stuff.

"We have to get together," the woman said, winding down. "With Jack and Barry. I think they'd get along."

"Definitely."

Grace took advantage of the pause to wave good-bye, pull open the door, and disappear inside the Fotomat. The glass door closed with a snap, ringing a little bell. The chemical smell, not unlike model glue, hit her first. She wondered about the long-term effects of working in such an environment and decided the short-term ones were annoying enough.

The kid working—Grace's use of the term *working* being overly generous here—behind the counter had a white fuzz pellet under his chin, hair dyed a color that'd intimidate Crayola, and enough piercings to double as a wind instrument. A pair of those wrap-around-low headphones snaked around the back of his neck. The music was so loud that Grace could feel it in her chest. He had tattoos, lots of them. One read STONE. Another read KILLJOY. Grace thought that a third should read SLACKER.

"Excuse me?"

He did not look up.

"Excuse me?" she said a little louder.

Still nothing.

"Yah, like, dude?"

That got his attention. He snarled, narrowed his eyes, offended by the interruption. He removed the headphones but grudgingly. "Stub."

"Pardon me?"

"Stub."

Ah. Grace handed him the receipt. Fuzz Pellet then asked her for her name. This reminded Grace of those damn customer service phones that ask you to dial in your home phone, and then as soon as you get a real live person, they ask you for the same phone number. Like the first request was just for practice.

Fuzz Pellet—Grace was warming up to this nickname—flipped through a file of photo packets before extracting one. He ripped off the tag and told her an exorbitant price. She handed him a Val-Pak coupon, one dug out of her purse in an excavation that rivaled the search for the Dead Sea Scrolls, and watched the price drop to something closer to reasonable.

He handed her the packet of photographs. Grace thanked him, but he already had the music plugged back into his cerebrum. She waved in his direction. "I come not for the pictures," Grace said, "but for the sparkling repartee."

Fuzz Pellet yawned and picked up his magazine. The latest issue of *Modern Slacker*.

Grace hit the sidewalk. The weather was brisk. Autumn had shoved summer aside with a patented gust. The leaves hadn't really started turning yet, but the air had that apple cider quality to it. The shop windows had started up with the Halloween decorations. Emma, her third grader, had convinced Jack to buy an eight-foot blow-up Homer-

Simpson-as-Frankenstein balloon. It looked, she had to admit, terrific. Her children liked *The Simpsons*, which meant that maybe, despite their best efforts, she and Jack were raising them right.

Grace wanted to slit open the envelope now. There was always an excitement with a newly developed roll of film, an opening-a-gift expectation, a hurry-to-the-mailbox-even-though-it's-always-bills rush that digital photography, for all its conveniences, could never duplicate. But there wasn't time before school let out.

As her Saab climbed up Heights Road, she took a small detour so that she could pass the town's lookout. From here, the skyline of Manhattan, especially at night, lay spread out like diamonds on black velvet. The longing tugged at her. She loved New York City. Until four years ago, that wonderful island had been their home. They'd had a loft on Charles Street down in the Village. Jack worked on medical research for a large pharmaceutical company. She painted in her home studio while scoffing at her suburban counterparts and their SUVs and corduroy pants and toddler-referencing dialogues. Now she was one of them.

Grace parked behind the school with the other mothers. She turned the engine off, picked up the Fotomat envelope, and ripped it open. The roll was from last week's annual trip to Chester for apple picking. Jack had snapped away. He liked being the family photographer. He considered it paternal work, taking the photos, as if this was a sacrifice a father was supposed to make for his family.

The first image was of Emma, their eight-year-old daughter, and Max, their six-year-old son, on the hayride, shoulders hunched, their cheeks reddened by wind. Grace stopped and stared for a moment. Feelings of, yes, maternal warmth, both primitive and evolutionary, rocked her back. That was the thing with kids. It was the little things that got to you. She remembered that it had been cold that day. The orchard, she'd known, would be too crowded. She had not wanted to go. Now, looking at this photograph, she wondered about the idiocy of her priorities.

The other mothers were gathering by the school fence, making small talk and planning playdates. It was, of course, the modern era, post-feminist America, and yet, of the roughly eighty parents waiting for their charges, only two were male. One, she knew, was a father who'd been laid off for more than a year. You could see it in his eyes, his slow shuffle, the missed spots when he shaved. The other guy was a stay-at-home journalist who always seemed a little too anxious to chat up the moms. Lonely maybe. Or something else.

Someone knocked on the car window. Grace looked up. Cora Lindley, her best friend in town, signaled for her to unlock the door. Grace did. Cora slid into the passenger's seat next to her.

"So how did the date go last night?" Grace asked.

"Poorly."

"Sorry."

"Fifth-date syndrome."

Cora was a divorcée, a little too sexy for the nervous, ever-protective "ladies who lunch." Clad in a low-cut leopard-print blouse with spandex pants and pink pumps, Cora most assuredly did not fit in with the stream of khakis and loose sweaters. The other mothers eyed her with suspicion. Adult suburbia can be a lot like high school.

"What's fifth-date syndrome?" Grace asked.

"You're not dating much, are you?"

"Well, no," Grace said. "The husband and two kids have really cramped my style."

"Pity. See—and don't ask me why—but on the fifth date, the guys always raise the subject . . . how should I word this delicately? . . . of a ménage à trois."

"Please tell me you're joking."

"I joke with you not. Fifth date. At the latest. The guy asks me, on a purely theoretical basis, what my opinion is on ménage à trois. Like it's peace in the Middle East."

"What do you say?"

"That I usually enjoy them, especially when the two men start French-kissing."

Grace laughed and they both got out of the car. Grace's bad leg ached. After more than a decade, she shouldn't be self-conscious about it anymore, but Grace still hated for people to see the limp. She stayed by the car and watched Cora walk away. When the bell rang, the kids burst out as if they'd been fired from a cannon. Like every other parent, Grace only had eyes for her own. The rest of the pack, uncharitable as this might sound, was scenery.

Max emerged in the second exodus. When Grace saw her son— one sneaker lace untied, his Yu-Gi-Oh! backpack looking four sizes too big, his New York Rangers knit hat tilted to the side like a tourist's beret—the warmth rushed over her anew. Max made his way down the stairs, adjusting the backpack up his shoulders. She smiled. Max spotted her and smiled back.

He hopped in the back of the Saab. Grace strapped him into the booster seat and asked him how his day was. Max answered that he didn't know. She asked him what he did in school that day. Max answered that he didn't know. Did he learn math, English, science, arts and crafts? Answer: shrug and dunno. Grace nodded. A classic case of the epidemic known as Elementary School Alzheimer's. Were the kids drugged to forget or sworn to secrecy? One of life's mysteries.

It was not until after she got home and gave Max his Go-Gurt snack—think yogurt in a toothpaste-like squeeze tube—that Grace had the chance to take a look at the rest of the photographs.

The message light on the answering machine was blinking. One message. She checked the caller ID and saw that the number was blocked. She pressed PLAY and was surprised. The voice belonged to an old . . . friend, she guessed. Acquaintance was too casual. Father figure was probably more accurate, but only in the most bizarre sense.

"Hi, Grace. It's Carl Vespa."

He did not have to say his name. It had been years, but she'd always know the voice.

"Could you give me a call when you have the chance? I need to talk to you about something."

The message beeped again. Grace did not move, but she felt an old fluttering in her belly. Vespa. Carl Vespa had called. This could not be good. Carl Vespa, for all his kindnesses to her, was not one for idle chit-chat. She debated calling him back and decided for the time being against it.

Grace moved into the spare bedroom that had become her make-shift studio. When she was painting well—when she was, like any artist or athlete, "in the zone"—she saw the world as if preparing to put it on canvas. She would look at the streets, the trees, the people and imagine the type of brush she would use, the stroke, the mix of colors, the differ-ing lights and casts of shadows. Her work should reflect what she wanted, not reality. That was how she looked at art. We all see the world through our own prism, of course. The best art tweaked reality to show the artist's world, what she saw or, more precisely, what she wanted others to see. It was not always a more beautiful reality. It was often more provocative, uglier maybe, more gripping and magnetic. Grace wanted a reaction. You might enjoy a beautiful setting sun—but Grace wanted you immersed in her sunset, afraid to turn away from it, afraid not to.

Grace had spent the extra dollar and ordered a second set of prints. Her fingers dipped into the envelope and plucked out the photographs. The first two were the ones of Emma and Max on the hayride. Next came Max with his arm stretched up to pick a Gala apple. There was the compulsory blurry shot of flesh, the one where Jack's hand had slipped too close to the lens. She smiled and shook her head. Her big doofus. There were several more shots of Grace and the children with a variety of apples, trees, baskets. Her eyes grew moist, the way they always did when she looked at photographs of her children.

Grace's own parents had died young. Her mother was killed when a semi crossed the divide on Route 46 in Totowa. Grace, an only child, was eleven at the time. The police did not come to the door like in the movies. Her father had learned what happened from a phone call. Grace still remembered the way her father, wearing blue slacks and a gray sweater-vest, had answered the phone with his customary musical hello, how his face had drained of color, how he suddenly collapsed to the floor, his sobs first strangled and then silent, as if he could not gather enough air to express his anguish.

Grace's father raised her until his heart, weakened from a child-hood bout of rheumatic fever, gave out during Grace's freshman year of college. An uncle out in Los Angeles volunteered to take her in, but Grace was of age by then. She decided to stay east and make her own way.

The deaths of her parents had been devastating, of course, but they had also given Grace's life a strange sense of urgency. There is a left-behind poignancy for the living. Those deaths added amplification to the mundane. She wanted to jam in the memories, get her fill of the life moments and—morbid as it sounds—make sure her kids had plenty to remember her by when she too was no more.

It was at that moment—thinking about her own parents, thinking about how much older Emma and Max looked now than in last year's apple-picking photo shoot—when she stumbled across the bizarre photograph.

Grace frowned.

The picture was near the middle of the pack. Closer to the back maybe. It was the same size, fitting neatly in with the others, though the backing sheet was somewhat flimsier. Cheaper stock, she thought. Like a high-end office-supply photocopy maybe.

Grace checked the next picture. No duplicate this time. That was strange. Only one copy of this photograph. She thought about that. The picture must have fallen in somehow, mixed up with another roll.

Because this photograph did not belong to her.

It was a mistake. That was the obvious explanation. Think for a moment about the quality workmanship of, say, Fuzz Pellet. He was more than capable of screwing up, right? Of putting the wrong photograph in the middle of her pack?

That was probably what was going on here.

Someone else's photograph had gotten mixed in with hers.

Or maybe . . .

The photograph had an old look about it—not that it was black-and-white or antique sepia. Nothing like that. The print was in color, but the hues seemed . . . off somehow—saturated, sun-faded, lacking the vibrancy one would expect in this day and age. The people in it too. Their clothes, their hair, their makeup—all dated. From fifteen, maybe twenty years ago.

Grace put it down on the table to take a closer look.

The images in the photograph were all slightly blurred. There were four people—no, wait, one more in the corner—five people in the photograph. There were two men and three women, all in their late teens, early twenties maybe—at least, the ones she could see clearly enough appeared to be around that age.

College students, Grace thought.

They had the jeans, the sweatshirts, the unkempt hair, that attitude, the casual stance of budding independence. The picture looked as if it'd been snapped when the subjects were not quite ready, in midgather. Some of the heads were turned so you only saw a profile. One dark-haired girl, on the very right edge of the photo, you could only see the back of her head, really, and a denim jacket. Next to her there was another girl, this one with flaming-red hair and eyes spaced wide apart.

Near the middle, one girl, a blonde, had—God, what the hell was that about?—her face had a giant X across it. Like someone had crossed her out.

How had this picture . . . ?

As Grace kept staring, she felt a small ping in the center of her chest. The three women—she didn't recognize them. The two men looked somewhat alike, same size, same hair, same attitude. The guy on the far left too was not someone she knew.

She was sure, however, that she recognized the other man. Or boy. He wasn't really old enough to be called a man. Old enough to join the army? Sure. Old enough to be called a man? He was standing in the middle, next to the blonde with the X through her face. . . .

But it couldn't be. His head was in midturn for one thing. That adolescent thin beard covered too much of his face. . . .

Was it her husband?

Grace bent closer. It was, at best, a profile shot. She hadn't known Jack when he was this young. They had met thirteen years ago on a beach in the Côte d'Azur in southern France. After more than a year of surgery and physical therapy, Grace was still not all the way back. The headaches and memory loss remained. She had the limp—still had it now—but with all the publicity and attention from that tragic night still suffocating her, Grace had just wanted to get away for a while. She matriculated at the University of Paris, studying art in earnest. It was while on break, lying in the sun on the Côte d'Azur, that she met Jack for the first time.

Was she sure it was Jack?

He looked different here, no doubt about it. His hair was a lot longer. He had this beard, though he was still too young and baby-faced for it to come in full. He wore glasses. But there was something in the way he stood, the tilt of his head, the expression.

This was her husband.

She quickly sifted through the rest of the roll. There were more hayrides, more apples, more arms raised in midpick. She saw one that she'd taken of Jack, the one time he'd let her have the camera, control freak that he was. He was reaching so high, his shirt had moved up enough to show his belly. Emma had told him that it was eeuw, gross.

That, of course, made Jack pull up the shirt more. Grace had laughed. "Work it, baby!" she'd said, snapping the next photo. Jack, much to Emma's ultimate mortification, obliged and undulated.

"Mom?"

She turned. "What's up, Max?"

"Can I have a granola bar?"

"Let's grab one for the car," she said, rising. "We need to take a ride."

Fuzz Pellet was not at the Fotomat.

Max checked out the various themed picture frames—"Happy Birthday," "We Love You, Mom," that kind of thing. The man behind the counter, resplendent in a polyester tie, pocket protector, and short-sleeve dress shirt flimsy enough to see the V-neck tee beneath it, wore a name tag that informed one and all that he, Bruce, was an assistant manager.

"May I help you?"

"I'm looking for the young man who was here a couple of hours ago," Grace said.

"Josh is gone for the day. Something I can do for you?"

"I picked up a roll of film a little before three o'clock. . . ."

"Yes?"

Grace had no idea how to put this. "There was a photo in there that shouldn't have been."

"I'm not sure I understand."

"One of the pictures. I didn't take it."

He gestured toward Max. "I see you have young children."

"Excuse me?"

Assistant Manager Bruce pushed his glasses up off the end of his nose. "I was just pointing out that you have young children. Or at least, one young child."

"What does that have to do with anything?"

"Sometimes a child picks up the camera. When the parent isn't looking. They snap a picture or two. Then they put the camera back."

"No, it's not that. This picture had nothing to do with us."

"I see. Well, I'm sorry for the inconvenience. Did you get all the photos you took?"

"I think so."

"None were missing?"

"I really didn't check that closely, but I think we got them all."

He opened a drawer. "Here. This is a coupon. Your next roll will be developed for free. Three by fives. If you want the four by sixes, there is a small surcharge."

Grace ignored his outstretched hand. "The sign on the door says you develop all the pictures on-site."

"That's right." He petted the large machine behind him. "Old Betsy here does the job for us."

"So my roll would have been developed here?"

"Of course."

Grace handed him the Fotomat envelope. "Could you tell me who developed this roll?"

"I'm sure it was just an honest error."

"I'm not saying it wasn't. I just want to know who developed my roll."

He took a look at the envelope. "May I ask why you want to know?"

"Was it Josh?"

"Yes, but—"

"Why did he leave?"

"Pardon me?"

"I picked up the photos a little before three o'clock. You close at six. It's nearly five now."

"So?"

"It seems strange that a shift would end between three and six for a store that closes at six."

Assistant Manager Bruce straightened up a bit. "Josh had a family emergency."

"What kind of emergency?"

"Look, Miss . . ."—he checked the envelope—"Lawson, I'm sorry for the error and inconvenience. I'm sure a photograph from another set fell into your packet. I can't recall it happening before, but none of us are perfect. Oh, wait."

"What?"

"May I see the photograph in question please?"

Grace was afraid he'd want to keep it. "I didn't bring it," she lied.

"What was it a picture of?"

"A group of people."

He nodded. "I see. And were these people naked?"

"What? No. Why would you ask that?"

"You seem upset. I assumed that the photograph was in some way offensive."

"No, nothing like that. I just need to speak to Josh. Could you tell me his last name or give me a home phone number?"

"Out of the question. But he'll be in tomorrow first thing. You can talk to him then."

Grace chose not to protest. She thanked the man and left. Might be better anyway, she thought. By driving here she had merely reacted. Check that. She had probably overreacted.

Jack would be home in a few hours. She would ask him about it then.

Grace had homebound car pool duties for the swim practice. Four girls, ages eight and nine, all delightfully energetic, piled two into the backseat and two into the "way, way" back of the minivan. There was a swirl of giggles, of "Hello, Ms. Lawson," wet hair, the gentle perfume of both YMCA chlorine and bubble gum, the sound of backpacks being shucked off, of seat belts fastening. No child sat in the front—new safety rules—but despite the chauffeur feel, or maybe because of it, Grace liked doing car pool. It was time spent seeing her child interact with her friends. Children spoke freely during car pool; the driving adult might as well have been in another time zone. A parent could learn much. You could find out who was cool, who was not, who was in, who was out, what teacher was totally rad, what teacher was most assuredly not. You could, if you listened closely enough, decipher where on the pecking order your child was currently perched.

It was also entertaining as all get-out.

Jack was working late again, so when they got home, Grace quickly made Max and Emma dinner—veggie chicken nuggets (purportedly healthier and, once dipped in ketchup, the kids can never tell the difference), Tater Tots, and Jolly Green Giant frozen corn. Grace peeled two oranges for dessert. Emma did her homework—too big a load for an eight-year-old, Grace thought. When she had a free second, Grace headed down the hallway and flipped on the computer.

Grace might not be into digital photography, but she understood the necessity and even advantages of computer graphics and the World Wide Web. There was a site that featured her work, how to buy it, how to commission a portrait. At first, this had hit her as too much like shilling, but as Farley, her agent, reminded her, Michelangelo painted for money and on commission. So did da Vinci and Raphael and pretty much every great artist the world has ever known. Who was she to be above it?

Grace scanned in her three favorite apple-picking photos for safekeeping and then, more on a whim than anything else, she decided to scan in the strange photograph too. That done, she started bathing the children. Emma went first. She was just getting out of the tub when Grace heard Jack's keys jangle in the back door.

"Hey," Jack called up in a whisper. "Any hot love monkeys up there waiting for their stud muffin?"

"Children," she said. "Children are still awake."

"Oh."

"Care to join us?"

Jack bounded up the stairs, taking them two at a time. The house shook from the onslaught. He was a big man, six-two, two-ten. She loved the substance of him sleeping beside her, the rise and fall of his chest, the manly smell of him, the soft hairs on his body, the way his arm snaked around her during the night, the feeling of not only intimacy but safety. He made her feel small and protected, and maybe it was un-PC, but she liked that.

Emma said, "Hi, Daddy."

"Hey, Kitten, how was school?"

"Good."

"Still have a crush on that Tony boy?"

"Eeuw!"

Satisfied with the reaction, Jack kissed Grace on the cheek. Max came out of his room, stark naked.

"Ready for your bath, mah man?" Jack asked.

"Ready," Max said.

They high-fived. Jack scooped Max up in a sea of giggles. Grace helped Emma get in her pajamas. Laughter spilled from the bath. Jack was singing a rhyming song with Max where some girl named Jenny Jenkins couldn't decide what color to wear. Jack would start off with the color and Max filled in the rhyme line. Right now they were singing that Jenny Jenkins couldn't wear "yellow" because she'd look like a "fellow." Then they both cracked up anew. They did pretty much the same rhymes every night. And they laughed their asses off over them every night.

Jack toweled Max off, got him into his pajamas, and put him to bed. He read two chapters of *Charlie and the Chocolate Factory*. Max listened to every word, totally riveted. Emma was old enough to read by herself. She lay in her bed, devouring the latest tale of the Baudelaire orphans from Lemony Snicket. Grace sat with her and sketched for half an hour. This was her favorite time of the day—working in silence in the same room as her elder child.

When Jack finished, Max begged for just one more page. Jack stayed firm. It was getting late, he said. Max grudgingly acquiesced. They talked for another moment or two about Charlie's impending visit to Willy Wonka's factory. Grace listened in.

Roald Dahl, both her men agreed, totally rocked.

Jack turned down the lights—they had a dimmer switch because Max didn't like complete darkness—and then he entered into Emma's room. He bent down to give Emma a kiss good night. Emma, a total daddy's girl, reached up, grabbed his neck, and wouldn't let him go. Jack melted at Emma's nightly technique for both showing affection and stalling going to sleep.

"Anything new for the journal?" Jack asked.

Emma nodded. Her backpack was next to her bed. She dug through it and produced her school journal. She turned the pages and handed it to her father.

"We're doing poetry," Emma said. "I started one today."

"Cool. Want to read it?"

Emma's face was aglow. So was Jack's. She cleared her throat and began:

> "Basketball, basketball,
> Why are you so round?
> So perfectly bumpy,
> So amazingly brown.
> Tennis ball, tennis ball,
> Why are you so fizzy,
> When you're hit with a racket,
> Do you feel kind of dizzy?"

Grace watched the scene from the doorway. Jack's hours had gotten bad lately. Most of the time Grace didn't mind. Quiet moments were becoming scarce. She needed the solace. Loneliness, the precursor to boredom, is conducive to the creative process. That was what artistic meditation was all about—boring yourself to the point where inspiration must emerge if only to preserve your sanity. A writer friend once explained that the best cure for writer's block was to read a phone book. Bore yourself enough and the Muse will be obligated to push through the most slog-filled of arteries.

When Emma was done, Jack fell back and said, "Whoa."

Emma made the face she makes when she's proud of herself but doesn't want to show it. She tucks her lips over and back under her teeth.

"That was the most brilliant poem I've ever heard ever ever," Jack said.

Emma gave a head-down shrug. "It's only the first two verses."

"That was the most brilliant first two verses I've ever heard ever ever."

"I'm going to write a hockey one tomorrow."

"Speaking of which . . ."

Emma sat up. "What?"

Jack smiled. "I got tickets for the Rangers at the Garden on Saturday."

Emma, part of the "jock" group as opposed to the group who worshipped the latest boy band, gave a yippee and reached up for another hug. Jack rolled his eyes and accepted it. They discussed the team's recent performance and set odds on their chances of beating the Minnesota Wild. A few minutes later, Jack disentangled himself. He told his daughter that he loved her. She told him that she loved him too. Jack started for the door.

"Gotta grab something to eat," he whispered to Grace.

"There's leftover chicken in the fridge."

"Why don't you slip into something more comfortable?"

"Hope springs eternal."

Jack arched an eyebrow. "Still afraid you're not enough woman for me?"

"Oh, that reminds me."

"What?"

"Something about Cora's date last night."

"Hot?"

"I'll be down in a second."

He arched the other eyebrow and hustled downstairs with a whistle. Grace waited until she heard Emma's breathing deepen before following. She turned off the light and watched for a moment. This was Jack's bit. He paced the corridors at night, unable to sleep, guarding them in their beds. There were nights she'd wake up and find the spot next to her empty. Jack would be standing in one of their doorways, his eyes glassy. She'd approach and he'd say, "You love them so much . . ." He didn't need to say more. He didn't even need to say that.

Jack didn't hear her approach, and for some reason, a reason Grace wouldn't want to articulate, she tried to stay quiet. Jack stood stiffly, his back to her, his head down. This was unusual. Jack was usually hyper, in constant motion. Like Max, Jack could not stay still. He fidgeted. His leg shook whenever he sat. He was high energy.

But right now he was staring down at the kitchen counter—more specifically, at the strange photograph—still as a stone.

"Jack?"

He startled upright. "What the hell is this?"

His hair, she noticed, was a shade longer than it should be. "Why don't you tell me?"

He didn't say anything.

"That's you, right? With the beard?"

"What? No."

She looked at him. He blinked and looked away.

"I picked up this roll of film today," she said. "At the Fotomat."

He said nothing. She stepped closer.

"That photograph was in the middle of the pack."

"Wait." He looked up sharply. "It was in with our roll of film?"

"Yes."

"Which roll?"

"The one we took at the apple orchard."

"That doesn't make any sense."

She shrugged. "Who are the other people in the photo?"

"How should I know?"

"The blonde standing next to you," Grace said. "With the X through her. Who is she?"

Jack's cell phone rang. He snapped it up like a gunfighter on a draw. He mumbled a hello, listened, put his hand over the mouthpiece, and said, "It's Dan." His research partner at Pentocol Pharmaceuticals. He lowered his head and headed into the den.

Grace headed upstairs. She started getting ready for bed. What had started as a gentle nagging was growing stronger, more persistent. She flashed back to their years living in France. He would never talk about his past. He had a wealthy family and a trust fund, she knew—and he wanted nothing to do with either. There was a sister, a lawyer out in Los Angeles or San Diego. His father was still alive but very old. Grace had wanted to know more, but Jack refused to elaborate, and sensing something foreboding, she had not pushed him.

They fell in love. She painted. He worked in a vineyard in Saint-Emilion in Bordeaux. They lived in Saint-Emilion until Grace had gotten pregnant with Emma. Something called her home then—a yearning, corny as it might sound, to raise her children in the land of the free and the home of the brave. Jack wanted to stay, but Grace had insisted. Now Grace wondered why.

Half an hour passed. Grace slipped under the covers and waited. Ten minutes later, she heard a car engine start up. Grace looked out the window.

Jack's minivan was pulling out.

He liked to shop at night, she knew—hit the grocery store when it wasn't crowded. So going out like this was not unusual for him. Except, of course, he hadn't called up to tell her he was going or to ask if they needed anything in particular.

Grace tried his cell phone but the voice mail picked up. She sat back and waited. Nothing. She tried to read. The words swam by in a meaningless haze. Two hours later, Grace tried Jack's cell phone again. Still voice mail. She checked on the children. They slept soundly, appropriately oblivious.

When she could stand it no longer Grace headed downstairs. She looked through the packet of film.

The strange photograph was gone.

CHAPTER 2

Most people check out the online personals to find a date.
Eric Wu found victims.

He had seven different accounts using seven different made-up personas—some male and some female. He tried to stay in e-mail contact with an average of six "potential dates" per account. Three of the accounts were on standard any-age straight personals. Two were for singles over the age of fifty. One was for gay men. The final site hooked up lesbians looking for serious commitment.

At any one time Wu would be conducting online flirtations with as many as forty or even fifty of the forlorn. He would slowly get to know them. Most were cautious, but that was okay. Eric Wu was a patient man. Eventually they would give him enough tidbits to find out if he should pursue the relationship or cut them loose.

He only dealt with women at first. The theory was that they would be the easiest victims. But Eric Wu, who received no sexual gratification from his work, realized that he was leaving untapped an entire market that would be less likely to worry about online safety. A man does not, for example, fear rape. He does not fear stalkers. A man is less cautious, and that makes him more vulnerable.

Wu was seeking singles with few ties. If they had children, they were no good to him. If they had family living close by, they were no good to him. If they had roommates, important jobs, too many close friends, well, ditto. Wu wanted them lonely, yes, but also secluded and shut off from the many ties and bonds that connect the rest of us to something greater than the individual. Right now, he also required one with geographical proximity to the Lawson household.

He found such a victim in Freddy Sykes.

Freddy Sykes worked for a storefront tax-filing company in Waldwick, New Jersey. He was forty-eight years old. His parents were both deceased. He had no siblings. According to his online flirtations at Bi-Men.com, Freddy had taken care of his mother and never had the time for a relationship. When she passed away two years ago, Freddy inherited the house in Ho-Ho-Kus, a scant three miles from the Lawson residence. His online photograph, a head shot, hinted that Freddy was probably on the plump side. His hair was shoe-polish black, thin, styled in a classic comb-over. His smile seemed forced, unnatural, as if he were wincing before a blow.

Freddy had spent the past three weeks flirting online with one Al Singer, a fifty-six-year-old retired Exxon executive who'd been married twenty-two years before admitting that he was interested in "experimenting." The Al Singer persona still loved his wife, but she didn't understand his need to be with both men and women. Al was interested in European travel, fine dining, and watching sports on TV. For his Singer persona, Wu used a photograph he'd grabbed off a YMCA online catalogue. His Al Singer looked athletic but not too handsome. Someone too attractive might raise Freddy's suspicion. Wu wanted him to buy the fantasy. That was the key thing.

Freddy Sykes's neighbors were mostly young families who paid him no attention. His house looked like every other on the block. Wu watched now as Sykes's garage door opened electronically. The garage was attached. You could enter and exit your car without being seen. That was excellent.

Wu waited ten minutes and then rang his doorbell.

"Who is it?"

"Delivery for Mr. Sykes."

"From whom?"

Freddy Sykes had not opened the door. That was strange. Men usually did. Again that was part of their vulnerability, part of the reason that they were easier prey than their female counterparts. Overconfidence. Wu spotted the peephole. Sykes would no doubt be peering at the twenty-six-year-old Korean man with baggy pants and a squat, compact build. He might notice Wu's earring and bemoan how today's youth mutilated their bodies. Or maybe the build and earring would turn Sykes on. Who knew?

"From Topfit Chocolate," Wu said.

"No, I mean, who sent them?"

Wu pretended to read the note again. "A Mr. Singer."

That did it. The dead bolt slid open. Wu glanced about him. No one. Freddy Sykes opened the door with a smile. Wu did not hesitate. His fingers formed a spear and then darted for Sykes's throat like a bird going for food. Freddy went down. Wu moved with a speed that defied his bulk. He slid inside and closed the door behind him.

Freddy Sykes lay on his back, his hands wrapped around his own neck. He was trying to scream, but all he could make were small squawking noises. Wu bent down and flipped him onto his stomach. Freddy struggled. Wu pulled up his victim's shirt. Freddy kicked at him. Wu's expert fingers traced up his spine until he found the right spot between the fourth and fifth vertebrae. Freddy kicked some more. Using his index finger and thumb like bayonets, Wu dug into the bone, nearly breaking skin.

Freddy stiffened.

Wu applied a bit more pressure, forcing the facet joints to sublux. Still burrowing deeper between the two vertebrae, he took hold and plucked. Something in Freddy's spine snapped like a guitar string.

The kicking stopped.

All movement stopped.

But Freddy Sykes was alive. That was good. That was what Wu wanted. He used to kill them right away, but now he knew better. Alive, Freddy could call his boss and tell him that he was taking time off. Alive, he could offer up his PIN if Wu wanted money from the ATM. Alive, he could answer messages in case someone did indeed call.

And alive, Wu would not have to worry about the smell.

Wu jammed a gag in Freddy's mouth and left him naked in the bathtub. The pressure on the spine had made the facet joints jump out of position. This dislocation of the vertebrae would contuse rather than completely sever the spinal column. Wu tested the results of his handiwork. Freddy could not move his legs at all. His deltoids might work, but the hands and lower arms would not function. Most important, he could still breathe on his own.

For all practical purposes, Freddy Sykes was paralyzed.

Keeping Sykes in the tub would make it easier to rinse off any mess. Freddy's eyes were open a little too wide. Wu had seen this look before: somewhere past terror but not yet death, a hollowness that fell in that awful cusp between the two.

There was obviously no need to tie Freddy up.

Wu sat in the dark and waited for night to fall. He closed his eyes and let his mind drift back. There were prisons in Rangoon where they studied spinal fractures during hangings. They learned where to place the knot, where to apply force, what effects different placements would have. In North Korea, in the political prison Wu had called home from the ages of thirteen to eighteen, they had taken the experiments one step further. Enemies of the state were killed creatively. Wu had done many with his bare hands. He had hardened his hands by punching boulders. He had studied the anatomy of the human body in a way most medical students would envy. He had practiced on human beings, perfecting his techniques.

The exact spot between the fourth and fifth vertebrae. That was key. Any higher and you could paralyze them completely. That would lead to death fairly quickly. Forget their arms and legs—their internal organs would stop working. Any lower and you would only get the legs. The arms would still work. If the pressure applied was too great, you'd snap the entire spinal column. It was all about precision. Having the right touch. Practice.

Wu turned on Freddy's computer. He wanted to keep up with the other singles on his list because he never knew when he would need a new place to live. When he was finished, Wu allowed himself to sleep. Three hours later he awoke and looked in on Freddy. His eyes were glassier now, staring straight up, blinking without focus.

When his contact called Wu's cell phone, it was nearly ten p.m.

"Are you settled in?" the contact asked.

"Yes."

"We have a situation."

Wu waited.

"We need to move things up a bit. Is that a problem?"

"No."

"He needs to be taken now."

"You have a place?"

Wu listened, memorizing the location.

"Any questions?"

"No," Wu said.

"Eric?"

Wu waited.

"Thanks, man."

Wu hung up. He found the car keys and took off in Freddy's Honda.

CHAPTER 3

G race couldn't call the police yet. She couldn't sleep either.

The computer was still on. Their screen saver was a family photo taken last year at Disney World. The four of them posed with Goofy at Epcot Center. Jack was wearing mouse ears. His grin was ear to ear. Hers was more reserved. She'd felt silly, which just encouraged Jack. She touched the mouse—the other mouse, the computer mouse—and her family disappeared.

Grace clicked the new icon and the strange photograph of the five college-aged kids appeared. The image came up with Adobe Photoshop. For several minutes Grace just stared at the young faces, searching for—she didn't know—a clue maybe. Nothing came to her. She cropped each face, blowing them up into something approaching four inches by four inches. Any bigger and the already-blurred image became undecipherable. The good paper was in the color ink-jet, so she hit the PRINT button. She grabbed a pair of scissors and went to work.

Soon she had five separate head shots, one for each person in the picture. She studied them again, this time taking extra care with the young blonde next to Jack. She was pretty with that girl-next-door complexion and long flaxen hair. The young woman's eyes were on Jack, and the look was more than casual. Grace felt a pang of, what, jealousy? How bizarre. Who was this woman? Obviously an old girlfriend—one

Jack had never mentioned. But so what? Grace had a past. So did Jack. Why would the look in that photograph bother her?

So what now?

She would have to wait for Jack. When he came home, she would demand answers.

But answers about what?

Back up here a second. What was really going on? An old photograph, probably of Jack, had popped up in her packet of pictures. It was weird, sure. It was even a little creepy, what with the blonde crossed out like that. And Jack had stayed out late before without calling. So really, what was the big deal here? Something in the photo had probably upset him. He turned off his phone and was probably in a bar. Or at Dan's house. This whole thing was probably just a bizarre joke.

Yeah, Grace, sure. A joke. Like the one about the car pool to the pool.

Sitting alone, the room dark except for the glow from the computer monitor, Grace tried a few more ways to rationalize away what was going on. She stopped when she realized that this was only scaring her more.

Grace clicked onto the face of the young woman, the one who stared at her husband with longing, zooming in for a better view. She stared at the face, really stared, and a tingle of dread began to travel across her scalp. Grace did not move. She just kept looking at the woman's face. She didn't know the wheres or whens or hows, but she now realized something with thudding certainty.

Grace had seen this young woman before.

CHAPTER 4

Rocky Conwell took up his post by the Lawson residence.

He tried to get comfortable in his 1989 Toyota Celica, but that was impossible. Rocky was too big for this piece-of-crap car. He pulled harder on that damned seat lever, nearly ripping it out, but the seat would go back no farther. It would have to do. He settled in and let his eyes start to close.

Man, was Rocky tired. He was working two jobs. The first, his steady gig to impress his parole officer, was a ten-hour shift on the Budweiser assembly line in Newark. The second, sitting in this damn car and staring at a house, was strictly off the books.

Rocky jerked up when he heard a noise. He picked up his binoculars. Damn, someone had started up the minivan. He focused in. Jack Lawson was on the move. He lowered the binoculars, shifted into drive, and prepared to follow.

Rocky needed two jobs because he needed cash in a big, bad way. Lorraine, his ex, was making overtures about a possible reconciliation. But she was still skittish about it. Cash, Rocky knew, could tip the balance in his favor. He loved Lorraine. He wanted her back in a big, bad way. He owed her some good times, didn't he? And if that meant he had to work his butt off, well, he'd been the one to screw up. It was a price he was willing to pay.

It hadn't always been like this for Rocky Conwell. He'd been an all-state defensive end at Westfield High. Penn State—Joe Paterno himself—had recruited him and transformed him into a hard-hitting inside linebacker. Six-four, two-sixty, and blessed with a naturally aggressive nature, Rocky had been a standout for four years. He'd been All Big-Ten for two years. The St. Louis Rams drafted him in the seventh round.

For a while, it was like God Himself had perfectly planned out his life from the get-go. His real name was Rocky, his parents naming him that when his mother went into labor as they watched the movie *Rocky* in the summer of 1976. You gonna have a name like Rocky, you better be big and strong. You better be ready to rumble. Here he was, a pro football draft pick itching to get to camp. He and Lorraine—a knockout who could not only stop traffic but make it go backward—hooked up during his junior year. They fell for each other pretty hard. Life was good.

Until, well, it wasn't.

Rocky was a great college player, but there is a big difference between Division 1-A and the pros. At the Rams rookie camp, they loved his hustle. They loved his work ethic. They loved the way he would sacrifice his body to make a play. But they didn't love his speed—and in today's game, what with the emphasis on passing and coverage, Rocky was simply not good enough. Or so they said. Rocky would not surrender. He started taking more steroids. He got bigger but still not big enough for the front line. He managed to hang around one season playing special teams for the Rams. The next year he was cut.

The dream wouldn't die. Rocky wouldn't let it. He pumped iron nonstop. He began 'roiding big time. He had always taken some kind of anabolic supplement. Every athlete does. But desperation had made him less cautious. He didn't worry about cycling or overdoing it. He just wanted mass. His mood darkened from either the drugs or the disappointment—or more likely, the potent blend of the two.

To make ends meet, Rocky took up work with the Ultimate Fighting Federation. You may remember their octagon grudge matches. For a while, they were all the rage on pay-per-view—real, bloody, no-holds-barred brawls. Rocky was good at it. He was big and strong and a natural fighter. He had great endurance and knew how to wear down an opponent.

Eventually the violence in the ring got to be too much for people's sensibilities. States began to outlaw ultimate fighting. Some of the guys started battling in Japan, where it was still legal—Rocky guessed that they had different sensibilities over there—but he didn't go. Rocky still believed that the NFL was within his grasp. He just had to work harder. Get a little bigger, a little stronger, a little faster.

Jack Lawson's minivan pulled onto Route 17. Rocky's instructions were clear. Follow Lawson. Write down where he went, who he talked to, every detail of his trip, but do not—repeat not—engage him. He was to observe. Nothing more.

Right, easy cash.

Two years ago, Rocky got into a bar fight. It was typical stuff. Some guy stared at Lorraine too long. Rocky had asked him what he was looking at, and the guy responded, "Not much." You know the drill. Except Rocky was juiced up from the 'roids. He pulverized the guy—put him in traction—and got nailed on an assault beef. He spent three months in jail and was now on probation. That had been the final straw for Lorraine. She called him a loser and moved out.

So now he was trying to make it up to her.

Rocky had quit the junk. Dreams die hard, but he now realized that the NFL was not going to be. But Rocky had talents. He could be a good coach. He knew how to motivate. A friend of his had an in at his old alma mater, Westfield High. If Rocky could get his record cleared, he'd be made varsity defensive coordinator. Lorraine could get a job there as a guidance counselor. They'd be on their way.

They just needed a little setup cash.

Rocky kept the Celica a decent distance back from the minivan. He was not too worried about being spotted. Jack Lawson was an amateur. He wouldn't be looking for a tail. That was what Rocky's boss had told him.

Lawson crossed the New York border and took the thruway north. The time was ten p.m. Rocky wondered if he should call it in, but no, not yet. There was nothing here to report. The man was taking a ride. Rocky was following him. That was his job.

Rocky felt his calf start cramping. Man, he wished this piece of junk had more legroom.

Half an hour later Lawson pulled off by the Woodbury Commons, one of those massive outdoor malls where all the stores were purportedly "outlets" for their more expensive counterparts. The Commons was closed. The minivan pulled down a quiet stretch of road on the side. Rocky hung back. If he followed now, he'd be spotted for sure.

Rocky found a position on the right, shifted into park, turned off his headlights, and picked up his binoculars.

Jack Lawson stopped the minivan, and Rocky watched him step out. There was another car not too far away. Must be Lawson's girl-friend. Strange place for a romantic rendezvous, but there you go. Jack looked both ways and then headed toward the wooded area. Damn. Rocky would have to follow on foot.

He put down the binoculars and slid out. He was still seventy, eighty yards away from Lawson. Rocky didn't want to get any closer. He squatted down and peered through the binoculars again. Lawson stopped walking. He turned around and . . .

What's this?

Rocky swung the binoculars to the right. A man was standing to Lawson's left. Rocky took a closer look. The man wore fatigues. He was short and squat, built like a perfect square. Looked like he worked out, Rocky thought. The guy—he looked Chinese or something—stood perfectly still, stonelike.

At least for a few seconds.

Gently, almost like a lover's touch, the Chinese guy reached up and put his hand on Lawson's shoulder. For a fleeting moment Rocky thought that maybe he had stumbled across a gay tryst. But that wasn't it. That wasn't it at all.

Jack Lawson dropped to the ground like a puppet with his strings cut.

Rocky stifled a gasp. The Chinese guy looked down at the crumpled form. He bent down and picked Lawson up by . . . hell, it looked like the neck. Like you'd pick up a puppy or something. By the scruff of his neck.

Oh damn, Rocky thought. I better call this in.

Without breaking a sweat, the Chinese guy started carrying Lawson toward his car. With one hand. Like the guy was a briefcase or something. Rocky reached for his cell phone.

Crap, he'd left it in the car.

Okay, think, Rocky. The car the Chinese guy was driving. It was a Honda Accord. New Jersey plates. Rocky tried to memorize the number. He watched while the Chinese guy opened the trunk. He dumped Lawson in as if he were a load of laundry.

Oh man, now what?

Rocky's orders were firm. Do not engage. How many times had he heard that? Whatever you do, just observe. Do not engage.

He didn't know what to do.

Should he just follow?

Uh-uh, no way. Jack Lawson was in the trunk. Look, Rocky did not know the man. He didn't know why he was supposed to follow him. He'd figured that they'd been hired to follow Lawson for the usual reason—his wife suspected him of having an affair. That was one thing. Follow and prove infidelity. But this . . . ?

Lawson had been assaulted. For crying out loud, he'd been locked in the trunk by this muscle-headed Jackie Chan. Could Rocky just sit back and let that happen?

No.

Whatever Rocky had done, whatever he had become, he was not

about to let that stand. Suppose he lost the Chinese guy? Suppose there wasn't enough air in the trunk? Suppose Lawson had been seriously injured already and was dying?

Rocky had to do something.

Should he call the police?

The Chinese guy slammed the trunk closed. He started for the front seat.

Too late to call anyone. He had to make his move now.

Rocky remained six-four, two-sixty, and rock solid. He was a professional fighter. Not a show boxer. Not a phony, staged wrestler. A real fighter. He didn't have a gun, but he knew how to take care of himself.

Rocky started running toward the car.

"Hey!" he shouted. "Hey, you! Stop right there!"

The Chinese guy—as he got closer, Rocky could see he was more like a kid—looked up. His expression did not change. He just stared as Rocky ran toward him. He did not move. He did not try to get in the car and drive away. He waited patiently.

"Hey!"

The Chinese kid stayed still.

Rocky stopped a yard in front of him. Their eyes met. Rocky did not like what he saw. He had played football against some true head cases. He'd fought pain-happy crazies in the Ultimate Fighting ring. He had stared into the eyes of pure psychos—guys who got off on hurting people. This was not like that. This was like staring into the eyes of . . . something not alive. A rock maybe. An inanimate object of some kind. There was no fear, no mercy, no reason.

"May I help you?" the Chinese kid said.

"I saw . . . Let that man out of the trunk."

The kid nodded. "Of course."

The kid glanced toward the trunk. So did Rocky. And that was when Eric Wu struck.

Rocky never saw the blow. Wu ducked down, twisted his hips for power, and smashed his fist into Rocky's kidney. Rocky had taken shots before. He had been punched in the kidney by men twice this size. But nothing had ever hit him like this. The blow landed like a sledgehammer.

Rocky gasped but stayed on his feet. Wu moved in and jabbed something hard into Rocky's liver. It felt like a barbecue skewer. The pain exploded through him.

Rocky's mouth opened, but the scream wouldn't come out. He fell to the ground. Wu dropped down next to him. The last thing Rocky saw—the last thing he would ever see—was Eric Wu's face, calm and serene, as he placed his hands under Rocky's rib cage.

Lorraine, Rocky thought. And then nothing more.

CHAPTER 5

Grace caught herself midscream. She jerked upright. The light was still on in the hallway. A silhouette stood in her doorway. But it wasn't Jack.

She awoke, still gasping. A dream. She knew that. On some elusive level, she had known that midway through. She'd had this dream before, plenty of times, though not in a long time. Must be the upcoming anniversary, she thought.

She tried to settle back. It wouldn't happen. The dream always started and ended the same. The variations occurred in the middle.

In the dream Grace was back at the old Boston Garden. The stage was directly in front of her. There was a steel blockade, short, maybe waist-high, like something you might use to lock your bike. She leaned against it.

The loudspeaker played "Pale Ink," but that was impossible because the concert hadn't even started yet. "Pale Ink" was the big hit from the Jimmy X Band, the bestselling single of the year. You still hear it on the radio all the time. It would be played live, not on some waiting-time recording. But if this dream was like some movie, "Pale Ink" was, if you will, the sound track.

Was Todd Woodcroft, her boyfriend at the time, standing next to her? She sometimes imagined holding his hand—though they were never the hand-holding kind of couple—and then, when it went wrong, the stomach-dropping feeling of his hand slipping away from hers. In reality, Todd was probably right next to her. In the dream, only sometimes. This time, no, he was not there. Todd had escaped that night unscathed. She never blamed him for what happened to her. There was nothing he could have done. Todd had never even visited her in the hospital. She didn't blame him for that either. Theirs was a college romance already on the skids, not a soul-mate situation. Who needed a scene at this stage of the game? Who'd want to break up with a girl in the hospital? Better for both, she thought, to let it just sort of drift away.

In the dream, Grace knows that tragedy is about to strike, but she does nothing about it. Her dream self does not call out a warning or try to make for the exit. She often wondered why, but wasn't that how dreams worked? You are powerless even with foreknowledge, a slave to some advanced hardwiring in your subconscious. Or perhaps the answer is simpler: There was no time. In the dream, the tragedy begins in seconds. In reality, according to witnesses, Grace and the others had stood in front of that stage for more than four hours.

The crowd's mood had slid from excited to antsy to restless before stopping at hostile. Jimmy X, real name James Xavier Farmington, the gorgeous rocker with the glorious hair, was supposed to take the stage at eight thirty p.m., though no one really expected him before nine. Now it was closing in on midnight. At first the crowd had been chanting Jimmy's name. Now a chorus of boos had started up. Sixteen thousand people, including those, like Grace, who had been lucky enough to get standing seats in the pit, rose as one, demanding their performance. Ten minutes passed before the loudspeaker finally offered up some feedback. The crowd, having reverted to their earlier state of fevered excitement, went wild.

But the voice that came over the loudspeaker did not introduce the band. In a straight monotone, it announced that tonight's performance had been delayed again for at least an hour. No explanation. For a moment nobody moved. Silence filled the arena.

This was where the dream began, during that lull before the devastation. Grace was there again. How old was she? She had been twenty-one, but in the dream she seemed to be older. It was a different, parallel Grace, one who was married to Jack and mother to Emma and Max and yet was still at that concert during her senior year of college. Again that was how it worked in dreams, a dual reality, your parallel self overlapping with your actual one.

Was all this, these dream moments, coming from her subconscious or from what she had read about the tragedy after the fact? Grace did not know. It was, she'd long surmised, probably a combination of both. Dreams open up memories, don't they? When she was awake, she couldn't recall that night at all—or for that matter, the few days before. The last thing she remembered was studying for a political science final she'd taken five days earlier. That was normal, the doctors assured her, with her type of head trauma. But the subconscious was a strange terrain. Perhaps the dreams were actual memories. Perhaps imagination. Most likely, as with most dreams or even memories, both.

Either way, be it from memory or press reports, it was at this very moment that someone fired a shot. Then another. And another.

This was before the days of metal detector sweeps when you entered an arena. Anyone could carry in a gun. For a while, there had been much debate over the origins of those shots. Conspiracy nuts still argued over the point, as if the arena had a grassy knoll in the upper tier. Either way, the young crowd, already in a frenzy, snapped. They screamed. They broke. They rushed for exits.

They rushed toward the stage.

Grace was in the wrong spot. Her waist was crushed against the top of the steel girder. It dug into her belly. She could not pry herself free. The crowd cried out and surged as one. The boy next to her—she would later learn that he was nineteen years old and named Ryan Vespa—didn't get his hands up in time. He smacked the girder at a bad angle.

Grace saw—again was it just in the dream or in reality too?—the

48 · HARLAN COBEN

blood shoot from Ryan Vespa's mouth. The girder finally gave way. It tilted over. She fell to the floor. Grace tried to get her footing, tried to stand, but the current of screaming humans drove her back down.

This part, she knew, was real. This part, being buried under a mass of people, haunted more than just her dreams.

The stampede continued. People stomped on her. Trampled her arms and legs. Tripped and fell, slamming down on her like stone tablets. The weight grew. Crushing her. Dozens of desperate, struggling, slithering bodies rushed over her.

Screams filled the air. Grace was underneath it now. Buried. There was no light anymore. Too many bodies on top of her. It was impossible to move. Impossible to breathe. She was suffocating. Like someone had buried her in concrete. Like she was being dragged underwater.

There was too much weight on her. It felt as if a giant hand was pressing down on her head, squashing her skull like it was a Styrofoam cup.

There was no escape.

And that, mercifully, was when the dream ended. Grace woke up, still gulping for air.

In reality, Grace had woken up four days later and remembered almost nothing. At first she thought it was the morning of her political science final. The doctors took their time explaining the situation. She had been seriously injured. She had, for one, a skull fracture. That, the doctors surmised, explained the headaches and memory loss. This was not a case of amnesia or repressed memory or even anything psychological. The brain was damaged, which is not infrequent with this kind of severe head trauma and loss of consciousness. Losing hours, even days, was not unusual. Grace also shattered her femur, her tibia, and three ribs. Her knee had split in two. Her hip had been ripped out of its joint.

Through a haze of painkillers, she eventually learned that she had been "lucky." Eighteen people, ranging in age from fourteen to twenty-six, had been killed in the stampede that the media dubbed the Boston Massacre.

The silhouette in the doorway said, "Mom?"

It was Emma. "Hi, sweetheart."

"You were screaming."

"I'm okay. Even moms have bad dreams sometimes."

Emma stayed in the shadows. "Where's Daddy?"

Grace checked the bedside clock. It was nearly four forty-five a.m. How long had she been asleep? No more than ten, fifteen minutes. "He'll be home soon."

Emma did not move.

"You okay?" Grace asked.

"Can I sleep with you?"

Plenty of bad dreams tonight, Grace thought. She pulled back the blanket. "Sure, honey."

Emma crawled onto Jack's side of the bed. Grace threw the blanket back over her and held tight. She kept her eyes on the bedside clock. At exactly seven a.m.—she watched the digital clock switch from six fifty-nine a.m.—she let panic in.

Jack had never done anything like this before. If it had been a normal night, if he had come up and told her that he was going grocery shopping, if he had made some clumsy double entendre before leaving, something about melons or bananas, something funny and stupid like that, she'd have been on the phone with the police already.

But last night had not been normal. There had been that photograph. There had been his reaction. And there had been no kiss good-bye.

Emma stirred beside her. Max entered in mid-eye rub a few minutes later. Jack was usually the one who made breakfast. He was more the early riser. Grace managed to whip up the morning meal—Cap'n Crunch with sliced banana—and deflected their questions about their father's absence. While they were busy wolfing down breakfast, she slid into the den and tried Jack's office, but nobody picked up the line. Still too early.

She threw on a pair of Jack's Adidas sweats and walked the kids to the bus stop. Emma used to hug her before she boarded, but she was too old for that. She hurried aboard, before Grace could mumble something idiotically parental about Emma being too old for hugs but not too old to visit Mom when she was scared at night. Max still gave her a hug but it was quick and with a serious lack of enthusiasm. He stepped inside, the bus door swooshing to a close as though swallowing him whole.

Grace blocked the sun with her hand and, as always, watched the bus until it turned down Bryden Road. Even now, even after all this time, she still longed to hop in her car and follow just to be sure that that seemingly fragile box of yellow tin made it safely to school.

What had happened to Jack?

She started back toward the house, but then, thinking better of it, she sprinted toward her car and took off. Grace caught up to the bus on Heights Road and followed it the rest of the way to Willard School. She shifted into park and watched the children disembark. When Emma and Max appeared, weighed down by their backpacks, she felt the familiar flutter. She sat and waited until they both headed up the path, up the stairs, and disappeared through the school doors.

And then, for the first time in a long time, Grace cried.

Grace expected cops in plainclothes. And she expected two of them. That was how it always worked on television. One would be the gruff veteran. The other would be young and handsome. So much for TV. The town police had sent one officer in the regulation stop-you-for-speeding uniform and matching car.

He had introduced himself as Officer Daley. He was indeed young, very young, with a smattering of acne on his shiny baby face. He was gym muscular. His short sleeves worked like tourniquets on his bloated biceps. Officer Daley spoke with annoying patience, a suburban-cop monotone, as if addressing a class of first graders on bike safety.

He had arrived ten minutes after her call on the non-emergency police line. Normally, the dispatcher told her, they would ask her to come in and fill out a report on her own. But it just so happened that Officer Daley was in the area, so he'd be able to swing by. Lucky her.

Daley took a letter-size sheet of paper and placed it on the coffee table. He clicked his pen and started asking questions.

"The missing person's name?"

"John Lawson. But he goes by Jack."

He started down the list.

"Address and phone number?"

She gave them.

"Place of birth?"

"Los Angeles, California."

He asked his height, weight, eye and hair color, sex (yes, he actually asked). He asked if Jack had any scars, marks, or tattoos. He asked for a possible destination.

"I don't know," Grace said. "That's why I called you."

Officer Daley nodded. "I assume that your husband is over the age of emancipation."

"Pardon?"

"He is over eighteen years old."

"Yes."

"That makes this harder."

"Why?"

"We got new regulations on filling out a missing-person report. It was just updated a couple weeks back."

"I'm not sure I understand."

He gave a theatrical sigh. "See, in order to put someone in the computer, he needs to meet the criteria." Daley pulled out another sheet of paper. "Is your husband disabled?"

"No."

"Endangered?"

"What do you mean?"

Daley read from the sheet. " 'A person of age who is missing and in the company of another person under circumstances indicating that his/her physical safety is in danger.' "

"I don't know. I told you. He left here last night . . ."

"Then that would be a no," Daley said. He scanned down the sheet. "Number three. Involuntary. Like a kidnapping or abduction."

"I don't know."

"Right. Number four. Catastrophe victim. Like in a fire or airplane crash."

"No."

"And the last category. Is he a juvenile? Well, we covered that already." He put the sheet down. "That's it. You can't put the person into the system unless he fits in one of those categories."

"So if someone goes missing like this, you do nothing?"

"I wouldn't put it that way, ma'am."

"How would you put it?"

"We have no evidence that there was any foul play. If we receive any, we will immediately upgrade the investigation."

"So for now you do nothing?"

Daley put down the pen. He leaned forward, his forearms on his thighs. His breathing was heavy. "May I speak frankly, Mrs. Lawson?"

"Please."

"Most of these cases—no, more than that, I'd say ninety-nine out of a hundred—the husband is just running around. There are marital problems. There is a mistress. The husband doesn't want to be found."

"That's not the case here."

He nodded. "And in ninety-nine out of a hundred cases, that's what we hear from the wife."

The patronizing tone was starting to piss her off. Grace hadn't felt comfortable confiding in this youth. She'd held back, as if she feared telling the entire truth would be a betrayal. Plus, when you really thought about it, how would it sound?

Well, see, I found this weird photo from the Fotomat in the middle of my pack from the apple orchard, in Chester, right, and my husband said it wasn't him and really, it's hard to tell because the picture is old and then Jack left the house . . .

"Mrs. Lawson?"

"Yes."

"Do you understand what I'm telling you?"

"I think so. That I'm hysterical. My husband ran off. I'm trying to use the police to drag him back. That sound about right?"

He remained unruffled. "You have to understand. We can't fully investigate until we have some evidence that a crime has been committed. Those are the rules set up by the NCIC." He pointed to the sheet of paper again and said in his gravest tone: "That's the National Crime Information Center."

She almost rolled her eyes.

"Even if we find your husband, we wouldn't tell you where he was. This is a free country. He is of age. We can't force him to come back."

"I'm aware of that."

"We could make a few calls, maybe make a few discreet inquiries."

"Great."

"I'll need the vehicle make and license plate number."

"It's a Ford Windstar."

"Color?"

"Dark blue."

"Year?"

She didn't remember.

"License plate?"

"It begins with an M."

Officer Daley looked up. Grace felt like a moron.

"I have a copy of the registration upstairs," she said. "I can check."

"Do you use E-ZPass at tollbooths?"

"Yes."

Officer Daley nodded and wrote that down. Grace headed upstairs and found the file. She made a copy with her scanner and gave it to Officer Daley. He wrote something down. He asked a few questions. She stuck with the facts: Jack had come home from work, helped put the children to bed, gone out, probably for groceries . . . and that was it.

After about five minutes, Daley seemed satisfied. He smiled and told her not to worry. She stared at him.

"We'll check back with you in a few hours. If we hear nothing by then, let's talk some more."

He left. Grace tried Jack's office again. Still no answer. She checked the clock. It was nearly ten a.m. The Fotomat would be opening now. Good.

She had some questions for Josh the Fuzz Pellet.

CHAPTER 6

Charlaine Swain slipped on her new online lingerie purchase—a Regal Lace babydoll with matching G-string—and pulled up her bedroom shade.

Something was wrong.

The day was Tuesday. The time was ten thirty a.m. Charlaine's children were at school. Her husband, Mike, would be at his desk in the city, the phone wedged between shoulder and ear, his fingers busy rolling and unrolling his shirtsleeves, his collar tighter by the day but his ego too proud to admit the need for a bigger size.

Her neighbor, the scuzzy creepazoid named Freddy Sykes, should be home by now.

Charlaine glanced toward the mirror. She didn't do that often. There was no need to remind herself that she was over forty. The image that stared back was still shapely, she guessed, helped no doubt by the babydoll's underwired support—but what had once been considered buxom and curvaceous had weakened and loosened. Oh, Charlaine worked out. There was yoga class—yoga being this year's Tae Bo or Step—three mornings a week. She stayed fit, battling against the obvious and unbeatable, holding tight even as it slipped away.

What had happened to her?

Forget the physical for a second. The young Charlaine Swain had been a bundle of energy. She had a zest for life. She was ambitious and a go-getter. Everyone said it. There was always a spark with Charlaine, a crackle in the air, and somewhere, somehow, life—just plain living—had extinguished it.

Were the children to blame? Was it Mike? There was a time when he couldn't get enough of her, when an outfit like this would make his eyes widen and his mouth water. Now when she strutted by, he would barely look up.

When had that started?

She couldn't put her finger on it. She knew the process had been gradual, the change so slow as to be almost indiscernible, until, alas, it was a fait accompli. It hadn't all been his fault. She knew that. Her drive had waned, especially during the years of pregnancies, nursing, the ensuing exhaustion of infants. That was natural, she supposed. Everyone went through that. Still she wished that she had made more of an effort before the temporary changes hardened into something apathetic and enduring.

The memories, however, were still there. Mike used to romance her. He used to surprise her. He used to lust after her. He used to—and yes, this might sound crude—jump her bones. Now what he wanted was efficiency, something mechanical and precise—the dark, a grunt, a release, sleep.

When they talked, it was about the kids—the class schedules, the pickups, the homework, the dentist appointments, the Little League games, the Biddy Basketball program, the playdates. But that wasn't just Mike's fault either. When Charlaine had coffee with the women in the neighborhood—the Mommy and Me meetings at Starbucks—the conversations were so cloying, so boring, so stuffed with all things children, that she wanted to scream.

Charlaine Swain was being smothered.

Her mother—the idle queen of the country-club lunch—told her that this was life, that Charlaine had everything a woman could want, that her expectations were simply unrealistic. The saddest part was, Charlaine feared that her mother was right.

She checked her makeup. She applied more lipstick and rouge and then sat back and appraised herself. Yep, she looked like a whore. She grabbed a Percodan, the mommy equivalent of the lunchtime cocktail, and swallowed it. Then she took a closer look in the mirror, squinting even.

Was the old Charlaine still there somewhere?

There was this woman who lived two blocks down, a nice mother of two like Charlaine. Two months ago, this nice mother of two walked up to the Glen Rock train tracks and committed suicide by stepping in front of the eleven ten a.m. Bergen line heading south. Horrible story. Everyone talked about it for weeks. How could this woman, this nice mother of two, just abandon her children like that? How could she be so selfish? And yet, as Charlaine tsk-tsked with her fellow suburbanites, she felt a small pang of jealousy. For this nice mother, it was over. There had to be relief in that.

Where was Freddy?

Charlaine actually looked forward to this, her Tuesdays at ten, and perhaps that was the saddest thing of all. Her initial reaction to Freddy's peeping had been revulsion and rage. When and how had that slid into acceptance and even, God forgive her, arousal? No, she thought. It wasn't arousal. It was . . . something. That was all. It was a spark. It was something to feel.

She waited for his shade to come up.

It didn't.

Strange. Come to think of it, Freddy Sykes never pulled down his shades. Their properties backed up to each other, so that only they could see in each other's window. Freddy never pulled down the shade in the back. Why would he?

Her eyes roamed toward the other windows. All the shades were pulled down. Curious. The curtains in what she assumed was the den— she had never, of course, stepped foot in his house—were drawn closed.

Was Freddy traveling? Had he perhaps gone away?

Charlaine Swain caught her reflection in the window and felt a fresh wave of shame. She grabbed a robe—her husband's ratty terry cloth—and slipped into it. She wondered if Mike was having an affair, if another woman had drained that once insatiable sex drive, or was he just not interested in her? She wondered which was worse.

Where was Freddy?

And how degrading, how truly scraping-the-bottom pitiful it was, that this meant so much to her. She stared at the house.

There was movement.

It was slight. A shadow had crossed the side of a shade. But movement nonetheless. Maybe, just maybe, Freddy was truly peeping again, upping, if you will, his excitement level. That could be it, right? Most peepers got off on the stealth, *I Spy* aspects of the act. Maybe he simply didn't want her to see him. Maybe he was watching her right now, surreptitiously.

Could that be it?

She loosened the robe and let it slide down her shoulders. The terry cloth reeked of man sweat and the aging remnants of cologne she'd bought Mike, what, eight, nine years ago. Charlaine felt the tears sting her eyes. But she didn't turn away.

Something else suddenly appeared between the window shades. Something . . . blue?

She squinted. What was it?

The binoculars. Where were they? Mike kept a box of crap like that in his closet. She found it, dug through the many power cords and adapters, and unearthed the Leicas. She remembered when they bought them. They were on a cruise in the Caribbean. The stop was one of the Virgin Islands—she didn't remember which one—and the purchase had been spontaneous. That was why she remembered it, the buying of the binoculars, because of the spontaneity of such a mundane act.

Charlaine put the binoculars up to her eyes. They were autofocus, so there was nothing to adjust. It took her a moment or two to find the space between the window and the shade. But the blue spot was there. She saw the flicker and her eyes closed. She should have known.

The television. Freddy had turned on the television.

He was home.

Charlaine stood without moving. She didn't know how she felt anymore. The numb was back. Her son Clay liked to play a song from the *Shrek* movie about a guy forming an L with his fingers on his forehead. Loser. That was Freddy Sykes. And now Freddy, this scuzzy creepazoid, this Loser with a finger-capital L, would rather watch television than her lingerie-clad body.

Something was still strange.

All those shades pulled down. Why? She had lived next to the Sykes house for eight years. Even when Freddy's mother was alive, the shades were never pulled down, the curtains never closed. Charlaine took another look through her binoculars.

The television flicked off.

She stopped, waiting for something to happen. Freddy had lost track of the time, she thought. The shade would open now. They would begin their perverted ritual.

But that's not what happened.

Charlaine heard the slight whir and knew immediately what it was. Freddy's electric garage door had been activated.

She moved closer to the window. There was the sound of a car starting up, and then Freddy's hunk-of-junk Honda pulled out. Sunlight reflected off the windshield. The glare made her squint. She blocked it by cupping her hand above her eyes.

The car moved and the glare cleared. She could now see who was driving.

It wasn't Freddy.

Something, something base and primitive, commanded Charlaine to duck out of sight. She did. She dropped down and crawled for the robe. She pressed the terry cloth against herself. The smell—that combination of Mike and stale cologne—now seemed oddly comforting.

Charlaine moved toward the side of the window. She pressed her back against the wall and peeked out.

The Honda Accord had stopped. The driver—the Asian man behind the wheel—was staring at her window.

Charlaine quickly flattened herself back against the wall. She stayed still, holding her breath. She stayed that way until she heard the car start moving again. And then, just to be on the safe side, she stayed down another ten minutes.

When she looked again, the car was gone.

The house next door was still.

CHAPTER 7

At exactly ten fifteen a.m., Grace arrived at the Fotomat.

Josh the Fuzz Pellet was not there. As a matter of fact, nobody was there. The sign in the store window, probably left from the night before, read CLOSED.

She checked the printed hours: OPENS AT TEN A.M. She waited. At ten twenty, the first customer, a harried woman in her midthirties, spotted the CLOSED sign, read the hours, tried the door. She sighed in high drama. Grace gave her a commiserating shrug. The woman huffed off. Grace waited.

When the store had still not opened at ten thirty a.m., Grace knew that it was bad. She decided to try Jack's office again. His line kept going into voice mail—eerie hearing Jack's too-formal recorded voice—so she tried Dan's line this time. The two men had, after all, spoken last night. Maybe Dan could offer a clue.

She dialed his work number.

"Hello?"

"Hi, Dan. It's Grace."

"Hey!" he said with a tad too much enthusiasm. "I was just about to call you."

"Oh?"

"Where's Jack?"

"I don't know."

He hesitated. "When you say you don't know—"

"You called him last night, right?"

"Yes."

"What did you two talk about?"

"We're supposed to be making a presentation this afternoon. On the Phenomytol studies."

"Anything else?"

"What do you mean, anything else? Like what?"

"Like what else did you talk about?"

"Nothing. I wanted to ask him about a PowerPoint slide. Why? What's going on, Grace?"

"He went out after that."

"Right, so?"

"I haven't seen him since."

"Wait, when you say you haven't seen him . . . ?"

"I mean, he hasn't come home, he hasn't called, I have no idea where he is."

"Jesus, did you call the police?"

"Yes."

"And?"

"And nothing."

"My God. Look, let me get out of here. I'll be right over."

"No," she said. "I'm fine."

"You sure?"

"Positive. I have some things to do," she said lamely. She moved the phone to the other ear, unsure how to put this. "Has Jack been okay?"

"You mean, at work?"

"I mean anywhere."

"Yeah, sure, he's Jack. You know."

"You haven't noticed any change?"

"We've both been stressed about these drug trials, if that's what you mean. But nothing unusual. Grace, are you sure I shouldn't come up?"

There was a beep on her phone. Call-waiting. "I need to go, Dan. That's the other line."

"Probably Jack. Call me if you need anything."

She clicked him off and checked the caller ID. Not Jack. At least, not his cell. The number was blocked.

"Hello?"

"Ms. Lawson, this is Officer Daley. Has there been any word from your husband?"

"No."

"We tried you at home."

"Right, I'm out."

There was a pause. "Where are you?"

"In town."

"Where in town?"

"I'm at the Fotomat store."

A longer pause. "I don't mean to sound judgmental, but isn't that a strange place to be when you're concerned about your husband?"

"Officer Daley?"

"Yes?"

"There's this new invention. It's called the cell phone. In fact, you're calling me on it right now."

"I didn't mean to—"

"Have you learned anything about my husband?"

"That's why I'm calling, actually. My captain is in now. He'd like to do a follow-up interview."

"A follow-up?"

"Yes."

"Is that standard?"

"Sure." He sounded like it was anything but.

"Have you found something?"

"No, I mean, nothing to be alarmed about."

"What does that mean?"

"Captain Perlmutter and I just need more information, Mrs. Lawson."

Another Fotomat customer, a recently streaked quasi-blonde about Grace's own age, approached the empty store. She cupped her hands around her eyes and peered inside. She too frowned and scoffed away.

"You're both at the station now?" Grace asked.

"Yes."

"I'll be there in three minutes."

Captain Perlmutter asked, "How long have you and your husband lived in town?"

They were jammed into an office more fitting for the school custodian than the police captain of a town. The Kasselton cops had moved their station house to the former town library, a building with history and tradition but very little comfort. Captain Stu Perlmutter sat behind his desk. He leaned back at the first question, hands resting on a tidy paunch. Officer Daley leaned against the doorframe, trying to look comfortable.

Grace said, "Four years."

"Like it here?"

"Well enough."

"Great." Perlmutter smiled at her, a teacher approving of the answer. "And you have kids, right?"

"Yes."

"How old?"

"Eight and six."

"Eight and six," he repeated with a wistful smile. "Man, those are great ages. Not babies, and not teens yet."

Grace decided to wait him out.

"Mrs. Lawson, has your husband ever disappeared before?"

"No."

"Are there any problems with the marriage?"

"None."

Perlmutter gave her a skeptical look. He didn't wink, but he came close. "Everything is perfect, eh?"

Grace said nothing.

"How did you and your husband meet?"

"Pardon?"

"I asked—"

"What does that have to do with anything?"

"I'm just trying to get a feel here."

"A feel for what? Have you found something or not?"

"Please." Perlmutter tried on what he must have believed was a disarming smile. "I just need to get some stuff down. For background, okay? Where did you and Jack Lawson meet?"

"In France."

He wrote it down. "You're an artist, aren't you, Mrs. Lawson?"

"Yes."

"So you were overseas studying your art?"

"Captain Perlmutter?"

"Yes."

"No offense, but this line of questioning is bizarre."

Perlmutter glanced at Daley. He shrugged to signal that he meant no harm. "Maybe you're right."

"Have you learned something or not?"

"I believe Officer Daley explained to you that your husband is of age, that we really aren't obligated to tell you anything."

"He did."

"Right, well, we don't think he's met up with foul play, if that's your concern."

"What makes you say that?"

"No evidence of such."

"Meaning," she said, "that you haven't found bloodstains or anything like that?"

"That's correct. But more than that"—Perlmutter looked over at Daley again—"we did find something that, well, we probably shouldn't share with you."

Grace adjusted herself in the seat. She tried very hard to meet his eye, but he wouldn't face her. "I'd very much appreciate knowing what you found."

"It's not much," Perlmutter said.

She waited.

"Officer Daley called your husband's office. He's not there, of course. I'm sure you know that already. He also didn't call in sick. So we decided to investigate a little more. Unofficially, you understand."

"Right."

"You were helpful enough to give us your car's E-ZPass number. We ran it through the computer. What time did you say your husband went out last night?"

"Around ten o'clock."

"And you thought that maybe he went to the grocery store?"

"I didn't know. He didn't tell me."

"He just up and left?"

"Right."

"And you never asked him where he was going?"

"I was upstairs. I heard the car start up."

"Okay, here's what I need to know." Perlmutter let go of the paunch. His chair creaked as he leaned forward. "You called him on the cell phone. Pretty much right away. Is that correct?"

"Yes."

"Well, see, that's the problem. Why didn't he answer you? I mean, if he wanted to talk to you?"

Grace saw where he was going with this.

"Do you think your husband—what?—got in an accident right away? Or maybe someone grabbed him within minutes of leaving your house?"

Grace hadn't really thought about that. "I don't know."

"Do you ever drive up the New York Thruway?"

The change of subject threw her. "Not often, but sure, I've taken it."

"Ever go to Woodbury Commons?"

"The outlet mall?"

"Yes."

"I've been, yes."

"How long do you figure it takes to get there?"

"Half an hour. Is that where he went?"

"I doubt it, not at that hour. The stores are all closed. But he used his E-ZPass at the tollbooth on that exit at precisely ten twenty-six p.m. It leads to Route 17, and heck, that's how I go to the Poconos. Give or take ten minutes either way, that would fit a scenario where your husband left your house and drove straight in that direction. From there, well, who knows where he went? It's fifteen miles to Interstate 84. From there you can go straight to California if you'd like."

She sat there.

"So add it up, Mrs. Lawson. Your husband leaves the house. You call him immediately. He doesn't answer. Within a half hour or so, we know he's driving in New York. If someone had attacked him or if he got in an accident, well, there's no way he could have been snatched and then used his E-ZPass up there in that short a time frame. Do you understand what I'm telling you?"

Grace met his eye. "That I'm a hysterical bimbo whose husband ran out on her."

"That's not what I'm saying at all. It's just . . . Well, we really can't investigate any further at this point. Unless . . ." He leaned a little closer. "Mrs. Lawson, is there anything else you can think of that could help us here?"

Grace tried not to squirm. She glanced behind her. Officer Daley had not moved. She had a copy of the strange photograph in her purse. She thought about Fuzz Pellet Josh and the store not opening. It was time to tell them. In hindsight she should have told Daley about it when it first showed up.

"I'm not sure it's relevant," she began, reaching into her purse. She pulled out a copy of the photograph and passed it to Perlmutter. Perlmutter took out a pair of reading glasses, cleaned them on his shirt, and pushed them into place. Daley walked around and bent down over the captain's shoulder. She told them about finding the photograph mixed in with her others. The two officers stared at her as if she'd taken out a razor and started shaving her head.

When Grace was done, Captain Perlmutter pointed to the picture and said, "And you're sure that's your husband?"

"I think so."

"But you're not sure?"

"I'm pretty sure."

He nodded in that way people do when they think you're a lunatic. "And the other people in the photo? The young lady somebody crossed out?"

"I don't know them."

"But your husband. He said it wasn't him, right?"

"Right."

"So if it isn't him, well, this is irrelevant. And if it is him"—Perlmutter took off the glasses—"he lied to you. Isn't that correct, Mrs. Lawson?"

Her cell phone rang. Grace grabbed it fast and checked the number. It was Jack.

For a moment she went very still. Grace wanted to excuse herself, but Perlmutter and Daley were both looking at her. Asking for privacy was not really an option here. She hit the ANSWER button and brought the phone to her ear.

"Jack?"

JUST ONE LOOK · 69

"Hey."

The sound of his voice should have filled her with relief. It didn't.

Jack said, "I tried you at home. Where are you?"

"Where am *I*?"

"Listen, I can't talk long. I'm sorry about running out on you like that."

His tone was aiming for casual, but it wasn't hitting the mark.

"I need a few days," he said.

"What are you talking about?"

"Where are you, Grace?"

"I'm at the police station."

"You called the police?"

Her eyes met Perlmutter's. He wiggled his fingers, as if to say, *Give me the phone, little lady. I'll handle it.*

"Look, Grace, just give me a few days. I . . ." Jack stopped. And then he said something that made the dread grow tenfold. "I need some space."

"Space," she repeated.

"Yes. A little space. That's all. Please tell the police that I apologize. I have to go now. Okay? I'll be back soon."

"Jack?"

He didn't reply.

"I love you," Grace said.

But the phone was dead.

CHAPTER 8

S pace. Jack said he needed space. And that was all wrong.

Never mind that "needing space" was one of those lame, cloying, namby-pamby, New Age we-are-the-world terms that was worse than meaningless—"needing space"—a terrible euphemism for "I'm soooo outta here." That would have been a clue perhaps, but this went much deeper.

Grace was home now. She had mumbled an apology to Perlmutter and Daley. Both men looked at her with pity and told her that it was all part of the job. They said that they were sorry. Grace offered up a solemn nod and headed for the door.

She had learned something crucial from the phone call.

Jack was in trouble.

She had not been overreacting. His disappearance had nothing to do with running away from her or fear of commitment. It was no accident. It had not been expected or planned. She had picked up the photograph from the store. Jack had seen it and run out.

And now he was in serious danger.

She could never explain this to the police. First off, they wouldn't believe her. They would claim that she was either delusional or naïve to the point of a learning disability. Maybe not to her face. Maybe they would humor her, which would be both a tremendous irritant and a waste of time. They'd been convinced that Jack was on the run before the call. Her explanation would not change their minds.

And maybe that was best.

Grace was trying to read between the lines here. Jack had been concerned about police involvement. That was obvious. When she said that she was at the police station, the regret in his voice was real. That was no act.

Space.

That was the main clue. If he had just told her that he was leaving for a few days, blowing off steam, running off with a stripper he'd met at the Satin Dolls, okay, she might not believe him, but it would be in the realm of possibility. But Jack hadn't done that. He had been specific about his reasons for disappearing. He even repeated himself.

Jack needed space.

Marital codes. All couples have them. Most were pretty stupid. For example, there was a scene in the Billy Crystal movie *Mr. Saturday Night* when the comic Crystal played—Grace couldn't remember the name, barely remembered the movie—pointed at an old man with a terrible toupee and said, "Is that a toupee? I, for one, was fooled." So now, whenever she and Jack saw a man with a possible toupee, one would turn to the other and say, "I for one?" and the spouse would either agree or disagree. Grace and Jack started using "I for one" for other vanity enhancements too—nose jobs, breast implants, whatever.

The origin of "Need space" was a bit more risqué.

Despite her current predicament, Grace's cheeks couldn't help but flush from the memory. Sex had always been very good with Jack, but in any long-term relationship, there are ebbs and flows. This was two years ago, during a time of, uh, great flow. A stage of more corporeal creativity, if you will. Public creativity, to be more specific.

There had been the quick nooky in the changing room at one of those upscale hair salons. There had been under-the-coat manipulation in a private balcony at a lush Broadway musical. But it was midway through a particularly daring encounter in a British-style red phone booth located on, of all places, a quiet street in Allendale, New Jersey, when Jack suddenly panted, "I need space."

Grace had looked up at him. "Excuse me?"

"I mean, literally. Back up! The phone receiver is pressing into my neck!"

They'd both laughed. Grace closed her eyes now, a faint smile on her lips. "Need space" had thus joined the ranks of their private marital language. Jack would not use that phrase haphazardly. He was sending her a message, warning her, letting her know that he was saying something he didn't mean.

Okay, so what did he mean then?

Jack couldn't speak freely for one thing. Someone was listening. Who? Was someone with him—or was he afraid because she was with the cops? She hoped the latter, that he was alone and simply didn't want police involvement.

But when she considered all the facts, that possibility seemed unlikely.

If Jack had been free to talk, why hadn't he called her back? He'd have to realize that she'd be out of the police station by now. If he were okay, if he was alone, Jack would have called again, just to let her know what was going on. He hadn't done that.

Conclusion: Jack was with somebody and in serious trouble.

Did he want her to react or sit tight? In the same way she knew Jack—in the same way she knew that he'd been sending her a signal—Jack would know that Grace's reaction would not be to go quietly into that good night. That was not her personality. Jack understood that. She would try to find him.

He had probably counted on that.

Of course, this was all no more than conjecture. She knew her husband well—or maybe she didn't?—so her conjectures were more than mere fancy. But how much more? Maybe she was just justifying her decision to take action.

Didn't matter. Either way, she was involved.

Grace thought about what she'd already learned. Jack had taken the Windstar up the New York Thruway. Who did they know up there? Why would he have gone that way so late at night?

She had no idea.

Hold up.

Roll it back to the start: Jack comes home. Jack sees the photograph. That was what set it off. The photograph. He sees it on the kitchen counter. She starts asking him about it. He gets a call from Dan. And then he goes into his study . . .

Stop. His study.

Grace hurried down the hall. *Study* was a rather ornate word for this converted screened-in porch. The plaster was cracking in spots. There was always a draft in the winter and a stifling lack of anything approaching air in the summer. There were photographs of the kids in cheap frames and two of her paintings in expensive ones. The study felt strangely impersonal to her. Nothing in here told you about the past of the room's main occupant—no mementos, no softball signed by friends, no photo of a golf foursome taking to the links. Other than some pharmaceutical freebies—pens, pads, a paper clip holder—there were no clues as to who Jack really was other than a husband, father, and researcher.

But maybe that was all there was.

Grace felt weird, snooping. There had been strength, she thought, in respecting each other's privacy. They each had a room closed off to the other. Grace had always been okay with that. She'd even convinced herself it was healthy. Now she wondered about looking away. She wondered if it'd derived from a desire to give Jack privacy—needing space?!—or because she feared poking a beehive.

His computer was up and online. Jack's default page was the "official" Grace Lawson Web site. Grace stared at the chair for a moment, the ergonomic gray from the local Staples store, imagining Jack there, turning on the computer every morning, having her face greet him. The site's home page had a glam shot of Grace along with several examples of her work. Farley, her agent, had recently insisted that she include the photograph in all her sales material because, as he put it, "You a babe." She reluctantly acquiesced. Looks had always been used by the arts to promote the work. Onstage and in movies, well, the importance of looks was obvious. Even writers, with their glossy touched-up portraits, the smoldering dark eyes of the next literati wunderkind, marketed appearances. But Grace's world—painting—had been fairly immune to this pressure, ignoring the creator's physical beauty, perhaps because the form itself was all about the physical.

But not anymore.

An artist appreciates the importance of the aesthetical, of course. Aesthetics do more than alter perception. They alter reality. Prime example: If Grace had been fat or homely, the TV crews would not have been monitoring her vital signs after she'd been pulled from the Boston Massacre. If she'd been physically unappealing, she would have never been adopted as the "people's survivor," the innocent, the "Crushed Angel," as one tabloid headline dubbed her. The media always broadcasted her image while giving medical updates. The press—nay, the country— demanded constant updates on her condition. The families of victims visited her room, spent time with her, searched her face for ghostly wisps of their own lost children.

Would they have done the same had she been unattractive?

Grace didn't want to speculate. But as one too-honest art critic had told her: "We have little interest in a painting that has little aesthetic appeal—why should it be different with a human being?"

Even before the Boston Massacre Grace had wanted to be an artist. But something—something elusive and impossible to explain—had been missing. The whole experience had helped take her artistic sensibilities to the next level. Yes, she knew how pretentious that sounded. She had disdained that art-school clatter: You have to suffer for your art; you need tragedy to give your work texture. It had always rung hollow before, but now she understood that there was indeed something to it.

Even though she hadn't changed her conscious viewpoint, her work developed that vague intangible. There was more emotion, more life, more . . . swirl. Her work was darker, angrier, more vivid. People often wondered if she'd ever painted any scenes from that horrible day. The simple answer was only one portrait—a young face so full of hope that you knew it would soon be crushed—but the truer answer was that the Boston Massacre shaded and colored everything she touched.

Grace sat down at Jack's desk. The phone was to her right. She reached for it, deciding to try the simplest thing first: hit REDIAL on Jack's phone.

The phone—a new Panasonic model she'd picked up at Radio Shack—had an LCD screen so she could see the redialed number come up. The 212 area code. New York City. She waited. On the third ring a woman answered and said, "Burton and Crimstein, law office."

Grace wasn't sure how to proceed.

"Hello?"

"This is Grace Lawson calling."

"How may I transfer your call?"

Good question. "How many attorneys work at the firm?"

"I really couldn't say. Would you like me to connect you with one?"

"Yes, please."

There was a pause. The voice had a shade of that trying-to-be-helpful impatience now. "Is there one in particular?"

Grace checked the caller ID. There were too many numbers. She saw that now. Usually long distance calls had eleven numbers. But here there were fifteen, including an asterisk. She mulled that over. If Jack had made the call, it would have been late last night. The receptionists would not have been on duty. Jack probably hit the asterisk button and plugged in an extension.

"Ma'am?"

"Extension four-six-three," she said, reading off the screen.

"I'll connect you."

The phone rang three times.

"Sandra Koval's line."

"Ms. Koval please."

"May I ask who is calling?"

"My name is Grace Lawson."

"And what is this in reference to?"

"My husband, Jack."

"Please hold."

Grace gripped the phone. Thirty seconds later, the voice came back on.

"I'm sorry. Ms. Koval is in a meeting."

"It's urgent."

"I'm sorry—"

"I just need a second of her time. Tell her it's very important."

The sigh was intentionally audible. "Please hold."

The hold music was a Muzak version of Nirvana's "Smells Like Teen Spirit." It was strangely calming.

"Can I help you?" The voice was all clipped professionalism.

"Ms. Koval?"

"Yes?"

"My name is Grace Lawson."

"What do you want?"

"My husband, Jack Lawson, called your office yesterday."

She did not reply.

"He's missing."

"Pardon?"

"My husband is missing."

"I'm sorry to hear that, but I don't see—"

"Do you know where he is, Ms. Koval?"

"Why on earth would I know?"

"He made a phone call last night. Before he disappeared."

"So?"

"I hit the redial button. This number came up."

"Ms. Lawson, this firm employs more than two hundred attorneys. He could have been calling any of them."

"No. Your extension is here, on the redial display. He called you."

No reply.

"Ms. Koval?"

"I'm here."

"Why did my husband call you?"

"I have nothing more to say to you."

"Do you know where he is?"

"Ms. Lawson, are you familiar with attorney-client privilege?"

"Of course."

More silence.

"Are you saying my husband called you for legal advice?"

"I cannot discuss the situation with you. Good-bye."

CHAPTER 9

It didn't take Grace long to put it together.

The Internet could be a wonderful tool when used properly. Grace had Googled the words "Sandra Koval," for Web hits, for newsgroups, for images. She checked the Burton and Crimstein Web site. There were bios of all their lawyers. Sandra Koval had graduated from Northwestern. She had gotten her law degree at UCLA. Based on the years of graduation, Sandra Koval would be forty-two or so. She was married, according to the site, to one Harold Koval. They had three children.

They lived in Los Angeles.

That had been the giveaway.

Grace had done a little more research, some the old-fashioned way: with a telephone. The pieces started to come together. The problem was, the picture made no sense.

The drive into Manhattan had taken less than an hour. Burton and Crimstein's reception desk was on the fifth floor. The receptionist/security guard gave her a closed-mouth smile. "Yes?"

"Grace Lawson to see Sandra Koval."

The receptionist made a call, speaking in a voice below a whisper. A moment later, she said, "Ms. Koval will be right out."

That was something of a surprise. Grace had been prepared to launch threats or accept a long wait. She knew what Koval looked like—there had been a photograph of her on the Burton and Crimstein Web site—so she'd even accepted the fact that she might have to confront her as she left.

In the end Grace had decided to take the chance and drive into Manhattan without calling first. Not only did she feel she'd need the element of surprise, but she very much wanted to confront Sandra Koval face-to-face. Call it necessity. Call it curiosity. Grace had to see this woman for herself.

It was still early enough. Emma had a playdate after school. Max attended an "enrichment program" today. She wouldn't need to pick either of them up for several hours yet.

The reception area of Burton and Crimstein was part old-world attorney—rich mahogany, lush carpeting, tapestry-clad seating, the décor that foreshadows the billing—and part Sardi's celebrity wall. Photographs, mostly of Hester Crimstein, the famed TV attorney, adorned the walls. Crimstein had a show on Court TV cleverly dubbed *Crimstein on Crime*. The photos included Ms. Crimstein with a bevy of actors, politicos, clients, and, well, combinations of all three.

Grace was studying a photograph of Hester Crimstein standing alongside an attractive olive-skinned woman when a voice behind her said, "That's Esperanza Diaz. A professional wrestler falsely accused of murder."

Grace turned. "Little Pocahontas," she said.

"Excuse me?"

Grace pointed at the photograph. "Her wrestling name. It was Little Pocahontas."

"How do you know that?"

Grace shrugged. "I'm a swarm of useless facts."

For a moment Grace openly stared at Sandra Koval. Koval cleared her throat and made a big production of looking at her watch. "I don't have much time. Please come this way."

Neither woman spoke as they headed down the corridor and into a conference room. There was a long table, maybe twenty chairs, one of those gray speakerphones in the middle that looks suspiciously like a dropped octopus. There was a variety of soft drinks and bottled water on a counter in the corner.

Sandra Koval kept her distance. She crossed her arms and made a gesture that said, *Well?*

"I did some research on you," Grace said.

"Care to sit?"

"No."

"Mind if I do?"

"Suit yourself."

"How about a drink?"

"No."

Sandra Koval poured herself a Diet Coke. She was what you'd call a handsome woman rather than pretty or beautiful. Her hair was going a gray that worked for her. Her figure was slim, her lips full. She had one of those lick-the-world postures that let your adversaries know that you were comfortable with yourself and more than ready to do battle.

"Why aren't we in your office?" Grace asked.

"You don't care for this room?"

"It's a tad large."

Sandra Koval shrugged.

"You don't have an office here, do you?"

"You tell me."

"When I called, the woman answered, 'Sandra Koval's line.' "

"Uh-huh."

"Line, she said. Line. Not office."

"And that's supposed to mean something?"

"On its own, no," Grace said. "But I looked up the law firm on the Web. You live in Los Angeles. Near the Burton and Crimstein West Coast office."

"True enough."

"That's your home base. You're visiting here. Why?"

"A criminal case," she said. "An innocent man wrongly accused."

"Aren't they all?"

"No," Sandra Koval said slowly. "Not all."

Grace moved closer to her. "You're not Jack's lawyer," she said. "You're his sister."

Sandra Koval stared at her drink.

"I called your law school. They confirmed what I suspected. Sandra Koval was the married name. The woman who graduated was named Sandra Lawson. I double-checked it through LawMar Securities. Your grandfather's firm. Sandra Koval is listed as a member of the board."

She smiled without humor. "My, aren't we the little Sherlock?"

"So where is he?" Grace asked.

"How long have you two been married?"

"Ten years."

"And in all that time, how many times has Jack talked about me?"

"Pretty much never."

Sandra Koval spread her hands. "Precisely. So why would I know where he is?"

"Because he called you."

"So you say."

"I hit the redial button."

"Right, you told me that on the phone."

"Are you saying he didn't call you?"

"When did this call purportedly take place?"

"Purportedly?"

Sandra Koval shrugged. "Always the lawyer."

"Last night. Around ten o'clock."

"Well, there's your answer then. I wasn't here."

"Where were you?"

"At my hotel."

"But Jack called your line."

"If he did, nobody would have answered. Not at that hour. It would have gone into voice mail."

"You checked the messages today?"

"Of course. And no, none from Jack."

Grace tried to digest that. "When was the last time you spoke to Jack?"

"A long time ago."

"How long?"

Her gaze flicked away. "We haven't spoken since he went overseas."

"That was fifteen years ago."

Sandra Koval took another sip.

"How would he still know your phone number?" Grace asked.

She didn't reply.

"Sandra?"

"You live at 221 North End Avenue in Kasselton. You have two phone lines, one the phone, one the fax." Sandra repeated the two numbers from memory.

The two women looked at each other, and Grace said, "But you've never called?"

Sandra's voice was soft. "Never."

The speakerphone squawked. "Sandra?"

"Yes."

"Hester wants to see you in her office."

"On my way." Sandra Koval broke the eye contact. "I have to go now."

"Why would Jack try to call you?"

"I don't know."

"He's in trouble."

"So you say."

"He's disappeared."

"Not for the first time, Grace."

The room felt smaller now. "What happened between you and Jack?"

"It's not my place to say."

"The hell it isn't."

Sandra shifted in her seat. "You said he disappeared?"

"Yes."

"And Jack hasn't called?"

"Actually, he has."

That puzzled her. "And when he called, what did he say?"

"That he needed space. But he didn't mean it. It was code."

Sandra made a face. Grace took out the photograph and placed it on the table. The air rushed out of the room. Sandra Koval looked down and Grace could see her body jolt.

"What the hell is this?"

"Funny," Grace said.

"What?"

"Those are the exact words Jack used when he saw it."

Sandra was still staring at the picture.

"That's him, right? In the middle with the beard?" Grace asked.

"I don't know."

"Sure you do. Who's the blonde next to him?"

Grace dropped the blowup of the young woman onto the table. Sandra Koval looked up. "Where did you get these?"

"The Fotomat." Grace quickly explained. Sandra Koval's face clouded over. She wasn't buying it. "Is it Jack, yes or no?"

"I really can't say. I've never seen him with a beard."

"Why would he call you immediately after seeing this picture?"

"I don't know, Grace."

"You're lying."

Sandra Koval pushed herself to a stand. "I have a meeting."

"What happened to Jack?"

"What makes you so sure he didn't just run away?"

"We're married. We have two kids. You, Sandra, have a niece and nephew."

"And I had a brother," she countered. "Maybe neither one of us knows him that well."

"Do you love him?"

Sandra stood there, shoulders slumped. "Leave it alone, Grace."

"I can't."

Shaking her head, Sandra turned toward the door.

"I'm going to find him," Grace said.

"Don't count on it."

And then she was gone.

CHAPTER 10

O kay, Charlaine thought, mind your own business.

She drew the curtains and changed back into her jeans and sweater. She put the babydoll back in the bottom of her drawer, taking her time, folding it very carefully for some reason. As if Freddy would notice if it was wrinkled. Right.

She took a bottle of seltzer water and mixed in a little of her son's fruit punch Twister. Charlaine sat on a stool at the marble kitchen block. She stared at the glass. Her finger traced loops in the condensation. She glanced at the Sub-Zero refrigerator, the new 690 model with the stainless-steel front. There was nothing on it—no kid pictures, no family photographs, no finger smears, not even magnets. When they had the old yellow Westinghouse, the front had been blanketed with that stuff. There had been vitality and color. The remodeled kitchen, the one she had wanted so much, was sterile, lifeless.

Who was the Asian man driving Freddy's car?

Not that she kept tabs on him, but Freddy had very few visitors. She could, in fact, recall none. That didn't mean he didn't have any, of course. She did not spend her entire day watching his house. Still a neighborhood has a routine of its own. A vibe, if you will. A neighborhood is an entity, a body, and you can feel when something is out of place.

The ice in her drink was melting. Charlaine had not yet taken a sip. There was food shopping to be done. Mike's shirts would be ready at the cleaner. She was having lunch with her friend Myrna at Baumgart's on Franklin Avenue. Clay had karate with Master Kim after school.

She mentally ran through the rest of her to-do list and tried to come up with an order. Mindless stuff. Would there be time before lunch to do the food shopping and get back to the house? Probably not. The frozen goods would melt in the car. That errand would have to wait.

She stopped. To hell with this.

Freddy should be at work now.

That was how it'd always worked. Their perverted little dance lasted from around ten to ten-thirty. By ten forty-five, Charlaine always heard that garage door open. She'd watch his Honda Accord pull out. Freddy worked, she knew, for H&R Block. It was in the same strip mall as the Blockbuster where she rented DVDs. His desk was near the window. She avoided walking past it, but some days, when she parked, she would look over and see Freddy staring out the window, pencil resting against his lips, lost.

Charlaine found the yellow pages and looked up the number. A man identifying himself as a supervisor said that Mr. Sykes was not in but was expected at any moment. She pretended to be put out. "He told me he'd be in by now. Doesn't he normally get in at eleven?"

The supervisor admitted that he did.

"So where is he? I really need those figures."

The supervisor apologized and assured her that Mr. Sykes would call the moment he arrived at his desk. She hung up.

Now what?

Something still felt very wrong here.

But so what? Who was Freddy Sykes to her anyway? Nothing. In a way, less than nothing. He was a reminder of her failures. He was a symptom of how pathetic she had become. She owed him nothing.

More than that, imagine, just imagine, if poking around got her caught. Imagine if somehow the truth came out.

Charlaine looked over at Freddy's place. The truth coming out.

Somehow that no longer bothered her all that much.

She grabbed her coat and headed toward Freddy's house.

CHAPTER 11

E ric Wu had seen the lingerie-clad woman in the window.

The previous night had been a long one for Wu. He had not anticipated any interference, and while the large man—his wallet said his name was Rocky Conwell—had presented no threat, Wu now had to get rid of a body and another car. That meant an extra trip back up to Central Valley, New York.

First things first. He packed Rocky Conwell into the trunk of his Toyota Celica. He moved Jack Lawson, whom he had originally jammed into the Honda Accord's trunk, to the back of the Ford Windstar. Once the bodies were out of sight, Wu changed license plates, got rid of the E-ZPass, and drove the Ford Windstar back to Ho-Ho-Kus. He parked the minivan in Freddy Sykes's garage. There was still enough time to catch a bus back up to Central Valley. Wu searched Conwell's car. Satisfied that it was cleared out, he took it to the Park-n-Ride on Route 17. He found a remote spot near the fence. A car being left there for days, even weeks, was not unusual. The smell would eventually bring attention, but that would not be anytime soon.

The Park-n-Ride was only three miles from Sykes's house in Ho-Ho-Kus. Wu walked. Early the next morning, he rose and caught the bus back to Central Valley. He picked up Sykes's Honda Accord. On the way back, he took a brief detour past the Lawson residence.

A patrol car was in the driveway.

Wu considered that. It did not cause him great concern, but perhaps he should nip any police involvement in the bud. He knew just how.

Wu drove back to Freddy's residence and turned on the television. Wu liked daytime TV. He enjoyed watching shows like *Springer* and *Ricki Lake*. Most people pooh-poohed them. Wu did not. Only a truly great society, a free one, could allow such nonsense to air. But more than that, stupidity made Wu happy. People were sheep. The weaker they are, the stronger you are. What could be more comforting or entertaining?

During a commercial—the theme of the show, according to a graphic on the bottom: "Mommy Won't Let Me Get a Nipple Ring!"—Wu rose. It was time to take care of the potential police problem.

Wu didn't need to touch Jack Lawson. All he had to say was one sentence: "I know that you have two children."

Lawson cooperated. He made the call to his wife's cell phone and told her he needed space.

At ten forty-five—with Wu watching a mother and daughter wrestle across a stage while a crowd chanted "Jerry!"—a call came in from a prison acquaintance.

"All okay?"

Wu said yes.

He pulled the Honda Accord out of the garage. As he did, he noticed the woman who lived next door standing in the window. She was wearing lingerie. Wu might not have thought much about the scene—a woman still in her unmentionables after ten in the morning—but for something about the way she suddenly ducked away. . . .

That might have been a natural reaction. You parade around in lingerie, forgetting to pull down your shade, and then you spot a stranger. Many people, perhaps most people, would move away or cover up. So it could be nothing.

But the woman had moved very fast, as if in a panic. More than that, she had not moved when the car first pulled out—only when she'd spotted Wu. If she had been afraid of being seen, wouldn't she have pulled the shade or ducked down when she first heard or saw the car?

Wu pondered that. He had, in fact, been pondering it all day.

He picked up his cell phone and hit the button to dial the last incoming number.

A voice said, "Problem?"

"I don't think so." Wu turned the car around and started back toward the Sykes house. "But I may be late."

CHAPTER 12

Grace didn't want to make the phone call.

She was still in New York City. There was a law against using a cell phone while driving unless it was hands-free, though that had nothing to do with her hesitation. With one hand on the steering wheel, she felt around on the floor of the car. She located the ear attachment, managed to untangle the cord, and jammed the earpiece deep into the canal.

This was supposed to be safer than using a handheld?

She turned on the cell phone. Though Grace hadn't called the number in years, she still had it programmed into the cell. For emergencies, she supposed. Like this one.

The phone was answered on the first ring.

"Yes?"

No name. No hello. No company greeting.

"This is Grace Lawson."

"Hold."

The wait was not long. First Grace heard the static and then, "Grace?"

"Hello, Mr. Vespa."

"Please call me Carl."

"Carl, right."

"You got my message?" he asked.

"Yes." She did not tell Carl Vespa that it had nothing to do with why she was calling now. There was feedback on the line. "Where are you?" she asked.

"My jet. We're about an hour outside of Stewart."

Stewart was an air force base and airport about an hour and a half from her house.

Silence.

"Is something wrong, Grace?"

"You said to call if I ever needed anything."

"And now, fifteen years later, you do?"

"I think so."

"Good. And your timing couldn't be better. There's something I want to show you."

"What's that?"

"Listen, are you home?"

"I'll be there soon."

"I'll pick you up in two, two and a half hours. We can talk then, okay? Do you have someone to watch the kids?"

"I should be able to find someone."

"If you can't, I'll leave my assistant at your house. See you then."

Carl Vespa hung up. Grace kept driving. She wondered what he wanted from her now. She wondered about the wisdom of calling him in the first place. She hit the first number on her speed dial again—Jack's cell phone—but there was still no answer.

Grace had another idea. She called her friend of the no-ménage, Cora.

"Didn't you used to date a guy who worked in e-mail spam?" Grace asked.

"Yep," Cora said. "Obsessive creep named—get this—Gus. Hard to get rid of. I had to use my own version of a bunker buster on him."

"What did you do?"

"I told Gus he had a small wee-wee."

JUST ONE LOOK · 93

"Ouch."

"Like I said, the bunker buster. Works every time, but there's often, uh, collateral damage."

"I might need his help."

"How?"

Grace was not sure how to put this. She decided to concentrate on the blonde with the X across her face, the one she was sure she'd seen before. "I found this photograph . . ." she began.

"Right."

"And there's this woman in it. She's probably late teens, early twenties."

"Uh-huh."

"It's an old picture. I'd say fifteen, twenty years old. Anyway, I need to find out who the girl is. I was thinking maybe I could send it out via spam mail. I could ask if anyone can identify the girl for a research project, something like that. I know most people erase those e-mails, but if a few looked, I don't know, maybe I could get a response."

"Long shot."

"Yeah, I know."

"And wow, talk about creeps coming out of the woodwork. Imagine the replies."

"Got a better idea?"

"Not really, no. It could work, I guess. By the way, you notice I'm not asking you why you need to find the identity of a woman in a picture from fifteen, twenty years ago?"

"I do."

"I just wanted it noted for the record."

"So noted. It's a long story."

"You need someone to tell it to?"

"I might. I might also need someone to watch the kids for a few hours."

"I'm available and alone." Pause. "Sheesh, I have to stop saying that."

"Where's Vickie?" Vickie was Cora's daughter.

"She's spending the night at the McMansion with my ex and his horse-faced wife. Or as I prefer to put it, she's spending the night in the bunker with Adolf and Eva."

Grace managed a smile.

"My car is in the shop," Cora said. "Can you pick me up on the way?"

"I'll be there right after I grab Max."

Grace swung by the Montessori Enrichment Program and grabbed her son. Max had that near-tears thing going on, having lost several of his Yu-Gi-Oh! cards to a classmate in some dumb game. Grace tried to humor him, but he wasn't in the mood. She gave up. She helped him get his jacket on. His hat was missing. So was one of his gloves. Another mother smiled and whistled while bundling up her little bundle in color-coordinated knit (hand-knit, no doubt) hat, scarf, and yes, matching gloves. She looked over at Grace and faked a sympathetic smile. Grace did not know this woman, but she disliked her intensely.

Being a mother, Grace thought, was a lot like being an artist—you are always insecure, you always feel like a phony, you know that everybody else is better at it than you. The mothers who doted obsessively on their offspring, the ones who performed their numbing tasks with that Stepford-ready smile and supernatural patience—you know, those mothers who always, *always*, have the right supplies for the ideal after-school craft . . . Grace suspected that these women were profoundly disturbed.

Cora was waiting in the driveway of her bubble-gum-pink house. Everybody on the block hated the color. For a while, one neighbor, a prissy thing properly named Missy, had started up a petition demanding that Cora repaint it. Grace had seen Prissy Missy passing around the petition at a first-grade soccer game. Grace had asked to see it, ripped it up, and walked away.

The color was hardly to Grace's taste, but memo to the Missys of the world: Get over yourselves.

Cora teetered toward them in her stiletto heels. She was dressed slightly more demurely—a sweatshirt over the leotard—but it really didn't matter. Some women oozed sex, even if dressed in a burlap sack. Cora was one of them. When she moved, new curves were formed even as old ones disappeared. Every line from her husky voice, no matter how innocuous, came out as a double entendre. Every tilt of the head was a come-on.

Cora slid in and looked back at Max. "Hey, handsome."

Max grunted and didn't look up.

"Just like my ex." Cora spun back around. "You got that photo?"

"I do."

"I called Gus. He'll do it."

"Did you promise anything in return?"

"Remember what I said about fifth-date syndrome? Well, are you free Saturday night?"

Grace looked at her.

"Kidding."

"I knew that."

"Good. Anyway, Gus said to scan the photo and e-mail it to him. He can set up an anonymous e-mail address for you to receive replies. No one will know who you are. We'll keep the text to a minimum, just say that a journalist is doing a story and needs to know the origin of the photograph. That sound okay?"

"Yeah, thanks."

They arrived at the house. Max stomped upstairs and then shouted down, "Can I watch *SpongeBob*?"

Grace acquiesced. Like every parent, Grace had strict rules about no TV during the day. Like every parent, she knew that rules were made to be broken. Cora headed straight for the cupboard and made coffee. Grace thought about which photograph to send and decided to use a blowup of the right side, the blonde with the X on her face and the red-head on her left. She left Jack's image—again, assuming that *was* Jack—

out. She didn't yet want him involved. She decided that having two people increased the chances of getting an identity hit and made the solicitation look less like the work of a crazed stalker.

Cora looked at the original photograph. "May I make an observation?"

"Yes."

"This is pretty weird."

"The guy over here"—Grace pointed—"the one with the beard. Who does that look like to you?"

Cora squinted. "I guess it could be Jack."

"Could be or is?"

"You tell me."

"Jack's missing."

"Come again?"

She told Cora the story. Cora listened, tapping a too-long fingernail painted up in Chanel's Rouge Noir, a color not unlike blood, on the tabletop. When Grace finished, Cora said, "You know, of course, that I have a low opinion of men."

"I know."

"I believe that, for the most part, they are two floors below dog turd."

"I know that too."

"So the obvious answer is that, yes, this is a picture of Jack. That, yes, this little blondie, the one gazing up at him like he's the messiah, is an old flame. That yes, Jack and Mary Magdalene here are having an affair. That someone, maybe her current husband, wanted you to find out about it, so he sent you that picture. That everything came to a head when Jack realized that you were on to him."

"And that's why he ran away?"

"Correct."

"That doesn't add up, Cora."

"You have a better theory?"

"I'm working on it."

"Good," Cora said, "because I don't buy it either. I'm just talking. The rule is this: Men are scum. Jack, however, has always hit me as the exception that proves the rule."

"I love you, you know."

Cora nodded. "Everybody does."

Grace heard a sound and glanced out the window. A stretch limousine of glistening black slid up the driveway with the smoothness of a Motown background singer. The chauffeur, a rat-faced man with the build of a whippet, hurried to open the car's back door.

Carl Vespa had arrived.

Despite his rumored vocation, Carl Vespa did not dress in *Sopranos*-style velour or shiny, sealant-coated suits. He preferred khakis, Joseph Abboud sports coats, and loafers sans socks. He was midsixties but looked a solid decade younger. His hair was tickling-the-shoulders long, the color a distinguished shade of blond-gone-to-gray. His face was tanned and had the sort of waxy smoothness that suggests Botox. His teeth were aggressively capped, as if the front cuspids had taken growth hormones.

He nodded an order at the whippetlike driver and approached the house on his own. Grace opened the door to greet him. Carl Vespa gave her the toothy dazzler. She smiled back, glad to see him. He greeted her with a kiss on the cheek. No words were exchanged. They didn't need them. He held both her hands and looked at her. She could see his eyes start to well up.

Max moved to his mother's right. Vespa let go and took a step back.

"Max," Grace began, "this is Mr. Vespa."

"Hello, Max."

"That your car?" Max asked.

"Yes."

Max looked at the car, then at Vespa. "Got a TV inside?"

"It does."

"Whoa."

Cora cleared her throat.

"Oh, and this is my friend, Cora."

"Charmed," Vespa said.

Cora looked at the car, then at Vespa. "You single?"

"I am."

"Whoa."

Grace repeated the babysitting instructions for the sixth time. Cora pretended to listen. Grace gave her twenty dollars to order pizza and that cheesy bread Max had become enamored with of late. A classmate's mom would bring Emma home in an hour.

Grace and Vespa headed toward the limousine. The rat-faced driver had the door open and at the ready. Vespa said, "This is Cram," gesturing to the driver. When Cram shook her hand, Grace had to bite back a scream.

"A pleasure," Cram said. His smile brought on visions of a Discovery Channel documentary on sea predators. She slid in first, and Carl Vespa followed.

There were Waterford glasses and a matching decanter half-filled with a liquid that appeared both caramel and luxurious. There was, as noted, a television set. Above her seat was a DVD player, a multiple-CD player, climate controls, and enough buttons to confuse an airline pilot. The whole thing—the crystal, the decanter, the electronics—was overstated, but maybe that was what you wanted in a stretch limousine.

"Where are we going?" Grace asked.

"It's a little hard to explain." They were sitting next to each other, both facing forward. "I'd rather just show it to you, if that's okay."

Carl Vespa had been the first lost parent to loom over her hospital bed. When Grace first came out of the coma, his was the first face she saw. She had no idea who he was, where she was, what day it was. More than a week was gone from her memory banks. Carl Vespa ended up sitting in her hospital room for days on end, sleeping in the chair next to her. He made sure that plenty of flowers surrounded her. He made sure that she had a good view, soothing music, enough pain medication, private nursing. He made sure that once Grace was able to eat, the hospital staff didn't give her the standard slop.

He never asked her for details of that night because, in truth, she really could not provide any. Over the next few months they talked for countless hours. He told her stories, mostly about his failures as a father. He had used his connections to get into her hospital room that first night. He had paid off security—interestingly enough, the security firm at the hospital was actually controlled by organized crime—and then he had simply sat with her.

Eventually other parents followed his lead. It was weird. They wanted to be around her. That was all. They found comfort in it. Their child had died in Grace's presence and it was as if maybe a small part of their souls, their forever-lost son or daughter, somehow still lived inside of her. It made no sense and yet Grace thought that maybe she understood.

These heartbroken parents came to talk about their dead children, and Grace listened. She figured that she owed them at least that much. She knew that these relationships were probably unhealthy, but there was no way she could turn them away. The truth was, Grace had no family of her own. She'd thrived, for a little while at least, on the attention. They needed a child; she needed a parent. It wasn't that simple—this malaise of cross-projection—but Grace wasn't sure she could explain it any better.

The limo headed south on the Garden State Parkway now. Cram flipped on the radio. Classical music, a violin concerto from the sound of it, came through the speakers.

Vespa said, "You know, of course, that the anniversary is coming up."

"I do," she said, though she had done her best to ignore it all. Fifteen years. Fifteen years since that awful night at the Boston Garden. The papers had run all the expected "Where Are They Now?" commemorative pieces. The parents and survivors all handled it differently. Most participated because they felt it was one way to keep the memory of what happened alive. There had been heart-wrenching articles on the Garrisons and the Reeds and the Weiders. The security guard, Gordon MacKenzie, who was credited with saving many by forcing open locked emergency exits, now worked as a police captain in Brookline, a Boston suburb. Even Carl Vespa had allowed a picture of him and his wife, Sharon, sitting in their yard, both still looking as if someone had just hollowed out their insides.

Grace had gone the other way. With her art career in full swing, she did not want even the appearance of capitalizing on the tragedy. She had been injured, that was all, and to make more of it than that reminded her of those washed-up actors who come out of the woodwork to shed crocodile tears when a hated costar suddenly dies. She wanted no part of it. The attention should be given to the dead and those they left behind.

"He's up for parole again," Vespa said. "Wade Larue, I mean."

She knew, of course.

The stampede that night had been blamed on Wade Larue, currently a resident of Walden Prison outside Albany, New York. He was the one who fired the shots creating the panic. The defense's claim was interesting. They argued that Wade Larue didn't do it—forget the gun residue found on his hands, the gun belonging to him, the bullet match to the gun, the witnesses who saw him fire—but if he *did* do it, he was too stoned to remember. Oh, and if neither of those rationales floated your boat, Wade Larue couldn't have known that firing a gun would cause the death of eighteen people and the injury of dozens more.

The case proved to be controversial. The prosecutors went for eighteen counts of murder, but the jury didn't see it that way. Larue's lawyer ended up cutting a deal for eighteen counts of manslaughter. Nobody really worried too much about sentencing. Carl Vespa's only son had died that night. Remember what happened when Gotti's son was killed in a car accident? The man driving the car, a family man, has never been heard from again. A similar fate, most agreed, would befall Wade Larue, except this time, the general public would probably applaud the outcome.

For a while, Larue was kept isolated in Walden Prison. Grace didn't follow the story closely, but the parents—parents like Carl Vespa—still called and wrote all the time. They needed to see her every once in a while. As a survivor, she had become a vessel of some sort, carrying the dead. Putting aside the physical recuperation, this emotional pressure—this awesome, impossible responsibility—was a big part of the reason for Grace's going overseas.

Eventually Larue had been put in the general population. Rumor had it he was beaten and abused by his fellow inmates, but for whatever reason, he lived. Carl Vespa had decided to forgo the hit. Maybe it was a sign of mercy. Or maybe it was just the opposite. Grace didn't know.

Vespa said, "He finally stopped claiming total innocence. Did you hear that? He admits he fired his gun, but that he just freaked out when the lights went out."

Which made sense. For her part, Grace had seen Wade Larue only once. She had been called to testify, though her testimony had nothing to do with guilt and innocence—she had almost no memory of the stampede, never mind who fired the gun—and everything to do with inflaming the passion of the jury. But Grace didn't need revenge. To her Wade Larue was stoned out of his mind, a souped-up punk more worthy of pity than hate.

"Do you think he'll get out?" she asked.

"He has a new lawyer. She's damn good."

"And if she gets him released?"

Vespa smiled. "Don't believe everything you read about me." Then he added, "Besides, Wade Larue isn't the only one to blame for that night."

"What do you mean?"

He opened his mouth and then fell silent. Then: "It's like I said. I'd rather show you."

Something about his tone told her to change subjects. "You said you were single," Grace said.

"Pardon?"

"You told my friend you were single."

He waved his finger. No ring. "Sharon and I divorced two years ago."

"I'm sorry to hear that."

"It hasn't been right for a long time." He shrugged, looking off. "How is your family?"

"Okay."

"I sense some hesitation."

She may have shrugged.

"On the phone, you said you needed my help."

"I think so."

"So what's wrong?"

"My husband . . ." She stopped. "I think my husband is in trouble."

She told him the story. His eyes stayed straight ahead, avoiding her gaze. He nodded every once in a while, but the nods seemed strangely out of context. His expression didn't change, which was strange. Carl Vespa was usually more animated. After she stopped talking, he didn't say anything for a long time.

"This photograph," Vespa said. "Do you have it with you?"

"Yes." She handed it to him. His hand, she noticed, had a small quake. Vespa stared at the picture for a very long time.

"Can I keep this?" he asked.

"I have copies."

Vespa's eyes were still on the images. "Do you mind if I ask you a few personal questions?" he asked.

"I guess not."

"Do you love your husband?"

"Very much."

"Does he love you?"

"Yes."

Carl Vespa had only met Jack once. He had sent a wedding gift when they got married. He sent gifts on Emma's and Max's birthday too. Grace wrote him thank-you notes and gave the gifts to charity. She didn't mind being connected to him, she guessed, but she didn't want her children . . . what was the phrase? . . . tainted by the association.

"You two met in Paris, right?"

"Southern France, actually. Why?"

"And how did you meet again?"

"What's the difference?"

He hesitated a second too long. "I guess I'm trying to learn how well you know your husband."

"We've been married ten years."

"I understand that." He shifted in his seat. "You were there on vacation when you met?"

"I don't know if I'd call it a vacation exactly."

"You were studying. You were painting."

"Yes."

"And, well, mostly you were running away."

She said nothing.

"And Jack?" Vespa continued. "Why was he there?"

"Same reason, I guess."

"He was running away?"

"Yes."

"From what?"

"I don't know."

"May I state the obvious then?"

She waited.

"Whatever he was running from"—Vespa gestured toward the photograph—"it caught up to him."

The thought had occurred to Grace too. "That was a long time ago."

"So was the Boston Massacre. Your running away. Did it make it go away?"

In the rearview mirror she saw Cram glance at her, waiting for an answer. She kept still.

"Nothing stays in the past, Grace. You know that."

"I love my husband."

He nodded.

"Will you help me?"

"You know I will."

The car veered off the Garden State Parkway. Up ahead, Grace saw an enormous bland structure with a cross on it. It looked like an airplane hangar. A neon sign stated that tickets were still available for the CONCERTS WITH THE LORD. A band called Rapture would be playing. Cram pulled the limo into a parking lot big enough to declare statehood.

"What are we doing here?"

"Finding God," Carl Vespa said. "Or maybe His opposite. Let's go inside. I want to show you something."

CHAPTER 13

This was nuts, Charlaine thought.

She moved steadily toward Freddy Sykes's yard without thought or emotion. It had crossed her mind that she could be raising the danger stakes out of desperation, hungry as she was for any kind of drama in her life. But okay, again, so what? Really, when she thought about it, what was the worst that could happen? Suppose Mike did find out. Would he leave her? Would that be so bad?

Did she want to get caught?

Oh, enough with the amateur self-analysis. It wouldn't hurt to knock on Freddy's door, pretend to be neighborly. Two years ago, Mike had put up a four-foot-high stockade fence in the backyard. He had wanted one higher, but the town ordinance wouldn't allow it unless you owned a swimming pool.

Charlaine opened the gate separating her backyard from Freddy's. Odd. This was a first. She had never opened the gate before.

As she got closer to Freddy's back door, she realized how weathered his house was. The paint was peeling. The garden was overgrown. Weeds sprouted up through the cracks in the walk. There were patches of dead grass everywhere. She turned and glanced at her own house. She had never seen it from this angle. It too looked tired.

She was at Freddy's back door.

Okay, now what?

Knock on it, stupid.

She did. She started with a soft rap. No answer. She pounded louder. Nothing. She pressed her ear against the door. Like that would do any good. Like she'd hear a muffled cry or something.

There was no sound.

The shades were still down, but there were wedges that the shades couldn't quite cover. She put an eye up to an opening and peered in. The living room had a lime green couch so worn it looked like it was melting. There was a maroon vinyl recliner in the corner. The television looked new. The wall had old paintings of clowns. The piano was loaded with old black-and-white photographs. There was one of a wedding. Freddy's parents, Charlaine figured. There was another of the groom looking painfully handsome in an army uniform. There was one more photograph of the same man holding a baby, a smile spread across his face. Then the man—the soldier, the groom—was gone. The rest of the photographs were of either Freddy alone or with his mother.

The room was immaculate—no, preserved. Stuck in a time warp, unused, untouched. There was a collection of small figurines on a side table. More photographs too. A life, Charlaine thought. Freddy Sykes had a life. It was a strange thought, but there you have it.

Charlaine circled toward the garage. There was one window in the back. A flimsy curtain of pretend lace hung across it. She stood on her tiptoes. Her fingers gripped the window ledge. The wood was so old it almost broke away. Peeling paint flaked off like dandruff.

She looked into the garage.

There was another car.

Not a car actually. A minivan. A Ford Windstar. When you live in a town like this, you know all the models.

Freddy Sykes did not own a Ford Windstar.

Maybe his young Asian guest did. That would make sense, right?

She was not convinced.

So what next?

Charlaine stared down at the ground and wondered. She had been wondering since she first decided to approach the house. She had known before leaving the safety of her own kitchen that there would be no answer to her knocks. She also knew that peeking in the windows—peeping on the peeper?—would do no good.

The rock.

It was there, in what had once been a vegetable garden. She had seen Freddy use it once. It wasn't a real rock. It was one of those hide-a-keys. They were so common now that criminals probably looked for them before checking under the mat.

Charlaine bent down, picked up the rock, and turned it over. All she had to do was slide the little panel back and take the key out. She did so. The key rested in her palm, glistening in the sunlight.

Here was the line. The no-going-back line.

She moved toward the back door.

CHAPTER 14

S till wearing the sea-predator smile, Cram opened the door and Grace stepped out of the limousine. Carl Vespa slid out on his own. The huge neon sign listed a church affiliation that Grace had never heard of. The motto, according to several signs around the edifice, seemed to indicate that this was "God's House." If that were true, God could use a more creative architect. The structure held all the splendor and warmth of a highway megastore.

The interior was even worse—tacky enough to make Graceland look understated. The wall-to-wall carpeting was a shiny shade of red usually reserved for a mall girl's lipstick. The wallpaper was darker, more blood colored, a velvet affair adorned with hundreds of stars and crosses. The effect made Grace dizzy. The main chapel, or house of worship—or, most suitably, arena—held pews rather than seats. They looked uncomfortable, but then again wasn't standing encouraged? The cynical side of Grace suspected that the reason all religious services had you sporadically stand had nothing to do with devotion and everything to do with keeping congregants from falling asleep.

As soon as she entered the arena, Grace felt a flutter in her heart.

The altar, done up in the green and gold of a cheerleader's uniform, was being wheeled offstage. Grace looked for preachers with bad toupees, but none were to be found. The band—Grace assumed this was

Rapture—was setting up. Carl Vespa stopped in front of her, his eyes on the stage.

"Is this your church?" she asked him.

A small smile came to his lips. "No."

"Is it safe to assume that you're not a fan of, uh, Rapture?"

Vespa didn't answer the question. "Let's move down closer to the stage."

Cram took the lead. There were security guards, but they swept aside as if Cram were toxic.

"What's going on here?" Grace asked.

Vespa kept moving down the steps. When they reached what a theater would call the orchestra—what do you call the good seats in a church?—she looked up and got a whole new feel for the size of the place. It was a huge theater-in-the-round. The stage was in the center, surrounded on all sides. Grace felt the constriction in her throat.

Dress it up in a religious cloak, but there was no mistake.

This felt like a rock concert.

Vespa took her hand. "It'll be okay."

But it wouldn't be. She knew that. She had not been to a concert or sporting event in any "arena venue" in fifteen years. She used to love going to concerts. She remembered seeing Bruce Springsteen and the E Street Band at Asbury Park Convention Center during her high school days. What was strange to her, what she had realized even back then, was that the line between rock concert and intense religious service was not all that thick. There was a moment when Bruce played "Meeting Across the River" followed by "Jungleland"—two of Grace's favorites— when she was on her feet, her eyes closed, sheen of sweat on her face, when she was simply gone, lost, shaking with bliss, the same bliss she'd witnessed on TV when a televangelist got the crowd on its feet, hands raised and shaking.

She loved that feeling. And she knew that she never wanted to experience it again.

Grace pulled her hand away from Carl Vespa's. He nodded as if he understood. "Come on," he said gently. Grace limped behind him. The limp, it seemed to her, was getting more pronounced. Her leg throbbed. Psychological. She knew that. Tight spaces did not terrify her; huge auditoriums, especially jammed with people, did. The place was fairly empty now, thank He Who Lives Here, but her imagination entered the fray and provided the absent commotion.

Shrill feedback from the amplifier made her pull up. Someone was doing a sound check.

"What's this all about?" she asked Vespa.

His face was set. He veered to the left. Grace followed. There was a scoreboard-type sign above the stage announcing that Rapture was in the middle of a three-week gig and that they, Rapture, were: WHAT GOD HAS ON HIS MP3.

The band came onstage now for a sound check. They gathered at center stage, had a brief discussion, and then started playing. Grace was surprised. They sounded pretty good. The lyrics were syrupy, full of stuff about skies and spread wings and ascensions and being lifted up. Eminem told a potential girlfriend to "sit your drunk ass on that f***ing runway, ho." These lyrics, in their own way, were equally jarring.

The lead singer was female. She had platinum blond hair, cut with bangs, and sang with her eyes cast toward the heavens. She looked about fourteen years old. A guitarist stood to her right. He was more heavy-metal rock, what with the Medusa black locks and a tattoo of a giant cross on his right biceps. He played hard, slashing at the strings as if they had pissed him off.

When there was a lull, Carl Vespa said, "The song was written by Doug Bondy and Madison Seelinger."

She shrugged.

"Doug Bondy wrote the music. Madison Seelinger—that's the singer up there—wrote the lyrics."

"And I care because?"

"Doug Bondy is playing the drums."

They moved to the side of the stage for a better look. The music started again. They stood by a speaker. Grace's ears took the pounding, but under normal conditions, she would actually have been enjoying the sound. Doug Bondy, the drummer, was pretty much hidden by the array of cymbals and snares surrounding him. She moved a little more to the side. She could see him better now. He was banging the skins, as they say, his eyes closed, his face at peace. He looked older than the other members of the band. He had a crew cut. His face was clean shaven. He wore those black Elvis Costello glasses.

Grace felt that flutter in her chest expand. "I want to go home," she said.

"It's him, isn't it?"

"I want to go home."

The drummer was still smacking the skins, lost in the music, when he turned and saw her. Their eyes met. And she knew. So did he.

It was Jimmy X.

She didn't wait. She started limping toward the exit. The music chased her down.

"Grace?"

It was Vespa. She ignored him. She pushed through the emergency exit door. The air felt cool in her lungs. She sucked it down, tried to let the dizziness fade. Cram was outside now, as if he knew that she'd take this exit. He smiled at her.

Carl Vespa came up behind her. "It's him, right?"

"And what if it is?"

"What if...?" Vespa repeated, surprised. "He's not innocent here. He's as much to blame—"

"I want to go home."

Vespa stopped short as if she'd slapped him.

Calling him had been a mistake. She knew that now. She had lived. She had recovered. Sure, there was the limp. There was some pain. There was the occasional nightmare. But she was okay. She had gotten over it. They, the parents, never would. She saw it that first day—the shatter in their eyes—and while progress had been made, lives had been lived, pieces had been picked up, the shatter had never left. She looked now at Carl Vespa—at the eyes—and saw it all over again.

"Please," she said to him. "I just want to go home."

CHAPTER 15

Wu spotted the empty hide-a-key.

The rock was on the path by the back door, turned over like a dying crab. The cover had been slid open. Wu could see the key was gone. He remembered the first time he had approached a house that had been violated. He was six years old. The hut—it was one room, no plumbing—had been his own. The Kim government had not bothered with the niceties of keys. They had knocked the door down and dragged his mother away. Wu found her two days later. They had hanged her from a tree. No one was allowed to cut her down, under penalty of death. A day later the birds found her.

His mother had been wrongly accused of being a traitor to the Great Leader, but guilt or innocence was irrelevant. An example was made of her anyway. This is what happens to those who defy us. Check that: This is what happens to anyone we *think may be* defying us.

No one took in the six-year-old Eric. No orphanage picked him up. He did not become a ward of the state. Eric Wu ran away. He slept in the woods. He ate out of garbage cans. He survived. At thirteen, he was arrested for stealing and thrown in jail. The chief guard, a man more crooked than anyone he housed, saw Wu's potential. And so it began.

Wu stared down at the empty hide-a-key.

Someone was in the house.

He glanced at the house next door. His best guess would be that it was the woman who lived there. She liked to watch out the window. She would know where Freddy Sykes hid a key.

He considered his options. There were two.

One, he could simply leave.

Jack Lawson was in the trunk. Wu had a vehicle. He could take off, steal another car, begin his journey, set up residence elsewhere.

Problem: Wu's fingerprints were inside the house, along with the severely wounded, perhaps dead, Freddy Sykes. The lingerie-clad woman, if it was the woman, would be able to identify him too. Wu was fresh out of prison and on parole. The DA had suspected him of terrible crimes, but he could not prove them. So they cut a deal in exchange for his testimony. Wu had spent time in a maximum security penitentiary in Walden, New York. Next to what he had experienced in his homeland, the prison might as well have been a Four Seasons.

But that didn't mean he wanted to go back.

No, option one was no good. So that left option two.

Wu silently opened the door and slid inside.

Back in the limousine, Grace and Carl Vespa fell into silence.

Grace kept flashing back to the last time she'd seen Jimmy X's face—fifteen years ago in her hospital. He'd been forced to visit, a photo op arranged by his promoter, but he couldn't even look at her, never mind speak. He just stood by her bed, flowers clutched in his hand, his head down like a little boy's waiting for the teacher to scold him. She never said a word. Eventually he handed her the flowers and walked out.

Jimmy X quit the business and ran off. Rumor had it he moved to a private island near Fiji. Now, fifteen years later, here he was in New Jersey, playing drums for a Christian rock band.

When they pulled onto her street, Vespa said, "It hasn't gotten any better, you know."

Grace looked out the window. "Jimmy X didn't fire the gun."

"I know that."

"So what do you want from him?"

"He's never said he's sorry."

"And that would be enough?"

He thought about that, and then said, "There was a boy who survived. David Reed. You remember him?"

"Yes."

"He was standing next to Ryan. They were body to body. But when the crush began, this Reed kid somehow got lifted up on someone's shoulder. He got on the stage."

"I know."

"You remember what his parents said?"

She did but she said nothing.

"Jesus lifted up their son. It was God's will." Vespa's voice had not changed, but Grace could feel the hidden rage like a blast furnace. "You see, Mr. and Mrs. Reed prayed and God responded. It was a miracle, they said. God looked out for their son—that's what they kept repeating. As if God didn't have the desire or inclination to save mine."

They fell into silence. Grace wanted to tell him that many good people died that day, many people with good parents who prayed, that God does not discriminate. But Vespa knew all that. It would not comfort him.

By the time they pulled into the driveway, night was falling. Grace could see the silhouettes of Cora and the kids in the kitchen window. Vespa said, "I want to help you find your husband."

"I'm not even sure what you can do."

"You'd be surprised," he said. "You have my number. No matter what you need, call me. No matter what time it is, I don't care. I'll be there."

Cram opened the door. Vespa walked her to the door.

"I'll be in touch," he said.

"Thank you."

"I'm also going to assign Cram here to watch your house."

She looked at Cram. Cram sort of smiled back.

"That won't be necessary."

"Humor me," he said.

"No, really, I don't want that. Please."

Vespa thought about it. "If you change your mind . . . ?"

"I'll let you know."

He turned to leave then. She watched him walk back to the car and wondered about the wisdom of making deals with the devil. Cram opened the door. The limo seemed to swallow Vespa whole. Cram nodded at her. Grace did not move. She considered herself pretty good at reading people, but Carl Vespa had changed her view. She never saw or even sensed a hint of evil in him. Yet she knew it was there.

Evil—real evil—was like that.

Cora put on boiling water for the Ronzoni penne. She threw a jar of Prego into a saucepan and then leaned close to Grace's ear.

"I'm going to check the e-mail to see if we got any replies," Cora whispered.

Grace nodded. She was helping Emma do her homework and trying like hell to care. Her daughter was dressed in a Jason Kidd Nets basketball jersey. She called herself Bob. She wanted to be a jock. Grace didn't know how she felt about it, but she guessed it was better than buying *Teen Beat* magazine and lusting after nonthreatening boy bands.

Mrs. Lamb, Emma's young-but-quickly-aging teacher, had the kids working on the multiplication tables. They were doing the sixes. Grace tested Emma. At six times seven, Emma paused for a long time.

"You should know it by heart," Grace said.

"Why? I can figure it out."

"That's not the point. You learn it by heart so you can build off that when you start multiplying numbers with multiple digits."

"Mrs. Lamb didn't say to memorize them."

"You should."

"But Mrs. Lamb—"

"Six times seven."

And so it went.

Max had to find an item to put in the "Secret Box." You put something in the box—in this case, a hockey puck—and you made up three clues so that your fellow kindergartners could guess what it was. Clue one: The item is black. Clue two: It's used in a sport. Clue three: Ice. Fair enough.

Cora came back from the computer shaking her head. Nothing yet. She grabbed a bottle of Lindemans, a decent-yet-cheap Chardonnay from Australia, and popped the cork. Grace put the kids to bed.

"Where's Daddy?" Max asked.

Emma echoed the sentiment. "I wrote the hockey verse for my poem."

Grace said something vague about Jack having to work. The kids looked wary.

"I'd love to hear the poem," Grace said.

Grudgingly Emma produced her journal.

"Hockey stick, hockey stick,
Do you love to score?
When you are used to shoot,
Do you feel like you want more?"

Emma looked up. Grace said, "Wow" and clapped, but she was simply not as good at the enthusiasm game as Jack. She kissed them both good night and headed back downstairs. The wine bottle was open. She and Cora began to drink. She missed Jack. He'd been gone less than twenty-four hours—he'd been gone longer on business trips plenty of times—and yet the house seemed to sag somehow. Something felt lost, irretrievably so. The missing of him had already become a physical ache.

Grace and Cora drank some more. Grace thought about her children. She thought about a life, a whole life, without Jack. We do anything to shield our children from pain. Losing Jack would, no doubt, crush Grace. But that was okay. She could take it. Her pain, however, would be nothing next to what it would do to the two children upstairs, who, she knew, lay awake, sensing something was amiss.

Grace looked at the photographs lining the walls.

Cora moved next to her. "He's a good man."

"Yeah."

"You okay?"

"Too much wine," Grace said.

"Not enough, if you ask me. Where did Mr. Mobster take you?"

"To see a Christian rock band."

"Quite the first date."

"It's a long story."

"I'm all ears."

But Grace shook her head. She didn't want to think about Jimmy X. An idea came to her. She mulled it over, let it settle.

"What?" Cora said.

"Maybe Jack made more than one call."

"You mean, besides the call to his sister?"

"Yes."

Cora nodded. "Have you set up an online account?"

"We have AOL."

"No, I mean for your phone bill."

"Not yet."

"No time like the present then." Cora stood up. There was a teeter to her step now. The wine was making them both warm. "Who do you use for long distance?"

"Cascade."

They were back by Jack's computer. Cora sat at the desk, cracked her knuckles, and went to work. She brought up Cascade's Web site. Grace gave her the necessary information—address, social security number, credit card. They came up with a password. Cascade sent an e-mail to Jack's account verifying that he'd just signed up for online billing.

"We're in," Cora said.

"I don't get it."

"An online billing account. I just set it up. You can now view and pay your phone bill over the Internet."

Grace looked over Cora's shoulder. "That's last month's bill."

"Yep."

"But it won't have the calls from last night."

"Hmm. Let me e-mail a request. We can also call Cascade and ask."

"They're not open twenty-four/seven. Part of the discount service." Grace leaned closer to the monitor. "Let me see if he called his sister before last night."

Her eyes skimmed down the list. Nothing. No unfamiliar numbers either. She no longer felt weird doing this, spying on the husband she loved and trusted, which of course felt weird in and of itself.

"Who pays the bills?" Cora asked.

"Jack does most of them."

"The phone bill comes to the house?"

"Yes."

"You look at it?"

"Sure."

Cora nodded. "Jack has a cell phone, right?"

"Right."

"What about that bill?"

"What about it?"

"Do you look at it?"

"No, it's his."

Cora smiled.

"What?"

"When my ex was cheating on me, he used the cell because I never looked at those bills."

"Jack isn't cheating."

"But he may be keeping secrets, right?"

"Could be," Grace allowed. "Okay, yeah, probably."

"So where would he keep the phone bills for his mobile?"

Grace checked the file cabinet. He saved the bills from Cascade. She checked under the Vs for Verizon Wireless. Nothing. "They're not here."

Cora rubbed her hands together. "Ooo, suspicious." She was into it now. "So let's do that voodoo that we do."

"And what exactly do we do?"

"Let's say Jack is keeping something from you. He would probably destroy the bills the minute he gets them, right?"

Grace shook her head. "This is so bizarre."

"But am I right?"

"Yeah, okay, if Jack is keeping secrets from me—"

"Everyone has secrets, Grace. C'mon, you know that. Are you telling me that this all comes as a total surprise?"

This truth would normally have made Grace pause, but there was no time for such indulgences. "Okay, so let's say Jack did destroy the cell phone bills—how are we going to get them?"

"Same way I just did. We set up another online account, this time under Verizon Wireless." Cora started typing.

"Cora?"

"Yep."

"Can I ask you something?"

"Shoot."

"How do you know how to do all this?"

"Practical experience." She stopped typing and looked back at Grace. "How do you think I found out about Adolf and Eva?"

"You spied on them?"

"Yup. I bought a book called *Spying for Dodoes* or something like that. It's all in there. I wanted to make sure I had all the facts before I confronted his sorry ass."

"What did he say when you showed it to him?"

"That he was sorry. That he'd never do it again. That he'd give up Ivana of the Implant and never see her again."

Grace watched her friend type. "You really love him, don't you?"

"More than life itself." Still typing, Cora added, "How about opening another bottle of wine?"

"Only if we're not driving tonight."

"You want me to sleep here?"

"We shouldn't drive, Cora."

"Okay, deal."

Grace stood and felt her head reel from the drink. She headed back into the kitchen. Cora often drank too much, but tonight Grace was happy to join her. She opened another bottle of the Lindemans. The wine was warm so she put an ice cube in both. Gauche, but they liked it cold.

When Grace got back into the office, the printer was whirring. She handed Cora a glass and sat. Grace stared at the wine. She started shaking her head.

"What?" Cora said.

"I finally met Jack's sister."

"So?"

"I mean, think about it. Sandra Koval. I didn't even know her name before now."

"You never asked Jack about her?"

"Not really."

"Why not?"

Grace took a sip. "I can't really explain it."

"Try."

She looked up and wondered how to put it. "I thought it was healthy. You know, keeping parts of yourself private. I was running away from something. He never pushed me on it."

"So you never pushed him either?"

"It was more than that."

"What?"

Grace thought about it. "I never bought into that 'we have no secrets' stuff. Jack had a wealthy family and he wanted no part of it. There had been a falling out. I knew that much."

"Wealthy from what?"

"What do you mean?"

"What business are they in?"

"Some kind of securities firm. Jack's grandfather started it. They have trust funds and options and voting shares, stuff like that. Nothing Onassis-like, but enough, I guess. Jack won't have anything to do with it. He won't vote. He won't touch the money. He set it up so the trust skips a generation."

"So Emma and Max will get it?"

"Yep."

"How do you feel about that?"

Grace shrugged. "You know what I'm realizing?"

"I'm all ears."

"The reason I never pushed Jack? It had nothing to do with respecting privacy."

"Then what?"

"I loved him. I loved him more than any man I'd ever met . . ."

"I feel a 'but' coming here."

Grace felt the tears press against her eyes. "But it all felt so fragile.

Does that make sense? When I was with him—this is going to sound so stupid—but when I was with Jack, it was the first time I was happy since, I don't know, since my father died."

"You've had a lot of pain in your life," Cora said.

Grace did not reply.

"You were scared it would go away. You didn't want to open yourself up to more."

"So I chose ignorance?"

"Hey, ignorance is supposed to be bliss, right?"

"You buy that?"

Cora shrugged. "If I never checked up on Adolf, he probably would have had his fling and gotten over it. Maybe I'd be living with the man I love."

"You could still take him back."

"Nope."

"Why not?"

Cora thought about it. "I need the ignorance, I guess." She picked up her glass and took a long sip.

The printer finished whirring. Grace picked up the sheets and started examining them. Most of the phone numbers she knew. Point of fact, she knew almost all of them.

But one immediately jumped out at her.

"Where's the six-oh-three area code?" Grace asked.

"Beats me. Which call?"

Grace showed her on the monitor. Cora moved the cursor over it.

"What are you doing?" Grace asked.

"You click the number, they tell you who you called."

"For real?"

"Man, what century do you live in? They have talkies now."

"So all you have to do is click the link?"

"And it'll tell all. Unless the number is unlisted."

Cora clicked the left mouse button. A box appeared saying:

NO RECORD OF THAT NUMBER.

"There you go. Unlisted."

Grace checked her watch. "It's only nine thirty," she said. "Not too late to call."

"Under the missing-husband rule, no, not too late at all."

Grace picked up the phone and inputted the number. A piercing feedback, not unlike the one at the Rapture concert, slapped her eardrum. Then: "The number you have called"—the robotic voice stated the number—"has been disconnected. No further information is available."

Grace frowned.

"What?"

"When was the last time Jack called it?"

Cora checked. "Three weeks ago. He talked for eighteen minutes."

"It's disconnected."

"Hmm, six-oh-three area code," Cora said, moving to another Web site. She typed in "603 area code" and hit the ENTER button. The answer came right up. "It's in New Hampshire. Hold on, let's Google it."

"Google what? New Hampshire?"

"The phone number."

"What will that do?"

"Your number is unlisted, right?"

"Right."

"Hold on. Let me show you something. This doesn't work every time, but watch." Cora typed Grace's phone number into the search engine. "What it will do is search the entire Web for those numbers in a row. Not just phone directories. That won't do it because, like you said, your number is unlisted. But . . ."

Cora hit ENTER. There was one search hit. The site was for an art prize offered at Brandeis University, her alma mater. Cora clicked the link. Grace's name and number came up. "You were judging some painting award?"

Grace nodded. "They were giving out an art scholarship."

"Yep, there you are. Your name, address, and phone number with other judges'. You must have given it to them."

Grace shook her head.

"Throw away your eight-tracks and welcome to the Information Age," Cora said. "And now that I know your name, I can do a million different searches. Your gallery Web page will come up. Where you went to college. Whatever. Now let's try with this six-oh-three number. . . ."

Cora's fingers flew again. She hit RETURN. "Hold on. We got something." She squinted at the screen. "Bob Dodd."

"Bob?"

"Yes. Not Robert. Bob." Cora looked back at Grace. "Is the name familiar?"

"No."

"The address is a PO box in Fitzwilliam, New Hampshire. You ever been?"

"No."

"How about Jack?"

"I don't think so. I mean, he went to college in Vermont, so he might have visited New Hampshire, but we've never been there together."

There was a sound from upstairs. Max cried out in his sleep.

"Go," Cora said. "I'll see what I can dig up on our friend Mr. Dodd."

As Grace headed up toward her son's bedroom, another pang struck deep in her chest: Jack was the house's night sentinel. He handled nightmares and nocturnal requests for water. He was the one who held the kids' foreheads at three a.m. when they woke up to, er, throw up. During the day, Grace took care of the sniffles, the taking of temperatures, the heating of chicken soup, the forcing down of Robitussin. The night shift was Jack's.

Max was sobbing when she reached his room. His cries were soft now, more a whimper, and somehow that was more pitiful than the loudest of screams. Grace wrapped her arms around him. His little body was shaking. She rocked back and forth and gently shushed him. She whispered that Mommy was here, that everything was okay, that he was safe.

It took Max a while to settle. Grace brought him to the bathroom. Even though Max was barely six, he peed like a man—that is to say, he missed the bowl entirely. He swayed, falling back asleep as he stood. When he finished, she helped him pull up his *Finding Nemo* pajamas. She tucked him back in and asked if he wanted to tell her about his dream. He shook his head and fell back asleep.

Grace watched his little chest rise and fall. He looked very much like his father.

After a while she headed back downstairs. There was no sound. Cora was no longer clacking the keyboard. Grace entered the office. The chair was empty. Cora stood in the corner. She gripped the wineglass.

"Cora?"

"I know why Bob Dodd's phone was disconnected."

There was a tightness in Cora's voice, one Grace had never heard. She waited for her friend to continue, but Cora seemed to be shrinking into the corner.

"What happened?" Grace asked.

Cora downed a quick sip. "According to an article in the *New Hampshire Post*, Bob Dodd is dead. He was murdered two weeks ago."

CHAPTER 16

E ric Wu stepped inside the Sykes house.

The house was dark. Wu had left all the lights out. The intruder—whoever had taken the key out of the rock—had not turned them on. Wu wondered about that.

He had assumed the intruder was the nosy woman in the lingerie. Would she be smart enough to know not to turn the lights on?

He stopped. More than that: If you have the forethought not to turn on the lights, wouldn't you have the foresight not to leave the hide-a-key in plain sight?

Something did not add up.

Wu lowered himself and moved behind the recliner. He stopped and listened. Nothing. If someone was in the house, he would hear them move. He waited some more.

Still nothing.

Wu mulled it over. Could the intruder have come and gone?

He doubted it. A person who would take the risk of entering with a hidden key would look around. They would probably find Freddy Sykes in the upstairs bathroom. They would call for help. Or if they left, if they found nothing amiss, they would have put the key back in the rock. None of that had happened.

What then was the most logical conclusion?

The intruder was still in the house. Not moving. Hiding.

Wu treaded gently. There were three exits. He made sure all the doors were locked. Two doors had bolt locks. He carefully slid them into place. He took the dining room chairs and placed them in front of all three exits. He wanted something, anything, to block or at least slow down an easy escape.

Trap his adversary.

The stairway was carpeted. That made it easier to pad up in silence. Wu wanted to check the bathroom, to see if Freddy Sykes was still in the tub. He thought again about the hide-a-key in plain sight. Nothing about this setup made sense. The more he thought about it, the slower his step.

Wu tried to think it through. Start from the beginning: A person who knows where Sykes keeps a hide-a-key opens the door. He or she comes inside. Now what? If he finds Sykes, panic would ensue. He would call the police. If he doesn't find Sykes, well, he leaves. He puts the key back in the rock and puts the rock away.

But neither one of those things had happened.

So again, what could Wu conclude?

The only other possibility that came to mind—unless he was missing something—was that the intruder had indeed found Sykes, just as Wu entered the house. There had been no time to call for help. There had only been time to hide.

But that scenario had problems too. Wouldn't the intruder have turned on a light? Perhaps she had. Perhaps she had turned on the light, but then seen Wu approach. She might have turned off the light and hidden where she was.

In the bathroom with Sykes.

Wu was in the master bedroom now. He could see the crack under the bathroom door. The light was still off. Do not underestimate your foe, he reminded himself. He had made mistakes recently. Too many of them. First, Rocky Conwell. Wu had been sloppy enough to allow him to follow. That had been mistake one. Second, Wu had been spotted by the woman next door. Sloppy.

And now this.

It was tough to look at yourself critically, but Wu tried to step away and do just that. He was not infallible. Only fools believe that. Perhaps his time in prison had rusted him somehow. Didn't matter. Wu needed to focus now. He needed to concentrate.

There were more photographs in Sykes's bedroom. This had been Freddy's mother's room for fifty years. Wu knew that from his online encounters. Sykes's father had died during the Korean War. Sykes had been an infant. The mother had never gotten over it. People react differently to the death of a loved one. Mrs. Sykes had decided to dwell with her ghost instead of the living. She spent the rest of her life in this same bedroom—in the same bed even—that she'd shared with her soldier husband. She slept on her side, Freddy said. She never let anyone, not even when young Freddy had a nightmare, touch the side of the bed where her beloved had once lain.

Wu's hand was on the doorknob now.

The bathroom, he knew, was small. He tried to picture an angle someone might use to attack. There really was none. Wu had a gun in his duffel bag. He wondered if he should take it out. If the intruder was armed, then it could be a problem.

Overconfident? Maybe. But Wu didn't think he'd need a weapon.

He turned the knob and pushed hard.

Freddy Sykes was still in the tub. The gag was in his mouth. His eyes were closed. Wu wondered if Freddy was dead. Probably. No one else was here. There was no place to hide. Nobody had come to Freddy's rescue.

Wu moved toward the window. He looked out at the house now, at the house next door.

The woman—the one who'd been in the lingerie—was there.

In her house. Standing by the window.

She stared back at him.

That was when Wu heard the car door slam. There was no siren, but now, as he turned toward the driveway, he could see the red cruiser lights.

The police were here.

Charlaine Swain was not crazy.

She watched movies. She read books. Lots of them. Escapism, she had thought. Entertainment. A way to numb the boredom every day. But maybe these movies and books were oddly educational. How many times had she shouted at the plucky heroine—the oh-so-guileless, witch-skinny, raven-haired beauty—not to go into that damned house?

Too many. So now, when it had been her turn . . . uh-uh, no way. Charlaine Swain was not about to make that mistake.

She had stood in front of Freddy's back door staring at that hide-a-key. She couldn't go inside per her movie and book training, but she couldn't just leave it alone either. Something was wrong. A man was in trouble. You can't just walk away from that.

So she came up with an idea.

It was simple really. She took the key out of the rock. It was in her pocket now. She left the hide-a-key in plain view, not because she wanted the Asian guy to see it, but because that would be her excuse for calling the police.

The moment the Asian guy entered Freddy's house, she dialed 911. "Someone is in the neighbor's house," she told them. The clincher: The hide-a-key was lying on the walkway.

Now the police were here.

One cruiser had made the turn onto her block. The siren was silent. The car was not speeding bat-out-of-hell style, just moving at a clip solidly above the speed limit. Charlaine risked a look back at Freddy's house.

The Asian man was watching her.

CHAPTER 17

G race stared at the headline. "He was murdered?"

Cora nodded.

"How?"

"Bob Dodd was shot in the head in front of his wife. Gangland style, they called it, whatever that means."

"They catch who did it?"

"Nope."

"When?"

"When was he murdered?"

"Yeah, when?"

"Four days after Jack called him."

Cora moved back toward the computer. Grace considered the date.

"It couldn't have been Jack."

"Uh-huh."

"It would be impossible. Jack hasn't traveled out of the state in more than a month."

"You say so."

"What's that supposed to mean?"

"Nothing, Grace. I'm on your side, okay? I don't think Jack killed anybody either, but c'mon, let's get a grip here."

"Meaning?"

"Meaning stop with the 'hasn't traveled out of state' nonsense. New Hampshire is hardly California. You can drive up in four hours. You can fly up in one."

Grace rubbed her eyes.

"Something else," Cora went on. "I know why he's listed as Bob, not Robert."

"Why?"

"He's a reporter. That's his byline. Bob Dodd. Google listed one hundred and twenty-six hits on his name over the past three years for the *New Hampshire Post*. The obituary called him—where's the line?—'a hard-nosed investigative reporter, famous for his controversial exposés'—like the New Hampshire mob rubbed him out to keep him quiet."

"And you don't think that's the case?"

"Who knows? But skimming through his articles, I'd say Bob Dodd was more like an 'On Your Side' reporter, you know—he finds dishwasher repairmen scamming old ladies, wedding photographers who bail out with the deposit, that sorta thing."

"He could have pissed someone off."

Cora's tone was flat. "Yup, could have. And, what, you think it's a coincidence—Jack calling the guy before he died?"

"No, there's no coincidence here." Grace tried to process what she was hearing. "Hold up."

"What?"

"That photograph. There were five people in it. Three women, two men. This is a long shot...."

Cora was already typing. "But maybe Bob Dodd is one of them?"

"There are image search engines, right?"

"Already there."

Cora's fingers flew, her cursor blinked, her mouse slid. There were two pages, a total of twelve picture hits for Bob Dodd. The first page featured a hunter with the same name living out in Wisconsin. On the second page—the eleventh hit—they found a table photograph taken at a charity function in Bristol, New Hampshire.

Bob Dodd, a reporter for the *New Hampshire Post*, was the first face on the left.

They didn't need to study it closely. Bob Dodd was African-American. Everyone in the mystery photograph was white.

Grace frowned. "There still has to be a connection."

"Let me see if I can dig up a bio on him. Maybe they went to college together or something."

There was a gentle rapping at the front door. Grace and Cora looked at each other. "Late," Cora said.

The knocking came again, still soft. There was a doorbell. Whoever was there had chosen not to use it. Must know she had kids. Grace rose and Cora followed. At the door she flicked on the outside light and peered out the window on the side of the door. She should have been more surprised, but Grace guessed that maybe she was beyond that.

"Who's that?" Cora asked.

"The man who changed my life," Grace said softly.

She opened the door. Jimmy X stood on the stoop looking down.

Wu had to smile.

That woman. As soon as he saw those siren lights, he put it together. Her ingenuity was both admirable and grating.

No time for that.

What to do . . . ?

Jack Lawson was tied up in the trunk. Wu realized now that he should have fled the moment he saw that hide-a-key. Another mistake. How many more could he afford?

Minimize the damage. That was the key here. There was no way to prevent it all—the damage, that is. He would be hurt here. It would cost him. His fingerprints were in the house. The woman next door had probably already given the police a description. Sykes, alive or dead, would be found. There was nothing he could do about that either.

Conclusion: If he was caught, he would go to jail for a very long time.

The police cruiser pulled into the driveway.

Wu snapped into survival mode. He hurried downstairs. Through the window he saw the cruiser glide to a stop. It was dark out now, but the street was well lit. A tall black man in full uniform came out. He put on his police cap. His gun remained in his holster.

That was good.

The black police officer was barely on the walk when Wu opened the front door and smiled widely. "Something I can do for you, Officer?"

He did not draw his weapon. Wu had counted on that. This was a family neighborhood in the great American expanse known as the suburbs. A Ho-Ho-Kus police officer probably responds to several hundred possible burglaries during his career. Most, if not all, were false alarms.

"We got a call about a possible break-in," the officer said.

Wu frowned, feigning confusion. He took a step outside but kept his distance. Not yet, he thought. Be nonthreatening. Wu's moves were intentionally laconic, setting a slow pace. "Wait, I know. I forgot my key. Someone probably saw me going in through the back."

"You live here, Mr. . . . ?"

"Chang," Wu said. "Yes, I do. Oh, but it's not my house, if that's what you mean. It belongs to my partner, Frederick Sykes."

Now Wu risked another step.

"I see," the officer said. "And Mr. Sykes is . . . ?"

"Upstairs."

"May I see him please?"

"Sure, come on in." Wu turned his back to the officer and yelled up the stairs. "Freddy? Freddy, throw something on. The police are here."

Wu did not have to turn around. He knew the tall black man was moving up behind him. He was only five yards away now. Wu stepped back into the house. He held the door open and gave the officer what he thought was an effeminate smile. The officer—his name tag read RICHARDSON—moved toward the door.

When he was only a yard away, Wu uncoiled.

Officer Richardson had hesitated, perhaps sensing something, but it was too late. The blow, aimed for the center of his gut, was a palm strike. Richardson folded in half like a deck chair. Wu moved closer. He wanted to disable. He did not want to kill.

An injured policeman produces heat. A dead policeman raises the temperature tenfold.

The cop was doubled over. Wu hit him behind the legs. Richardson dropped to his knees. Wu used a pressure point technique. He dug the knuckles of his index fingers into both sides of Richardson's head, up and into the ear cavity under the cartilage, an area known as Triple Warmer 17. You need to get the right angle. Go full strength and you could kill someone. You need precision here.

Richardson's eyes went white. Wu released the hold. Richardson dropped like a marionette with its strings cut.

The knockout would not last long. Wu took the handcuffs from the man's belt and cuffed his wrist to the stairwell. He ripped the radio from his shoulder.

Wu considered the woman next door. She'd be watching.

She would surely call the police again. He wondered about that, but there was no time. If he tried to attack, she would see him and lock the door. It would take too long. His best bet was to use time and surprise here. He hurried to the garage and got into Jack Lawson's minivan. He checked the cargo area in the back.

Jack Lawson was there.

Wu moved to the driver's seat now. He had a plan.

Charlaine had a bad feeling the moment she saw the policeman step out of the car.

For one thing, he was alone. She had assumed that there would be two of them, partners, again from TV—*Starsky and Hutch, Adam-12,* Briscoe and Green. She realized now that she had made a mistake. Her call had been too casual. She should have claimed to see something menacing, something frightening, so that they would have arrived more wary and prepared. Instead she had simply come across as a nosy neighbor, a dotty woman who had nothing better to do but call the cops for any little thing.

The policeman's body language too was all wrong. He sauntered toward the door, slack and casual, not a care in the world. Charlaine couldn't see the front door from where she was, only the driveway. When the officer disappeared from view, Charlaine felt her stomach drop.

She considered shouting out a warning. The problem was—and this might sound strange—the new Pella windows they had installed last year. They opened vertically, with a hand crank. By the time she slid open both locks and cranked the handle, well, the officer would already be out of sight. And really, what could she yell? What kind of warning? What in the end did she really know?

So she waited.

Mike was in the house. He was downstairs in the den, watching the Yankees on the YES Network. The divided night. They never watched TV together anymore. The way he flipped the remote was maddening. They liked different shows. But really, she didn't think that was it. She could watch anything. Still Mike took the den; she had the bedroom. They both watched alone, in the dark. Again she didn't know when that had started. The children weren't home tonight—Mike's brother had taken them to the movies—but when they were, they stayed in their own rooms. Charlaine tried to limit the Web surf time, but it was impossible. In her youth, friends talked on the phone for hours. Now they instant-messaged and Lord-knew-what over the Internet.

This was what her family had become—four separate entities in the dark, interacting with one another only when necessary.

She saw the light go on in the Sykes garage. Through the window, the one covered with flimsy lace, Charlaine could see a shadow. Movement. In the garage. Why? There would be no need for the police officer to be in there. She reached for the phone and dialed 911, even as she began to head for the stairs.

"I called you a little while ago," she told the 911 operator.

"Yes?"

"About a break-in at my neighbor's house."

"An officer is responding."

"Yeah, I know that. I saw him pull up."

Silence. She felt like a dope.

"I think something might have happened."

"What did you see?"

"I think he may have been attacked. Your officer. Please send someone quickly."

She hung up. The more she'd explain, the stupider it would sound.

The familiar churning noise started up. Charlaine knew what it was. Freddy's electric garage door. The man had done something to the cop. He was going to escape.

And that was when Charlaine decided to do something truly stupid.

She thought back to those wicked-witch-thin heroines, the ones with the mind-scooped stupidity, and wondered if any of them, even the most brain dead, had ever done something so colossally stupid. She doubted it. She knew that when she looked back on the choice she was about to make—assuming she survived it—she would laugh and maybe, just maybe, have a little more respect for the protagonists who enter dark homes in just their bra and panties.

Here was the thing: The Asian guy was about to escape. He had hurt Freddy. He had hurt a cop; she was sure of it. By the time the cops responded, he would be gone. They wouldn't find him. It would be too late.

And if he got away, then what?

He had seen her. She knew that. At the window. He had probably already figured out that she was the one who called the police. Freddy could be dead. So too the cop. Who was the only witness left?

Charlaine.

He would come back for her, wouldn't he? And even if he didn't, even if he decided to let her be, well, at best, she would live in fear. She'd be jumpy in the night. She'd look for him in crowds during the days. Maybe he would simply want revenge. Maybe he would go after Mike or the kids. . . .

She could not let that happen. She had to stop him now.

How?

Wanting to prevent his escape was all fine and good, but let's stay real here. What could she do? They didn't own a gun. She couldn't just run outside and jump on his back and try to claw his eyes. No, she had to be cleverer than that.

She had to follow him.

On the surface it sounded ridiculous, but add it up. If he got away, the result would be fear. Pure, unadulterated, probably unending terror until he was captured, which might be never. Charlaine had seen the man's face. She had seen his eyes. She couldn't live with that.

Following him—running a tail, as they say on TV—made sense, when you considered the alternatives. She would follow him in her car. She would keep her distance. She would have the cell phone. She would be able to tell the police where he was. The plan did not involve following him long, just until the police could take over. Right now, if she didn't act, she knew what would happen: The police would arrive; the Asian man would be gone.

There was no alternative.

The more she thought about it, the less nutsy it sounded. She'd be in a moving car. She'd stay comfortably behind him. She'd be on her cell phone with a 911 operator.

Wasn't that safer than letting him go?

She ran downstairs.

"Charlaine?"

It was Mike. He stood there, in the kitchen, standing over the sink eating peanut-butter crackers. She stopped for a second. His eyes probed her face in a way only he could, in a way only he ever had. She fell back to her days at Vanderbilt, when they first fell in love. The way he looked at her then, the way he looked at her now. He was skinnier back then and so handsome. But the look, the eyes, they were the same.

"What's wrong?" he asked.

"I need"—she stopped, caught her breath—"I need to go somewhere."

His eyes. Probing. She remembered the first time she ever saw him, that sunny day at Centennial Park in Nashville. How far had they come? Mike still saw. He still saw her in a way that no one else ever had. For a moment Charlaine could not move. She thought that she might cry. Mike dropped the crackers into the sink and started toward her.

"I'll drive," Mike said.

CHAPTER 18

Grace and the famous rocker known as Jimmy X were alone in the den-cum-playroom. Max's Game Boy was lying on its back. The battery case had broken, so now the two double A's were held in place by Scotch tape. The game cartridge, lying next to it as if it'd been spit out, was called Super Mario Five, which, according to Grace's less than sophisticated eye, appeared to be exactly the same as Super Mario One through Four.

Cora had left them alone and returned to her role as cybersleuth. Jimmy had still not spoken. He sat with his forearms against his thighs, his head hanging, reminding Grace of the first time she'd seen him, in her hospital room not long after she regained consciousness.

He wanted her to talk first. She could see that. But she had nothing to say to him.

"I'm sorry to stop by so late," he said.

"I thought you had a gig tonight."

"Already over."

"Early," she said.

"The concerts usually end by nine. It's how the promoters like it."

"How did you know where I live?"

Jimmy shrugged. "I guess I've always known."

"What's that supposed to mean?"

He didn't answer and she didn't push it. For several seconds the room was dead silent.

"I'm not sure how to begin," Jimmy said. Then, after a brief pause, he added, "You still limp."

"Good opening," she said.

He tried to smile.

"Yes, I limp."

"From . . . ?"

"Yes."

"I'm sorry."

"I got off easy."

The shadow crossed his face. His head, the one he'd finally worked up the nerve to lift, dropped back down as if it had learned its lesson.

Jimmy still had the cheekbones. The famed blond locks were gone, from either genetics or a razor's edge, she couldn't tell which. He was older, of course. His youth was over and she wondered if that was true for her too.

"I lost everything that night," he began. Then he stopped and shook his head. "That didn't come out right. I'm not here for pity."

She said nothing.

"Do you remember when I came to see you at the hospital?"

She nodded.

"I'd read every newspaper story. Every magazine story. I watched all the news reports. I can tell you about every kid that died that night. Every one of them. I know their faces. I close my eyes, I still see them."

"Jimmy?"

He looked up again.

"You shouldn't be telling me this. Those kids had families."

"I know that."

"I'm not the one to give you absolution."

"You think that's what I came here for?"

Grace did not reply.

"It's just . . ." He shook his head. "I don't know why I came, okay? I saw you tonight. At the church. And I could see you knew who I was." He tilted his head. "How did you find me anyway?"

"I didn't."

"The man you were with?"

"Carl Vespa."

"Oh Christ." He closed his eyes. "Father of Ryan."

"Yes."

"He brought you?"

"Yes."

"What does he want?"

Grace thought about that. "I don't think he knows."

Now it was Jimmy's turn to stay silent.

"He thinks he wants an apology."

"Thinks?"

"What he really wants is his son back."

The air felt heavy. She shifted in her chair. Jimmy's face had no color.

"I tried, you know. To apologize, I mean. He's right about that. I owe them that. At the very least. And I'm not talking about that stupid photo op with you at the hospital. My manager wanted that. I was so stoned I just went along. I could barely stand." He stared at her. He had those same intense eyes that had made him an instant MTV darling. "Do you remember Tommy Garrison?"

She did. He had died in the stampede. His parents were Ed and Selma.

"His picture touched me. I mean, they all did, you know. These lives, they were all just starting out. . . ." He took a deep breath, tried again. "But Tommy, he looked like my kid brother. I couldn't get him out of my head. So I went to his house. I wanted to apologize to his parents. . . ." He stopped.

"What happened?"

"I got there. We sat at their kitchen table. I remember I put my elbows on it and the whole thing teetered. They had this linoleum floor, half coming up. The wallpaper, this awful yellow flowered stuff, was peeling off the walls. Tommy was their only child. I looked at their lives, at their empty faces . . . I couldn't bear it."

She said nothing.

"That was when I ran."

"Jimmy?"

He looked at her.

"Where have you been?"

"Lot of places."

"Why?"

"Why what?"

"Why did you just give it all up?"

He shrugged. "There wasn't all that much, really. The music business, well, I won't go into it, but let's just say I hadn't received much money yet. I was new. It takes a while to get serious money. I didn't care. I just wanted out."

"So where did you go?"

"I started in Alaska. Worked gutting fish, if you can believe that. Did that for about a year. Then I started traveling, played with a couple of small bar bands. In Seattle I found a group of old hippies. They used to do IDs for members of the Weather Underground, that kinda thing. They got me new papers. The closest I came back here, I played with a cover band in an Atlantic City casino for a while. At the Tropicana. I dyed my hair. I stuck to the drums. Nobody recognized me, or if they did, they didn't much care."

"Were you happy?"

"You want the truth? No. I wanted to come back. I wanted to make amends and move on. But the longer I was gone, the harder it was, the more I longed for it. The whole thing was a vicious circle. And then I met Madison."

"The lead singer of Rapture?"

"Yeah. Madison. Can you believe that name? It's huge now. You remember that movie *Splash*, the one with Tom Hanks and what's-her-name?"

"Daryl Hannah," Grace said automatically.

"Right, the blond mermaid. Remember that scene where Tom Hanks is trying to come up with a name for her and he says all kinds of stuff like Jennifer or Stephanie and they're walking past Madison Avenue and he just mentions the street name and she wants it to be her name and that's a big laugh in the movie, right, a woman named Madison. Now it's a top-ten name."

Grace let it go.

"Anyway, she's from a farm town in Minnesota. She ran away to the Big Apple when she was fifteen, ended up strung out and homeless in Atlantic City. She landed at a homeless shelter for runaway teens. She found Jesus—you know the deal, trading one addiction for another—and started singing. She has a voice like a Janis Joplin angel."

"Does she know who you are?"

"No. You know how Shania has Mutt Lange in the background? That's what I wanted. I like working with her. I like the music, but I wanted to stay out of the spotlight. At least that's what I tell myself. Madison is painfully shy. She won't perform unless I'm onstage with her. She'll get over that, but for now I figured drums are a pretty good disguise."

He shrugged, tried a smile. There was still a hint of the old knock-'em-back charisma. "Guess I was wrong about that."

They were silent for a moment.

"I still don't understand," Grace said.

He looked at her.

"I said before I'm not the one to give you absolution. I meant that. But the truth is, you didn't fire a gun that night."

Jimmy stayed still.

"The Who. When they had that stampede in Cincinnati, they got over it. And the Stones, when that Hell's Angel killed a guy at their concert. They're still playing. I can see wanting out for a little while, a year or two . . ."

Jimmy looked to the right. "I should leave."

He stood.

"Going to disappear again?" she asked.

He hesitated and then reached into his pocket. He pulled out a card and handed it to her. There were ten digits on it and nothing more. "I don't have a home address or anything, just this mobile phone."

He turned and started for the door. Grace did not follow. Under normal circumstances, she might have pushed him, but in the end, his visit was an aside, a not very important one in the scheme of things. Her past had a curious pull—that was all. Especially now.

"Take care of yourself, Grace."

"You too, Jimmy."

She sat in the den, feeling the exhaustion begin to weigh on her shoulders, and wondered where Jack was right now.

Mike did indeed drive. The Asian man had nearly a minute head start, but what was good about their twisty development of cul-de-sacs, tract houses, nicely wooded lots—this wondrous serpentine sprawl of suburbia—was that there was only one true entrance and exit road.

In this stretch of Ho-Ho-Kus, all roads led to Hollywood Avenue.

Charlaine filled Mike in as quickly as possible. She told him most of it, about how she'd looked out the window and spotted the man and grown suspicious. Mike listened without interrupting. There were holes the size of a heartache in her story. She left out why she had been looking out the window in the first place, for example. Mike must have seen the holes, but right now he was letting it go.

Charlaine studied his profile and traveled back to the first time they met. She had been a freshman at Vanderbilt University. There was a park in Nashville, not far from campus, with a replica of the Parthenon, the one in Athens. Originally built in 1897 for the Centennial Expo, the structure was thought to be the most realistic replica of the famed site atop the Acropolis anywhere in the world. If you wanted to know what the actual Parthenon looked like in its heyday, well, people would travel to Nashville, Tennessee.

She was sitting there on a warm fall day, just eighteen years old, staring at the edifice, imagining what it must have been like in ancient Greece, when a voice said, "It doesn't work, does it?"

She turned. Mike had his hands in his pockets. He looked so damned handsome. "Excuse me?"

He took a step closer, a half smile on his lips, moving with a confidence that drew her. Mike gestured with his head toward the enormous structure. "It's an exact replica, right? You look at it, and this is what they saw, great philosophers like Plato and Socrates, and all I can think is"—he stopped, shrugged—"is that all there is?"

She smiled at him. She saw his eyes widen and knew that the smile had landed hard. "It leaves nothing to the imagination," she said.

Mike tilted his head. "What do you mean?"

"You see the ruins of the real Parthenon and you try to imagine what it would have looked like. But the reality, which this is, can never live up to what your mind conjures up."

Mike nodded slowly, considering.

"You don't agree?" she asked.

"I had another theory," Mike said.

"I'd like to hear it."

He moved closer and bent down on his haunches. "There are no ghosts."

Now she did the head tilt.

"You need the history. You need the people in their sandals walking through it. You need the years, the blood, the deaths, the sweat from, what, four hundred years B.C. Socrates never prayed in there. Plato didn't argue by its door. Replicas never have the ghosts. They're bodies without souls."

The young Charlaine smiled again. "You use this line on all the girls?"

"It's new, actually. I'm trying it out. Any good?"

She lifted her hand, palm down, and turned it back and forth. "Eh."

Charlaine had been with no other man since that day. For years they returned to the fake Parthenon on their anniversary. This had been the first year they hadn't gone back.

"There he is," Mike said.

The Ford Windstar was traveling west on Hollywood Avenue toward Route 17. Charlaine was back on the phone with a 911 operator. The operator was finally taking her seriously.

"We lost radio contact with our officer at the scene," she said.

"He's heading onto Route 17 south at the Hollywood Avenue entrance," Charlaine said. "He's driving a Ford Windstar."

"License plate?"

"I can't see it."

"We have officers responding to both scenes. You can drop your pursuit now."

She lowered the phone. "Mike?"

"It's okay," he said.

She sat back and thought about her own house, about ghosts, about bodies without souls.

Eric Wu was not easily surprised.

Seeing the woman from the house and this man he assumed was her husband following him—that definitely registered as something he would not have predicted. He wondered how to handle it.

The woman.

She had set him up. She was following him. She had called the police. They had sent an officer. He knew then that she would call again.

What Wu had counted on, however, was putting enough distance between himself and the Sykes household before the police responded to her call. When it comes to tracking down vehicles the police are far from omnipotent. Think about the Washington sniper a few years back. They had hundreds of officers. They had roadblocks. For an embarrassingly long time they couldn't locate two amateurs.

If Wu could get enough miles ahead, he would be safe.

But now there was a problem.

That woman again.

That woman and her husband were following him. They would be able to tell the police where he was going, what road he was on, what direction he was heading. He would not be able to put the distance between him and the authorities.

Conclusion: Wu had to stop them.

He spotted the sign for the Paramus Park Mall and took the jughandle back over the highway. The woman and her husband followed. It was late at night. The stores were closed. The lot was empty. Wu pulled into it. The woman and her husband kept their distance.

That was okay.

Because it was time to call their bluff.

Wu had a gun, a Walther PPK. He didn't like using it. Not that he was squeamish. Wu simply preferred his hands. He was decent with a gun; he was expert with his hands. He had perfect control with them. They were a part of him. With a gun you are forced to trust the mechanics, an outside source. Wu did not like that.

But he understood the need.

He stopped the car. He made sure the gun was loaded. His car door was unlocked. He pulled the handle, stepped out of the vehicle, and aimed his weapon.

Mike said, "What the hell is he doing?"

Charlaine watched the Ford Windstar enter the mall lot. There were no other cars. The lot was well lit, bathed in a shopping-center fluorescent glow. She could see Sears up ahead, the Office Depot, Sports Authority.

The Ford Windstar drifted to a stop.

"Keep back," she said.

"We're in a locked car," Mike said. "What can he do?"

The Asian man moved with fluidity and grace, and yet there was also deliberation, as if each movement had been carefully planned in advance. It was a strange combination, the way he moved, almost inhuman. But right now the man stood next to his car, his entire body still. His arm swept forward, only the arm, the rest of him so undisturbed by the motion that you might think it was an optical illusion.

And then their windshield exploded.

The noise was sudden and deafening. Charlaine screamed. Something splashed on her face, something wet and syrupy. There was a coppery smell in the air now. Instinctively Charlaine ducked. The glass from the windshield rained down on her head. Something slumped against her, pushing her down.

It was Mike.

She screamed again. The scream mixed with the sound of another bullet being fired. She had to move, had to get out, had to get them out of here. Mike was not moving. She shoved him off her and risked raising her head.

Another shot whistled past her.

She had no idea where it landed. Her head was back down. There was a screaming in her ears. A few seconds passed. Charlaine finally risked a glance.

The man was walking toward her.

What now?

Escape. Flee. That was the only thought that came through.

How?

She shifted the car into reverse. Mike's foot was still on the brake. She dropped low. Her hand stretched out and took hold of his slack ankle. She slid his foot off the brake. Still wedged into the foot area Charlaine managed to jam her palm on the accelerator. She pushed down with everything she had. The car jerked back. She could not move. She had no idea where she was going.

But they were moving.

She kept her palm pressed down to the floor. The car jolted over something, a curb maybe. The bounce banged her head against the steering column. Using her shoulder blades, she tried to keep the wheel steady. Her left hand still pressed down on the accelerator. They hit another bump. She held on. The road was smoother now. But just for a moment. Charlaine heard the honking of horns, the screech of tires and brakes, and the awful whir of cars spinning out of control.

There was an impact, a terrible jarring, and then, a few seconds later, darkness.

CHAPTER 19

The color in Officer Daley's face had ebbed away.

Perlmutter sat up. "What is it?"

Daley stared at the sheet of paper in his hand as if he feared it might flee. "Something doesn't make sense here, Cap."

When Captain Perlmutter had started working as a cop, he hated the night shift. The quiet and solitude got to him. He had grown up in a big family, one of seven kids, and he liked that life. He and his wife, Marion, planned on having a big family. He had the whole thing figured out—the barbecues, the weekends coaching one kid or the other, the school conferences, the family movies on Friday night, the summer nights on the front porch—the life he'd experienced growing up in Brooklyn, but with a suburban, bigger-house twist.

His grandmother used to spew Yiddish quotes all the time. Stu Perlmutter's personal favorite had been this: "Man plans and God laughs." Marion, the only woman he had ever loved, died of an embolism when she was thirty-one. She'd been in the kitchen, making Sammy—that was their son, their only child—a sandwich when the embolism hit. She was dead before she landed on the linoleum.

Perlmutter's life pretty much ended that day. He did what he could to raise Sammy, but the truth was, his heart was never really in it. He loved the boy and enjoyed his job, but he had lived for Marion. This precinct, his work, had become his solace. Home, being with Sammy, reminded him of Marion and all they'd never have. Here, alone, he could almost forget.

All of that was a long time ago. Sammy was in college now. He had turned into a good man, despite his father's inattentiveness. There was something to be said for that, but Perlmutter did not know what.

Perlmutter signaled for Daley to sit down. "So what's up?"

"That woman. Grace Lawson."

"Ah," Perlmutter said.

"Ah?"

"I was just thinking about her too."

"Something about her case bothering you, Captain?"

"Yep."

"I thought it was just me."

Perlmutter tipped his chair back. "Do you know who she is?"

"Ms. Lawson?"

"Yup."

"She's an artist."

"More than that. You notice the limp?"

"Yes."

"Her married name is Grace Lawson. But once upon a time, her name—her maiden name, I guess—was Grace Sharpe."

Daley looked at him blankly.

"You ever hear of the Boston Massacre?"

"Wait, you mean that rock concert riot?"

"More of a stampede, but yeah. Lot of people died."

"She was there?"

Perlmutter nodded. "Badly injured too. In a coma for a while. Press gave her the full fifteen minutes and then some."

"How long ago was that?"

"What, fifteen, sixteen years ago maybe?"

"But you remember?"

"It was big news. And I was a big fan of the Jimmy X Band."

Daley looked surprised. "You?"

"Hey, I wasn't always an old fart."

"Heard their CD. It was pretty damn good. Radio still plays 'Pale Ink' all the time."

"One of the best songs ever."

Marion had liked the Jimmy X Band. Perlmutter remembered her constantly blasting "Pale Ink" on an old Walkman, her eyes closed, her lips moving as she silently sang along. He blinked the image away.

"So what happened to them?"

"The massacre destroyed the band. They broke up. Jimmy X—I don't remember his real name anymore—was the front man and wrote all the songs. He just up and quit." Perlmutter pointed to the piece of paper in Daley's hand. "So what's that?"

"That's what I wanted to talk to you about."

"Something to do with the Lawson case?"

"I don't know." Then: "Yeah, maybe."

Perlmutter put his hands behind his head. "Start talking."

"DiBartola got a call early tonight," Daley said. "Another missing-husband case."

"Similarities to Lawson?"

"No. I mean, not at first. This guy wasn't even her husband anymore. An ex. And he isn't exactly squeaky clean."

"He's got a record?"

"Did time for assault."

"Name?"

"Rocky Conwell."

"Rocky? For real?"

"Yep, that's what it says on his birth certificate."

"Parents." Perlmutter made a face. "Wait, why does that name ring a bell?"

"He played a little pro ball."

Perlmutter searched the memory banks, shrugged. "So what's the deal?"

"Okay, like I said, this case looks even more cut-and-dry than Lawson. Ex-husband who was supposed to take his wife out shopping this morning. I mean, it's nothing. It's less than nothing. But DiBartola sees the wife—her name is Lorraine—well, she's a royal babe. So you know DiBartola."

"A pig," Perlmutter said with a nod. "Ranked in the top ten by both the AP and UPI."

"Right, so he figures, what the hell, humor her, right? She's separated, so you never know. Maybe something would swing his way."

"Very professional." Perlmutter frowned. "Go on."

"This is where it gets weird." Daley licked his lips. "DiBartola, he does the simple thing. He runs the E-ZPass."

"Like you."

"*Exactly* like me."

"What do you mean?"

"He gets a hit." Daley took another step into the room. "Rocky Conwell crossed the tollbooth off Exit 16 on the New York Thruway. At exactly ten twenty-six last night."

Perlmutter looked at him.

"Yeah, I know. Exact same time and place as Jack Lawson."

Perlmutter scanned the report. "You're sure about this? DiBartola didn't accidentally run the same number we did or something?"

"Checked it twice. There's no mistake. Conwell and Lawson crossed the toll at the exact same time. They had to be together."

Perlmutter mulled it over and shook his head. "No."

Daley looked confused. "You think it's a coincidence?"

"Two separate cars, crossing the toll at the same time? Not likely."

"So how do you figure it?"

"I'm not sure," Perlmutter said. "Let's say they, I don't know, ran away together. Or Conwell kidnapped Lawson. Or hell, Lawson kidnapped Conwell. Whatever. They'd be in the same car. There would be only one E-ZPass hit, not two."

"Right, okay."

"But they were in two separate cars. That's what's throwing me. Both men in separate cars cross the toll at the same time. And now both men are missing."

"Except Lawson called his wife," Daley added. "He needed space, remember?"

They both thought about it.

Daley said, "You want me to call Ms. Lawson? See if she knows this Conwell guy?"

Perlmutter plucked on his bottom lip and thought about it. "Not yet. Besides, it's late. She's got kids."

"So what should we do?"

"A little more investigating. Let's talk to Rocky Conwell's ex-wife first. See if we dig up a connection between Conwell and Lawson. Put his car out there, see if we get a hit."

The phone rang. Daley was working the switchboard as well. He picked it up, listened, and then turned to Perlmutter.

"Who was that?"

"Phil over at the Ho-Ho-Kus station."

"Something wrong?"

"They think an officer might be down. They want our help."

CHAPTER 20

B eatrice Smith was a fifty-three-year-old widow.

Eric Wu was back in the Ford Windstar. He took Ridgewood Avenue to the Garden State Parkway north. He headed east on Interstate 287 toward the Tappan Zee Bridge. He exited at Airmont in New York. He was on side roads now. He knew exactly where he was going. He had made mistakes, yes, but the basics were still with him.

One of those basics: Have a backup residence lined up.

Beatrice Smith's husband had been a popular cardiologist, even serving a term as town mayor. They'd had lots of friends, but they were all "couple" friends. When Maury—that was her husband's name—died of a sudden heart attack, the friends stayed around for a month or two and then faded away. Her only child, a son, and a doctor like his father, lived in San Diego with his wife and three children. She kept the house, the same house she had shared with Maury, but it was big and lonely. She was thinking about selling it and moving into Manhattan, but the prices were just too steep right now. And she was afraid. Airmont was all she knew. Would it be jumping from the frying pan into the fire?

She had confided all of this online to the fictional Kurt McFaddon, a widower from Philadelphia who was considering relocating to New York City. Wu pulled onto her street and slowed. The surroundings were quiet and woodsy and very private. It was late. A fake delivery would not work at this hour. There would be no time or even need for subtlety. Wu would not be able to keep this host alive.

There could be nothing to connect Beatrice Smith to Freddy Sykes.

In short, Beatrice Smith could not be found. Not ever.

Wu parked the car, put on his gloves—no fingerprints this time—and approached the house.

CHAPTER 21

At five a.m., Grace threw on a bathrobe—Jack's robe—and headed downstairs. She always wore Jack's clothes. He'd kindly request lingerie, but she preferred his pajama tops. "Well?" she'd ask, modeling the top. "Not bad," he'd reply, "but why not try wearing just the bottoms instead? Now *that* would be a look." She shook her head at the memory and reached the computer room.

The first thing Grace did was check the e-mail address they were using to receive replies from their spam of the photograph. What she saw surprised her.

There were no replies.

Not one.

How could that be? It was conceivable, she guessed, that nobody recognized the women in the photograph. She'd been prepared for that possibility. But by now they had sent out hundreds of thousands of e-mails to people. Even with spam blocks and all that, *someone* should have responded with at the very least an expletive, some crackpot with time on his hands, someone fed up with the overflow of spam who'd need to vent.

Someone.

But she had not received even one reply.

What should she make of that?

The house was quiet. Emma and Max were still asleep. So too was Cora. Cora was snoring, stretched out on her back, her mouth open.

Switch gears, Grace thought.

She knew that Bob Dodd, the murdered reporter, was now her best, perhaps only, lead, and let's face it, it was a pretty flimsy one. She had no phone contact for him, no next of kin, not even a street address. Still, Dodd had been a reporter for a fairly major newspaper, the *New Hampshire Post*. She decided that was the best place to start.

Newspapers don't really close—at least, that was what Grace figured. Someone had to be manning the *Post* desk in case a big story broke. It also figured that the reporter stuck working at five a.m. might be bored and more apt to talk to her. So she picked up the phone.

Grace was not sure how to approach this. She considered various angles, pretending, for example, to be a reporter doing a story, asking for collegial assistance, but she wasn't sure she'd be able to talk the talk.

In the end she decided to try to keep as close to the truth as possible.

She pressed *67 to block the caller ID. The newspaper had a toll-free line. Grace didn't use it. You can't block caller ID from toll-free numbers. She had learned that somewhere and stockpiled it in the back brain closet, the same closet where she stored information about Daryl Hannah being in *Splash* and Esperanza Diaz being the wrestler dubbed Little Pocahontas, the same closet that helped make Grace, in Jack's words, "Mistress of the Useless Factoid."

The first two calls to the *New Hampshire Post* went nowhere. The guy at the news desk simply could not be bothered. He hadn't really known Bob Dodd and barely listened to her pitch. Grace waited twenty minutes and tried again. This time she got routed to Metro, where a woman who sounded very young informed Grace that she had just started at the paper, that this was her first job ever, that she didn't know Bob Dodd, but gee, wasn't it awful what happened to him?

Grace checked the e-mail again. Still nothing.

"Mommy!"

It was Max.

"Mommy, come quick!"

Grace hurried up the stairs.

"What is it, honey?"

Max sat in his bed and pointed to his foot. "My toe is growing too fast."

"Your toe?"

"Look."

She moved next to him and sat down.

"See?"

"See what, honey?"

"My second toe," he began. "It's bigger than my big toe. It's growing too fast."

Grace smiled. "That's normal, honey."

"Huh?"

"Lots of people have a second toe that's longer than their big one. Your daddy has that."

"No way."

"Yup, way. His second toe is longer than the big one on the end."

That seemed to appease him. Grace felt another pang. "You want to watch *The Wiggles*?" she asked him.

"That's a baby show."

"Let's see what's on *Playhouse Disney*, okay?"

Rolie Polie Olie was on, and Max settled onto the couch to watch. He liked to use the cushions as blankets, making a total mess of the place. Grace was beyond caring. She tried the *New Hampshire Post* again. This time she asked for Features.

JUST ONE LOOK · 161

The man who answered had a voice like old tires on a gravel road. "What's up?"

"Good morning," Grace said, too cheerfully, smiling into the phone like a dimwit.

The man made a noise which, loosely translated, said: *Get on with it.*

"I'm trying to get some information on Bob Dodd."

"Who is this?"

"I'd rather not say."

"You're kidding, right? Look, sweetheart, I'm going to hang up now—"

"Wait a second. I can't go into details, but if it turns into a major scoop—"

"Major scoop? Did you just say major scoop?"

"Yes."

The man started cackling. "And what, you think I'm like Pavlov's dog or something? Say major scoop and I'll salivate?"

"I just need to know about Bob Dodd."

"Why?"

"Because my husband is missing and I think it might have something to do with his murder."

That made him pause. "You're kidding me, right?"

"No," Grace said. "Look, I just need to find someone who knew Bob Dodd."

The voice was softer now. "I knew him."

"Did you know him well?"

"Well enough. What do you want?"

"Do you know what he was working on?"

"Look, lady, do you have information on Bob's murder? Because if you do, forget the major scoop crap and tell the police."

"Nothing like that."

"Then what?"

"I was going through some old phone bills. My husband talked to Bob Dodd not long before he was murdered."

"And your husband is?"

"I'm not going to tell you that. It's probably just a coincidence."

"But you said your husband is missing?"

"Yes."

"And you're concerned enough to be following up on this old phone call?"

"I've got nothing else," Grace said.

There was a pause. "You're going to have to do better than that," the man said.

"I don't think I can."

Silence.

"Ah, what's the harm? I don't know anything. Bob didn't confide in me."

"Who would he confide in?"

"You can try his wife."

Grace almost slapped herself in the head. How could she not have thought of something so obvious? Man, she was over her head here. "Do you know how I can locate her?"

"Not sure. I only met her, what, once, maybe twice?"

"What's her name?"

"Jillian. That's with a J, I think."

"Jillian Dodd?"

"I guess."

She wrote it down.

"There's another person you might try. Bob's father, Robert Senior. He must be in his eighties, but I think they were pretty close."

"Do you have an address for him?"

"Yeah, he's in some nursing home in Connecticut. We shipped Bob's stuff there."

"Stuff?"

"Cleaned out his desk myself. Put the stuff in a cardboard box for him."

Grace frowned. "And you sent it to his father's nursing home?"

"Yup."

"Why not to Jillian, the wife?"

There was a brief pause. "Don't know actually. I think she freaked after the murder. She was there, you know. Hold on a second—let me find the number of the nursing home. You can ask yourself."

Charlaine wanted to sit next to the hospital bed.

You always see that in movies and on TV—doting wives sitting bedside, holding the hand of their beloved—but in this room there was no chair made for that. The one chair in the room was too low to the ground, the sort of thing that opened up into a sleeper, and yes, that might come in handy later, but now, right now, Charlaine just wanted to sit and hold her husband's hand.

She stood instead. Every once in a while she sat on the bed's edge, but she feared that might disturb Mike. So she'd stand again. And maybe that was good. Maybe that felt a little like penance.

The door behind her opened. Her back was to it. She did not bother turning around. A man's voice, one she hadn't heard before, said, "How are you feeling?"

"I'm fine."

"You were lucky."

She nodded. "I feel like I won the lottery."

Charlaine reached up and touched the bandage on her forehead. A few stitches and a possible slight concussion. That was all she had suffered during the accident. Scrapes, bruises, a few stitches.

"How is your husband?"

She did not bother replying. The bullet had hit Mike in the neck. He still had not regained consciousness, though the doctors had informed her that they believed "the worst was over," whatever that meant.

"Mr. Sykes is going to live," the man behind her said. "Because of you. He owes you his life. A few more hours in that tub . . ."

The man—she assumed that he was yet another police officer—let his voice drift off. She finally turned and faced him. Yep, a cop. In uniform no less. The patch on his arm said he was from the Kasselton Police Department.

"I already talked to the Ho-Ho-Kus detectives," she said.

"I know that."

"I really don't know any more, Officer . . . ?"

"Perlmutter," he said. "Captain Stuart Perlmutter."

She turned back toward the bed. Mike had his shirt off. His belly rose and fell as if it were being inflated at a gas station. He was overweight, Mike, and the act of breathing, just breathing, seemed to put undue stress on him. He should have taken better care of his health. She should have insisted on it.

"Who's with your kids?" Perlmutter asked.

"Mike's brother and sister-in-law."

"Anything I can get you?"

"No."

Charlaine changed her grip on Mike's hand.

"I was going over your statement."

She did not reply.

"Do you mind if I ask you a few follow-up questions?"

"I'm not sure I understand," Charlaine said.

"Pardon?"

"I live in Ho-Ho-Kus. What does Kasselton have to do with it?"

"I'm just helping out."

She nodded, though she had no idea why. "I see."

"According to your statement, you were looking out your bedroom window when you saw the hide-a-key on Mr. Sykes's back path. Is that correct?"

"Yes."

"And that's why you called the police?"

"Yes."

"Do you know Mr. Sykes?"

She shrugged, keeping her eyes on that rising and falling stomach. "To say hello."

"You mean like a neighbor?"

"Yes."

"When was the last time you talked to him?"

"I didn't. I mean, I never really talked to him."

"Just the neighborly hellos."

She nodded.

"And the last time you did that?"

"Waved hello?"

"Yes."

"I don't know. A week ago maybe."

"I'm a little confused, Mrs. Swain, so maybe you can help me out here. You saw a hide-a-key on the path and just decided to call the police—"

"I also saw movement."

"Pardon?"

"Movement. I saw something move in the house."

"Like someone was inside?"

"Yes."

"How did you know it wasn't Mr. Sykes?"

She turned around. "I didn't. But I also saw the hide-a-key."

"Lying there. In plain sight."

"Yes."

"I see. And you put two and two together?"

"Right."

Perlmutter nodded as if suddenly understanding. "And if Mr. Sykes had been the one to use the hide-a-key, he wouldn't have just tossed it onto the path. Was that your thinking?"

Charlaine said nothing.

"Because, see, that's what's weird to me, Mrs. Swain. This guy who broke into the house and assaulted Mr. Sykes. Why would he have left the hide-a-key out in plain sight like that? Wouldn't he have hidden it or taken it inside with him?"

Silence.

"And there's something else. Mr. Sykes sustained his injuries at least twenty-four hours before we found him. Do you think the hide-a-key was out on that path the whole time?"

"I wouldn't know."

"No, I guess you wouldn't. It's not like you stare at his backyard or anything."

She just looked at him.

"Why did you and your husband follow him, the guy who broke into the Sykes place, I mean?"

"I told the other officer—"

"You were trying to help out so we wouldn't lose him."

"I was also afraid."

"Of what?"

"That he'd know I called the police."

"Why would you worry about that?"

"I was watching from the window. When the police arrived. He turned and looked out and saw me."

"And you thought, what, he'd go after you?"

"I don't know. I was scared, that's all."

Perlmutter did that over-nod bit again. "I guess that fits. I mean some of the pieces, well, you have to force them down, but that's normal. Most cases don't make perfect sense."

She turned away from him again.

"You say he was driving a Ford Windstar."

"That's right."

"He pulled out of the garage in that vehicle, right?"

"Yes."

"Did you see the license plate?"

"No."

"Hmm. Why do you think he did that?"

"Did what?"

"Parked in the garage."

"I have no idea. Maybe so no one would see his car."

"Yeah, okay, that adds up."

Charlaine took her husband's hand again. She remembered the last time they'd held hands. Two months ago, when they went to see a romantic comedy starring Meg Ryan. Strangely enough Mike was a sucker for "chick flicks." His eyes welled up during bad romance movies. In real life, she could only remember seeing him cry once, when his father died. But at movies Mike sat in the dark and you would see a little quake in the face and then, yes, the tears would start. That night he reached out and took her hand, and what Charlaine remembered most—what tormented her now—was being unmoved. Mike had tried to interlace their fingers, but she shifted hers just enough to block him. That was how little it meant to Charlaine, nothing really, this overweight man with the comb-over reaching out to her.

"Could you please leave now?" she asked Perlmutter.

"You know I can't."

She closed her eyes.

"I know about your tax problem."

She stayed still.

"In fact, you called H&R Block this morning about it—isn't that right? That's where Mr. Sykes worked."

She didn't want to let go of the hand, but it felt as though Mike was pulling away.

"Mrs. Swain?"

"Not here," Charlaine said to Perlmutter. She let the hand drop and stood. "Not in front of my husband."

CHAPTER 22

Nursing home residents are always in and happy to have a visitor. Grace called the number and a perky woman answered.

"Starshine Assisted Living!"

"I'd like to know about visiting hours," Grace said.

"We don't have them!" She spoke in exclamations.

"Excuse me?"

"No visiting hours. You can visit anytime, twenty-four/seven."

"Oh. I'd like to visit Mr. Robert Dodd."

"Bobby? Well, let me connect you to his room. Oh wait, it's eight. He'll be at exercise class. Bobby likes to keep in shape."

"Is there a way I can make an appointment?"

"To visit?"

"Yes."

"No need, just stop by."

The drive would take her a little under two hours. It would be better than trying to explain over the phone, especially in light of the fact that she didn't have a clue what she wanted to ask him about. The elderly are better in person anyway.

"Do you think he'll be in this morning?"

"Oh sure. Bobby stopped driving two years ago. He'll be here."

"Thank you."

"My pleasure."

At the breakfast table, Max dug his hand deep into the box of Cap'n Crunch. The sight—her child going for the toy—made her pause. It was all so normal. Children sense things. Grace knew that. But sometimes, well, sometimes children are wonderfully oblivious. Right now she was grateful for that.

"You already got the toy out," she said.

Max stopped. "I did?"

"So many boxes, so crummy a toy."

"What?"

The truth was, she had done the same thing when she was a kid—digging to get the worthless prize. Come to think of it, with the same cereal. "Never mind."

She sliced up a banana and mixed it in with the cereal. Grace always tried to be sneaky here, gradually adding more banana and less of the Cap'n. For a while she added Cheerios—less sugar—but Max quickly caught on.

"Emma! Get up now!"

A groan. Her daughter was too young to start with the trouble-getting-out-of-bed bit. Grace hadn't pulled that until she was in high school. Okay, maybe middle school. But certainly, definitely, not when she was eight. She thought about her own parents, dead for so long now. Sometimes one of the kids did something that reminded Grace of her mother or father. Emma pursed her lips so much like Grace's mom that Grace sometimes froze in place. Max's smile was like her dad's. You could see the genetic echo, and Grace never knew if it was a comfort or a painful reminder.

"Emma, now!"

A sound. Might have been a child getting out of bed.

Grace started making one lunch. Max liked to buy it at school and Grace was all for the ease of that. Making lunches in the morning was a pain in the ass. For a while Emma would buy the school lunch too, but something recently grossed her out, some indiscernible smell in the cafeteria that caused an aversion so strong Emma would gag. She ate outside, even in the cold, but the smell, she soon realized, was also in the food. Now she stayed in the cafeteria and brought a Batman lunchbox with her.

"Emma!"

"I'm here."

Emma wore her standard gym-rat garb: maroon athletic shorts, blue high-top Converse All-Stars, and a New Jersey Nets jersey. Total clash, which may have been the point. Emma wouldn't wear anything the least bit feminine. Putting on a dress usually required a negotiation of Middle East sensitivity, with often an equally violent result.

"What would you like for lunch?" Grace asked.

"Peanut butter and jelly."

Grace just stared at her.

Emma played innocent. "What?"

"You've been attending this school for how long now?"

"Huh?"

"Four years, right? One year of kindergarten. And now you're in third grade. That's four years."

"So?"

"In all that time how many times have you asked me for peanut butter in school?"

"I don't know."

"Maybe a hundred?"

Shrug.

"And how many times have I told you that your school doesn't allow peanut butter because some children might have an allergic reaction?"

"Oh yeah."

"Oh yeah." Grace checked the clock. She had a few Oscar Mayer "Lunchables," a rather disgustingly processed premade lunch, that she kept around for emergencies—i.e., no time or desire to fix a lunch. The

JUST ONE LOOK · 171

kids, of course, loved them. She asked Emma softly if she'd like one—softly because if Max heard, that would be the end of buying lunch. Emma graciously accepted it and jammed it into the Batman lunchbox.

They sat down to breakfast.

"Mom?" It was Emma.

"Yep."

"When you and Dad got married . . ." She stopped.

"What about it?"

Emma started again. "When you and Dad got married—at the end, when the guy said now you may kiss the bride . . ."

"Right."

"Well"—Emma cocked her head and closed one eye—"did you have to?"

"Kiss him?"

"Yeah."

"Have to? No, I guess not. I wanted to."

"But do you have to?" Emma insisted. "I mean, can't you just high-five instead?"

"High-five?"

"Instead of kiss. You know, turn to each other and high-five." She demonstrated.

"I guess. If that's what you want."

"That's what I want," Emma said firmly.

Grace took them to the bus stop. This time she did not follow the bus to school. She stayed in place and bit down on her lower lip. The calm façade was slipping off again. Now that Emma and Max were gone, that would be okay.

When she got back to the house, Cora was awake and at the computer and groaning.

"Can I get you something?" Grace asked.

"An anesthesiologist," Cora said. "Straight preferred but not required."

"I was thinking more like coffee."

"Even better." Cora's fingers danced across the keyboard. Her eyes narrowed. She frowned. "Something's wrong here."

"You mean with the e-mails off our spam, right?"

"We're not getting any replies."

"I noticed that too."

Cora sat back. Grace moved next to her and started biting a cuticle. After a few seconds, Cora leaned forward. "Let me try something." She brought up an e-mail, typed something in, sent it.

"What was that all about?"

"I just sent an e-mail to our spam address. I want to see if it arrives."

They waited. No e-mail appeared.

"Hmm." Cora leaned back. "So either something is wrong with the mail system . . ."

"Or?"

"Or Gus is still ticked about that small wee-wee line."

"How do we find out which?"

Cora kept staring at the computer. "Who were you on the phone with before?"

"Bob Dodd's nursing home. I'm going to pay him a visit this morning."

"Good." Cora's eyes stayed on the screen.

"What is it?"

"I want to check something out," she said.

"What?"

"Nothing probably, just something with the phone bills." Cora started typing again. "I'll call you if I learn anything."

Perlmutter left Charlaine Swain with the Bergen County sketch artist. He had forced the truth out of her, thereby unearthing a tawdry secret that would have been better left deep in the ground. Charlaine Swain had been right to keep it from him. It offered no help. The revelation was, at best, a sleazy and embarrassing distraction.

He sat with a doodle pad, wrote the word "Windstar" and spent the next fifteen minutes circling it.

A Ford Windstar.

Kasselton was not a sleepy small town. They had thirty-eight cops on the payroll. They worked robberies. They checked on suspicious cars. They kept the school drug problems—suburban white-kid drugs—under control. They worked vandalism cases. They dealt with congestion in town, illegal parking, car accidents. They did their best to keep the urban decay of Paterson, a scant three miles from the border of Kasselton, at a safe distance. They answered too many false alarms emanating from the technological mating call of too many overpriced motion detectors.

Perlmutter had never fired his service revolver, except on a range. He had, in fact, never drawn his weapon in the line of duty. There had only been three deaths in the last three decades that fell under the possible heading of "suspicious" and all three perpetrators were caught within hours. One was an ex-husband who got drunk and decided to profess his undying love by planning to kill the woman he purportedly adored before turning the shotgun on himself. Said ex-husband managed to get the first part right—two shotgun blasts to the ex's head—but like everything else in his pathetic life, he messed up the second part. He had only brought two shells. An hour later he was in custody. Suspicious Death Two was a teenage bully stabbed by a skinny, tormented elementary-school victim. The skinny kid served three years in juvie, where he learned the real meaning of being bullied and tormented. The final case was of a man dying of cancer who begged his wife of forty-eight years to end his suffering. She did. She got parole and Perlmutter suspected that it was worth it to her.

As for gunshots, well, there had been plenty in Kasselton but almost all were self-inflicted. Perlmutter wasn't much on politics. He wasn't sure of the relative merits of gun control, but he knew from personal experience that a gun bought for home protection was more likely—much, much, much more likely—to be used by the owner to commit suicide than to ward off a home invasion. In fact, in all his years in law enforcement, Perlmutter had never seen a case where the home gun had been used to shoot, stop, or scare away an intruder. Suicides by handguns, well, they were more plentiful than anyone wanted to let on.

Ford Windstar. He circled it again.

Now, after all these years, Perlmutter had a case involving attempted murder, bizarre abduction, unusually brutal assault—and, he suspected, much more. He started doodling again. He wrote the name *Jack Lawson* in the top left-hand corner. He wrote the name *Rocky Conwell* in the top right-hand corner. Both men, possibly missing, had crossed a toll plaza in a neighboring state at the same time. He drew a line from one name to the other.

Connection One.

Perlmutter wrote out Freddy Sykes's name, bottom left. The victim of a grievous assault. He wrote *Mike Swain* on the bottom right. Shot, attempted murder. The connection between these two men, Connection Two, was obvious. Swain's wife had seen the perpetrator of both acts, a stout Chinese guy she made sound like the Son of Oddjob from the old James Bond film.

But nothing really connected the four cases. Nothing connected the two disappearing men to the work of Oddjob's offspring. Except perhaps for one thing:

The Ford Windstar.

Jack Lawson had been driving a blue Ford Windstar when he disappeared. Mini Oddjob had been driving a blue Ford Windstar when he left the Sykes residence and shot Swain.

Granted this was a tenuous connection at best. Saying "Ford Windstar" in this suburb was like saying "implant" at a strip club. It wasn't much to go on, but when you add in the history of this town, the fact that stable fathers do not really just go missing, that this much activity never happens in a town like Kasselton . . . no, it wasn't a strong tie, but it wasn't far off for Perlmutter to draw a conclusion:

All of this was related.

Perlmutter had no idea how this was all related, and he really didn't want to think about it too much quite yet. Let the techies and lab guys do their jobs first. Let them scour the Sykes residence for fingerprints and hairs. Let the artist finish the sketch. Let Veronique Baltrus, their resident computer weenie and an honest-to-God knockout, sift through the Sykes computer. It was simply too early to make a guess.

"Captain?"

It was Daley.

"What's up?"

"We found Rocky Conwell's car."

"Where?"

"You know the Park-n-Ride on Route 17?"

Perlmutter took off his reading glasses. "The one down the street?"

Daley nodded. "I know. It doesn't make sense. We know he left the state, right?"

"Who found it?"

"Pepe and Pashaian."

"Tell them to secure the area," he said, rising. "We'll check the vehicle out ourselves."

CHAPTER 23

G race threw on a Coldplay CD for the ride, hoping it'd distract her. It did and it didn't. On one level she understood exactly what was happening to her with no need for interpretation. But the truth, in a sense, was too stark. To face it straight on would paralyze her. That was where the surrealism probably derived from—self-preservation, the need to protect and even filter what one saw. Surrealism gave her the strength to go on, to pursue the truth, to find her husband, as opposed to the eye of reality, stark and naked and alone, which made her want to crouch into a small ball or maybe scream until they took her away.

Her cell phone rang. She instinctively glanced at the display before hitting the hands-free. Again, no, not Jack. It was Cora. Grace picked up and said, "Hey."

"I won't classify the news as bad or good, so let me put it this way. Do you want the weird news first or the really weird news?"

"Weird."

"I can't reach Gus of the small wee-wee. He won't answer his calls. I keep getting his voice mail."

Coldplay started singing, appropriately enough, a haunting number entitled "Shiver." Grace kept both hands on the wheel, perfectly placed at ten and two o'clock. She stayed in the middle lane and drove exactly the speed limit. Cars flew by on both her right and left.

"And the really weird news?"

"Remember how we tried to see the calls from two nights ago? I mean, the ones Jack might have made?"

"Right."

"Well, I called the cell phone company. I pretended I was you. I assumed you wouldn't mind."

"Correct assumption."

"Right. Anyway, it didn't matter. The only call Jack's made in the past three days was to your cell phone yesterday."

"The call he made when I was at the police station."

"Right."

"So what's weird about that?"

"Nothing. The weird part was on your home phone."

Silence. She stayed on the Merritt Parkway, her hands on the wheel at ten and two o'clock.

"What about it?"

"You know about the call to his sister's office?" Cora asked.

"Yeah. I found that one by hitting redial."

"And his sister—what's her name again?"

"Sandra Koval."

"Sandra Koval, right. She told you that she wasn't there. That they never talked."

"Yes."

"The phone call lasted nine minutes."

A small shudder skipped through Grace. She forced her hands to stay at two and ten. "Ergo she lied."

"It would seem."

"So what did Jack say to her?"

"And what did she say back?"

"And why did she lie about it?"

"Sorry to have to tell you," Cora said.

"No, it's good."

"How do you figure?"

"It's a lead. Before this, Sandra was a dead end. Now we know she's somehow involved."

"What are you going to do about it?"

"I don't know," Grace said. "Confront her, I guess."

They said good-bye and Grace hung up. She drove a little farther, trying to run the scenarios through her head. "Trouble" came on the CD player. She pulled into an Exxon station. New Jersey didn't have self-serve, so for a moment Grace just sat in her car, not realizing that she had to fill it up herself.

She bought a bottle of cold water at the station's mini-mart and dropped the change into a charity can. She wanted to think this through some more, this connection to Jack's sister, but there wasn't time for finesse here.

Grace remembered the number of the Burton and Crimstein law firm. She took out her phone and pressed in the digits. Two rings later she asked to be connected to Sandra Koval's line. She was surprised when Sandra herself said, "Hello?"

"You lied to me."

There was no reply. Grace walked back toward her car.

"The call lasted nine minutes. You talked to Jack."

More silence.

"What's going on, Sandra?"

"I don't know."

"Why did Jack call you?"

"I'm going to hang up now. Please don't try to contact me again."

"Sandra?"

"You said he called you already."

"Yes."

"My advice is to wait until he calls again."

"I don't want your advice, Sandra. I want to know what he said to you."

"I think you should stop."

"Stop what?"

"You're on a cell phone?"

"Yes."

"Where are you?"

"I'm at a gas station in Connecticut."

"Why?"

"Sandra, I want you to listen to me." There was a burst of static. Grace waited for it to pass. She finished filling the tank and grabbed her receipt. "You're the last person to talk to my husband before he disappeared. You lied to me about it. You still won't tell me what he said to you. Why should I tell you anything?"

"Fair point, Grace. Now you listen to me. I'm going to leave you with one last thought before I hang up: Go home and take care of your children."

The line went dead. Grace was back in the car now. She hit redial and asked to be connected to Sandra's office. Nobody answered. She tried again. Same thing. So now what? Try to show up in person again?

She pulled out of the gas station. Two miles later Grace saw a sign that said STARSHINE ASSISTED LIVING CENTER. Grace was not sure what she'd been expecting. The nursing homes of her youth, she guessed, those one-level edifices of plain brick, the purest form of substance-over-style that, in a perverse way, reminded her of elementary schools. Life, alas, was cyclical. You start in one of those plain brick buildings, you end there. Turn, turn, turn.

But the Starshine Assisted Living Center was a three-story faux Victorian hotel. It had the turrets and the porches and the bright yellow of the painted ladies of old, all set against ghastly aluminum siding. The grounds were manicured to the point where everything looked a tad too done, almost plastic. The place was aiming for cheery but it was trying too hard. The whole effect reminded Grace of Epcot Center at Disney World—a fun reproduction but you'd never mistake it for the real thing.

An old woman sat on a rocking chair on the front porch. She was reading the paper. She wished Grace a good morning and Grace did likewise. The lobby too tried to force up memories of a hotel from a bygone era. There were oil paintings in gaudy frames that looked like the kind of thing you'd buy at one of those Holiday Inn sales where everything was $19.99. It was obvious that they were reproductions of classics, even if you had never seen Renoir's *Luncheon of the Boating Party* or Hopper's *Nighthawks*.

The lobby was surprisingly busy. There were elderly people, of course, lots of them, in various states of degeneration. Some walked with no assistance, some shuffled, some had canes, some had walkers, some had wheelchairs. Many seemed spry; others slept.

The lobby was clean and bright but still had that—Grace hated herself for thinking like this—old-people smell, the odor of a sofa turning moldy. They tried to cover it up with something cherry, something that reminded Grace of those dangling tree fresheners in gypsy cabs, but there are some smells that you can never mask.

The single young person in the room—a woman in her midtwenties—sat behind a desk that was again aiming for the era but looked like something just bought at the Bombay Company. She smiled up at Grace.

"Good morning. I'm Lindsey Barclay."

Grace recognized the voice from the phone. "I'm here to see Mr. Dodd."

"Bobby's in his room. Second floor, room 211. I'll take you."

She rose. Lindsey was pretty in a way that only the young are, with that enthusiasm and smile that belong exclusively to the innocent or the cult recruiter.

"Do you mind taking the stairs?" she asked.

"Not at all."

Many of the residents stopped and said hello. Lindsey had time for every one of them, cheerfully returning each greeting, though Grace

JUST ONE LOOK · 181

the cynic couldn't help but wonder if this was a bit of a show for the visitor. Still Lindsey knew all the names. She always had something to say, something personal, and the residents seemed to appreciate that.

"Seems like mostly women," Grace noted.

"When I was in school, they told us the national ratio in assisted living is five women for every one man."

"Wow."

"Yes. Bobby jokes that he's waited his whole life for that kind of odds."

Grace smiled.

She waved a hand. "Oh, but he's all talk. His wife—he calls her 'his Maudie'—died almost thirty years ago. I don't think he's looked at a woman since."

That silenced them. The corridor was done up in forest green and pink, the walls lined with the familiar—Rockwell prints, dogs playing poker, black-and-whites from old movies like *Casablanca* and *Strangers on a Train*. Grace limped along. Lindsey noticed it—Grace could tell the way she cut quick glances—but like most people, she said nothing.

"We have different neighborhoods at Starshine," Lindsey explained. "That's what we call the corridors like this. Neighborhoods. Each has a different theme. The one we're in now is called Nostalgia. We think the residents find it comforting."

They stopped at a door. A nameplate on the right said B. DODD. She knocked on the door. "Bobby?"

No reply. She opened the door anyway. They stepped into a small but comfortable room. There was a tiny kitchenette on the right. On the coffee table, ideally angled so that you could see it from both the door and the bed, was a large black-and-white photograph of a stunning woman who looked a bit like Lena Horne. The woman in the picture was maybe forty but you could tell that the picture was old.

"That's his Maudie."

Grace nodded, lost for a moment in this image in the silver frame.

She thought again about "her Jack." For the first time she allowed herself to consider the unthinkable: Jack might never come home. It was something she'd been avoiding from the moment she'd heard the minivan start up. She might never see Jack again. She might never hold him. She might never laugh at one of his corny jokes. She might never—and this was apropos to think here—grow old with him.

"Are you okay?"

"Fine."

"Bobby must be up with Ira on Reminiscence. They play cards."

They began to back out of the room. "Is Reminiscence another, uh, neighborhood?"

"No. Reminiscence is what we call our third floor. It's for our residents with Alzheimer's."

"Oh."

"Ira doesn't recognize his own children, but he still plays a mean game of pinochle."

They were back in the hall. Grace noticed a cluster of images next to Bobby Dodd's door. She took a closer look. It was one of those box frames people use to display trinkets. There were army medals. There was an old baseball, brown with age. There were photographs from every era of the man's life. One photograph was of his murdered son, Bob Dodd, the same one she'd seen on the computer last night.

Lindsey said, "Memory box."

"Nice," Grace said, because she didn't know what else to say.

"Every patient has one by their door. It's a way to let everyone know about you."

Grace nodded. Summing up a life in a twelve-by-eight box frame. Like everything else about this place, it managed to be both appropriate and creepy at the exact same time.

To get to the Reminiscence floor you had to use an elevator that worked by a coded numeric keypad. "So the residents don't wander,"

Lindsey explained, which again fit into the "making sense yet giving the willies" style of this place.

The Reminiscence floor was comfortable, well appointed, well staffed, and terrifying. Some residents were functional, but most wilted in wheelchairs like dying flowers. Some stood and shuffled. Several muttered to themselves. All had that glazed hundred-yard stare.

A woman deep into her eighties jangled her keys and started for the elevator.

Lindsey asked, "Where are you going, Cecile?"

The old woman turned toward her. "I have to pick up Danny from school. He'll be waiting for me."

"It's okay," Lindsey said. "School won't be out for another two hours."

"Are you sure?"

"Of course. Look, let's have some lunch and then you can pick up Danny, okay?"

"He has piano lessons today."

"I know."

A staff member came over and steered Cecile away. Lindsey watched her go. "We use validation therapy," she said, "with our advanced Alzheimer's patients."

"Validation therapy?"

"We don't argue with them or try to make them see the truth. I don't, for example, tell her that Danny is now a sixty-two-year-old banker with three grandchildren. We just try to redirect them."

They walked down a corridor—no, "neighborhood"—filled with life-size dolls of babies. There was a changing table and teddy bears.

"Nursery neighborhood," she said.

"They play with dolls?"

"Those that are more high functioning. It helps them prepare for visits from great-grandchildren."

"And the others?"

Lindsey kept walking. "Some think they're young mothers. It helps soothe them."

Subconsciously, or maybe not, they picked up the pace. A few seconds later, Lindsey said, "Bobby?"

Bobby Dodd rose from the card table. The first word that came to mind: dapper. He looked sprightly and fresh. He had dark black skin, thick wrinkles like something you might see on an alligator. He was a snappy dresser in a tweed jacket, two-tone loafers, a red ascot with a matching hanky. His gray hair was cropped close and slicked down.

His manner was upbeat, even after Grace explained that she wanted to talk to him about his murdered son. She looked for some signs of devastation—a wetness in the eye, a tremor in the voice—but Bobby Dodd showed nothing. Okay, yes, Grace was dealing in heavy generalities, but could it be that death and big-time tragedy did not hit the elderly as hard as the rest of us? The elderly could be easily agitated by the little stuff—traffic delays, lines at airports, poor service. But it was as if the big things never quite reached them. Was there a strange selfishness that came with age? Was there something about being closer to the inevitable—having that perspective—that made one either internalize, block, or brush off the big calamities? Can frailty not handle the big blows, and thus a defense mechanism, a survival instinct, runs interference?

Bobby Dodd wanted to help, but he really didn't know much. Grace could see that almost right away. His son had visited twice a month. Yes, Bob's stuff had been packed up and sent to him, but he hadn't bothered opening it.

"It's in storage," Lindsey told Grace.

"Do you mind if I look through it?"

Bobby Dodd patted her leg. "Not at all, child."

"We'll need to ship it to you," Lindsey said. "The storage facility is off-site."

"It's very important."

"I can have it overnighted."

"Thank you."

Lindsey left them alone.

"Mr. Dodd—"

"Bobby, please."

"Bobby," Grace said. "When was the last time your son visited you?"

"Three days before he was killed."

The words came quickly and without thought. She finally saw a flicker behind the façade, and she wondered about her earlier observations, about old age making tragedy less hurtful—or does it merely make the mask more deft?

"Did he seem different at all?"

"Different?"

"More distracted, anything like that."

"No." Then: "Or at least I didn't notice, if he did."

"What did you talk about?"

"We never have much to say. Sometimes we talk about his momma. Most of the time we just watch TV. They got cable here, you know."

"Did Jillian come with him?"

"No."

He said that too quickly. Something in his face closed down.

"Did she ever come?"

"Sometimes."

"But not the last time?"

"That's right."

"Did that surprise you?"

"That? No, *that*"—big emphasis—"didn't surprise me."

"What did?"

He looked off and bit his lower lip. "She wasn't at the funeral."

Grace thought that she must have heard wrong. Bobby Dodd nodded as if he could read her thoughts.

"That's right. His own wife."

"Were they having marital issues?"

"If they were, Bob never said anything to me."

"Did they have any children?"

"No." He adjusted the ascot and glanced away for a moment. "Why are you bringing this all up, Mrs. Lawson?"

"Grace, please."

He did not reply. He looked at her with eyes that spoke of wisdom and sadness. Maybe the answer to elderly coldness is far simpler: Those eyes had seen bad. They didn't want to see more.

"My own husband is missing," Grace said. "I think—I don't know—I think they're connected."

"What's your husband's name?"

"Jack Lawson."

He shook his head. The name meant nothing to him. She asked if he had a phone number or any idea how she could contact Jillian Dodd. He shook his head again. They headed to the elevator. Bobby didn't know the code, so an orderly escorted them down. They rode from floor three to one in silence.

When they reached the door, Grace thanked him for his time.

"Your husband," he said. "You love him, don't you?"

"Very much."

"Hope you're stronger than me." Bobby Dodd walked away then. Grace thought of that silver-framed picture in his room, of his Maudie, and then she showed herself out.

CHAPTER 24

Perlmutter realized that they had no legal right to open Rocky Conwell's car. He pulled Daley over. "Is DiBartola on duty?"

"No."

"Call Rocky Conwell's wife. Ask her if she had a set of keys to the car. Tell her we found it and want her permission to go through it."

"She's the ex-wife. Does she have any standing?"

"Enough for our purposes," Perlmutter said.

"Okay."

It took Daley no time. The wife cooperated. They stopped by the Maple Garden apartments on Maple Street. Daley ran up and retrieved the keys. Five minutes later they pulled into the Park-n-Ride.

There was no reason to be suspicious of foul play. If anything, finding the car here, at this depot, would lead one to the opposite conclusion. People parked here so that they could go elsewhere. One bus whisked the weary to the heart of midtown Manhattan. Another brought you to the northern tip of the famed isle, near the George Washington Bridge. Other buses took you to the three nearby major airports—JFK, La Guardia, Newark Liberty—and ultimately anywhere in the world. So, no, finding Rocky Conwell's car did not lead one to suspect foul play.

At least, not at first.

Pepe and Pashaian, the two cops who were watching the car, had not seen it. Perlmutter's eyes slid toward Daley. Nothing on his face either. They all looked complacent, expecting this would lead to a dead end.

Pepe and Pashaian hoisted their belts and sauntered toward Perlmutter. "Hey, Captain."

Perlmutter kept his eyes on the car.

"You want us to start questioning the ticket agents?" Pepe asked. "Maybe one of them remembers selling Conwell a ticket."

"I don't think so," Perlmutter said.

The three younger men caught something in their superior's voice. They looked at one another and shrugged. Perlmutter did not explain.

Conwell's vehicle was a Toyota Celica. A small car, old model. But the size and age didn't really matter. Neither did the fact that there was rust along the wheel trims, that two hubcaps were gone, that the other two were so dirty you could not tell where metal ended and rubber began. No, none of that bothered Perlmutter.

He stared at the back of the car and thought about those small-town sheriffs in horror movies—you know the ones, where something is very wrong, where townspeople start acting strangely and the body count keeps rising and the sheriff, that good, smart, loyal, out-of-his-league law enforcement officer, is powerless to do anything about it. That was what Perlmutter felt now because the back of the car, the trunk area, was low.

Much too low.

There was only one explanation. Something heavy was in the trunk.

It could be anything, of course. Rocky Conwell had been a football player. He probably lifted weights. Maybe he was transferring a set of dumbbells. The answer could be as simple as that, good old Rocky moving his weights. Maybe he was bringing them back to the garden apartment on Maple Street, the one where his ex lived. She had worried about him. They were reconciling. Maybe Rocky loaded his car—okay, not his whole car, just his trunk, because Perlmutter could see that there was nothing in the backseat—anyway, maybe he loaded it up to move back in with her.

Perlmutter jangled the keys as he moved closer to the Toyota Celica. Daley, Pepe, and Pashaian hung back. Perlmutter glanced down at the set of keys. Rocky's wife—he thought that her name was Lorraine but he couldn't be sure—had a Penn State football helmet key chain. It looked old and scraped up. The Nittany Lion was barely visible. Perlmutter wondered what she thought about when she looked at the key chain, why she still used it.

He stopped at the trunk and sniffed the air. Not a hint. He put the key in the lock and turned. The trunk's lock popped open, the sound echoing. He began to open the trunk. The air escaping was almost audible. And now, yes, the smell was unmistakable.

Something large had been squished into the trunk, like an oversize pillow. Without warning it sprang free like a giant jack-in-the-box. Perlmutter jumped back as the head fell out first, smacking the pavement hard.

Didn't matter, of course. Rocky Conwell was already dead.

CHAPTER 25

Now what?

Grace was starved for one thing. She drove over the George Washington Bridge, took the Jones Road exit, and stopped to grab a bite at a Chinese restaurant called, interestingly enough, Baumgart's. She ate in silence, feeling as lonely as she had ever felt, and tried to hold herself together. What had happened? The day before yesterday—was it really only then?—she had picked up photographs at Fotomat. That was all. Life was good. She had a husband she adored and two wonderful, inquisitive kids. She had time to paint. They all had their health, enough money in the bank. And then she had seen a photograph, an old one, and now . . .

Grace had almost forgotten about Josh the Fuzz Pellet.

He was the one who developed the roll of film. He was the one who mysteriously left the store not long after she picked up the pictures. He had to be the one, she was sure, who put that damn photograph in the middle of her pack.

She grabbed her cell phone, asked directory assistance for the number of the Fotomat in Kasselton, and even paid the extra fee to be directly connected. On the third ring, the phone was picked up.

"Fotomat."

Grace said nothing. No question about it. She would recognize that bored yah-dude slur anywhere. It was Fuzz Pellet Josh. He was back at the store.

She considered just hanging up, but maybe, somehow, that would—she didn't know—tip him off. Make him run. She changed her voice, added a little extra lilt, and asked what time they closed.

"Like, six," Fuzz Pellet told her.

She thanked him, but he had hung up. The check was already on the table. She paid and tried not to sprint to her car. Route 4 was wide open. She sped past the plethora of malls and found a parking spot not far from the Fotomat. Her cell phone rang.

"Hello?"

"It's Carl Vespa."

"Oh, hi."

"I'm sorry about yesterday. About springing Jimmy X on you like that."

She debated telling him about Jimmy's late-night visit, decided now was not the time. "It's okay."

"I know you don't care, but it looks like Wade Larue is going to get released."

"Maybe it's the right thing," she said.

"Maybe." But Vespa sounded far from convinced. "You sure you don't need any protection?"

"Positive."

"If you change your mind . . ."

"I'll call."

There was a funny pause. "Any word from your husband?"

"No."

"Does he have a sister?"

Grace changed hands. "Yes. Why?"

"Her name Sandra Koval?"

"Yes. What does she have to do with this?"

"I'll talk to you later."

He hung up. Grace stared at the phone. What the hell was that all about? She shook her head. It would be useless to call back. She tried to refocus.

Grace grabbed her purse and hurry-limped toward the Fotomat. Her leg hurt. Walking was a chore. It felt as though someone were on the ground clinging to her ankle and she had to drag him along. Grace kept moving. She was three stores away when a man in a business suit stepped in her path.

"Ms. Lawson?"

A weird thought struck Grace as she looked at this stranger: His sandy hair was nearly the same color as his suit. It almost looked like they were both made from the same material.

"May I help you?" she said.

The man reached into his coat pocket and pulled out a photograph. He held it up to her face so that she could see it. "Did you post this on the Web?"

It was the cropped mystery photograph of the blonde and the redhead.

"Who are you?"

The sandy-haired man said, "My name is Scott Duncan. I'm with the U.S. attorney's office." He pointed to the blonde, the one who'd been looking up at Jack, the one with the X across her face.

"And this," Scott Duncan said, "is a picture of my sister."

CHAPTER 26

Perlmutter had broken the news to Lorraine Conwell as gently as he could.

He had delivered bad news plenty of times. Usually it involved car accidents on Route 4 or the Garden State Parkway. Lorraine Conwell had exploded into tears when he told her, but now the numbness had seeped in and dried her eyes.

The stages of grief: Supposedly the first is denial. That was wrong. The first is just the opposite: Total acceptance. You hear the bad news and you understand exactly what is being said to you. You understand that your loved one—your spouse, your parent, your child—will never come home, that they are gone for good, that their life is over, and that you will never, ever, see them again. You understand that in a flash. Your legs buckle. Your heart gives out.

That was the first step—not just acceptance, not just understanding, but total truth. Human beings are not built to withstand that kind of hurt. That then is when the denial begins. Denial floods in quickly, salving the wounds or at least covering them. But there is still that moment, mercifully quick, the real Stage One, when you hear the news and stare into the abyss, and horrible as it is, you understand everything.

Lorraine Conwell sat ramrod straight. There was a quiver on her

lips. Her eyes were dry. She looked small and alone, and it took all Perlmutter had not to put his arms around her and pull her in close.

"Rocky and me," she said. "We were going to get back together."

Perlmutter nodded, encouraging.

"It's my fault, you know. I made Rocky leave. I shouldn't have." She
looked up at him with those violet eyes. "He was different when we met,
you know? He had dreams then. He was so sure of himself. But when he
couldn't play ball anymore, it just ate away at him. I couldn't live with that."

Perlmutter nodded again. He wanted to help her out, wanted to
stay in her company, but he really did not have time for the unabridged
life story. He needed to move this along and get out of here. "Was there
anyone who wanted to hurt Rocky? Did he have enemies or anything
like that?"

She shook her head. "No. No one."

"He spent time in prison."

"Yes. It was stupid. He got into a fight in a bar. It got out of hand."

Perlmutter looked over at Daley. They knew about the fight. They
were already on that, seeing if his victim had sought late revenge. It
seemed doubtful.

"Was Rocky working?"

"Yes."

"Where?"

"In Newark. He worked at the Budweiser plant. The one near the
airport."

"You called our office yesterday," Perlmutter said.

She nodded, her eyes staring straight ahead.

"You spoke to an Officer DiBartola."

"Yes. He was very nice."

Right. "You told him that Rocky hadn't come home from work."

She nodded.

"You called in the early morning. You said he'd been working the
night before."

"That's right."

"Did he work a night shift at the plant?"

"No. He'd taken a second job." She squirmed a little. "It was off the books."

"Doing what?"

"He worked for this lady."

"Doing what?"

She used one finger to wipe a tear. "Rocky didn't talk about it much. He delivered subpoenas, I think, stuff like that."

"Do you know the lady's name?"

"Something foreign. I can't pronounce it."

Perlmutter did not need to think about it long. "Indira Khariwalla?"

"That's it." Lorraine Conwell looked up at him. "You know her?"

He did. It had been a long time, but yes, Perlmutter knew her very well.

Grace had handed Scott Duncan the photograph, the one with all five people in it. He could not stop staring, especially at the image of his sister. He ran his finger over her face. Grace could barely look at him.

They were back at Grace's house now, sitting in the kitchen. They had been talking for the better part of half an hour.

"You got this two days ago?" Scott Duncan asked.

"Yes."

"And then your husband . . . He's this one, right?" Scott Duncan pointed to Jack's image.

"Yes."

"He ran off?"

"He vanished," she said. "He didn't run off."

"Right. You think he was, what, kidnapped?"

"I don't know what happened to him. I only know he's in trouble."

Scott Duncan's eyes stayed on the old photograph. "Because he gave you some kind of warning? Something about needing space?"

"Mr. Duncan, I'd like to know how you came across this picture. And how you found me, for that matter."

"You sent it out via some kind of spam. Someone recognized the picture and forwarded it to me. I traced back the spammer and put a little pressure on him."

"Was that why we didn't receive any answers?"

Duncan nodded. "I wanted to talk to you first."

"I've told you everything I know. I was on my way to confront the guy in the Fotomat when you showed up."

"We'll question him—don't worry about that."

He couldn't take his eyes off the picture. She had done all the talking. He had told her nothing, except that the woman in the photograph was his sister. Grace pointed at the crossed-out face. "Tell me about her," she said.

"Her name was Geri. Does her name mean anything to you?"

"I'm sorry. It doesn't."

"Your husband never mentioned her? Geri Duncan."

"Not that I remember." Then: "You said 'was.'"

"What?"

"You said 'was.' Her name *was* Geri."

Scott Duncan nodded. "She died in a fire when she was twenty-one years old. In her dorm room."

Grace froze. "She went to Tufts, right?"

"Yes. How did you know?"

Now it made sense—why the girl's face had seemed familiar. Grace hadn't known her, but there had been pictures in the newspapers at the time. Grace had been undergoing physical therapy and ripping through way too many periodicals. "I remember reading about it. Wasn't it an accident? Electrical fire or something?"

"That was what I thought. Until three months ago."

"What changed?"

"The U.S. attorney's office captured a man who goes by the name Monte Scanlon. He's a hired assassin. His job was to make it look like an accident."

Grace tried to take it in. "And you just learned this three months ago?"

"Yes."

"Did you investigate?"

"I'm still investigating, but it's been a long time." His voice was softer now. "Not many clues after all these years."

Grace turned away.

"I found out that Geri was dating a boy at the time, a local kid named Shane Alworth. The name mean anything to you?"

"No."

"You're sure?"

"Pretty sure, yeah."

"Shane Alworth had a rap sheet, nothing serious, but I checked him out."

"And?"

"And he's gone."

"Gone?"

"No sign of him. I can't find work records for him. I can't find any sign of a Shane Alworth on the tax payroll. I can't find any hit on his social security number."

"For how long?"

"How long has he been gone?"

"Yes."

"I've gone back ten years. Nothing." Duncan reached into his coat pocket and pulled out another photograph. He handed it to Grace. "Recognize him?"

She took a long look at the photograph. No question about it. It was the other guy in her photograph. She looked up at him for confirmation. Duncan nodded.

"Creepy, huh?"

"Where did you get this?" she asked.

"From Shane Alworth's mother. She claims her son lives in a small town in Mexico. That he's a missionary or something and that's why his name doesn't pop up. Shane also has a brother who lives in Saint Louis. Works as a psychologist. He backs up what the mother said."

"But you don't buy it."

"Do you?"

Grace put the mystery photograph on the table. "So we know about three people in this photograph," she said, more to herself than Duncan. "We have your sister, who was murdered. We have her boyfriend, Shane Alworth, the guy over here. He's missing. We have my husband, who disappeared right after seeing this photograph. That about right?"

"Pretty much."

"What else did the mother say?"

"Shane was unreachable. He was in the Amazon jungle, she thought."

"The Amazon jungle? In Mexico?"

"Her geography was fuzzy."

Grace shook her head and pointed at the picture. "So that leaves the other two women. Any clue who they are?"

"No, not yet. But we know more now. The redhead, we should get a bead on her pretty soon. The other one, the one with her back to the camera, I don't know if we'll ever know."

"Did you learn anything else?"

"Not really. I've had Geri's body exhumed. That took some time to arrange. A full autopsy is being done, to see if they can find any physical evidence, but it's a long shot. This"—he held up the picture from the Web—"this is the first real lead I've had."

She didn't like the pitch of hope in his voice. "It might just be a picture," she said.

"You don't believe that."

Grace put her hands on the table. "Do you think my husband had something to do with your sister's death?"

Duncan rubbed his chin. "Good question," he said.

She waited.

"Something to do with it, probably. But I don't think he killed her, if that's what you're asking. Something happened to them a long time ago. I don't know what. My sister was killed in a fire. Your husband ran overseas, I guess. France, you said?"

"Yes."

"And Shane Alworth, too. I mean, it's all connected. It has to be."

"My sister-in-law knows something."

Scott Duncan nodded. "You said she's a lawyer?"

"Yes. With Burton and Crimstein."

"That's not good. I know Hester Crimstein. If she doesn't want to tell us anything, I won't be able to apply much pressure."

"So what do we do?"

"We keep shaking the cage."

"Shaking the cage?"

He nodded. "Shaking cages is the only way you make progress."

"So we should start with shaking Josh at the Fotomat," Grace said. "He's the one who gave me that photograph."

Duncan stood. "Sounds like a plan."

"You're going there now?"

"Yes."

"I'd like to come along."

"Let's go then."

"As I live and breathe. Captain Perlmutter. To what do I owe the pleasure?"

Indira Khariwalla was small and wizened. Her dark skin—she was, as her name implied, from India, more specifically Bombay—had started to harden and thicken. She was still attractive but not the exotic temptress she had been in her heyday.

"Been a long time," he said.

"Yes." The smile, once a dazzler, took great effort now, almost cracking the skin. "But I'd prefer not to rehash the past."

"Me either."

When Perlmutter started working in Kasselton, he had been part-nered with a veteran a year from retirement named Steve Goedert, a great guy. They struck up a deep friendship. Goedert had three kids, all grown, and a wife named Susan. Perlmutter did not know how Goedert met Indira, but they started up. Susan found out.

Fast-forward past the ugly divorce.

Goedert had no money left once the lawyers were through with him. He ended up working as a private investigator but with a twist: He specialized in infidelity. Or at least that was what he claimed. To Perlmutter's thinking it was a scam—entrapment at its very worst. He would use Indira as bait. She would approach the husband, lure him in, and then Goedert would take pictures. Perlmutter told him to stop. Fidelity was not a game. It was not a prank, testing a man like that.

Goedert must have known it was wrong. He hit the bottle pretty good and never came out. He too had a gun in his house, and in the end he too did not use it to stop a home invasion. After his death, Indira struck out on her own. She took over the agency, keeping Goedert's name on the door.

"A long time ago," she said softly.

"Did you love him?"

"None of your business."

"You ruined his life."

"Do you really think I can wield that kind of power over a man?" She shifted in her chair. "What can I do for you, Captain Perlmutter?"

"You have an employee named Rocky Conwell."

She did not respond.

"I know he's off the books. I don't care about that."

Still nothing. He slapped down a crude Polaroid of Conwell's dead body.

Indira's eyes flicked to it, ready to dismiss, and then stared there. "Dear Lord."

Perlmutter waited, but Indira said nothing. She stared for a little while longer and then let her head drop back.

"His wife says he worked for you."

She nodded.

"What did he do?"

"Night shifts."

"What did he do on the night shifts?"

"Mostly repossession. He did a little subpoena work too."

"What else?"

She said nothing.

"There was stuff in his car. We found a long-range camera and a pair of binoculars."

"So?"

"So was he doing surveillance?"

She looked at him. There were tears in her eyes. "You think he was killed on the job?"

"It's a logical assumption, but I won't know for certain until you tell me what he was doing."

Indira looked away. She began to rock in the chair.

"Was he working a job the night before last?"

"Yes."

More silence.

"What was he doing, Indira?"

"I can't say."

"Why not?"

"I have clients. They have rights. You know the drill, Stu."

"You're not a lawyer."

"No, but I can work for one."

"Are you saying this case was attorney work product?"

"I'm not saying anything."

"You want to take another look at that photograph?"

She almost smiled. "You think that will make me talk?" But Indira did take another look. "I don't see any blood," she said.

"There wasn't any."

"He wasn't shot?"

"Nope. No gun, no knife."

She looked confused. "How was he killed?"

"I don't know yet. He's on the table. But I have a guess, if you want to hear it."

She didn't. But she nodded slowly.

"He suffocated."

"You mean like he was garroted?"

"Doubtful. There are no ligature marks on the neck."

She frowned. "Rocky was huge. He was strong as an ox. It had to be poison, something like that."

"I don't think so. The ME said there was substantial damage to the larynx."

She looked confused.

"In other words, his throat was crushed like an eggshell."

"You mean he was strangled by hand?"

"We don't know."

"He was too strong for that," she said again.

"Who was he following?" Perlmutter asked.

"Let me make a call. You can wait in the hall."

He did. The wait was not long.

When Indira came out, her voice was clipped. "I can't speak to you," she said. "I'm sorry."

"Attorney's orders?"

"I can't speak to you."

"I'll be back. I'll get a warrant."

"Good luck," she said, turning away. And Perlmutter thought that maybe she meant it.

CHAPTER 27

Grace and Scott Duncan headed back to the Fotomat. Her heart sank when they entered and she saw no Fuzz Pellet.

Assistant Manager Bruce was there. He puffed out his chest. When Scott Duncan flashed his badge, the chest deflated. "Josh is out on lunch break," he said.

"Do you know where?"

"He usually goes to the Taco Bell. It's right down the block."

Grace knew it. She hurried out first, afraid to lose his scent again. Scott Duncan followed. As soon as she entered the Taco Bell, the fragrance of lard rising up to assault her, she spotted Josh.

Equally important, Josh spotted her. His eyes widened.

Scott Duncan stood at her side. "That him?"

Grace nodded.

Fuzz Pellet Josh sat alone. His head was tilted down, his hair hanging in front of his face like a curtain. His expression—and Grace guessed that he only had this one—was sullen. He bit into the taco as if it had insulted his favorite grunge group. The earphones were jammed into place. The cord fell into the sour cream. Grace hated to sound like an old biddy, but having this kind of music plugged directly into the brain all day could not be good for a person. Grace enjoyed music. When she was alone, she would turn the music up, sing along, dance, whatever. So it wasn't the music or even the volume. But what did it do to the mental health of a young mind to have music, probably angry and harsh, pounding in the ears all the time? An aural confinement, solitary walls of sound, to paraphrase Elton John, inescapable. No life noises let in. No talking. An artificial sound track to your life.

It could not be healthy.

Josh lowered his head, pretending he didn't see them. She watched him as they approached. He was so young. He looked pitiful, sitting there alone like that. She thought about his hopes and dreams and how he already looked set on the road of lifelong disappointments. She thought about Josh's mother, about how she must have tried and how she must worry. She thought about her own son, her little Max, and about how she'd handle it if he started slipping in this direction.

She and Scott Duncan stopped in front of Josh's table. He took another bite and then slowly looked up. The music coming from his earphones was so loud that Grace could actually make out the lyrics. Something about bitches and hos. Scott Duncan took the lead. She let him.

"Do you recognize this lady?" Scott asked.

Josh shrugged. He lowered the volume.

"Take those off," Scott said. "Now."

He did as he was told, but he took his time.

"I asked you if you recognized this lady."

Josh glanced in her direction. "Yeah, I guess."

"How do you know her?"

"From where I work."

"You work at the Fotomat, correct?"

"Yeah."

"And Ms. Lawson here. She's a customer."

"That's what I said."

"Do you remember the last time she was in the store?"

"No."

"Think."

He shrugged.

"Does two days ago sound about right?"

Another shrug. "Could be."

Scott Duncan had the envelope from the Fotomat. "You developed this roll of film, correct?"

"You say so."

"No, I'm asking you. Look at the envelope."

He did. Grace stayed still. Josh had not asked Scott Duncan who he was. He had not asked them what they wanted. She wondered about that.

"Yeah, I developed that roll."

Duncan took out the photograph with his sister in it. He put it on the table. "Did you put this picture in Ms. Lawson's packet?"

"No," Josh said.

"You sure?"

"Positive."

Grace waited a beat. She knew that he was lying. She spoke for the first time. "How do you know?" she asked.

They both looked at her. Josh said, "Huh?"

"How do you develop rolls?"

He said, "Huh?" again.

"You put the roll in that machine," Grace said. "They come out in a pile. Then you put the pile in an envelope. Isn't that right?"

"Yeah."

"Do you look at every picture you develop?"

He said nothing. He looked around as if asking for help.

"I've seen you work," Grace said. "You read your magazines. You listen to your music. You do not check through all the pictures. So my question is, Josh, how do you know what pictures were in that pile?"

Josh glanced at Scott Duncan. No help there. He turned back to her. "It's weird—that's all."

Grace waited.

"That picture looks like it's a hundred years old or something. It's the right size, but that ain't Kodak paper. That's what I meant. I'd never seen it before." Josh liked that. His eyes lit up, warming to his lie. "Yeah, see, that's what I thought he meant. When he said did I put it in. Did I ever see it before?"

Grace just looked at him.

"Look, I don't know what goes through that machine. But I've never seen that print. That's all I know, okay?"

"Josh?"

It was Scott Duncan. Josh turned toward him.

"That picture ended up in Ms. Lawson's pack of pictures. Do you have any idea how that happened?"

"Maybe she took the picture."

"No," Duncan said.

Josh gave another elaborate shrug. He must have had very powerful shoulders from all the work they got.

"Tell me how it works," Duncan said. "How you develop the pictures."

"It's like she said. I put the film into the machine. It does the rest. I just set the size and the count."

"Count?"

"You know. One print from each negative, two prints, whatever."

"And they come out in a pile?"

"Yeah."

Josh was more relaxed now, on comfortable ground.

"And then you put them in an envelope?"

"Right. Same envelope the customer filled out. Then I file it in alphabetical order. That's it."

Scott Duncan looked over at Grace. She said nothing. He took out his badge. "Do you know what this badge means, Josh?"

"No."

"It means I work for the U.S. attorney's office. It means I can make your life miserable if you cross me. Do you understand?"

Josh looked a little scared now. He managed a nod.

"So I'm going to ask you one more time: Do you know anything about this photograph?"

"No. I swear." He looked around. "I gotta get back to work now."

He stood. Grace blocked his path. "Why did you leave work early the other day?"

"Huh?"

"About an hour after I picked up my roll of film, I went back to the store. You were gone. And the next morning too. So what happened?"

"I got sick," he said.

"Yeah?"

"Yeah."

"Feeling better now?"

"Guess so." He started pushing past her.

"Because," Grace went on, "your manager said you had a family emergency. Is that what you told him?"

"I gotta get back to work," he said, and this time he pushed past her and nearly ran out the door.

Beatrice Smith was not home.

Eric Wu broke in without any trouble. He checked through the house. No one was there. With the gloves still on Wu flicked on the computer. Her software PIM—a fancy term for a date and phone book—was Time & Chaos. He opened it and checked her calendar.

Beatrice Smith was visiting her son, the doctor, in San Diego. She'd be home in two days—far enough away to save her life. Wu considered that, the fickle winds of fate. He couldn't help it. He glanced through Beatrice Smith's calendar two months in the past and two months in the future. There were no overnight trips. If he had come at any other time,

Beatrice Smith would be dead. Wu liked to think about things like that, about how it was often the little things, the unconscious things, the things we can't know or control, that alter our lives. Call it fate, luck, odds, God. Wu found it fascinating.

Beatrice Smith had a two-car garage. Her tan Land Rover took up the right side. The left side was empty. There was an oil stain on the ground. This, Wu figured, had been where Maury parked his car. She kept it empty now—Wu couldn't help but think of Freddy Sykes's mother—as if it was his side of the bed. Wu parked there. He opened the back. Jack Lawson looked shaky. Wu untied his legs so he could walk. The hands remained bound at the wrist. Wu led him inside. Jack Lawson fell twice. The blood had not fully circulated through the legs. Wu held him up by the collar of his shirt.

"I'm taking the gag off," Wu said.

Jack Lawson nodded. Wu could see it in his eyes. Lawson was broken. Wu had not hurt him much—not yet anyway—but when you spend enough time in the dark, alone with your thoughts, your mind turns inward and feasts. That was always a dangerous thing. The key to serenity, Wu knew, was to keep working, keep moving forward. When you're moving, you don't think about guilt or innocence. You don't think about your past or your dreams, your joys or disappointments. You just worry about survival. Hurt or be hurt. Kill or be killed.

Wu removed the gag. Lawson did not plead and beg or ask questions. That stage was over. Wu tied his legs to a chair. He searched the pantry and refrigerator. They both ate in silence. When they finished, Wu washed off the dishes and cleaned up. Jack Lawson stayed tied to the chair.

Wu's cell phone rang. "Yes."

"We have a problem."

Wu waited.

"When you picked him up, he had a copy of that photograph, right?"

"Yes."

"And he said there were no other copies?"

"Yes."

"He was wrong."

Wu said nothing.

"His wife has a copy of the picture. She's flashing it everywhere."

"I see."

"Will you take care of it?"

"No," Wu said. "I can't return to the area."

"Why not?"

Wu did not respond.

"Forget I asked that. We'll use Martin. He has the information on her children."

Wu said nothing. He did not like the idea, but he kept it to himself.

The voice on the phone said, "We'll take care of it," before hanging up.

CHAPTER 28

G race said, "Josh is lying."

They were back on Main Street. Clouds threatened, but for now humidity ruled the day. Scott Duncan gestured a few stores up with his chin. "I could use a Starbucks," he said.

"Wait. You don't think he's lying?"

"He's nervous. There's a difference."

Scott Duncan pulled open the glass door. Grace entered. There was a line at Starbucks. There always seemed to be a line at Starbucks. The sound system played something old from a warbly female blues singer, a Billie Holiday or Dinah Washington or Nina Simone. The song ended and a girl-with-acoustic-guitar came on, Jewel or Aimee Mann or Lucinda Williams.

"What about his inconsistencies?" she asked.

Scott Duncan frowned.

"What?"

"Does our friend Josh look like the type who willingly cooperates with authority?"

"No."

"So what would you expect him to say?"

"His boss said that he had a family emergency. He told us he was sick."

212 · HARLAN COBEN

"It is an inconsistency," he agreed.

"But?"

Scott Duncan gave an exaggerated shrug, mimicking Josh. "I've worked a lot of cases. You know what I've learned about inconsistencies?"

She shook her head. In the background the milk did that froth thing, the machine making a noise like a car-wash vacuum.

"They exist. I'd be more suspicious if there weren't a few. The truth is always fuzzy. If his story had been clean, I'd be more concerned. I'd wonder if he rehearsed it. Keeping a lie consistent isn't that difficult, but in this guy's case, if you asked him what he ate for breakfast twice he'd mess it up."

They moved forward in line. The barista asked for a drink order. Duncan looked at Grace. She ordered a venti iced Americano, no water. He nodded and said, "Make that two." He paid using one of those Starbucks debit cards. They waited for the drinks at the bar.

"So you think he was being truthful?" Grace asked.

"I don't know. But nothing he said raised much of a red flag."

Grace wasn't so sure. "It had to be him."

"Why?"

"There was no one else."

They picked up their drinks and found a table near the window. "Run it through for me," he said.

"Run what?"

"Go back. You picked up the pictures. Josh handed them to you. Did you look at them right away?"

Grace's eyes went up and to the right. She tried to remember the details. "No."

"Okay, so you took the packet. Did you stick it in your purse or something?"

"I held it."

"And then what?"

"I got in my car."

"The packet was still with you?"

"Yes."

"Where?"

"On the console. Between the two front seats."

"Where did you go?"

"To pick up Max from school."

"Did you stop on the way?"

"No."

"Were the pictures in your possession the whole time?"

Grace smiled in spite of herself. "You sound like I'm checking in for a flight."

"They don't ask that anymore."

"It's been a while since I flew anywhere." She smiled stupidly and realized why she had taken this inane detour in their conversation. He did too. She had spotted something—something she really didn't want to pursue.

"What?" he asked.

She shook her head.

"I might not have been able to tell if Josh was hiding something. You, however, make for an easier interrogation. What is it?"

"Nothing."

"Come on, Grace."

"The pictures were never out of my possession."

"But?"

"Look, this is a waste of time. I know it was Josh. It had to be."

"But?"

She took a deep breath. "I'm just going to say this once, so we can dismiss it and get on with our lives."

Duncan nodded.

"There was one person who *may*—I stress the word *may*—have had access."

"Who?"

"I was sitting in the car waiting for Max. I opened the envelope and looked at the first few pictures. Then my friend Cora got in."

"Got in your car?"

"Yes."

"Where?"

"The passenger's seat."

"And the pictures were on the console next to it?"

"No, not anymore." Her voice cracked now with annoyance. She was not enjoying this. "I just told you. I was looking at them."

"But you put them down?"

"Eventually, yeah, I guess."

"On the console?"

"I guess. I don't remember."

"So she had access."

"No. I was there the whole time."

"Who got out first?"

"We both got out at the same time, I think."

"You limp."

She looked at him. "So?"

"So getting out must be something of an effort."

"I do fine."

"But come on, Grace, work with me here. It's possible—I'm not saying likely, I'm saying possible—that while you were stepping out, your friend could have slipped that picture into the envelope."

"Possible, sure. But she didn't."

"No way?"

"No way."

"You trust her that much?"

"Yes. But even if I didn't, I mean, think about it. What was she doing—carrying around this picture in the hopes I'd have a packet of developed photos in my car?"

"Not necessarily. Maybe her plan was to plant it in your pocket-book. Or in the glove compartment. Or under the seat, I don't know. Then maybe she saw the pictures and—"

"No." Grace held up a hand. "We're not going there. It's not Cora. It's a waste to even start down this road."

"What's her last name?"

"It's not important."

"Tell me that and I'll drop it."

"Lindley. Cora Lindley."

"Okay," he said. "I'll drop it." But he was jotting on a small pad.

"Now what?" Grace asked.

Duncan checked his watch. "I have to go back to work."

"What should I do?"

"Search your house. If your husband was hiding something, maybe you'll get lucky."

"Your suggestion is to spy on my husband?"

"Shake the cages, Grace." He started for the car. "Sit tight. I'll be back to you soon, promise."

CHAPTER 29

L ife does not stop.

Grace had to do some food shopping. That might sound odd considering the circumstances. Her two children, she was sure, would gladly survive on a steady diet of delivered pizzas, but they still needed the basics: milk, orange juice (the kind with calcium and never, ever, pulp), a dozen eggs, sandwich meats, a couple of boxes of cereal, a loaf of bread, a box of pasta, Prego sauce. Stuff like that. It might even feel good, food shopping. Doing the mundane, doing something so numbingly normal, would surely be, if not comforting, mildly therapeutic.

She hit the King's on Franklin Boulevard. Grace held no supermarket loyalties. Her friends had favorites and would never dream of shopping elsewhere. Cora liked the A&P in Midland Park. Her neighbor liked the Whole Foods in Ridgewood. Other acquaintances favored the Stop & Shop in Waldwick. Grace's selection was more haphazard because, to put it plainly, no matter where you shopped, Tropicana Orange Juice was Tropicana Orange Juice.

In this case the King's was the closest to Starbucks. Decision made.

She grabbed a cart and pretended that she was just an average citizen having an average day. That didn't last long. She thought about Scott Duncan, his sister, what that all meant.

Where, Grace wondered, do I go from here?

First off, the purported "Cora Connection"—Grace dismissed it. There was simply no way. Duncan did not know Cora. His job was to be suspicious. Grace knew better. Cora was out there, no question about it, but that was what had drawn Grace to her in the first place. They had met at a school concert when the Lawsons first moved to town. While their kids butchered the holiday standards, they'd both been forced to stand in the lobby because neither of them had arrived early enough to secure a seat. Cora had leaned over and whispered, "I had an easier time getting front row for Springsteen." Grace had laughed. And so, slowly, it began.

But forget that. Forget Grace's own biased viewpoint. What possible motive could Cora have? The smart money was still on Fuzz Pellet Josh. Yes, he would naturally be nervous. Yes, he was probably antiauthority. But there was more there, Grace was sure of it. So forget Cora. Concentrate on Josh. Figure an angle on that.

Max was on a bacon kick. There was some newfangled premade bacon he'd had at a friend's house during a playdate. He wanted her to buy it. Grace was checking the health claims. Like the rest of the country she was concentrating more on lowering the carb intake. This stuff had none. No carbs at all. Enough sodium to salt a large body of water. But no carbs.

She was checking the ingredients—an interesting potpourri of words she'd need to look up—when she felt, actually felt, someone's eyes on her. Still holding the box at eye level, she slowly shifted her gaze. Down the corridor, near the bologna and salami display, a man stood and openly stared at her. There was no one else in the aisle. He was average height, maybe five-ten or so. A razor hadn't glided across his face in at least two days. He wore blue jeans, a maroon T-shirt, and a shiny black Members Only Windbreaker. His baseball cap had a Nike swoosh on it.

Grace had never seen the man before. He stared at her for another moment before he spoke. His voice was barely a whisper.

"Mrs. Lamb," the man said to her. "Room 17."

For a moment the words did not register. Grace just stood there, unable to move. It wasn't that she hadn't heard him—she had—but his words were so out of context, so out of place coming from this stranger's lips, that her brain could not really comprehend the significance.

At first anyway. For a second or two. Then it all flooded in. . . .

Mrs. Lamb. Room 17. . . .

Mrs. Lamb was Emma's teacher. Room 17 was Emma's classroom.

The man was already on the move, hurrying down the aisle.

"Wait!" Grace shouted. "Hey!"

The man turned the corner. Grace went after him. She tried to pick up speed but the limp, that damn limp, kept her in check. She reached the end of the aisle, coming out on the back wall by the chicken parts. She looked left and right.

No sign of the man.

Now what?

Mrs. Lamb. Room 17. . . .

She moved to her right, checking down the aisles as she went. Her hand slid into her pocketbook, fumbled a bit, touched down on her cell phone.

Stay calm, she told herself. Call the school.

Grace tried to pick up the pace, but her leg dragged like a lead bar. The more she hurried, the more pronounced the limp became. When she really tried to run, she resembled Quasimodo heading up the belfry. Didn't matter, of course, what she looked like. The problem was function: She wasn't moving fast enough.

Mrs. Lamb. Room 17. . . .

If he's done anything to my baby, if he's so much as looked at her wrong . . .

Grace reached the last aisle, the refrigerated section that housed the milk and eggs, the aisle farthest from the entrance so as to encourage impulse buying. She started toward the front of the store, hoping that she'd find him when she doubled back. She fiddled with her phone as she moved, no easy task, scrolling through her saved phone numbers to see if she had the school's.

She didn't.

Damn. Grace bet those other mothers, the good mothers, the ones with the perky smiles and ideal after-school projects—she bet they had the school's phone number preprogrammed into their speed dial.

Mrs. Lamb. Room 17. . . .

Try directory assistance, stupid. Dial 411.

She hit the digits and the SEND button. When she reached the end of the aisle, she looked down the row of cashiers.

No sign of the man.

On the phone the thunder-deep voice of James Earl Jones announced: "Verizon Wireless four-one-one." Then a ding. A woman's voice now: "For English please stay on the line. *Para español, por favor numero dos.*"

And it was then, listening to this Spanish option, that Grace spotted the man again.

He was outside the store now. She could see him through the plate-glass window. He still wore the cap and the black Windbreaker. He was strolling casually, too casually, whistling even, swinging his arms. She was about to start moving again when something—something in the man's hand—made her blood freeze.

It couldn't be.

Again it did not register immediately. The sight, the stimuli the eye was sending to the brain, would not compute, the information causing some sort of short circuit. Again not for long. Only for a second or two.

Grace's hand, the one with the phone in it, dropped to her side. The man kept walking. Terror—terror unlike anything she had ever experienced before, terror that made the Boston Massacre feel like an amusement park ride—hardened and banged against her chest. The man was almost out of sight now. There was a smile on his face. He was still whistling. His arms were still swinging.

And in his hand, his right hand, the hand closest to the window, he held a Batman lunchbox.

CHAPTER 30

"**M**rs. Lawson," Sylvia Steiner, the principal of Willard School, said to Grace in that voice that principals use when dealing with hysterical parents, "Emma is fine. So is Max."

By the time Grace had made it to the door at King's, the man with the Batman lunchbox was gone. She started screaming, started asking for help, but her fellow shoppers looked at her as if she'd escaped from the county mental facility. There was no time to explain. She did her limp-run to her car, called the school while driving a speed that would have intimidated an Andretti, and burst straight into the main office.

"I spoke to both of their teachers. They're in class."

"I want to see them."

"Of course, that's your right, but may I make a suggestion?"

Sylvia Steiner spoke so damn slowly that Grace wanted to reach her hand down her throat and rip the words out.

"I'm sure you've had a terrible fright, but take a few deep breaths. Calm yourself first. You'll scare your children if they see you like this."

Part of Grace wanted to grab her patronizing, smug, overcoiffed 'do and pull it off her head. But another part of her, a bigger part, realized that the woman was speaking the truth.

"I just need to see them," Grace said.

JUST ONE LOOK · 221

"I understand. How about this? We can peek in on them from the window at the door. Would that work for you, Mrs. Lawson?"

Grace nodded.

"Come on then, I'll escort you." Principal Steiner shot the woman working the desk a look. The woman at the desk, Mrs. Dinsmont, did everything she could not to roll her eyes. Every school has a seen-it-all woman like this at the front desk. State law or something.

The corridors were explosions of color. The artwork of children always broke Grace's heart. The pieces were like snapshots, a moment that is forever gone, a life post, never to be repeated. Their artistic abilities will mature and change. The innocence will be gone, captured only in fingerpainting or coloring out of the lines, in uneven handwriting.

They reached Max's classroom first. Grace put her face to the glass. She spotted her son immediately. Max's back was to her, his face tilted up. He sat cross-legged in a circle on the floor. His teacher, Miss Lyons, was in a chair. She was reading a picture book, holding it up so the children could see it, while she read.

"Okay?" Principal Steiner asked.

Grace nodded.

They continued down the corridor. Grace saw number 17 . . .

Mrs. Lamb, Room 17. . . .

. . . on the door. She felt a fresh shiver and tried not to hurry. Principal Steiner, she knew, had noticed the limp. The leg ached in a way it hadn't in years. She peered through the glass. Her daughter was there, right where she should be. Grace had to fight back the tears. Emma had her head down. The eraser end of her pencil was in her mouth. She chewed on it, deep in thought. Why, Grace wondered, do we find such poignancy in watching our children when they don't know we're there? What exactly are we trying to see?

So now what?

Deep breaths. Calm. Her children were okay. That was the key thing. Think it through. Be rational.

Call the police. That was the obvious move.

Principal Steiner faked a cough. Grace looked at her.

"I know this is going to sound nuts," Grace said, "but I need to see Emma's lunchbox."

Grace expected a look of surprise or exasperation, but no, Sylvia Steiner just nodded. She did not ask why—had in fact not questioned her bizarre behavior in any way. Grace was grateful.

"All the lunchboxes are kept in the cafeteria," she explained. "Each class has their own bucket. Would you like me to show you?"

"Thank you."

The buckets were all lined up in grade order. They found the big blue bucket marked SUSAN LAMB, ROOM 17 and started going through it.

"What does it look like?" Principal Steiner asked.

Just as she was about to reply Grace saw it. Batman. The word *POW!* in yellow caps. She slowly lifted it into view. Emma's name was written on the bottom.

"Is that it?"

Grace nodded.

"A popular one this year."

It took all her effort not to clutch the lunchbox to her chest. She put it back as though it were Venetian glass. They headed back to the main office in silence. Grace was tempted to pull the kids out of school. It was two thirty. They'd be let out in a half an hour anyway. But no, that wouldn't work. That would probably just freak them out. She needed time to think, to consider her response, and when she thought about it, weren't Emma and Max safest right here, surrounded by others?

Grace thanked the principal again. They shook hands.

"Is there anything else I can do?" the principal asked.

"No, I don't think so."

Grace left then. She stood outside on the walk. She closed her eyes for a moment. The fear was not so much dissolving as solidifying, turning into pure, primitive rage. She could feel the heat running up her neck. That bastard. That bastard had threatened her daughter.

Now what?

The police. She should call them. That was the obvious move. The phone was in her hand. She was about to dial when a simple thought stopped her: What exactly would she say?

Hi, I was in the supermarket today, see, and this man near the bologna section? Well, he whispered the name of my kid's teacher. Right, teacher. Oh, and her classroom number. Yes, at the bologna section, right there with the Oscar Mayer meats. And then the man ran off. But I saw him later with my daughter's lunchbox. Outside the supermarket. What was he doing? Just walking, I guess. Well, no, it wasn't really Emma's lunchbox. It was the same kind. Batman. No, he didn't make any overt threats. Sorry? Yes, I'm the same woman who said her husband had been kidnapped yesterday. Right, then my husband called and said he needed space. Yep, that was me, the same hysterical broad. . . .

Was there another option?

She ran it through again. The police already thought she was a whack job. Could she convince them otherwise? Perhaps. What would the cops do anyway? Would they assign a man full-time to watch her children? Doubtful, even if she could somehow make them understand the urgency.

Then she remembered Scott Duncan.

He was with the U.S. attorney's office. That was like being a federal cop, right? He would have pull. He would have power. And most of all he would believe her.

Duncan had given her his cell number. She checked her pocket for it. Came up empty. Had she left it in the car? Probably. Didn't matter. He told her that he was heading back to work. The U.S. attorney's office was in Newark, she figured. Either that or Trenton. Trenton was too far a ride. Better to try Newark first. He should be there by now.

She stopped walking and turned to face the school. Her children were inside. Weird thought, but there it was. They spent their days here, away from her in this bastion of brick, and part of Grace found that oddly overwhelming. She dialed directory assistance and asked for the U.S. attorney's office in Newark. She spent the extra thirty-five cents to have the operator dial it for her.

"U.S. attorney for the state of New Jersey."

"Scott Duncan, please."

"Hold."

Two rings and a woman answered. "Goldberg," she said.

"I'm looking for Scott Duncan."

"What case?"

"Pardon?"

"What case is this in reference to?"

"No case. I just need to speak with Mr. Duncan."

"May I ask what it's about?"

"It's a personal matter."

"Sorry. I can't help you. Scott Duncan doesn't work here anymore. I'm covering most of his cases. If I can help you with that . . ."

Grace pulled the phone away from her ear. She looked at it as though from afar. She clicked the END button. She got into her car and again watched the brick building that currently housed her children. She watched it for a very long time, wondering if there was anyone she could truly trust, before deciding what to do.

She lifted the phone back into view. She pressed in the number.

"Yes?"

"This is Grace Lawson."

Three seconds later, Carl Vespa said, "Is everything okay?"

"I changed my mind," Grace said. "I do need your help."

CHAPTER 31

"His name is Eric Wu."

Perlmutter was back at the hospital. He had been working on getting a warrant compelling Indira Khariwalla to tell him who her client was, but the county prosecutor was running into more interference than expected. In the meantime the lab boys were doing their thing. The fingerprints had been sent down to the NCIC, and now, if Daley was to be believed, they had an ID on the perp.

"Does he have a record?" Perlmutter asked.

"He was let out of Walden three months ago."

"For?"

"Armed assault," Daley said. "Wu cut a deal on that Scope case. I called and asked around. This is one very bad man."

"How bad?"

"Poop-in-your-pants bad. If ten percent of the rumors about this guy are true, I'm sleeping with my Barney the Dinosaur night-light on."

"I'm listening."

"He grew up in North Korea. Orphaned at a young age. Spent time working for the state inside prisons for political dissidents. He has a talent with pressure points or something, I don't know. That's what he did with that Sykes guy, some kung-fu crap, practically severed his spine. One story I heard, he kidnapped some guy's wife, worked on her for like

225

two hours. He calls the husband and tells him to listen up. The wife starts screaming. Then she tells him, the husband, that she hates his guts. Starts cursing him. That's the last thing the husband ever hears."

"He killed the woman?"

Daley's face had never looked so solemn. "That's just it. He didn't."

The room's temperature dropped ten degrees. "I don't understand."

"Wu let her go. She hasn't spoken since. Just sits and rocks someplace. The husband comes near her, she freaks out and starts screaming."

"Jesus." Perlmutter felt the chill ease through him. "You got an extra night-light?"

"I got two, yeah, but I'm using both."

"So what would this guy want with Freddy Sykes?"

"Not a clue."

Charlaine Swain appeared down the corridor. She had not left the hospital since the shooting. They had finally gotten her to talk to Freddy Sykes. It had been a strange scene. Sykes kept crying. Charlaine had tried to get information. It'd worked to some extent. Freddy Sykes seemed to know nothing. He had no idea who his assailant was or why anyone would want to hurt him. Sykes was just a small-time accountant who lived alone—he seemed to be on no one's radar.

"It's all linked," Perlmutter said.

"You have a theory?"

"I have some of it. Strands."

"Let's hear."

"Start with the E-ZPass records."

"Okay."

"We have Jack Lawson and Rocky Conwell crossing that exit at the same time," Perlmutter said.

"Right."

"I think now we know why. Conwell was working for a private investigator."

"Your friend India Something."

"Indira Khariwalla. And she's hardly a friend. But that's not important. What makes sense here, the only thing that makes sense really, is that Conwell was hired to follow Lawson."

"Ipso facto, the E-ZPass timing explained."

Perlmutter nodded, trying to put it together. "So what happened next? Conwell ends up dead. The ME says he probably died that night before midnight. We know he crossed the tollbooth at ten twenty-six p.m. So sometime soon after that, Rocky Conwell met up with foul play." Perlmutter rubbed his face. "The logical suspect would be Jack Lawson. He realizes he's being followed. He confronts Conwell. He kills him."

"Makes sense," Daley said.

"But it doesn't. Think about it. Rocky Conwell was six-four, two-sixty, and in great shape. You think a guy like Lawson could have killed him like that? With his bare hands?"

"Sweet Jesus." Daley saw it now. "Eric Wu?"

Perlmutter nodded. "It adds up. Somehow Conwell met up with Wu. Wu killed him, stuffed his body into a trunk, and left him at the Park-n-Ride. Charlaine Swain said that Wu was driving a Ford Windstar. Same model and color as Jack Lawson's."

"So what's the connection between Lawson and Wu?"

"I don't know."

"Maybe Wu works for him."

"Could be. We just don't know. What we do know, however, is that Lawson's alive—or at least he was alive after Conwell was killed."

"Right, because he called his wife. When she was at the station. So what happened next?"

"Damned if I know."

Perlmutter watched Charlaine Swain. She just stood down the hall, staring through the window of her husband's room. Perlmutter considered going over, but really, what could he say?

Daley jostled him, and they both turned to see Officer Veronique

Baltrus walk off the elevator. Baltrus had been with the department three years. She was thirty-eight, with tousled black hair and a constant tan. She was in a regulation police uniform that somehow hugged as much as anything with a belt and holster could, but in her off-hours she preferred Lycra workout clothes or anything that revealed the flat tan of her stomach. She was petite, with dark eyes, and every guy in the station, even Perlmutter, had a thing for her.

Veronique Baltrus was both exquisitely beautiful and a computer expert—an interesting albeit heart-racing combination. Six years ago she had been working for a bathing suit retailer in New York City when the stalking began. The stalker would call her. He would send e-mail. He would harass her at work. His main weapon was the computer, the best bastion for the anonymous and gutless. The police did not have the manpower to hunt him down. They also believed that this stalker, whoever he was, would probably not take it to the next level.

But he did.

On a calm fall evening Veronique Baltrus was savagely attacked. Her assailant got away. But Veronique recovered. Already good with computers, she now upped her ability and became an expert. She used her new knowledge to hunt down her assailant—he continued to send her e-mail discussing an encore—and bring him to justice. Then she quit her job and became a police officer.

Now, even though Baltrus wore a uniform and worked a regular shift, she was the county's unofficial computer expert. Nobody in the department but Perlmutter knew her backstory. That was part of the deal when she applied for the job.

"You got something?" he asked her.

Veronique Baltrus smiled. She had a nice smile. Perlmutter's "thing" for her was different than the rest of the guys'. It was not built simply on lust. Veronique Baltrus was the first woman to make him feel something since Marion's death. He wouldn't take it anywhere. It would be

JUST ONE LOOK · 229

unprofessional. It would be unethical. And truth be told, Veronique was waaaaay out of his league.

She gestured down the corridor toward Charlaine Swain. "We might have to thank her."

"How so?"

"Al Singer."

That, Sykes had told Charlaine, was the name Eric Wu used when he pretended to be making a delivery. When Charlaine asked who Al Singer was, Sykes jolted a little and denied knowing any Mr. Singer. He said he opened the door anyway out of curiosity. Perlmutter said, "I thought Al Singer was a fake name."

"Yes and no," Baltrus said. "I went through Mr. Sykes's computer pretty thoroughly. He'd signed up for an online dating service and had been corresponding fairly regularly with a man named Al Singer."

Perlmutter made a face. "A gay dating service?"

"Bisexual, actually. That a problem?"

"No. So Al Singer was, what, his online lover?"

"Al Singer doesn't exist. It was an alias."

"Isn't that common online, especially at a gay dating service? Using an alias?"

"It is," Baltrus agreed. "But here's my point. Your Mr. Wu pretended to make a delivery. He used that name, Singer. How would Wu know about Al Singer unless . . . ?"

"You saying Eric Wu is Al Singer?"

Baltrus nodded, rested her hands on her hips. "That would be my guess, sure. Here's what I think: Wu goes online. He uses the name Al Singer. He meets some people—potential victims—that way. In this case, he meets Freddy Sykes. He breaks into his home and assaults him. My guess is, he would have eventually killed Sykes."

"You think he's done this before?"

"Yes."

"So he's, what, some kind of serial bisexual basher?"

"That I don't know. But it fits the action I'm seeing on the computer."

Perlmutter thought about it. "Does this Al Singer have any other online partners?"

"Three more."

"Have any of them been assaulted?"

"Not yet, no. They're all healthy."

"So what makes you think it's serial?"

"It's too early to say for sure one way or the other. But Charlaine Swain did us a huge favor. Wu was using Sykes's computer. He probably planned on destroying it before he left, but Charlaine flushed him out before he had time. I'm piecing it together now, but there's definitely another online persona in there. I don't know the name yet, but he's working out of yenta-match.com. Jewish singles."

"How do we know it's not Freddy Sykes?"

"Because whoever accessed this page did so in the past twenty-four hours."

"So it had to be Wu."

"Yes."

"I still don't get it. Why would he go to another online dating service?"

"To find more victims," she said. "Here's how I think it works: This Wu has a bunch of different names and personas at a bunch of different dating sites. Once he, shall we say, uses one, like Al Singer, he won't dip into that dating pool again. He used Al Singer to get to Freddy Sykes. He'd have to know that an investigator could track that down."

"So he stops using Al Singer."

"Right. But he's been using other aliases at other sites. So he's ready for his next victim."

"Do you have any of the other names yet?"

"Getting close," Baltrus said. "I just need a warrant for yenta-match.com."

"You think a judge will grant it?"

"The only identity we know Wu accessed recently is the one at the yenta-match site. I think he was seeking out his next victim. If we can get a list of what name he used and who he contacted . . ."

"Keep digging."

"Will do."

Veronique Baltrus hurried out. Wrong as it felt—he was, after all, her superior—Perlmutter watched her go with a longing that made him remember Marion.

CHAPTER 32

Ten minutes later Carl Vespa's driver—the infamous Cram—met Grace two blocks away from the school.

Cram arrived on foot. Grace did not know how or where his car was. She'd just been standing there, looking at the school from afar, when she felt the tap on her shoulder. She leapt, her heart pounding. When she turned and saw his face, well, the sight was hardly a comforting one.

Cram arched an eyebrow. "You rang?"

"How did you get here?"

Cram shook his head. Up close, now that she was able to get a really good look at him, the man was even more hideous than she remembered. His skin was pockmarked. His nose and mouth looked like an animal's snout, what with the sea-predator smile locked on autopilot. Cram was older than she'd thought, probably nearing sixty. He was wiry though. He had the wild-eyed look she'd always associated with serious psychosis, but there was a comfort to that element of danger right now, the kind of guy you'd want next to you in a foxhole and nowhere else.

"Tell me everything," Cram said.

Grace started with Scott Duncan and moved on to arriving at the supermarket. She told him what the unshaven man had said to her, about him darting down the aisle, about him carrying the Batman lunchbox. Cram chewed on a toothpick. He had thin fingers. His nails were too long.

"Describe him."

She did as best she could. When she was done, Cram spit out the toothpick and shook his head. "For real?" he said.

"What?"

"A Members Only jacket? What is this, 1986?"

Grace did not laugh.

"You're safe now," he said. "Your children are safe."

She believed him.

"What time do they get out?"

"Three o'clock."

"Fine." He squinted at the school. "Christ, I hated this place."

"You went here?"

Cram nodded. "A Willard graduate, 1957." She tried to picture him as a little boy coming to this school. The image would not hold. He started walking away.

"Wait," she said. "What do you want me to do?"

"Pick up your kids. Bring them home."

"Where will you be?"

Cram upped the grin. "Around." And then he was gone.

Grace waited by the fence. The mothers began to flock in, gather, chat. Grace folded her arms, trying to give off a "keep away" vibe. There were days she could participate in the clatter. This was not one of them.

The cell phone rang. She put it to her ear and said hello.

"You get the message now?"

The voice was male and muffled. Grace felt her scalp tingle.

"Stop looking, stop asking questions, stop flashing the picture. Or we'll take Emma first."

Click.

Grace did not scream. She would not scream. She put the phone away. Her hands shook. She looked down at them as if they belonged to someone else. She couldn't stop the shake. Her children would be coming out soon. She jammed her hands into her pockets and tried to force up a smile. It wouldn't come. She bit her lower lip and made herself not cry.

"Hey, you okay?"

Grace startled at the voice. It was Cora.

"What are you doing here?" Grace asked. The words came out with too sharp a snap.

"What do you think? I'm picking up Vickie."

"I thought she was with her father."

Cora looked puzzled. "Just for last night. He dropped her off at school this morning. Jesus, what the hell happened?"

"I can't talk about it."

Cora did not know how to react to that one. The bell sounded. Both women turned away. Grace did not know what to think. She knew that Scott Duncan was wrong about Cora—more than that, she now knew that Scott Duncan was a liar—and yet, once voiced, the suspicion about her friend would not leave. She couldn't flick it away.

"Look, I'm just scared, okay?"

Cora nodded. Vickie appeared first. "If you need me . . ."

"Thank you."

Cora moved away without another word. Grace waited alone, searching for the familiar faces in the stream of children pouring through the door. Emma stepped into the sunshine and shielded her eyes. When she spotted her mother, Emma's face broke into a smile. She waved.

Grace suppressed a cry of relief. Her fingers snaked through the chain-link, gripping hard, holding herself back so she wouldn't sprint over and scoop Emma into her arms.

When Grace, Emma, and Max reached home, Cram was already stand-ing on their front stoop.

Emma looked a question at her mother, but before Grace could re-spond, Max sprinted up the walk. He stopped dead in front of Cram and craned his neck to look up at the sea-predator smile.

"Hey," Max said to Cram.

"Hey."

Max said, "You were the guy driving that big car, right?"

"Right."

"That cool? Driving that big car?"

"Very."

"I'm Max."

"I'm Cram."

"Cool name."

"Yeah. Yeah, it is."

Max made a fist and held it up. Cram made one too and then they touched knuckles-against-knuckles in some newfangled high-five. Grace and Emma came up the walk.

"Cram is a family friend," Grace said. "He's going to help me a little."

Emma did not like it. "Help with what?" She aimed her "eeuw gross" face in Cram's direction, which, under the circumstances, was both understandable and rude, but this was hardly the time for a cor-rection. "Where's Daddy?"

"He's on a business trip," Grace said.

Emma did not say another word. She stepped into the house and ran upstairs.

Max squinted up at Cram. "Can I ask you something?"

"Sure," Cram said.

"Do all your friends call you Cram?"

"Yes."

"Just Cram?"

"One word." He wiggled his eyebrows. "Like Cher or Fabio."

"Who?"

Cram chuckled.

"Why do they call you that?" Max asked.

"Why do they call me Cram?"

"Yeah."

"My teeth." He opened his mouth wide. When Grace worked up the courage to look, she was greeted with a sight that resembled the mad experiment of a very deranged orthodontist. The teeth were all crammed together on the left, almost stacked. It looked like there were too many of them. Empty pockets of coarse pink where teeth should have been lined the right side of his mouth. "Cram," he said. "You see?"

"Whoa," Max said. "That's so cool."

"You want to know how my teeth got this way?"

Grace took that one. "No, thank you."

Cram glanced at her. "Good answer."

Cram. She took another look at the too-small teeth. Tic Tac might have been a more apt name.

"Max, you have homework?"

"Aw, Mom."

"Now," she said.

Max looked at Cram. "Scram," Cram said. "We'll talk later."

They shared another fist-knuckle salute before Max darted off with the abandon of a six-year-old. The phone rang. Grace checked the caller ID. It was Scott Duncan. She decided to let the machine pick that one up—more important that she talk to Cram. They moved into the kitchen. There were two men sitting at the table. Grace pulled up short. Neither of the men looked up at her. They were whispering to each other. Grace was about to say something, but Cram signaled her to step outside.

"Who are they?"

"They work for me."

"Doing?"

"Don't worry about it."

She did, but right now there were more pressing matters. "I got a call from the guy," she said. "On my cell phone." She told him what the voice on the phone had said. Cram's expression did not change. When she finished, he pulled out a cigarette.

"You mind if I smoke?"

She told him to go ahead.

"I won't do it in the house."

Grace looked around. "Is that why we're out here?"

Cram did not reply. He lit the cigarette, drew a deep breath, let the smoke pour out of both nostrils. Grace looked toward the neighbor's yard. There was no one in sight. A dog barked. A lawn mower ripped through the air like a helicopter.

Grace looked at him. "You've threatened people, right?"

"Yup."

"So if I do what he says—if I stop—do you think they'll leave us alone?"

"Probably." Cram took a puff so deep it looked like a doobie toke. "But the real question is, why do they want you to stop?"

"Meaning?"

"Meaning you must have been getting close. You must have struck a nerve."

"I can't imagine how."

"Mr. Vespa called. He wants to see you tonight."

"What about?"

Cram shrugged.

She looked off again.

"You ready for some more bad news?" Cram asked.

She turned to him.

"Your computer room. The one in the back."

"What about it?"

"It's bugged. One listening device, one camera."

"A camera?" She couldn't believe this. "In my house?"

"Yeah. Hidden camera. It's in a book on the shelf. Fairly easy to spot if you're looking for it. You can get one at any spy shop. You've probably seen them online. You hide it in a clock or a smoke detector, that kind of thing."

Grace tried to take this in. "Someone is spying on us?"

"Yup."

"Who?"

"No idea. I don't think it's the cops. It's a little too amateur for that. My boys have given the rest of the house a quick sweep. Nothing else so far."

"How long . . . ?" She tried to comprehend what he was telling her. "How long has the camera and—listening device, did you say?—how long have they been here?"

"No way to know. That's why I dragged you out here. So we could talk freely. I know you've been hit with a lot, but you're ready to deal with this now?"

She nodded, though her head was swimming.

"Okay, first off. The equipment. It's not all that sophisticated. It only has a range of maybe a hundred feet. If it's a live feed, it goes to a van or something. Have you noticed any vans parked on the street for long periods of time?"

"No."

"I didn't think so. It probably just goes to a video recorder."

"Like a VCR?"

"Exactly like a VCR."

"And it has to be within a hundred feet of the house?"

"Yep."

She looked around as if it might be in the garden. "How often would they need to change the tape?"

"Every twenty-four hours tops."

"Any idea where it is?"

"Not yet. Sometimes they keep the recorder in the basement or garage. They probably have access to the house, so they can fetch the tape and put in a new one."

"Wait a second. What do you mean, they have access to the house?"

He shrugged. "They got that camera and bug in somehow, right?"

The rage was back now, rising, smoldering behind her eyes. Grace started looking at her neighbors'. Access to the house. Who had access to the house? she asked herself. And a small voice replied . . .

Cora.

Uh-uh, no way. Grace shook it off. "So we need to find that recorder."

"Yes."

"And then we wait and watch," she said. "We see who picks up the tape."

"That's one way of doing it," Cram said.

"You have a better suggestion?"

"Not really."

"Then, what, we follow the guy, see where it leads?"

"That's a possibility."

"But . . . ?"

"It's risky. We could lose him."

"What would you do?"

"If it were up to me, I'd grab him. I'd ask him some hard questions."

"And if he refused to answer?"

Cram still wore the sea-predator smile. It was always a horrific sight, this man's face, but Grace was getting used to it. She also realized that he was not intentionally scaring her; whatever had been done to his mouth had made that become his permanent, natural expression. It spoke volumes, that face. It rendered her question rhetorical.

Grace wanted to protest, to tell him that she was civil and that they would handle this legally and ethically. But instead she said, "They threatened my daughter."

"So they did."

She looked at him. "I can't do what they asked. Even if I wanted to. I can't just walk away and leave it alone."

He said nothing.

"I have no choice, do I? I have to fight them."

"I don't see any other way."

"You knew that all along."

Cram cocked his head to the right. "So did you."

His cell phone went off. Cram flipped it open but did not speak, not even a hello. A few seconds later he snapped the phone shut and said, "Someone is pulling up the drive."

She looked out the screen door. A Ford Taurus came to a stop. Scott Duncan stepped out and approached the house.

"You know him?" Cram asked.

"That," she said, "is Scott Duncan."

"The guy who lied about working for the U.S. attorney?"

Grace nodded.

"Maybe," Cram said, "I'll stick around."

They remained outside. Scott Duncan stood next to Grace. Cram had stepped away. Duncan kept sneaking glances at Cram. "Who is that?"

"You don't want to know."

Grace gave Cram a look. He got the hint and headed back inside. She and Scott Duncan were alone now.

"What do you want?" she asked.

Duncan picked up on her tone. "Something wrong, Grace?"

"I'm just surprised you got out of work already. I figured it'd be busier at the U.S. attorney's office."

He said nothing.

"Cat got your tongue, Mr. Duncan?"

"You called my office."

She touched her nose with her pointer, indicating a direct hit. Then: "Oh wait, correction: I called the United States attorney's office. Apparently you don't work there."

"It's not what you think."

"How enlightening."

"I should have told you up front."

"Do tell."

"Look, everything I said was true."

"Except the part about working for the United States attorney. I mean, that wasn't true, was it? Or was Ms. Goldberg lying?"

"Do you want me to explain or not?"

Now his voice had a little steel. Grace gestured for him to continue.

"What I told you was true. I worked there. Three months ago this killer, this Monte Scanlon, he insisted on seeing me. No one could understand why. I was a low-level lawyer on political corruption. Why would a hit man insist on talking only to me? That was when he told me."

"That he killed your sister."

"Yes."

She waited. They moved toward the porch furniture and sat down. Cram stood in a window watching them. He let his gaze wander toward Scott Duncan, hang there for a few heavy seconds, survey the grounds, go back to Duncan.

"He looks familiar," Duncan said, gesturing toward Cram. "Or maybe I'm flashing back to the Pirates of the Caribbean ride at Disney World. Shouldn't he have an eye patch?"

Grace shifted in her seat. "You were telling me about why you lied."

Duncan ran his hand through the sandy hair. "When Scanlon said the fire was no accident . . . You can't understand what it did to me. I mean, one moment my life was one thing. The next . . ." He snapped his fingers with a magician's flourish. "It wasn't so much that everything was different now—it was more like the past fifteen years had all been different. Like someone had gone back in time and changed one event and it changed everything else. I wasn't the same guy. I wasn't a guy whose sister died in a tragic fire. I was a guy whose sister had been murdered and never avenged."

"But now you have the killer," Grace said. "He confessed."

Duncan smiled, but there was no joy there. "Scanlon said it best. He was just a weapon. Like a gun. I wanted the person who pulled the trigger. It became an obsession. I tried to do it part-time, you know, work my job while searching for the killer. But I started to neglect my cases. So my boss, she strongly suggested I take a leave." He looked up at her.

"Why didn't you just tell me?"

"I didn't think it would be a great opening line, you know, telling you I was forced out like that. I still have connections in the office. I still have friends in law enforcement. But just so we're clear, everything I'm doing is off the books."

Their eyes locked. Grace said, "You're still holding something back."

He hesitated.

"What is it?"

"We should get one thing straight." Duncan stood, did the run a hand through the sandy hair bit again, turned away from her. "Right now we're both trying to find your husband. It's a temporary alliance. The truth is, we have separate agendas. I won't lie to you. What happens after we find Jack, well, do we both want the truth?"

"I just want my husband."

He nodded. "That's what I mean about separate agendas. About our alliance being temporary. You want your husband. I want my sister's killer."

He looked at her now. She understood.

"So now what?" Grace asked.

He took out the mystery photograph and held it up. There was a hint of a smile on his face.

"What?"

Scott Duncan said, "I know the name of the redhead in the photograph." She waited.

"Her name is Sheila Lambert. Attended Vermont University at the same time as your husband"—he pointed at Jack and then slid his finger to the right—"and Shane Alworth."

"Where is she now?"

"That's just the thing, Grace. No one knows."

She closed her eyes. A shudder ran through her.

"I sent the photograph up to the school. A retired dean identified her. I ran a full check, but she's gone. There is no sign of Sheila Lambert's existence over the past decade—no payroll tax, no social security number hit, nothing."

"Just like with Shane Alworth."

"Exactly like Shane."

Grace tried to put it together. "Five people in the photograph. One, your sister, was murdered. Two others, Shane Alworth and Sheila Lambert, haven't been heard of in years. The fourth, my husband, ran overseas and is missing now. And the last one, well, we still don't know who she is."

Duncan nodded.

"So where do we go from here?"

"You remember I said I talked to Shane Alworth's mother?"

"The one with the fuzzy Amazonian geography."

"When I visited her the first time, I didn't know about this picture or your husband or any of that. I want to show her the picture now. I want to gauge her reaction. And I want you there."

"Why?"

"I just have a feeling, that's all. Evelyn Alworth is an old woman. She's emotional, and I think she's scared. I went in there the first time as an investigator. Maybe, I don't know, but maybe if you go in as a concerned mother, something will shake loose."

Grace hesitated. "Where does she live?"

"A condo in Bedminster. Shouldn't take us more than thirty minutes to get there."

Cram came back into view. Scott Duncan nodded toward him.

"So what's with that scary guy?" Duncan asked.

"I can't go with you now."

"Why not?"

"I have the kids. I can't just leave them here."

"Bring them along. There's a playground right there. We won't take long."

Cram came to the door now. He beckoned with his hand for Grace. She said, "Excuse me," and headed toward Cram. Scott Duncan stayed where he was.

"What is it?" she asked Cram.

"Emma. She's upstairs crying."

Grace found her daughter in classic cry position—facedown on her bed, pillow over her head. The sound was muted. It had been a while since Emma had cried like this. Grace sat on the edge of the bed. She knew what was coming. When Emma could speak, she asked where Daddy was. Grace told her that he was on a business trip. Emma said that she didn't believe her. That it was a lie. Emma demanded to know the truth. Grace repeated that Jack was just on a business trip. That everything was fine. Emma pushed. Where was he? Why hadn't Daddy called? When was he coming home? Grace made up rationales that sounded pretty believable in her ears—he was really busy, he was traveling in Europe, London right now, didn't know how long he'd be gone, he had called but Emma had been sleeping, remember that London is in a different time zone.

Did Emma buy it? Who knew?

Child-rearing experts—those namby-pamby, lobotomy-voiced Ph.D.s on cable TV—would probably tsk-tsk, but Grace was not one of those tell-kids-everything parents. Above all else a mother's job was to protect. Emma was not old enough to handle the truth. Plain and simple. Deception was a necessary part of parenting. Of course Grace could be wrong—she knew that—but the old adage is true: Kids don't come with instructions. We all mess up. Raising a child is pure impromptu.

A few minutes later she told Max and Emma to get ready. They were going for a ride. Both children grabbed their Game Boys and piled into the back of the car. Scott Duncan moved toward the passenger's seat. Cram cut him off.

"Problem?" Duncan said.

"I want to talk to Ms. Lawson before you go. Stay here."

Duncan snapped a sarcastic salute. Cram gave him a look that could have held back a weather front. He and Grace stepped into the back room. Cram closed the door.

"You know you shouldn't go with him."

"Maybe not. But I have to."

Cram chewed on his lower lip. He didn't like it, but he understood. "Do you carry a purse?"

"Yes."

"Let me see it."

She showed it to him. Cram pulled a gun out of his waist. It was small, almost toylike. "This is a Glock nine-millimeter, model 26."

Grace held up her hands. "I don't want that."

"Keep it in your purse. You can also wear it in an ankle holster but you'll need long pants."

"I've never fired a gun in my life."

"Experience is overrated. You aim for the middle of the chest, you squeeze the trigger. It's not complicated."

"I don't like weapons."

Cram shook his head.

"What?"

"Maybe I'm mistaken, but didn't somebody threaten your daughter today?"

That made her pause. Cram put the gun in her purse. She did not fight him.

"How long are you going to be gone?" Cram asked.

"Couple of hours, tops."

"Mr. Vespa will be here at seven p.m. He says it's important that he speak to you."

"I'll be here."

"You sure you trust this Duncan guy?"

"I'm not sure. But I think we're safe with him."

Cram nodded. "Let me add a little insurance on that front."

"How?"

Cram said nothing. He escorted her back. Scott Duncan was on his cell phone. Grace did not like what she saw on Duncan's face. He finished up his call when he spotted them.

"What?"

Scott Duncan shook his head. "Can we go now?"

Cram walked toward him. Duncan did not back down, but there was definitely an understandable flinch. Cram stopped directly in front of him, stuck out his hand, wiggled his fingers. "Let me see your wallet."

"Pardon me?"

"Do I look like the kind of guy who enjoys repeating himself?"

Scott Duncan glanced at Grace. She nodded. Cram still had the fingers wiggling. Duncan handed Cram his wallet. Cram brought it over to a table and sat down. He quickly rifled through the contents, taking notes.

"What are you doing?" Duncan asked.

"While you're gone, Mr. Duncan, I'm going to learn everything about you." He looked up. "If Ms. Lawson is harmed in any way, my response will be"—Cram stopped, looked up as though searching for the word—"disproportionate. I make myself clear?"

Duncan looked at Grace. "Who the hell is this guy?"

Grace was already moving toward the door. "We'll be fine, Cram."

Cram shrugged, tossed Duncan his wallet. "Have a delightful drive."

No one talked for the first five minutes of the ride. Max and Emma used their headphones with the Game Boys. Grace had bought the headphones recently because the beeps and buzzes and Luigi shouting, "Mamma mia!" every two minutes gave her a headache. Scott Duncan sat next to her with his hands in his lap.

"So who was on the phone?" Grace asked.

"A coroner."

Grace waited.

"Remember how I told you that I had my sister's body exhumed?" he said.

"Yes."

"The police didn't really see a need for it. Too expensive. I under-stand, I guess. Anyway I paid for it myself. I know this person, used to work for a county ME, who does private autopsies."

"And he's the one who called you?"

"It's a she. Her name is Sally Li."

"And?"

"And she says she needs to see me right away." Duncan looked over at her. "Her office is in Livingston. We can hit it on the way back." He turned back away. "I'd like you to come with me, if that's okay."

"To a morgue?"

"No, nothing like that. Sally does the actual autopsy work at St. Barnabas Hospital. This is just an office where she does her paperwork. There's a waiting room we can stick the kids in."

Grace did not reply.

The Bedminster condos were generic, which, when you're talking about condos, is something of a repetition in terms. They had the prefab light brown aluminum siding, three levels, garages underneath, every building identical to the one to its right and to its left and behind it and in front of it. The complex was huge and sprawling, a khaki-coated ocean stretching as far as the eye could see.

For Grace, the route here had been familiar. Jack drove by this on his way to work. They had, for a very brief moment, debated moving into this condo development. Neither Jack nor Grace was particularly good with their hands or enjoyed fix-the-old-home shows on cable. Condos held that appeal—you pay a monthly fee, you don't worry about the roof or an addition or the landscaping or any of that. There were tennis courts and a swimming pool and, yes, a playground for children. But in the end there was just so much conformity one could take. Suburbia is already a subworld of sameness. Why add insult to injury by making your physical abode conform too?

Max spotted the complicated, brightly hued playground before the car had come to a complete stop. He was raring to sprint for the swing set. Emma looked more bored with the prospect. She held on to her Game Boy. Normally Grace would have protested—Game Boy in the car only, especially when the alternative was fresh air—but again now did not seem the time.

Grace cupped her hand over her eyes as they started moving away. "I can't leave them alone."

"Mrs. Alworth lives right here," Duncan said. "We can stay in the doorway and watch them."

They approached the door on the first level. The playground was quiet. The air was still. Grace inhaled deeply and smelled the freshly cut grass. They stood side by side, she and Duncan. He rang the bell. Grace waited by the door, feeling oddly like a Jehovah's Witness.

A cackling voice not unlike the witch in an old Disney film said, "Who is it?"

"Mrs. Alworth?"

Again the cackle: "Who is it?"

"Mrs. Alworth, it's Scott Duncan."

"Who?"

"Scott Duncan. We spoke a few weeks ago. About your son, Shane."

"Go away. I have nothing to say to you."

Grace picked up an accent now. Boston area.

"We could really use your help."

"I don't know nothing. Go away."

"Please, Mrs. Alworth, I need to talk to you about your son."

"I told you. Shane lives in Mexico. He's a good boy. He helps poor people."

"We need to ask about some of his old friends." Scott Duncan looked at Grace, nodded for her to say something.

"Mrs. Alworth," Grace said.

The cackle was more wary now. "Who's that?"

"My name is Grace Lawson. I think my husband knew your son."

There was silence now. Grace turned away from the door and watched Max and Emma. Max was on a corkscrew slide. Emma sat cross-legged and played the Game Boy.

Through the door, the cackling voice asked, "Who's your husband?"

"Jack Lawson."

Nothing.

"Mrs. Alworth?"

"I don't know him."

Scott Duncan said, "We have a picture. We'd like to show it to you."

The door opened. Mrs. Alworth wore a housedress that couldn't have been manufactured after the Bay of Pigs. She was in her midseventies, heavyset, the kind of big aunt who hugs you and you disappear in the folds. As a kid you hate the hug. As an adult you long for it. She had varicose veins that resembled sausage casing. Her reading glasses dangled against her enormous chest from a chain. She smelled faintly of cigarette smoke.

"I don't have all day," she said. "Show me this picture."

Scott Duncan handed her the photograph.

For a long time the old woman said nothing.

"Mrs. Alworth?"

"Why did someone cross her out?" she asked.

"That was my sister," Duncan said.

She flicked a glance his way. "I thought you said you were an investigator."

"I am. My sister was murdered. Her name was Geri Duncan."

Mrs. Alworth's face went white. Her lip started to tremble. "She's dead?"

"She was murdered. Fifteen years ago. Do you remember her?"

She seemed to have lost her bearings. She turned to Grace and snapped, "What do you keep looking at?"

Grace was facing Max and Emma. "My children." She gestured toward the playground. Mrs. Alworth followed suit. She stiffened. She seemed lost now, confused.

"Did you know my sister?" Duncan asked.

"What does this have to do with me?"

His voice was stern now. "Yes or no, did you know my sister?"

"I can't remember. It was a long time ago."

"Your son dated her."

"He dated a lot of girls. Shane was a handsome boy. So was his brother, Paul. He's a psychologist in Missouri. Why don't you leave me alone and talk to him?"

"Try to think." Scott's voice rose a notch. "My sister was murdered." He pointed to the picture of Shane Alworth. "That's your son, isn't it, Mrs. Alworth?"

She stared down at the strange photograph for a long time before nodding.

"Where is he?"

"I told you before. Shane lives in Mexico. He helps poor people."

"When was the last time you spoke with him?"

"Last week."

"He called you?"

"Yes."

"Where?"

"What do you mean where?"

"Did Shane call you here?"

"Of course. Where else would he call?"

Scott Duncan took a step closer. "I checked your phone records, Mrs. Alworth. You haven't gotten or made an international call in the past year."

"Shane uses one of those phone cards," she said too quickly. "Maybe the phone companies don't pick those up—how should I know?"

Duncan took another step closer. "Listen to me, Mrs. Alworth. And please listen closely. My sister is dead. There is no sign of your son anywhere. This man here"—he pointed to the picture of Jack—"her husband, Jack Lawson, he's also missing. And this woman over here"—he pointed to the redheaded girl with the spaced-out eyes—"her name is Sheila Lambert. There's been no sign of her for at least ten years."

"This has got nothing to do with me," Mrs. Alworth insisted.

"Five people in the photograph. We've been able to identify four of them. They're all gone. One we know is dead. For all we know, they all are."

"I told you. Shane is—"

"You're lying, Mrs. Alworth. Your son graduated Vermont University. So did Jack Lawson and Sheila Lambert. They must have been friends. He dated my sister; we both know that. So what happened to them? Where is your son?"

Grace put a hand on Scott's arm. Mrs. Alworth was staring out now toward the playground, at the children. Her bottom lip was quivering. Her skin was ashen. Tears ran down both cheeks. She looked as if she'd fallen into a trance. Grace tried to step into her line of vision.

"Mrs. Alworth," she said gently.

"I'm an old woman."

Grace waited.

"I don't have nothing to say to you people."

Grace said, "I'm trying to find my husband." Mrs. Alworth was still staring at the playground. "I'm trying to find their father."

"Shane is a good boy. He helps people."

"What happened to him?" Grace asked.

"Leave me alone."

Grace tried to meet the older woman's gaze, but the focus was gone from her eyes. "His sister"—Grace gestured toward Duncan—"my husband, your son. Whatever happened affected us all. We want to help."

But the old woman shook her head and turned away. "My son doesn't need your help. Now go away. Please." She stepped back into her house and closed the door.

CHAPTER 33

When they were back in the car, Grace said, "When you told Mrs. Alworth you checked her phone records for international calls . . ."

Duncan nodded. "It was a bluff."

The children were plugged back in to their Game Boys. Scott Duncan called the coroner. She was waiting for them.

Grace said, "We're getting closer to the answer, aren't we?"

"I think so."

"Mrs. Alworth might be telling the truth. I mean, as far as she knows."

"How do you figure?" he asked.

"Something happened years ago. Jack ran away overseas. Maybe Shane Alworth and Sheila Lambert did too. Your sister, for whatever reason, hung around and ended up dead."

He did not reply. His eyes were suddenly moist. There was a tremor in the corner of his mouth.

"Scott?"

"She called me. Geri. Two days before the fire."

Grace waited.

"I was running out the door. You have to understand. Geri was a bit of a kook. She was always so melodramatic. She said she had to tell me something important, but I figured it could wait. I figured it was about whatever new thing she was into—aromatherapy, her new rock band, her etchings, whatever. I said I'd call her back."

He stopped, shrugged. "But I forgot."

Grace wanted to say something, but nothing came to her. Words of comfort would probably do more harm than good right now. She took hold of the wheel and glanced in the rearview mirror. Emma and Max both had their heads lowered, their thumbs working the buttons on the tiny consoles. She felt that overwhelmed thing coming on, that pure blast in the middle of normalcy, the bliss from the everyday.

"Do you mind if we stop at the coroner's now?" Duncan asked.

Grace hesitated.

"It's about a mile away. Just turn right at the next light."

In for a penny, Grace thought. She drove. He gave directions. A minute later he pointed up ahead. "It's that office building on the corner."

The medical office seemed dominated by dentists and orthodontists. When they opened the door, there was that antiseptic smell Grace always associated with a voice telling her to rinse and spit. An ophthalmology group called Laser Today was listed for the second floor. Scott Duncan pointed to the name SALLY LI, MD. The directory said she was on the lower level.

There was no receptionist. The door chimed when they entered. The office was properly sparse. The furniture consisted of two distressed couches and one flickering lamp that wouldn't muster a price tag at a garage sale. The lone magazine was a catalogue of medical-examiner tools.

An Asian woman, midforties and exhausted, stuck her head through the door of the inner office. "Hey, Scott."

"Hey, Sally."

"Who's this?"

"Grace Lawson," he said. "She's helping me."

"Charmed," Sally said. "Be with you in a sec."

Grace told the kids that they could keep playing their Game Boys. The danger of video games was that they shut the world out. The beauty of video games was that they shut the world out.

Sally Li opened the door. "Come on in."

She wore clean surgical scrubs with high heels. A pack of Marlboros was jammed into the breast pocket. The office, if you could call it that, had that Early American Hurricane look going for it. There were papers everywhere. They seemed to be cascading off her desk and bookshelves, almost like a waterfall. Pathology textbooks were open. Her desk was old and metal, something bought at an old elementary school garage sale. There were no pictures on it, nothing personal, though a really big ashtray sat front and center. Magazines, lots of them, were stacked high all over the place. Some of the stacks had already collapsed. Sally Li had not bothered to clean them up. She dropped herself in the chair behind her desk.

"Just knock that stuff to the floor. Sit."

Grace removed the papers from the chair and sat. Scott Duncan did the same. Sally Li folded her hands and put them on her lap.

"You know, Scott, that I'm not much with bedside manner."

"I know."

"The good thing is, my patients never complain."

She laughed. No one else did.

"Okay, so now you see why I don't get dates." Sally Li picked up a pair of reading glasses and started shuffling through files. "You know how the really messy person is always so well organized? They always say something like, 'It might look untidy but I know where everything is.' That's crap. I don't know where . . . Wait, here it is."

Sally Li pulled out a manila file.

"Is that my sister's autopsy?" Duncan asked.

"Yep."

She slid it toward him. He opened it. Grace leaned in next to him. On the top were the words DUNCAN, GERI. There were photographs too.

Grace spotted one, a brown skeleton lying on a table. She turned away, as if she'd been caught invading someone's privacy.

Sally Li had her feet on the desk, her hands behind her head. "Look, Scott, you want me to go through the rigmarole of how amazing the science of pathology has become, or do you want me to bottom-line it?"

"Skip the rigmarole."

"At the time of her death, your sister was pregnant."

Duncan's body convulsed as if she'd hit him with a cattle prod. Grace did not move.

"I can't tell you how long. No more than four, five months."

"I don't understand," Scott said. "They must have done an autopsy the first time around."

Sally Li nodded. "I'm sure."

"Why didn't they see it then?"

"My guess? They did."

"But I never knew . . ."

"Why would you? You were, what, in law school? They may have told your mom or dad. But you were just a sibling. And her pregnancy has nothing to do with the cause of death. She died in a fire. The fact that she was pregnant, if they knew, would be deemed irrelevant."

Scott Duncan just sat there. He looked at Grace and then back at Sally Li. "You can get DNA from the fetus?"

"Probably, yeah. Why?"

"How long will it take you to run a paternity test?"

Grace was not surprised by the question.

"Six weeks."

"Any way to rush it?"

"I might be able to get some kind of rejection earlier. In other words, rule people out. But I can't say for sure."

Scott turned to Grace. She knew what he was thinking. She said, "Geri was dating Shane Alworth."

"You saw the picture."

She had. The way Geri looked up at Jack. She had not known the camera was on her. They were all still getting ready to pose. But what was captured, the look on Geri Duncan's face, well, it was the way you look at someone who is much more than a friend.

"Let's run the test then," Grace said.

CHAPTER 34

Charlaine was holding Mike's hand when his eyes finally fluttered open. She screamed for a doctor, who declared, in a moment of true obviousness, that this was a "good sign." Mike was in tremendous pain. The doctor put a morphine pump on him. Mike did not want to go back to sleep. He grimaced and tried to ride it out. Charlaine stayed bedside and held his hand. When the pain got bad, he squeezed hard.

"Go home," Mike said. "The kids need you."

She shushed him. "Try to rest."

"Nothing you can do for me here. Go home."

"Shh."

Mike began to drift off. She looked down at him. She remembered the days at Vanderbilt. The range of emotions overwhelmed her. There was love and affection, sure, but what troubled Charlaine right now—even as she held his hand, even as she felt a strong bond with this man who shared her life, even as she prayed and made deals with a God she'd ignored for far too long—was that she knew that these feelings would not last. That was the terrible part. In the middle of this intensity Charlaine knew that her feelings would ebb away, that the emotions were fleeting, and she hated herself for knowing that.

Three years ago Charlaine attended a huge self-help rally at Continental Arena in East Rutherford. The speaker had been dynamic. Charlaine loved it. She bought all the tapes. She started doing exactly what he said—making goals, sticking to them, figuring out what she wanted from life, trying to put things in perspective, organizing and restructuring her priorities so that she could achieve—but even as she went through the motions, even as her life began to change for the better, she knew that it would not last. That this would all be a temporary change. A new regimen, an exercise program, a diet—that was how this felt too.

It would not be happily ever after.

The door behind her opened. "I hear your husband woke up."

It was Captain Perlmutter. "Yes."

"I was hoping to talk to him."

"You'll have to wait."

Perlmutter took another step into the room. "Are the children still with their uncle?"

"He took them to school. We want things to feel normal for them." Perlmutter moved next to her. She kept her eyes on Mike. "Have you learned anything?" she asked.

"The man who shot your husband. His name is Eric Wu. Does that mean anything to you?"

She shook her head. "How did you figure that out?"

"His fingerprints in Sykes's house."

"Has he been arrested before?"

"Yes. In fact he's on parole."

"What did he do?"

"He was convicted of assault and battery, but it's believed that he's committed a number of crimes."

She was not surprised. "Violent crimes?"

Perlmutter nodded. "Can I ask you something?"

She shrugged.

"Does the name Jack Lawson mean anything to you?"

Charlaine frowned. "Does he have two kids at Willard?"

"Yes."

"I don't know him personally, but Clay, my youngest, is still at Willard. I see his wife sometimes when we do pickups."

"That would be Grace Lawson?"

"I think that's her name. Pretty woman. She has a daughter named Emma, I think. She's a year or two behind my Clay."

"Do you know her at all?"

"Not really, no. I see her at the school holiday concert, stuff like that. Why?"

"It's probably nothing."

Charlaine frowned. "You just picked that name out of a hat?"

"Early conjecture," he said, trying to dismiss it. "I also wanted to thank you."

"For?"

"For talking to Mr. Sykes."

"He didn't tell me much."

"He told you that Wu used the name Al Singer."

"So?"

"Our computer expert found that name on Sykes's computer. Al Singer. We think Wu used that alias for an online dating service. That's how he met Freddy Sykes."

"He used the name Al Singer?"

"Yes."

"It was a gay dating service then?"

"Bisexual."

Charlaine shook her head and came close to chuckling. *Ain't that something?* She looked at Perlmutter, daring him to laugh. He was stone-faced. They both looked down at Mike again. Mike startled. He opened his eyes and smiled at her. Charlaine smiled back and smoothed his hair. He closed his eyes and drifted back to sleep.

"Captain Perlmutter?"

"Yes."

"Please leave," she said.

CHAPTER 35

W hile waiting for Carl Vespa to arrive, Grace started cleaning up the bedroom. Jack, she knew, was a great husband and father. He was smart, funny, loving, caring, and devoted. To counter that, God had blessed him with the organizational skills of a citrus beverage. He was, in sum, a slob. Nagging him about it—and Grace had tried—did no good. So she stopped. If living happily was about compromise, this seemed to her like a pretty good one to make.

Grace had long ago given up on Jack clearing out the pile of magazines next to his bed. His postshower wet towel never ended up back on the rack. Not every article of clothing made it to its ultimate destination. Right now, there was a T-shirt draped half-in, half-out of the hamper as if it'd been shot trying to escape.

For a moment Grace just stared down at the T-shirt. It was green with the word FUBU plastered across the front, and it might have one day been in vogue. Jack bought it for $6.99 at T.J.Maxx, a discount clothing store where hip goes to die. He'd put it on with a pair of too-baggy shorts. He stood in front of the mirror and started wrapping his arms around his body in a bizarre variety of ways.

"What are you doing?" Grace had asked him.

"Gangsta poses. Yo, whatchya think?"

"That I should get you seizure medication."

"Phat," he said. "Bling-bling."

"Right. Emma needs a ride to Christina's."

"Word. Dawg. Hit dat."

"Please go. Immediately."

Grace picked up the shirt now. She had always been cynical about the male species. She was guarded with her feelings. She did not open up easily. She had never believed in love at first sight—she still didn't—but when she met Jack, the attraction had been immediate, flutters in her stomach, and deny it now as much as she wanted, a small voice had told her right then and there, first meeting, that this was the man she was going to marry.

Cram was in the kitchen with Emma and Max. Emma had recovered from her earlier histrionics. She had recovered the way only kids can—fast and with very little residue. They were all eating fish sticks, Cram included, and ignoring the side dish of peas. Emma was reading a poem to Cram. Cram was a great audience. His laugh was the kind that not only filled a room but pushed against the panes of glass. You heard it, you had to either smile or cringe.

There was still time before Carl Vespa arrived. Grace didn't want to think about Geri Duncan, her death, her pregnancy, the way she looked at Jack in that damned photograph. Scott Duncan had asked her what she ultimately wanted. She'd said her husband back. That was still very much the case. But maybe, with all that was happening, she needed the truth too.

With that in mind Grace headed downstairs and flipped on the computer. She brought up Google and typed in JACK LAWSON. Twelve hundred hits. Too many to do any good. She tried SHANE ALWORTH. Hmm, no hits. Interesting. Grace tried SHEILA LAMBERT. Hits about a woman basketball player with the same name. Nothing relevant. Then she began trying combinations.

Jack Lawson, Shane Alworth, Sheila Lambert, and Geri Duncan: These four people were together in this picture. They had to be linked in some other way. She tried various combinations. She tried one first name, one last name. Nothing of interest popped. She was still typing, going through the useless 227 hits on the words LAWSON and ALWORTH when the phone rang.

Grace looked at the caller ID and saw it was Cora. She picked up. "Hey."

"Hey."

"I'm sorry," Grace said.

"Don't worry about it. Bitch."

Grace smiled and kept hitting the down arrow. The hits were useless.

"So do you still want my help?" Cora asked.

"Yeah, I guess."

"Enthusiasm. I love that. Okay, fill me in."

Grace kept it vague. She trusted Cora, but she didn't want to have to trust her. Yeah, that made little sense. It was like this: If Grace's life were in jeopardy, she'd call Cora immediately. But if the kids were in danger . . . well, she'd hesitate. The scary thing was, she probably trusted Cora more than anybody, which was to say that she had never felt more isolated in her life.

"So you're putting the names through search engines?" Cora asked.

"Yes."

"Any relevant hits so far?"

"Not a one." Then: "Wait, hold on."

"What?"

But now again, trust or no trust, Grace wondered what would be the point in telling Cora more than she needed to know. "I gotta run. I'll call you back."

"Okay. Bitch."

Grace hung up and stared at the screen. Her pulse started giddying up, just a little faster now. She had pretty much used up all the name combinations when she remembered an artist friend named Marlon Coburn. He was constantly complaining because his name was misspelled. Marlon would be spelled Marlin or Marlan or Marlen and Coburn would be Cohen or Corburn. Anyway Grace figured she'd give it a go.

The fourth "typo" combo she tried was "Lawson" and "Allworth"—two Ls instead of one.

There were three hundred hits—neither name was that uncommon—but it was the fourth one that jumped out at her. She looked at the top line first:

Crazy Davey's Blog

Grace knew vaguely that a blog was a sort of public diary. People wrote down their random thoughts. Other people, for some odd reason, enjoyed reading them. A diary used to be about being private. Now it was about trying to be shrill enough to reach the masses.

The little sample bit under the link line read:

...John Lawson on keyboards and Sean Allworth who was wicked on guitar...

John was Jack's real name. Sean was pretty close to Shane. Grace clicked the link. The page was forever long. She went back, clicked CACHE. When she returned to the page, the words Lawson and Allworth would be highlighted. She scrolled down and found an entry from two years ago:

April 26
Hey, gang. Terese and I took a weekend up in Vermont. We stayed at the Westerly's bed and breakfasts. It was great. They had a fireplace and at night we played checkers....

Crazy Davey went on and on. Grace shook her head. Who the hell read this nonsense? She skipped three more paragraphs.

That night I went with Rick, an old college bud, to Wino's. It's an old college bar. Total dump. We used to go when we went to Vermont University. Get this, we played Condom Roulette like the old days. Ever play? Every guy guesses a color—there's Hot Red, Stallion Black, Lemon Yellow, Orange Orange. Okay, the last two are jokes, but you get the point. There's this condom dispenser in the bathroom. It's still there! So each guy puts a buck on the table. One guy gets a quarter and buys a condom. He brings it to the table. You open it and whammo, if it's your color, you win! Rick guessed the first one right. He bought us a pitcher. The band that night sucked. I remembered hearing a group when I was a freshman named Allaw. There were two chicks in that band and two guys. I remember one chick played drums. The guys were John Lawson on keyboards and Sean Allworth who was wicked on guitar. That was how they got the name, I think. Allworth and Lawson. Combine it into Allaw. Rick never heard of them. Anyway we finished up the pitcher. A couple of hot chicks came in but they ignored us. We started feeling old....

That was it. Nothing more.

Grace did a search for "Allaw." Nothing.

She tried more combinations. Nothing else. Only this one mention in a blog. Crazy Davey had gotten both Shane's first and last name wrong. Jack had gone by Jack, well, for as long as Grace had known him, but maybe he was John back then. Or maybe the guy remembered it wrong or saw it written down.

But Crazy Davey had mentioned four people—two women, two men. There were five people in the picture, but the one woman, the one who was pretty much a blur near the edge of the photograph—maybe she wasn't part of the group. And what had Scott said about his sister's last phone call?

I figured it was about whatever new thing she was into— aromatherapy, her new rock band . . .

Rock band. Could that be it? Was it a picture of a rock group?

She searched Crazy Davey's site for a phone number or a full name. There was only an e-mail. Grace hit the link and typed quickly:

"I need your help. I have a very important question about Allaw, the band you saw in college. Please call me collect."

She listed her phone number and then hit the SEND button.

So what does this mean?

She tried to put it together in a dozen different ways. Nothing fit. A few minutes later the limousine pulled up the driveway. Grace glanced out the window. Carl Vespa was here.

He had a new driver now, a mammoth muscleman with a crew cut and matching scowl who did not look half as dangerous as Cram. She bookmarked Crazy Davey's blog before heading down the corridor to open the door.

Vespa stepped in without saying hello. He still looked natty, still wearing a blazer that seemed to have been tailored by the gods, but the rest of him looked strangely unruly. His hair was always unkempt—that was his look—but there is a fine line between unkempt and not touched at all. It had crossed that line. His eyes were red. The lines around his mouth were deeper, more pronounced.

"What's wrong?"

"Somewhere we can talk?" Vespa asked.

"The kids are with Cram in the kitchen. We can use the living room."

He nodded. From a distance they heard Max's full-bodied laugh. The sound made Vespa pull up. "Your son is six, right?"

"Yes."

Vespa smiled now. Grace did not know what he was thinking, but the smile broke her heart. "When Ryan was six, he was into baseball cards."

"Max is into Yu-Gi-Oh!"

"Yu-Gi-what?"

She shook her head to indicate that it wasn't worth explaining.

He went on: "Ryan used to play this game with his cards. He'd break them up into teams. Then he'd lay them out on the carpet like it was a ball field. You know, the third baseman—Graig Nettles back then—actually playing third, three guys in the outfield—he even kept the extra pitchers in a bull pen out in right field."

His face glowed in the memory. He looked at Grace. She smiled at him, as gently as she could, but the mood still burst. Vespa's face fell.

"He's getting released on probation."

Grace said nothing.

"Wade Larue. They're rushing his release. He'll be out tomorrow."

"Oh."

"How do you feel about it?"

"He's been in jail for almost fifteen years," she said.

"Eighteen people died."

She did not want to have this conversation with him. That number—eighteen—was not relevant. Just one mattered. Ryan. From the kitchen Max laughed again. The sound shredded the room. Vespa kept his face steady but Grace could see something going on inside of him. A roiling. He did not speak. He did not have to, the thoughts obvious: Suppose it had been Max or Emma. Would she rationalize it as a stoned loser getting high and panicking? Would she be so quick to forgive?

"Do you remember that security guard, Gordon MacKenzie?" Vespa asked.

Grace nodded. He had been the hero of the night, finding a way to open up two locked emergency exits.

"He died a few weeks ago. He had a brain tumor."

"I know." They had given Gordon MacKenzie the biggest spread in the anniversary pieces.

"Do you believe in life after death, Grace?"

"I don't know."

"How about your parents? Will you see them one day?"

"I don't know."

"Come on, Grace. I want to know what you think."

Vespa's eyes bored into hers. She shifted in her seat. "On the phone. You asked if Jack had a sister."

"Sandra Koval."

"Why did you ask me that?"

"In a minute," Vespa said. "I want to know what you think. Where do we go when we die, Grace?"

She could see that it would be useless to argue with him. There was a wrong vibe here, something out of sorts. He was not asking as a friend, a father figure, out of curiosity. There was challenge in his voice. Anger even. She wondered if he'd been drinking.

"There's a Shakespeare quote," she said. "From Hamlet. He says that death is—and I think I have the quote right—an undiscovered country from whose bourne no traveler returns."

He made a face. "In other words, we don't have a clue."

"Pretty much."

"You know that's crap."

She didn't say anything.

"You know that there's nothing. That I will never see Ryan again. It's just too hard for people to accept. The weak-minded invent invisible gods and gardens and reunions in paradise. Or some, like you, won't buy into that nonsense, but it's still too painful to admit the truth. So you come up with this 'how can we know?' rationale. But you do know, Grace, don't you?"

"I'm sorry, Carl."

"For what?"

"I'm sorry that you're in pain. But please don't tell me what I believe."

Something happened to Vespa's eyes. They expanded for a moment and it was almost as if something behind them exploded. "How did you meet your husband?"

"What?"

"How did you meet Jack?"

"What does that have to do with anything?"

He took a quick step closer. A threatening step. He looked down at her, and for the first time Grace knew that all the stories, all the rumors about what he was, what he did, they were true. "How did you two meet?"

Grace tried not to cringe. "You already know."

"In France?"

"Right."

He stared at her hard.

"What's going on, Carl?"

"Wade Larue is getting out."

"So you said."

"Tomorrow his lawyer is holding a press conference in New York. The families will be there. I want you there."

She waited. She knew there was more.

"His lawyer was terrific. She really dazzled the parole board. I bet she'll dazzle the press too."

He stopped and waited. Grace was puzzled for a few moments, but then something cold started in the center of her chest and spread through her limbs. Carl Vespa saw it. He nodded and stepped back.

"Tell me about Sandra Koval," he said. "Because, see, I can't understand how your sister-in-law, of all people, ended up representing someone like Wade Larue."

CHAPTER 36

ndira Khariwalla waited for the visitor.

Her office was dark. All the private detection was done for the day. Indira liked sitting with the lights out. The problem with the West, she was convinced, was overstimulation. She fell prey to it too, of course. That was the thing. No one was above it. The West seduced you with stimulation, a constant barrage of color and light and sound. It never stopped. So whenever possible, especially at the end of the day, Indira liked to sit with the lights off. Not to meditate, as one might assume because of her heritage. Not sitting in lotus position with her thumbs and forefingers making two circles.

No, just darkness.

At ten p.m., there was a light rap on the door. "Come on in."

Scott Duncan entered the room. He did not bother turning on the light. Indira was glad. It would make this easier.

"What's so important?" he asked.

"Rocky Conwell was murdered," Indira said.

"I heard about that on the radio. Who is he?"

"The man I hired to follow Jack Lawson."

Scott Duncan said nothing.

"Do you know who Stu Perlmutter is?" she continued.

"The cop?"

"Yes. He visited me yesterday. He asked about Conwell."

"Did you claim attorney-client?"

"I did. He wants to get a judge to compel me to answer."

Scott Duncan turned away.

"Scott?"

"Don't worry about it," he said. "You don't know anything."

Indira was not so sure. "What are you going to do?"

Duncan stepped out of the office. He reached behind him, grabbed the knob, and started closing the door behind him. "Nip this in the bud," he said.

CHAPTER 37

The press conference was at ten a.m. Grace took the children to school first. Cram drove. He wore an oversized flannel shirt left untucked. He had a gun under it, she knew. The children hopped out. They said good-bye to Cram and hurried away. Cram shifted the car into gear.

"Don't go yet," Grace said.

She watched until they were safely inside. Then she nodded that it was okay for the car to start moving again.

"Don't worry," Cram said. "I have a man watching."

She turned to him. "Can I ask you something?"

"Shoot."

"How long have you been with Mr. Vespa?"

"You were there when Ryan died, right?"

The question threw her. "Yes."

"He was my godson."

The streets were quiet. She looked at him. She had no idea what to do. She could not trust them—not with her children, not after she'd seen Vespa's face last night. But what choice did she have? Maybe she should try the police again, but would they really be willing or able to protect them? And Scott Duncan, well, even he had admitted that their alliance only went so far.

As if reading her thoughts, Cram said, "Mr. Vespa still trusts you."

"And what if he decides he doesn't anymore?"

"He'd never hurt you."

"You're that sure?"

"Mr. Vespa will meet us in the city. At the press conference. You want to listen to the radio?"

The traffic was not bad, considering the hour. The George Washington Bridge was still crawling with cops, a hangover from September 11 that Grace could not get used to. The press conference was being held at the Crowne Plaza Hotel in Times Square. Vespa told her that there'd been talk about conducting it in Boston—that would seem more appropriate—but someone in the Larue camp realized that it might be too emotionally jarring to return so close to the scene. They also hoped that fewer family members would show up if it were held in New York.

Cram dropped her off on the sidewalk and headed into the lot next door. Grace stood on the street for a moment and tried to gather herself. Her cell phone sounded. She checked the caller ID. The number was unfamiliar. Six-one-seven area code. That was the Boston area, if she remembered correctly.

"Hello?"

"Hi. This is David Roff."

She was in Times Square in New York. People were, of course, everywhere. No one seemed to be talking. No horns were honking. But the roar in her ear was still deafening. "Who?"

"Uh, well, I guess you might know me better as Crazy Davey. From my blog. I got your e-mail. Is this a bad time?"

"No, not at all." Grace realized that she was shouting to be heard. She stuck a finger in her free ear. "Thanks for calling me back."

"I know you said to call collect, but I got some new phone service where all long distance is included, so I figured what the hell, you know?"

"I appreciate it."

"You made it sound kind of important."

"It is. On your blog you mentioned a band named Allaw."

"Right."

"I'm trying to find out anything I can about them."

"I figured that, yeah, but I don't think I can really help you. I mean, I just saw them that one night. Me and some buddies got totally wasted, spent the whole night there. We met some girls, did a lot of dancing, did a lot more drinking. We talked to the band afterward. That's why I remember it so well."

"My name is Grace Lawson. My husband was Jack."

"Lawson? That was the lead guy, right? I remember him."

"Were they any good?"

"The band? Truth is, I don't remember, but I think so. I remember having a blast and getting wasted. Had a hangover that still makes me cringe to this day. You trying to put a surprise together for him?"

"A surprise?"

"Yeah, like a surprise party or a scrapbook about his old days."

"I'm just trying to find out anything I can about the people in the group."

"I wish I could help. I don't think they lasted that long. Never heard them again, though I know they had another gig at the Lost Tavern. That was in Manchester. That's all I know. I'm sorry."

"I appreciate your calling me back."

"Sure, no problem. Oh wait. This might be fun trivia for a scrapbook."

"What's that?"

"The gig Allaw played in Manchester? They opened for Still Night."

Waves of pedestrians rushed past her. Grace huddled near a wall, trying to avoid the masses. "I'm not familiar with Still Night."

"Well, only real music buffs would be, I guess. Still Night didn't last too long either. At least not in that incarnation." There was a static crackle, but Grace still heard Crazy Davey's next words too clearly: "But their lead singer was Jimmy X."

Grace felt her grip on the phone go slack.

"Hello?"

"I'm still here," Grace said.

"You know who Jimmy X is, right? 'Pale Ink'? The Boston Massacre?"

"Yes." Her voice sounded very far away. "I remember."

Cram came out of the parking lot. He spotted her face and picked up his pace again. Grace thanked Crazy Davey and hung up. She had his number on her cell phone now. She could always call him back.

"Everything okay?"

She tried to shake it off, this feeling of cold. It wouldn't happen. She managed to utter, "Fine."

"Who was that?"

"You my social secretary now?"

"Easy." He held up both hands. "Just asking."

They headed inside the Crowne Plaza. Grace tried to process what she had just heard. A coincidence. That was all. A bizarre coincidence. Her husband had played in a bar band in college. So had a zillion other people. He happened to play on the same bill once as Jimmy X. Again so what? They were both in the same area at around the same time. This would have been at least a year, probably two, before the Boston Massacre. And Jack might not have mentioned it to her because he figured that it was irrelevant and might, in any case, upset his wife. A Jimmy X concert had traumatized her. It had left her partially crippled. So he maybe didn't see a need to mention that slight connection.

No big deal, right?

Except that Jack had never even mentioned playing in a band. Except that the members of Allaw were all now either dead or missing.

She tried to gather some of the pieces. When exactly had Geri Duncan been murdered anyway? Grace had been undergoing physical therapy when she read about the fire. That meant it probably happened a few months after the massacre. Grace would need to check the exact date. She would need to check the entire time line because, let's face it, there was no way the Allaw–Jimmy X connection was a coincidence.

But how did it work? Nothing about it made sense.

She ran it through one more time. Her husband plays in a band. One time the band plays at the same time as a band featuring Jimmy X. A year or two later—depending on if Jack had been a senior or a year postgrad—the now famous Jimmy X plays a concert that she, young Grace Sharpe, attends. She gets injured in a melee that night. Another three years pass. She meets Jack Lawson on an entirely different continent and they fall in love.

It didn't mesh.

The elevator dinged on the ground level. Cram said, "You sure you're okay?"

"Groovy," she said.

"Still twenty minutes until the press conference begins. I figured it would be better if you went alone, try to grab your sister-in-law beforehand."

"You're a font of ideas, Cram."

The doors opened. "Third floor," he said. Grace stepped inside and let the elevator swallow her whole. She was alone. There would not be much time. She took out her cell phone and the card Jimmy X had given her. She pressed in the number and hit SEND. It went immediately into his voice mail. Grace waited for the beep:

"I know about Still Night playing with Allaw. Call me."

She left her number and hung up. The elevator came to a stop. When she stepped off, there was one of those black signs with the changeable white letters, the kind that tell you in what room the Ratzenberg bar mitzvah or Smith-Jones wedding is being held. This one read: BURTON-CRIMSTEIN PRESS CONFERENCE. Advertising the firm. She followed the arrow to a door, took a deep breath, and pushed it open.

The whole thing was like one of those courthouse movie scenes— that pinnacle cinematic moment when the surprise witness bursts

JUST ONE LOOK · 277

through the double doors. When Grace walked in, there was that sort of collective gasp. The room hushed. Grace felt lost. She glanced around and what she saw made her head spin. She took a step back. The faces of grief, older but no more at peace, swirled about her. There they were again—the Garrisons, the Reeds, the Weiders. She flashed back to the early days at the hospital. She had seen everything through the haze of Halcion, as if through a shower curtain. It felt the same today. They approached in silence. They hugged her. None of them said a word. They didn't have to. Grace accepted the embraces. She could still feel the sadness emanating from them.

She saw the widow of Lieutenant Gordon MacKenzie. Some said that he had been responsible for pulling Grace to safety. Like most true heroes, Gordon MacKenzie had rarely talked about it. He claimed not to remember what he did exactly, that yes, he opened doors and pulled people out, but that it was more out of reaction than anything approaching bravery.

Grace gave Mrs. MacKenzie an extra-long hug.

"I'm sorry for your loss," Grace said.

"He found God." Mrs. MacKenzie held on. "He's with Him now."

There was really nothing to say to that, so Grace just nodded. She let her go and looked over the woman's shoulder. Sandra Koval had entered the room from the other side. She spotted Grace at almost the same moment and a strange thing happened. Her sister-in-law smiled, almost as if she'd expected this. Grace stepped away from Mrs. MacKenzie. Sandra tilted her head, signaling her to step forward. There was a velvet rope. A security guard stepped in her way.

"It's okay, Frank," Sandra said. He let Grace pass.

Sandra led the way. She hurried down a corridor. Grace limped behind, unable to catch up. No matter. Sandra stopped and opened a door. They stepped into a huge ballroom. Waiters busily laid out the silverware. Sandra led her to a corner. She grabbed two chairs and turned them so that they faced each other.

"You don't seem surprised to see me," Grace said.

Sandra shrugged. "I figured you were following the case in the news."

"I wasn't."

"Doesn't matter, I guess. Until two days ago you didn't know who I was."

"What's going on, Sandra?"

She did not answer right away. The tinkling of the silverware provided background music. Sandra let her gaze wander toward the waiters in the center of the room.

"Why are you representing Wade Larue?"

"He was charged with a crime. I'm a criminal defense lawyer. It's what I do."

"Don't patronize me."

"You want to know how I stumbled upon this particular client, is that it?"

Grace said nothing.

"Isn't it obvious?"

"Not to me."

"You, Grace." She smiled. "You're the reason I represent Mr. Larue."

Grace opened her mouth, closed it, started again. "What are you talking about?"

"You never really knew about me. You just knew that Jack had a sister. But I knew all about you."

"I'm still not following."

"It's simple, Grace. You married my brother."

"So?"

"When I learned you were going to be my sister-in-law, I was curious. I wanted to learn about you. Makes sense, right? So I had one of my investigators do a background check. Your paintings are wonderful, by the way. I bought two. Anonymously. They're in my home out in Los Angeles. Spectacular stuff, really. My older daughter, Karen—she's seventeen—loves them. She wants to be an artist."

"I don't see what this has to do with Wade Larue."

"Really?" Her voice was strangely cheerful. "I've worked criminal defense since I graduated law school. I started by working with Burton and Crimstein in Boston. I lived there, Grace. I knew all about the Boston Massacre. And now my brother had fallen in love with one of the Massacre's major players. It piqued my curiosity even more. I started reading up on the case—and guess what I realized."

"What?"

"That Wade Larue had been railroaded by an incompetent lawyer."

"Wade Larue was responsible for the death of eighteen people."

"He fired a gun, Grace. He didn't even hit anyone. The lights went out. People were screaming. He was under the influence of drugs and alcohol. He panicked. He believed—or at least, honestly imagined—that he was in imminent danger. There was no way, no way at all, that he could have known what the outcome would be. His first lawyer should have cut a deal. Probation, eighteen months away tops. But no one really wanted to work this case. Larue was sent to jail to rot. So yes, Grace, I read about him because of you. Wade Larue had been shafted. His old attorney screwed him and ran."

"So you took the case?"

Sandra Koval nodded. "Pro bono. I came to him two years ago. We started preparing for the parole hearing."

Something clicked. "Jack knew, didn't he?"

"That I don't know. We don't talk, Grace."

"Are you still going to tell me you didn't talk to him that night? Nine minutes, Sandra. The phone company says the call lasted nine minutes."

"Jack's call had nothing to do with Wade Larue."

"What did it have to do with?"

"That photograph."

"What about it?"

Sandra leaned forward. "First you answer a question for me. And I need the truth here. Where did you get that picture?"

"I told you. It was in my packet of film."

Sandra shook her head, not believing her. "And you think the guy from the Fotomat stuck it in there?"

"I don't know anymore. But you still haven't explained—what about the picture made him call you?"

Sandra hesitated.

"I know about Geri Duncan," Grace said.

"You know what about Geri Duncan?"

"That she's the girl in the picture. And that she was murdered."

That made Sandra sit up. "She died in a fire. It was an accident."

Grace shook her head. "It was set intentionally."

"Who told you that?"

"Her brother."

"Wait, how do you know her brother?"

"She was pregnant, you know. Geri Duncan. When she died in that fire, she was carrying a baby."

Sandra stopped and looked up in horror. "Grace, what are you doing?"

"I'm trying to find my husband."

"And you think this is helping?"

"You told me yesterday you didn't know anyone in the picture. But you just admitted you knew Geri Duncan, that she died in a fire."

Sandra closed her eyes.

"Did you know Shane Alworth or Sheila Lambert?"

Her voice was soft. "Not really, no."

"Not really. So their names are not totally unfamiliar to you?"

"Shane Alworth was a classmate of Jack's. Sheila Lambert, I think, was a friend from a sister college or something. So what?"

"Did you know that the four of them played together in a band?"

"For a month maybe. Again so what?"

"The fifth person in the picture. The one with her head turned. Do you know who she is?"

"No."

"Is it you, Sandra?"

She looked up at Grace. "Me?"

"Yes. Is it you?"

There was a funny look on Sandra's face now. "No, Grace, it's not me."

"Did Jack kill Geri Duncan?"

The words just came out. Sandra's eyes opened as if she'd been slapped. "Are you out of your mind?"

"I want the truth."

"Jack had nothing to do with her death. He was overseas already."

"So why did the picture freak him out?"

She hesitated.

"Why, dammit?"

"Because he didn't know Geri was dead until then."

Grace looked confused. "Were they lovers?"

"Lovers," she repeated, as if she'd never heard the word before. "That's a pretty mature term for what they were."

"Wasn't she dating Shane Alworth?"

"I guess. But they were all just kids."

"Jack was fooling around with his friend's girlfriend?"

"I don't know how friendly Jack and Shane were. But yes, Jack slept with her."

Grace's head began to whirl. "And Geri Duncan got pregnant."

"I don't know anything about that."

"But you know she's dead."

"Yes."

"And you know Jack ran away."

"Before she died."

"Before she was pregnant?"

"I just told you. I never knew she was pregnant."

"And Shane Alworth and Sheila Lambert, they're both missing too. You want to tell me it's all a coincidence, Sandra?"

"I don't know."

"So what did Jack say when he called you?"

She let loose a deep sigh. Her head dropped. She was silent for a while.

"Sandra?"

"Look, that picture has to be, what, fifteen, sixteen years old? When you just gave it to him like that, out of the blue . . . how did you think he'd react? With Geri's face crossed out. So Jack went to the computer. He did a Web search—I think he used the *Boston Globe*'s archives. He found out she's been dead this whole time. That was why he called me. He wanted to know what happened to her. I told him."

"Told him what?"

"What I knew. That she died in a fire."

"Why would that make Jack run out?"

"That I don't know."

"What made him run overseas in the first place?"

"You have to let this go."

"What happened to them, Sandra?"

She shook her head. "Forget the fact that I'm his attorney and that it's protected. It is simply not my place. He's my brother."

Grace reached out and took Sandra's hands in hers. "I think he's in trouble."

"Then what I know can't help him."

"They threatened my children today."

Sandra closed her eyes.

"Did you hear what I said?"

A man in a business suit leaned into the room. He said, "It's time, Sandra." She nodded and thanked him. Sandra pulled her hands away, stood, smoothed out the lines of her suit.

"You have to stop this, Grace. You have to go home now. You have to protect your family. It's what Jack would want you to do."

CHAPTER 38

T he threat at the supermarket had not taken.

Wu was not surprised. He had been raised in an environment that stressed the power of men and the subordination of women, but Wu had always found it to be more hope than truth. Women were harder. They were more unpredictable. They handled physical pain better—he knew this from personal experience. When it came to protecting their loved ones, they were far more ruthless. Men would sacrifice themselves out of machismo or stupidity or the blind belief that they would be victorious. Women would sacrifice themselves without self-deception.

He had not been in favor of making the threat in the first place. Threats left enemies and uncertainty. Eliminating Grace Lawson earlier would have been routine. Eliminating her now would be riskier.

Wu would have to return and handle the job himself.

He was in Beatrice Smith's shower, dyeing his hair back to its original color. Wu usually wore it bleached blond. He did this for two reasons. The first reason was basic: He liked the way it looked. Vanity, perhaps, but when Wu looked in the mirror he thought the gel-spiked surfer blond style worked on him. Reason two, the color—a garish yellow—was useful because it was what most people remembered. When he brought his hair back to its natural state of everyday Asian black, flattened it down, when he changed his clothes from the modern hip style to something more conservative, donned a pair of wire-rimmed spectacles, well, the transformation was very effective.

He grabbed Jack Lawson and dragged him down into the basement. Lawson did not resist. He was barely conscious. He was not doing well. His mind, already stretched, had perhaps snapped. He would not survive much longer.

The basement was unfinished and damp. Wu remembered the last time he'd been in a similar setting, out in San Mateo, California. The instructions had been specific. He had been hired to torture a man for exactly eight hours—why eight Wu had never learned—and then break bones in both the man's legs and arms. Wu had manipulated the broken bones so that the jagged edges sat next to nerve bundles or near the surface of the skin. Any movement, even the slightest, would cause excruciating pain. Wu locked the basement and left the man by himself. He checked up on him once a day. The man would plead, but Wu would just stare silently. It took eleven days for the man to die of starvation.

Wu found a strong pipe and chained Lawson to it. He also cuffed his arms behind his back around a support wall. He put the gag back into his mouth.

Then he decided to test the binds.

"You should have gotten every copy of that photograph," Wu whispered.

Jack Lawson's eyes rolled up.

"Now I'll have to pay your wife a visit."

Their gazes locked. A second passed, no more, and then Lawson sprang to life. He began to flail. Wu watched him. Yes, this would be a good test. Lawson struggled for several minutes, a fish dying on the line. Nothing gave way.

Wu left him alone then, still fighting his chains, to find Grace Lawson.

CHAPTER 39

G race did not want to stay for the press conference.

Being in the same room with all these mourners . . . She didn't like to use the term "aura," but it seemed to fit. The room had a bad aura. Shattered eyes stared at her with a yearning that was palpable. Grace understood, of course. She was no longer the conduit to their lost children—too much time had passed for that. Now she was the survivor. She was there, alive and breathing, while their children rotted in the grave. On the surface there was still affection, but beneath that Grace could feel rage at the unfairness of it all. She had lived—their children had not. The years had offered no reprieve. Now that Grace had children of her own, she understood in a way that would have been impossible fifteen years ago.

She was about to slide out the back door when a hand took firm hold of her wrist. She turned and saw it was Carl Vespa.

"Where are you going?" he asked.

"Home."

"I'll give you a ride."

"That's okay. I can hire a car."

His hand, still on her wrist, tightened for a brief moment and again Grace thought she saw something detonate behind his eyes. "Stay," he said.

It was not a request. She searched his face, but it was oddly calm. Too calm. His demeanor—so off with the surroundings, so different from the flash of fury she'd seen last night—frightened her anew. Was this really the man she was trusting with her children's lives?

She sat next to him and watched Sandra Koval and Wade Larue take the podium. Sandra pulled the microphone closer and started up with the standard clichés about forgiveness and starting over and rehabilitation. Grace watched the faces around her shut down. Some cried. Some pursed their lips. Some visibly shook.

Carl Vespa did none of that.

He crossed his legs and leaned back. He surveyed the proceedings with a casualness that scared her more than the worst scowl. Five minutes into Sandra Koval's statement, Vespa's eyes shifted toward Grace. He saw that she'd been watching him. Then he did something that made her shiver.

He winked at her.

"Come on," he whispered. "Let's get out of here."

With Sandra still talking, Carl Vespa rose and headed for the door. Heads turned and there was a brief hush. Grace followed. They took the elevator down in silence. The limousine was right out front. The big burly guy was in the driver's seat.

"Where's Cram?" Grace asked.

"On an errand," Vespa said, and Grace thought she saw the trace of a smile. "Tell me about your meeting with Ms. Koval."

Grace recounted her conversation with her sister-in-law. Vespa stayed silent, gazing out the window, his index finger gently tapping his chin. When she finished, he asked, "Is that everything?"

"Yes."

"Are you sure?"

She did not like the lilt in his tone.

"What about your recent"—Vespa looked up, scanning for the word—"visitor?"

"You mean Scott Duncan?"

Vespa had the oddest grin. "You are aware, of course, that Scott Duncan works for the U.S. attorney's office."

"Used to," she corrected.

"Yes, used to." His voice was too relaxed. "What did he want with you?"

"I told you."

"Did you?" He shifted in his chair, but he still did not face her. "Did you tell me everything?"

"What's that supposed to mean?"

"Just a question. Was this Mr. Duncan your only recent visitor?"

Grace did not like how this was going. She hesitated.

"Nobody else you'd like to tell me about?" he continued.

She tried to search his face for a clue, but he kept it turned away from her. What was he talking about? She mulled it over, replayed the past few days . . .

Jimmy X?

Could Vespa somehow know about Jimmy stopping by after his concert? It was possible, of course. He had found Jimmy in the first place—it would stand to reason that he'd have someone following him. So what should Grace do here? Would saying something now just compound the issue? Maybe he didn't know about Jimmy. Maybe opening her mouth now would just get her in deeper trouble.

Play it vague, she thought. See where it goes. "I know I asked for your help," she said, her tone deliberate. "But I think I'd like to handle this on my own now."

Vespa finally turned toward her and faced her full. "Really?"

She waited.

"Why is that, Grace?"

"Truth?"

"Preferably."

"You're scaring me."

"You think I'd harm you?"

"No."

"Then?"

"I just think it might be best—"

"What did you tell him about me?"

The interruption caught her off guard. "Scott Duncan?"

"Is there anyone else you talked to about me?"

"What? No."

"So what did you say to Scott Duncan about me?"

"Nothing." Grace tried to think. "What could I tell him anyway?"

"Good point." He nodded, more to himself than at Grace. "But you were never very specific on why Mr. Duncan paid you this visit." Vespa folded his hands and put them on his lap. "I'd very much like to know the details."

She didn't want to tell him—didn't want him involved anymore—but there was no way to avoid it. "It's about his sister."

"What about her?"

"Do you remember the girl crossed out in that picture?"

"Yes."

"Her name was Geri Duncan. She was his sister."

Vespa frowned. "And that's why he came to you?"

"Yes."

"Because his sister was in the photograph?"

"Yes."

He sat back. "So what happened to her, this sister?"

"She died in a fire fifteen years ago."

Vespa surprised Grace then. He didn't ask a follow-up question. He didn't ask for clarification. He simply turned away and stared out the window. He did not speak again until the car pulled into the driveway. Grace opened the door to get out, but there was some kind of locking system on it, like the safety lock she'd used when the kids were small, and she could not open it from the inside. The burly driver came around and took hold of the door handle. She wanted to ask Carl Vespa what he planned on doing now, if he'd indeed leave them alone, but his body language was wrong.

Calling him in the first place had been a mistake. Telling him she wanted him out of this might have compounded it.

"I'll keep my men on until you pick up the children from school," he said, still not facing her. "Then you'll be on your own."

"Thank you."

"Grace?"

She looked back at him.

"You should never lie to me," he said.

His voice was ice. Grace swallowed hard. She wanted to argue, to tell him that she hadn't, but she worried that it would sound too defensive—protesting too much. So she simply nodded.

There were no good-byes. Grace headed up the walk alone. Her step teetered from something more than the limp.

What had she done?

She wondered about her next step. Her sister-in-law had said it best: Protect the children. If Grace were in Jack's shoes, if she had gone missing for whatever reason, that would be what she'd want. *Forget me,* she'd tell him. *Keep the children safe.*

So now, like it or not, Grace was out of the rescue business. Jack was on his own.

She'd pack now. She'd wait until three o'clock, until school was let out, and then she'd pick up the children and drive to Pennsylvania. She'd find a hotel where you didn't need a credit card. Or a B&B. Or a rooming house. Whatever. She'd call the police, maybe that Perlmutter even. She'd tell him what was going on. But first she needed her children. Once they were safe, once she had them in her car and was on the road, she'd be okay.

She reached her front door. There was a package on the step. She bent down and picked it up. The box had a *New Hampshire Post* logo on it. The return address read: BOBBY DODD, STARSHINE ASSISTED LIVING.

It was Bob Dodd's files.

CHAPTER 40

Wade Larue sat next to his lawyer, Sandra Koval.

He wore brand-new clothes. The room did not smell of prison, that horrid combination of decay and disinfectant, of fat guards and urine, of stains that never come out, and that in and of itself was a strange adjustment. Prison becomes your world, getting out an impossible daydream, like imagining life on other planets. Wade Larue had gone inside at the age of twenty-two. He was now thirty-seven. That meant he had spent pretty much all his adult years inside that place. That smell, that horrid smell, was all he knew. Yes, he was still young. He had, as Sandra Koval repeated mantralike, his whole life in front of him.

It didn't feel like that right now.

Wade Larue's life had been ruined by a school play. He had grown up in a small town in Maine, and everyone agreed that Wade had the acting chops. He was a crummy student. He was not much of an athlete. But he could sing and dance and, most important, he had what one local reviewer called—this after seeing Wade star as Nathan Detroit in *Guys and Dolls* during his sophomore year—"supernatural charisma." Wade had that something special, that intangible that separated talented wannabes from the real deals.

Before Wade's senior year of high school, Mr. Pearson, the high school play director, called Wade into his office to tell him about his "impossible dream." Mr. Pearson had always wanted to put on *Man of La Mancha*, but he never had a student, not until now, who could handle the role of Don Quixote. Now, for the first time, he wanted to give it a go with Wade.

But come September Mr. Pearson moved away and Mr. Arnett took over as director. He held tryouts—usually a formality for Wade Larue—but Mr. Arnett was hostile. To the shock of everyone in town he ended up picking Kenny Thomas, a total no-talent, to play Don Quixote. Kenny's father was a bookie, and Mr. Arnett, rumor had it, was into him for over twenty grand. You do the math. Wade was offered the role of the barber—one song!—and ended up quitting.

Here was how naïve Wade was: He thought that his quitting would cause a townwide uproar. High schools are made up of types. The handsome quarterback. The basketball captain. The school president. The lead in every school play. He thought the townsfolk would rally against the injustice that had befallen him. But no one said a thing. At first, Wade figured that they were scared of Kenny's father and his possible mob connections, but the truth was far simpler: They didn't care. Why should they?

It is so easy to inch your way into foul territory. The line is so thin, so flimsy. You just step over it, just for a second, and sometimes, well, sometimes you can't make your way back. Three weeks later Wade Larue got drunk, broke into the school, and vandalized the sets for the play. He was caught by the police and suspended from school.

And so the slide began.

Wade ended up taking too many drugs, moving to Boston to help sell and distribute, grew paranoid, carried a gun. And now here he was, sitting at this podium, a famous felon blamed for the death of eighteen people.

The faces glaring up at him were familiar from his trial fifteen years ago. Wade knew most of the names. At the trial they stared with a combination of grief and bewilderment, still woozy from the sudden blow. Wade had understood back then, sympathized even. Now, fifteen years later, the glares were more hostile. Their grief and bewilderment had crystallized into a purer cut of anger and hate. At the trial, Wade Larue had avoided the glares. But no more. He kept his head up. He met their eyes. His sympathy, his understanding, had been decimated by their lack of forgiveness. He had never meant to hurt anyone. They knew that. He had apologized. He had paid a huge price. They, these families, still chose hate.

To hell with them.

Sandra Koval waxed eloquent from the seat next to him. She spoke of apologies and forgiveness, of turning corners and transformations, of understanding and the human desire for a second chance. Larue tuned her out. He spotted Grace Lawson sitting next to Carl Vespa. He should have felt tremendous fear seeing Vespa in the flesh, but no, he was beyond that now. When Wade was first put in prison, he had been badly beaten—first by people working for Vespa and then by those hoping to curry favor. Guards included. There had been no escape from the constant fear. Fear, like the smell, had become a natural part of him, his world. Maybe that explained why he was immune to it now.

Larue eventually made friends at Walden, but prison is no character builder, despite what Sandra Koval was now telling this audience. Prison strips you down to your barest state, the state of nature, and what you do to survive is never pretty. No matter. He was out now. That was in the past. You move on.

But not quite yet.

The room was beyond silent, a vacuuming feel, as if the very air had been sucked out of it. The families all sat there, unmoved both physically and emotionally. But there was no energy there. They were hollow entities, devastated and powerless. They could not hurt him. Not anymore.

Without warning Carl Vespa rose. For a second—no longer than that—Sandra Koval was thrown. Grace Lawson stood too. Wade Larue could not understand why they were together. It made no sense. He wondered if it changed anything, if he would soon meet Grace Lawson.

Did it matter?

When Sandra Koval finished, she leaned over to him and whispered, "Come on, Wade. You can take the back way out."

Ten minutes later, out on the streets of Manhattan, Wade Larue was free for the first time in fifteen years.

He stared up at the skyscrapers. Times Square was his first destination. It would be noisy and crowded with people—real, live nonconvicts. Larue did not want solitude. He did not crave green grass or trees—you could see those from his prison cell in the sticks of Walden. He wanted lights and sounds and people, real people, not prisoners, and yes, perhaps, the company of a good (or better, bad) woman.

But that would have to wait. Wade Larue checked his watch. It was almost time.

He started west on Forty-third Street. There was still a chance to back out of this. He was achingly close to the Port Authority Bus Terminal. He could hop on a bus, any bus, and start anew someplace. He could change his name, maybe his face a little, and try out for local theater. He was still young. He still had the chops. He still had that supernatural charisma.

Soon, he thought.

He needed to clear this up. Put it behind him. When he was being released, one of the prison counselors had given him the standard lecture about this being either a new start or a bad end—it was all up to him. The counselor was right. Today he would either put this all behind him or he would die. Wade doubted that there would be an in-between.

Up ahead he saw a black sedan. He recognized the man leaning against the side, his arms crossed. It was the mouth you couldn't forget, the way the teeth were all twisted together. He had been the first to beat Larue all those years ago. He wanted to know what had happened the night of the Boston Massacre. Larue had told him the truth: He didn't know.

Now he did.

"Hey, Wade."

"Cram."

Cram opened the door. Wade Larue slid into the back. Five minutes later they were on the West Side Highway heading toward the endgame.

CHAPTER 41

E ric Wu watched the limousine pull up to the Lawson residence.

A large man who looked like anything but a chauffeur stepped out of the car, pulled his jacket together hard so he could work the button, and opened the back door. Grace Lawson stepped out. She headed for her front door without saying good-bye or looking behind her. The large man watched her pick up a package and go inside. Then he got back in the car and pulled out.

Wu wondered about him, the large man. Grace Lawson, he'd been told, might have protection now. She had been threatened. Her children had been threatened. The large chauffeur was not with the police. Wu was certain of that. But he was no simple driver either.

Best to be cautious.

Keeping a good distance away, Wu began to circle the perimeter. The day was clear, the foliage bursting with green. There were many places to hide. Wu did not have binoculars—it would have made the task easier—but that was not important. He spotted one man within minutes. The man was stationed behind the detached garage. Wu crept closer. The man was communicating with a cell-phone walkie-talkie. Wu listened. He only picked up snippets, but it was enough. There was someone in the house too. Probably another man on the perimeter, on the other side of the street.

This was not good.

Wu could still handle it. He knew that. But he would have to strike fast. He would first have to know the exact location of the other perimeter man. He would take one out with his hands and one with the gun. He would need to rush the house. It could be done. There would be lots of bodies. The man inside could be tipped off. But it could be done.

Wu checked his watch. Twenty minutes until three.

He started circling back toward the street when the back door of the Lawson home opened. Grace stepped out. She had a suitcase. Wu stopped and watched. She put the suitcase in the trunk. She went back inside. She came out with another suitcase and a package—the same one, he thought, that he'd seen her pick up at the front door.

Wu hurried back to the car he was using—ironically enough, her Ford Windstar, though he'd switched license plates at the Palisades Mall and slapped on some bumper stickers to draw attention away from that fact. People remembered bumper stickers more than license plates or even makes. There was one about him being a proud parent of an honor roll student. A second, for the New York Knicks, read ONE TEAM, ONE NEW YORK.

Grace Lawson got behind the wheel of her car and started it up. Good, Wu thought. It would be much easier to grab her wherever she stopped. His instructions were clear. Find out what she knows. Get rid of the body. He put the Windstar in gear but kept his foot on the brake. He wanted to see if anyone else followed. No one pulled out after her. Wu kept his distance.

There were no other tails.

The men had been ordered to protect the house, he guessed, not her. Wu wondered about the suitcases, about where she might be headed, about how long this journey might take. He was surprised when she started taking small side streets. He was even more surprised when she pulled to a stop near a schoolyard.

Of course. It was nearing three o'clock. She was picking up her children from school.

He thought again about the suitcases and what they might mean. Was her intention to pick up her children and take a trip? If that was the case, it might be someplace far away. It might be hours before she stopped.

Wu did not want to wait hours.

On the other hand she might head straight back home, back into the protection of the two men on the perimeter and the one in the house. That was not good either. He would have the old set of problems, plus, in either case, children would now be involved. Wu was neither bloodthirsty nor sentimental. He was pragmatic. Grabbing a woman whose husband had already run off might raise suspicions and even police involvement, but if you add dead bodies, possibly two dead children, the attention becomes nearly intolerable.

No, Wu realized. It would be best to grab Grace Lawson here and now. Before the children came out of the schoolyard.

That did not give him much time.

Mothers began to congregate and mingle, but Grace Lawson stayed in her car. She seemed to be reading something. The time was two fifty. That gave Wu ten minutes. Then he remembered the earlier threat. They had told her that they would take her children. If that was the case, it was entirely possible that there were men watching the school too.

He had to check fast.

It didn't take long. The van was parked a block away, at the end of a cul-de-sac. So obvious. Wu considered the possibility that there was more than one. He did a quick scan and saw nothing. No time anyway. He had to strike. The school would be letting out in five minutes. Once the kids were present, it would complicate everything exponentially.

Wu had dark hair now. He put on gold-framed glasses. He had the loose-fitting casual clothes. He tried to make himself look timid as he walked toward the van. He looked around as if lost. He moved straight to the back door and was about to open it when a bald man with a sweaty brow popped his head out.

"What do you want, pal?"

The man was dressed in a blue velour sweat suit. There was no shirt under the jacket, just mounds of chest hair. He was big and gruff. Wu reached out with his right hand and cupped the back of the man's head. He snapped his arm forward and planted his left elbow deep in the man's Adam's apple. The throat simply collapsed. The entire windpipe gave way like a brittle branch. The man went down, his body thrashing like a fish on the dock. Wu pushed him deeper into the van and slid inside.

There was the same cell-phone walkie-talkie, a pair of binoculars, a gun. Wu jammed the weapon into his waist. The man still thrashed. He would not live much longer.

Three minutes until the bell rang.

Wu locked the van's door behind him and hurried out. He made it back to the street where Grace Lawson was parked. Mothers lined the fence in anticipation of school being let out. Grace Lawson was out of her car now, standing by herself. That was good.

Wu walked toward her.

On the other side of the schoolyard, Charlaine Swain was thinking about chain reactions and falling dominoes.

If she and Mike hadn't had problems.

If she had not started up that perverted dance with Freddy Sykes.

If she had not looked out that window when Eric Wu was there.

If she had not opened the hide-a-key and called the police.

But right now, as she passed the playground, the dominoes were falling more in the present: If Mike had not woken up, if he had not insisted she take care of the children, if Perlmutter had not asked her about Jack Lawson, well, without all of that, Charlaine would not have been looking in Grace Lawson's direction.

But Mike had insisted. He had reminded her that the children needed her. So here she was. Picking up Clay from school. And Perlmutter had indeed asked Charlaine if she knew Jack Lawson. So when Charlaine arrived at the schoolyard, it was natural, if not inevitable, that she would start scanning the grounds for the man's wife.

That was how Charlaine came to be looking at Grace Lawson.

She had even been tempted to approach—hadn't that been part of the reason she had agreed to pick up Clay in the first place?—but then she saw Grace pick up her cell phone and start talking into it. Charlaine decided to keep her distance.

"Hi, Charlaine."

A woman, a popular yappy mom who had never deigned to give Charlaine the time before, now stood before her with a look of feigned concern. The newspaper had not mentioned Mike's name, just that there was a shooting, but small towns and gossip and all that.

"I heard about Mike. Is he okay?"

"Fine."

"What happened?"

Another woman sidled up to her right. Two others began to mosey over. Then two more. They came from every direction now, these approaching mothers, getting in her way, almost blocking Charlaine's view.

Almost.

For a moment Charlaine could not move. She stood frozen, watching as he approached Grace Lawson.

He had changed his appearance. He wore glasses now. His hair wasn't blond anymore. But there was no doubt. It was the same man.

It was Eric Wu.

From more than a hundred feet away Charlaine felt the shiver when Wu put his hand on Grace Lawson's shoulder. She saw him bend down and whisper something into her ear.

And then she saw Grace Lawson's whole body go rigid.

———

Grace wondered about the Asian man walking toward her.

She figured that he would just walk by her. He was too young to be a parent. Grace knew most of the teachers. He wasn't one of them. He was probably a new student teacher. That was probably it. She really did not give him much thought. Her mind was concerned with other things.

She had packed enough clothes for a few days anyway. Grace had a cousin who lived near Penn State, smack in the middle of Pennsylvania. Maybe she would drive out there. Grace had not called ahead to see. She did not want to leave any trail.

After throwing clothes in the suitcases, she had closed the door to her bedroom. She took out the small gun Cram had given her and set it on the bed. For a long time she just stared at it. She had always been fervently antigun. Like most rational people she was scared of what a weapon like this could do lying around the house. But Cram had put it succinctly yesterday: Hadn't her children been threatened?

The trump card.

Grace wrapped the nylon ankle holster around her good leg. It felt itchy and uncomfortable. She changed into jeans with a small flare at the bottom. The gun was covered now, but there was some room down there. There was still a small bulge in the area, but no more so than if she were wearing a boot.

She grabbed the Bob Dodd file from his office at the *New Hampshire Post* and drove to the school. She had a few minutes now, so she stayed in the car and started going through it. Grace had no idea what she expected to find. There were plenty of desk knickknacks—a small American flag, a Ziggy coffee mug, a return address stamper, a small Lucite paperweight. There were pens, pencils, erasers, paper clips, Wite-out, thumbtacks, Post-it notes, staples.

Grace wanted to skip past that stuff and dive into the files, but the pickings were slim. Dodd must have done all his work on a computer.

She found a few diskettes, all unmarked. Maybe there would be a clue on one of those. She'd check when she got access to a computer.

As for paperwork, all she found was press clippings. Articles written by Bob Dodd. Grace skimmed through them. Cora had been right. His stories were mostly small-time exposés. People would write in with a complaint. Bob Dodd would investigate. Hardly the sort of stuff that gets you killed, but who knows? The little things have a way of rippling.

She was just about to give up—had given up really—when she located the desk photo in the bottom. The frame was facedown. More out of curiosity than anything else she flipped the frame over and took a look. The photograph was a classic vacation shot. Bob Dodd and his wife, Jillian, stood on a beach, both smiling with dazzling white teeth, both wearing Hawaiian shirts. Jillian had red hair. Her eyes were widely spaced apart. Grace suddenly understood Bob Dodd's involvement. It had nothing to do with the fact that he was a reporter.

His wife, Jillian Dodd, was Sheila Lambert.

Grace closed her eyes and rubbed the bridge of her nose. Then she carefully put everything back in the package. She stuck it in the backseat and slipped out of the car. She needed time to think and put it together.

The four members of Allaw—it all came back to them. Sheila Lambert, Grace now knew, had stayed in the country. She had changed her identity and gotten married. Jack had taken off for a small village in France. Shane Alworth was either dead or in parts unknown—maybe, as his mother suggested, helping the poor in Mexico. Geri Duncan had been murdered.

Grace checked her watch. The bell would ring in a few minutes. She felt the buzz of her cell phone on her belt. "Hello?"

"Ms. Lawson, this is Captain Perlmutter."

"Yes, Captain, what can I do for you?"

"I need to ask you some questions."

"I'm picking up my children at school right now."

"Would you like me to come by your house? We can meet there."

"They'll be out in two more minutes. I'll swing by the station." A sense of relief rushed over her. This half-baked idea of running off to Pennsylvania—that might be too much. Maybe Perlmutter knew something. Maybe, with all she now knew about that picture, he would finally believe her. "Will that be okay?"

"That'll be fine. I'll be here waiting."

The very moment Grace snapped the receiver closed, she felt a hand touch down on her shoulder. She turned. The hand belonged to the young Asian man. He bent his head toward her ear.

"I have your husband," he whispered.

CHAPTER 42

"Charlaine? Are you okay?"

It was the popular yappy mother. Charlaine ignored her.

Okay, Charlaine, think.

What, she wondered, would the dumb heroine do? That was how she'd tried to play it in the past—imagine what the waif would do and do the opposite.

C'mon, c'mon . . .

Charlaine tried to battle through the near-paralyzing fear. She had not expected to see this man ever again. Eric Wu was wanted. He had shot Mike. He had assaulted Freddy and held him captive. The police had his fingerprints. They knew who he was. They would send him back to prison. So what was he doing here?

Who cares, Charlaine? Do something.

The answer was a no-brainer: Call the police.

She reached into her pocketbook and pulled out her Motorola. The mothers were still barking like small dogs. Charlaine flipped the phone open.

It was dead.

Typical, and yet it made sense. She had used it during the chase. She had left it on all this time. The phone was two years old. The damn thing was always going dead. She glanced back across the schoolyard. Eric Wu was talking to Grace Lawson. They both began to walk away.

The same woman asked again: "Is something wrong, Charlaine?"

"I need to use your cell phone," she said. "Now."

Grace just stared at the man.

"If you come with me quietly, I will take you to your husband. You will see him. You will be back in an hour. But the school bell rings in one minute. If you do not come with me, I will take out a gun. I will shoot your children. I will shoot random children. Do you understand?"

Grace could not speak.

"You don't have much time."

She found her voice. "I'll go with you."

"You drive. Just walk calmly with me. Please do not make the mistake of trying to signal someone. I will kill them. Do you understand?"

"Yes."

"You may be wondering about the man assigned to protect you," he went on. "Let me assure you that he will not interfere."

"Who are you?" Grace asked.

"The bell is about to ring." He looked off, a tiny smile on his lips. "Do you want me to be here when your children come out?"

Scream, Grace thought. Scream like a lunatic and start running. But she could see the bulge of the gun. She could see the man's eyes. This was no bluff. He meant it. He would kill people.

And he had her husband.

They began to walk to her car, side by side, like two friends. Grace's eyes darted about the playground. She spotted Cora. Cora gave her a puzzled look. Grace did not want to risk it. She looked away.

Grace kept walking. They reached her car. She had just unlocked the doors when the school bell rang.

———

The yappy woman rummaged through her purse. "We have a terrible calling plan. Hal is so cheap sometimes. We run out of minutes in the first week and then we need to watch ourselves the rest of the month."

Charlaine looked at the other faces. She did not want to cause a panic, so she kept her voice even. "Please, does anyone have a phone I can borrow?"

She kept her eyes on Wu and Lawson. They were across the street, by Grace's car now. She saw Grace use one of those remote controls to unlock the doors. Grace stood by the driver's door. Wu was by the passenger's. Grace Lawson made no move to run away. It was hard to see her face, but she didn't look as if she was being coerced.

The bell sounded.

The mothers all turned toward the doors, a Pavlovian response, and waited for their children to emerge.

"Here, Charlaine."

One of the mothers, eyes on the school door, handed Charlaine her cell phone. Charlaine tried not to grab it too quickly. She was raising it to her ear when she glanced over at Grace and Wu one more time. She stopped cold.

Wu was staring directly at her.

When Wu saw that woman again, he started for his gun.

He was going to shoot her. Right here. Right now. Right in front of everyone.

Wu was not a superstitious man. He realized that the odds of her being here were reasonable. She had children. She lived in the area. There must have been two or three hundred mothers here. It would make sense that she would be one of them.

But he still wanted to kill her.

On the superstitious side, he would kill this demon.

On the practical side, he would prevent her from calling the police. He would also cause a panic that would allow him to escape. If he shot her, everyone would run toward the fallen woman. It would be the ideal diversion.

But there were problems too.

First, the woman stood at least a hundred feet away. Eric Wu knew his strengths and weaknesses. In hand-to-hand he had no equal. With a gun, he was merely decent. He might only wound or, worse, miss altogether. Yes, there would be a panic, but without a body falling, it might not be the sort of diversion he wanted.

His real target—the reason he was here—was Grace Lawson. He had her now. She was listening to him. She was pliable because she still held out hope that her family could survive this. If she were to see him fire a shot, standing as she was out of his reach, there was a chance that Grace Lawson would panic and bolt.

"Get in," he said.

Grace Lawson opened her car door. Eric Wu stared at the woman across the schoolyard. When their eyes met, he slowly shook his head and gestured toward his waist. He wanted her to understand. She had crossed him before and he had fired. He would do so again.

He waited until the woman lowered the phone. Still keeping his eyes on her, Wu slid into the car. They pulled out and disappeared down Morningside Drive.

CHAPTER 43

Perlmutter sat across from Scott Duncan. They were in the captain's office at the station. The air-conditioning was on the fritz. Dozens of cops in full uniform all day and no air-conditioning—the place was starting to reek.

"So you're on leave from the U.S. attorney's office," Perlmutter said.

"That's correct," Duncan replied. "I'm working in private practice right now."

"I see. And your client hired Indira Khariwalla—check that, you hired Ms. Khariwalla on behalf of a client."

"I will neither confirm nor deny that."

"And you won't tell me if your client wanted Jack Lawson followed. Or why."

"That's correct."

Perlmutter spread his hands. "So what exactly do you want, Mr. Duncan?"

"I want to know what you've learned about Jack Lawson's disappearance."

Perlmutter smiled. "Okay, let me make sure I have this straight. I'm supposed to tell you everything I know about a murder and missing-person investigation, even though your client may very well be involved. You, in turn, are supposed to tell me squat. That about cover it?"

"No, that's not correct."

"Well, help me here."

"This has nothing to do with a client." Duncan crossed his ankle over his knee. "I have a personal involvement in the Lawson case."

"Come again?"

"Ms. Lawson showed you the photograph."

"Right, I remember."

"The girl with her face crossed out," he said, "was my sister."

Perlmutter leaned back and whistled low. "Maybe you should start at the beginning."

"It's a long story."

"I'd say I have all day, but that would be a lie."

As if proving the point, the door flew open. Daley jammed his head in.

"Line two."

"What is it?"

"Charlaine Swain. She says she just saw Eric Wu at the schoolyard."

Carl Vespa stared at the painting.

Grace was the artist. He owned eight of her paintings, though this was the one that moved him most. It was, he suspected, a portrait of Ryan's last moments. Grace's memory of that night was hazy. She hated to sound pompous about it, but this vision—this seemingly ordinary painting of a young man somehow on the verge of a nightmare—had come to her in something of an artistic trance. Grace Lawson claimed that she dreamed about that night. That, she said, was the only place that the memories existed.

Vespa wondered.

His home was in Englewood, New Jersey. The block had at one

time been old money. Now Eddie Murphy lived at the end of the street. A power forward for the New Jersey Nets was two houses down. Vespa's property, once owned by a Vanderbilt, was sprawling and secluded. In 1988 Sharon, his then-wife, had torn down the turn-of-the-century stone edifice and built what was then considered modern. It had not aged well. The house looked like a bunch of glass cubes, stacked haphazardly. There were too many windows. The house got ridiculously hot in the summer. It looked and felt like a damn greenhouse.

Sharon was gone now too. She had not wanted the house in the divorce. She really did not want very much at all. Vespa did not try to stop her. Ryan had been their main connection, in his death more than life. That was never a healthy thing.

Vespa checked the security monitor for the driveway. The sedan was pulling up.

He and Sharon had wanted more children, but it was not to be. Vespa's sperm count was too low. He told no one, of course, subtly implying that the fault lay with Sharon. Awful to say now, but Vespa believed that if they had more children, if Ryan had at least one sibling, it would have made the tragedy, if not easier, at least bearable. The problem with tragedy is that you have to go on. There is no choice. You cannot just pull off the road and wait it out—much as you might want to. If you have other children you understand that right away. Your life may be over, but you get out of bed for others.

Put simply, there was no reason for him to get out of bed anymore.

Vespa headed outside and watched the sedan come to a stop. Cram got out first, a cell phone glued to his ear. Wade Larue followed. Larue did not look frightened. He looked oddly at peace, gazing at the lush surroundings. Cram mumbled something to Larue—Vespa couldn't hear what he said—and then started up the stairs. Wade Larue wandered away as if he was on retreat.

Cram said, "We got a problem."

Vespa waited, following Wade Larue with his eyes.

"Richie is not answering his radio."

"Where was he stationed?"

"In a van near the kids' school."

"Where is Grace?"

"We don't know."

Vespa looked at Cram.

"It was three o'clock. We knew she'd gone to pick up Emma and Max. Richie was supposed to tail her from there. She got to the school—we know that. Richie radioed that in. Since then, nothing."

"Did you send someone over?"

"Simon went to check on the van."

"And?"

"It's still there. Parked in the same spot. But there are cops in the area now."

"What about the kids?"

"We don't know yet. Simon thinks he sees them in the schoolyard. But he doesn't want to get too close with the cops around."

Vespa closed his fists. "We have to find Grace."

Cram said nothing.

"What?"

Cram shrugged. "I think you have it wrong, that's all."

Neither one of them said anything after that. They stood and watched Wade Larue. He strolled the grounds, cigarette in tow. From the top of the property there was a magnificent view of the George Washington Bridge and, behind it, the distant skyline of Manhattan. It had been there that Vespa and Cram had watched the smoke billow as if from Hades when the towers fell. Vespa had known Cram for thirty-eight years. Cram was the best with a gun or a knife Vespa had ever seen. He scared people with little more than a glance. The vilest men, the most violent psychotics, begged for mercy before Cram even touched them. But on that day, standing silently in the yard, watching the smoke not dissipate, Vespa had seen even Cram break down and cry.

They looked over at Wade Larue.

"Did you talk to him at all?" Vespa asked.

Cram shook his head. "Not a word."

"He looks pretty calm."

Cram said nothing. Vespa started toward Larue. Cram stayed where he was. Larue did not turn around. Vespa stopped about ten feet away and said, "You wanted to see me?"

Larue kept staring out at the bridge. "Beautiful view," he said.

"You're not here to admire it."

He shrugged. "Doesn't mean I can't."

Vespa waited. Wade Larue did not turn around. "You confessed."

"Yes."

"Did you mean it?" Vespa asked.

"At the time? No."

"What does that mean, at the time?"

"You want to know if I fired those two shots that night." Wade Larue finally turned and faced Vespa full. "Why?"

"I want to know if you killed my boy."

"Either way I didn't shoot him."

"You know what I mean."

"Can I ask you something?"

Vespa waited.

"Are you doing this for you? Or your son?"

Vespa thought about that. "It's not for me."

"Then your son?"

"He's dead. It won't do him any good."

"Who then?"

"It doesn't matter."

"It does to me. If it's not about you or your son, why do you still need revenge?"

"It needs to be done."

Larue nodded.

"The world needs balance," Vespa went on.

"Yin and yang?"

"Something like that. Eighteen people died. Someone has to pay."

"Or the world is out of balance?"

"Yes."

Larue took out a pack of cigarettes. He offered one to Vespa. Vespa shook his head.

"Did you fire those shots that night?" Vespa asked.

"Yes."

That was when Vespa exploded. His temper was like that. He went from zero to uncontrolled rage in a snap. There was an adrenaline rush, like a thermometer spiking up in a cartoon. He cocked his fist and smashed it into Larue's face. Larue went down hard on his back. He sat up, put his hand to his nose. There was blood. Larue smiled at Vespa. "That give you balance?"

Vespa was breathing hard. "It's a start."

"Yin and yang," Larue said. "I like that theory." He wiped his face with his forearm. "Thing is, this universal balancing act—does it stretch across generations?"

"What the hell is that supposed to mean?"

Larue smiled. There was blood on his teeth. "I think you know."

"I'm going to kill you. You know that."

"Because I did something bad? So I should pay a price?"

"Yes."

Larue got to his feet. "But what about you, Mr. Vespa?"

Vespa tightened his fists, but the adrenaline rush was quieting.

"You've done bad. Did you pay the price?" Larue cocked his head. "Or did your son pay it for you?"

Vespa hit Larue deep in the gut. Larue folded. Vespa punched him in the head. Larue fell again. Vespa kicked him in the face. Larue was flat on his back now. Vespa took a step closer. Blood dripped out of Larue's mouth, but the man still laughed. The only tears were on Vespa's face, not Larue's.

"What are you laughing at?"

"I was like you. I craved revenge."

"For what?"

"For being in that cell."

"That was your fault."

Larue sat up. "Yes and no."

Vespa took a step back. He looked behind him. Cram stood perfectly still and watched. "You said you wanted to talk."

"I'll wait till you're done beating me."

"Tell me why you called."

Wade Larue sat up, checked his mouth for blood. He seemed almost happy to see it. "I wanted vengeance. I can't tell you how badly. But now, today, when I got out, when I was suddenly free . . . I don't want that anymore. I spent fifteen years in prison. But my sentence is over. Your sentence, well, the truth is yours will never end, will it, Mr. Vespa?"

"What do you want?"

Larue stood. He walked over to Vespa. "You're in such pain." His voice was soft now, as intimate as a caress. "I want you to know everything, Mr. Vespa. I want you to learn the truth. This has to end. Today. One way or another. I want to live my life. I don't want to look over my shoulder. So I'm going to tell you what I know. I'm going to tell you everything. And then you can decide what you need to do."

"I thought you said you fired those shots."

Larue ignored that. "Do you remember Lieutenant Gordon Mac-Kenzie?"

The question surprised Vespa. "The security guard. Of course."

"He visited me in prison."

"When?"

"Three months ago."

"Why?"

Larue smiled. "That balance thing again. Making things right. You call it yin and yang. MacKenzie called it God."

"I don't understand."

"Gordon MacKenzie was dying." Larue put his hand on Vespa's shoulder. "So before he went, he needed to confess his sins."

CHAPTER 44

T he gun was in Grace's ankle holster.

She started up the car. The Asian man sat next to her. "Head up the road and turn left."

Grace was scared, of course, but there was an odd calmness too. Something about being in the eye of the storm, she guessed. Something was happening. There was a potential to find answers here. She tried to prioritize.

First: Get him far away from the children.

That was the number one thing here. Emma and Max would be fine. The teachers stayed outside until all the children were picked up. When she didn't show, they would give an impatient sigh and bring them to the office. That old battle-ax of a receptionist, Mrs. Dinsmont, would gleefully cluck her tongue about the neglectful mother and make the children wait. There had been an incident about six months ago when Grace got caught up by construction and arrived late. She'd been racked with guilt, picturing Max waiting like a scene from *Oliver Twist*, but when she got there he was in the office coloring a picture of a dinosaur. He wanted to stay.

The school was out of sight now. "Turn right."

Grace obeyed.

Her captor, if that's what you wanted to call him, had said that he was taking her to Jack. She did not know if that was true or not, but she somehow suspected that it was. She was sure, of course, that he was not doing this out of the goodness of his heart. She had been warned. She had gotten too close. He was dangerous—she didn't need to see the gun in his waistband to know that. There was a crackle around him, an electricity, and you knew, just knew, that this man always left devastation in his path.

But Grace desperately needed to see where this led. She had her gun in the ankle holster. If she stayed smart, if she was careful, she would have the element of surprise. That was something. So for now she would go along. There was really no alternative anyway.

She was worried about working the gun and the holster. Would the gun come out smoothly? Would the gun really just fire when she pulled the trigger? Did you really just aim and pull? And even if she could get the gun from the holster in time—something doubtful with the way this guy was watching her—what would she do? Point it at him and demand he take her to Jack?

She couldn't imagine that working.

She couldn't just shoot him either. Forget the ethical dilemma or the question of if she'd be brave enough to pull the trigger. He, this man, might be her only connection to Jack. If she killed him, where would that leave her? She'd have silenced her only solid clue, maybe her only chance, to find Jack.

Better to wait and play it out. As if she had a choice.

"Who are you?" Grace asked.

Total stone face. He took hold of her purse and emptied the contents into his lap. He went through it, sifting and tossing items into the backseat. He found her cell phone, removed the battery, threw it in the back.

She kept peppering him with questions—where is my husband, what do you want with us?—but he continued to ignore her. When they reached a stoplight, the man did something that she did not expect.

He rested his hand on her bad knee.

"Your leg was damaged," he said.

Grace was not sure how to respond to this. His touch was light, almost feathery. And then without warning his fingers dug down with steel talons. They actually burrowed beneath the kneecap. Grace buckled. The tips of the man's fingers disappeared into the hollow where the knee meets the shinbone. The pain was so sudden, so enormous, that Grace could not even scream. She reached out and grabbed his fingers, tried to pry them out of her knee, but there was absolutely no give. His hand felt like a concrete block.

His voice was barely a whisper. "If I dig in a little more and then pull . . ."

Her head was swimming. She was close to losing consciousness.

". . . I could tear your kneecap right off."

When the light turned green, he let go. Grace nearly collapsed in relief. The whole incident had probably taken less than five seconds. The man looked at her. There was the smallest hint of a smile on his face.

"I'd like you to stop talking now, okay?"

Grace nodded.

He faced forward. "Keep driving."

Perlmutter called in the APB. Charlaine Swain had had the good sense to get both the make and license plate. The car was registered to Grace Lawson. No surprise there. Perlmutter was in an unmarked car now, heading toward the school. Scott Duncan was with him.

"So who is this Eric Wu?" Duncan asked.

Perlmutter debated what to tell him but saw no reason to hold this back. "To date we know he broke into a house, assaulted the owner in such a way as to leave him temporarily paralyzed, shot another man, and my guess is, he killed Rocky Conwell, the guy who was following Lawson."

Duncan had no response.

Two other police cars were already on the scene. Perlmutter did not like that—marked cars at a school. They'd had the good sense, at least, not to use their sirens. That was something. The parents picking up off-spring reacted in two ways. Some hurried their kids to their cars, hands on their shoulders, shielding them as though from gunfire. Others let curiosity rule the day. They walked over, oblivious or in a state of denial that there could be any danger in so innocent a setting.

Charlaine Swain was there. Perlmutter and Duncan hurried toward her. A young uniformed cop named Dempsey was asking her questions and taking notes. Perlmutter shooed him away and asked, "What happened?"

Charlaine told him about coming to school, keeping an eye out for Grace Lawson because of what he, Perlmutter, had said. She told him about seeing Eric Wu with Grace.

"There was no overt threat?" he asked.

Charlaine said, "No."

"So she might have gone with him voluntarily."

Charlaine Swain flicked a glance at Scott Duncan, then back to Perlmutter. "No. She didn't go voluntarily."

"How do you know?"

"Because Grace came alone to pick up her kids," Charlaine said.

"So?"

"So she wouldn't just voluntarily leave them like that. Look, I couldn't call you guys right away when I saw him. He was able to make me freeze from across a schoolyard."

Perlmutter said, "I'm not sure I understand."

"If Wu could do that to me from that far away," Charlaine said, "imagine what he'd be able to do to Grace Lawson when he was right next to her, whispering in her ear."

Another uniformed officer named Jackson came sprinting over to Perlmutter. His eyes were wide and Perlmutter could see he was trying everything he could not to panic. The parents picked up on it too. They took a step away.

"We found something," Jackson said.

"What?"

He leaned in closer so no one would overhear. "A van parked two blocks away. I think you should come see this."

She should use the gun now.

Grace's knee throbbed. It felt as if someone had set off a bomb inside the joint. Her eyes were wet from holding back tears. She wondered if she'd be able to walk when they stopped.

She sneaked glances at the man who had hurt her so. Whenever she did, he was watching her, that bemused look still on his face. She tried to think, tried to organize her thoughts, but she kept flashing back to his hand on her knee.

He had been so casual about causing her such pain. It would have been one thing if he'd been emotional about it, one way or the other, if he'd been moved to either ecstasy or revulsion, but there had been nothing there. Like hurting someone was paperwork. No strain, no sweat. His boast, if you want to call it that, had not been idle: If he'd so desired, he could have twisted off her kneecap like a bottle top.

They had crossed the state line and were in New York now. She was on Interstate 287 heading toward the Tappan Zee Bridge. Grace did not dare speak. Her mind, naturally enough, kept going back to the children. Emma and Max would have come out of the school by now. They would have looked for her. Would they have been brought to the office? Cora had seen Grace in the schoolyard. So had several other mothers, Grace was sure. Would they say or do something?

This was all irrelevant and, more than that, a waste of mental energy. Nothing she could do about it. Time to concentrate on the task at hand.

Think about the gun.

Grace tried to rehearse in her mind how it would go. She would reach down with both hands. She would pull her cuff up with her left and grab the weapon with her right. How was it strapped in? Grace tried to remember. There was a strip covering the top, wasn't there? She had snapped it into place. It kept the gun secure, so it wouldn't jerk around. She'd have to unsnap that. If she just tried to pull the gun free, it would get caught.

Okay, good. Remember that: Unsnap first. Then pull.

She thought about timing. The man was incredibly strong. She had seen that. He probably had a fair amount of experience with violence. She would have to wait for an opportunity. First—and this was obvious—she couldn't be driving when she made her move. They would either need to be at a stoplight or parked or . . . or better, wait until they were getting out of the car. That might work.

Second, the man would have to be distracted. He watched her a lot. He was also armed. He had a weapon in his waistband. He would be able to draw it out far faster than she could. So she had to make sure that he was not looking at her—that his attention was, in some way, diverted.

"Take this exit."

The sign read AIRMONT. They had only been on 287 for maybe three or four miles. They were not going to be crossing the Tappan Zee Bridge. She had thought that perhaps the bridge would have provided another opportunity. There were tollbooths there. She could have tried to escape or somehow signal the toll worker, though she couldn't imagine that working. Her captor would be watching her if they'd pulled up to the tollbooth. He would, she bet, have put his hand on her knee.

She veered to the right and up the ramp. She began to work it out in her head again. When you really thought about it, Grace's best bet would be to wait until they reached their destination. For one thing, if indeed he really was taking her to Jack, well, Jack would be there, right? That made some sense.

But more than that, when they stopped the car, they would both have to get out. Obvious, yes, but it would provide an opportunity. He would get out on his side. She would get out on hers.

This could be her diversion.

Again she started rehearsing it in her head. She would open the car door. As she swung her legs out, she'd pull up the cuff. Her legs would be on the ground and blocked by the car. He wouldn't see. If she timed it right, he would be getting out on his side of the car at the same time. He'd turn his back. She'd be able to pull out the weapon.

"Take the next right," he said. "And then the second left."

They were moving through a town Grace didn't know. There were more trees here than in Kasselton. The houses looked older, more lived-in, more private.

"Pull into the driveway over there. Third on the left."

Grace's hands stayed tight on the wheel. She pulled into the driveway. He told her to stop in front of the house.

She took a breath and waited for him to open the door and get out.

Perlmutter had never seen anything like it.

The guy in the van, an overweight man with a standard-issue mafioso sweat suit, was dead. His last few moments had not been pleasant. The big man's neck was, well, flat, totally flat, as if a steamroller had somehow managed to roll over only the man's throat, leaving his head and torso intact.

Daley, never one at a loss for words, said, "Serious grossness." Then he added, "He looks familiar."

"Richie Jovan," Perlmutter said. "Works low level for Carl Vespa."

"Vespa?" Daley repeated. "He's involved in this?"

Perlmutter shrugged. "This has to be Wu's handiwork."

Scott Duncan was turning white. "What the hell is going on?"

"It's simple, Mr. Duncan." Perlmutter turned to face him. "Rocky Conwell worked for Indira Khariwalla, a private investigator you hired. The same man—Eric Wu—murdered Conwell, killed this poor schmuck, and was last seen driving away from that school with Grace Lawson." Perlmutter moved toward him. "You want to tell us what's going on now?"

Another police car screeched to a stop. Veronique Baltrus came flying out. "Got it."

"What?"

"Eric Wu at yenta-match.com. He was using the name Stephen Fleisher." She sprinted over to them, the raven hair tied back in a tight bun. "Yenta-match sets up Jewish widows and widowers. Wu had three online flirtations going on at the same time. One woman is from Washington, D.C. Another lives in Wheeling, West Virginia. And the last one, a Beatrice Smith, resides in Airmont, New York."

Perlmutter broke into a run. No doubt, he thought. That was where Wu had gone. Scott Duncan followed. The ride to Airmont would take no more than twenty minutes.

"Call the Airmont Police Department," he shouted to Baltrus. "Tell them to send every available unit right away."

CHAPTER 45

G race waited for the man to get out.

The lot was wooded, so the house was hard to see from the road. There were cathedral points and lots of deck space. Grace could see an aging barbecue. There was a string of lights, the old lantern kind, but the lanterns were weathered and torn. There was a rusted swing set in the back, like ruins from another era. There had been parties here once. A family. People who liked to entertain friends. The house had the feel of a ghost town, as if you expected tumbleweeds to roll past.

"Turn off the ignition."

Grace ran over it again. Open the door. Swing the legs out. Pull out the gun. Take aim . . .

And then what? Tell him to put his hands up? Just shoot him in the chest? What?

She flicked off the ignition and waited for him to get out first. He reached for the door handle. She readied herself. His eyes were on the front door of the house. She slid her hand down a little.

Should she go for it now?

No. Wait until he starts getting out. Don't hesitate. Any hesitation and she would lose the edge.

The man stopped with his hand on the handle. Then he turned around, made a fist, and hit Grace so hard in the lower ribs she thought the whole cage would cave in like a bird's nest. There was a thud and a crack.

Pain exploded across Grace's side.

She thought that her whole body would simply give out. The man grabbed her head with one hand. With the other he traced his hand down the side of her rib cage. His index finger came to rest on the spot he'd just hit, at the bottom of the rib cage.

His voice was gentle. "Please tell me how you got that picture."

She opened her mouth but nothing came out. He nodded as if he'd expected that. His hand dropped off her. He opened the car door and got out. Grace was dizzy from the pain.

The gun, she thought. Get the goddamn gun!

But he was already on the other side of the car. He opened her door. His hand took hold of her neck, his thumb on one side, his index finger on the other. He squeezed the pressure points and started to lift. Grace tried to stay with him. The movement jarred her ribs. It felt like someone had jammed a screwdriver between two bones and was jerking it up and down.

He dragged her out by the neck. Every step was a new adventure in pain. She tried not to breathe. When she did, even that slight expansion of the ribs made the tendons feel like they were being freshly ripped. He yanked her toward the house. The front door was unlocked. He turned the knob, pushed it open, and tossed her inside. She fell hard, nearly passing out.

"Please tell me how you got that picture."

He slowly moved toward her. Fear cleared her head. She talked fast.

"I picked up a packet of film at the Fotomat," she began.

He nodded in the way someone does when they are not listening. He kept coming closer. Grace kept talking and tried to scoot back. There was nothing on his face, a man going about a mundane task, planting seeds, hammering a nail, putting in a buy order, whittling wood.

He was on her now. She tried to struggle but he was ridiculously strong. He lifted her enough to flip her onto her stomach. The ribs banged against the floor. A different pain, a new pain, seared through her. Her vision started going hazy. They were still in the front foyer. He straddled her back. She tried to kick, but there was nothing behind it. He pinned her down.

Grace couldn't move.

"Please tell me how you got that picture."

She felt the tears coming, but she would not let herself cry. Stupid. Macho. But she would not cry. She said it again, about going to the Fotomat, and getting that packet. Still straddling her back, his knees on each side of her hips, he put his index finger on the damaged bottom of the rib cage. Grace tried to buck. He found the spot where it hurt the most and rested the tip of his finger right there. For a moment he did not do anything. She bucked more. She flung her head back and forth. She flailed. He just waited a second. Then another.

And then he jammed the finger between two broken ribs.

Grace screamed.

The voice remained unchanged: "Please tell me how you got that picture."

Now she did cry. He let her. She started explaining again, changing her words, hoping it would sound more believable, more convincing. He did not say a word.

He rested the index finger on the damaged rib again.

That was when a cell phone rang.

The man sighed. He put his hands on her back and lifted himself off. The ribs screamed again. Grace heard a whimpering sound and realized that it was coming from her. She made herself stop. She managed to glance over her shoulder. He kept his eyes on her, took the phone from his pocket, snapped it open.

"Yes."

One thought in her head: Go for the gun.

He stared down at her. She almost didn't care. Going for the gun right now would be suicide, but her thoughts were base—escape the pain. Whatever the cost. Whatever the risk. Escape the pain.

The man kept the phone by his ear.

Emma and Max. Their faces floated toward her in something of a haze. Grace encouraged the vision. And something odd happened then.

Lying there, still on her stomach, her cheek pressed to the floor, Grace smiled. Actually smiled. Not from feelings of maternal warmth, though that might have been part of it, but with specific memory.

When she was pregnant with Emma, she told Jack that she wanted to do natural childbirth and that she did not want to take any drugs. She and Jack dutifully attended Lamaze class every Monday night for three months. They practiced breathing techniques. Jack would sit behind her and rub her belly. He would go "hee hee hoo hoo." She would copy him. Jack even bought a shirt that read COACH on the front and TEAM HEALTHY BABY on the back. He wore a whistle around his neck.

When the contractions began, they rushed to the hospital all prepared, all ready for their hard work to pay off dividends. Once there, Grace felt a stronger contraction. They started doing their breathing. Jack would go "hee hee hoo hoo." Grace would follow suit. It worked wonderfully well right up until the very moment Grace started to, well, started to feel pain.

Then the insanity of their plan—when did "breathing" become a euphemism for "painkiller"?—became apparent. It washed away the macho idiocy of "taking the hurt," a concept idiotically male in the first place, and reason, calm reason, finally came to her.

She reached out then, grabbed a part of Jack's anatomy, pulled him close so he could hear her. She told him to find an anesthesiologist. Now. Jack said he would, the moment she released said part of his anatomy. She obliged. He ran and found an anesthesiologist. But by then it was too late. The contractions were too far along.

And the reason Grace was smiling now, some eight years after the fact, was that the pain that day was at least this bad, probably worse. She had taken it. For her daughter. And then, miraculously, she had been willing to risk it again for Max.

So bring it on, she thought.

Maybe she was delirious. Nothing maybe about it. She was. But she didn't care. The smile stayed in place. Grace could see Emma's beautiful face. She saw Max's face too. She blinked and they were gone. But that didn't matter anymore. She looked at the cruel man on the phone.

Bring it on, you sick son of a bitch. Bring it on.

He finished with his phone call. He moved back toward her. She was still on her stomach. He straddled her again. Grace closed her eyes. Tears squeezed out of them. She waited.

The man took hold of both of her hands and pulled them behind her back. He wrapped duct tape around them and stood. He pulled her so that she was on her knees, her hands bound behind her back. The ribs ached but the pain was manageable for now.

She looked up at him.

He said, "Don't move."

He turned away and left her alone then. She listened. She heard a door open and then the sound of footsteps.

He was heading down into the basement.

She was alone.

Grace struggled to free her arms, but they were wrapped tightly. No way to reach the gun. She debated trying to stand and run, but that would be futile at best. The position of her arms, the searing pain in her ribs, and of course, the fact that she was a major gimp under the best of circumstances—add it up and it didn't look like a sound alternative.

But could she slip her hands under herself?

If she could do that, if she could get her hands, even bound, to the front of her body, she could go for the gun.

It was a plan.

Grace had no idea how long he'd be gone—not long, she figured—but she had to chance it.

Her shoulders rolled back in their sockets. Her arms straightened. Every movement—every breath—set the ribs afire. She fought through it. She stood and bent at the waist. She forced her hands down.

Progress.

Still standing, she bent the knees and squirmed. She was getting close. Footsteps again.

Damn, he was heading back up the stairs.

She was caught in the middle, her bound hands under her buttocks.

Hurry, dammit. One way or the other. Put the hands back behind her or keep going.

She chose to keep going. Keep going forward.

This was going to end here and now.

The footsteps were slow. Heavier. It sounded like he was dragging something with him.

Grace pushed harder. Her hands were stuck. She bent more at the waist and knees. The pain made her head swim. She closed her eyes and swayed. She pulled up, willing to dislocate her shoulders if it would help her get through this.

The footsteps stopped. A door closed. He was here.

She forced her arms through. It worked. They came out in front of her.

But it was too late. The man was back. He stood in the room, not five feet from her. He saw what she had done. But Grace did not notice that. She was, in fact, not looking at the man's face at all. She stared openmouthed at the man's right hand.

The man let go. And there, falling to the floor by his side, was Jack.

CHAPTER 46

Grace dove toward him.

"Jack? Jack?"

His eyes were closed. His hair was matted to his forehead. Her hands were still bound, but she was able to hold his face. Jack's skin was clammy. His lips were dry and caked over. There was duct tape around his legs. A handcuff hung around his right wrist. She could see scabs on his left wrist. It had been cuffed too, for a long time judging by the marks.

She called his name again. Nothing. She lowered her ear to his mouth. He was breathing. She could see that. Shallow, but he was breathing. She shifted around and put his head in her lap. Her rib pain screamed but that was irrelevant now. He lay flat on his back, her lap his pillow. Her mind fell back to the grape groves in that vineyard in Saint-Emilion. They'd been together about three months by then, totally infatuated, jammed neatly in that sprint-across-the-park, thumping-of-the-heart-whenever-you-see-the-person stage. She packed some pâté, some cheese, wine of course. The day had been sun-kissed, the sky the kind of blue that made you believe in the angels. They'd lain down on a red tartan blanket; his head in her lap like this, she stroked his hair. She'd spent more time staring at him than at the natural wonders that surrounded them. She'd traced his face with her fingers.

Grace made her voice soft, tried to ease up on the panic.

"Jack?"

His eyes fluttered open. His pupils were too large. It took him a moment to focus, and then he saw her. For a moment his caked lips cracked into a smile. Grace wondered if he too was flashing back to that same picnic. Her heart burst, but she managed to smile back. There was a serene moment, no more, and then reality flooded in. Jack's eyes widened in panic. The smile vanished. His face crumbled into anguish.

"Oh God."

"It's okay," she said, even though that was about as dumb a statement as one could make under the circumstances.

He was trying not to cry. "I'm so sorry, Grace."

"Shhh, it's okay."

Jack's eyes searched like beacons, finding their captor. "She doesn't know anything," he said to the man. "Let her go."

The man took a step closer. He bent down on his haunches. "If you speak again," he said to Jack, "I will hurt her. Not you. Her. I will hurt her very badly. Do you understand?"

Jack closed his eyes and nodded.

He stood back up. He kicked Jack off her lap, grabbed Grace by the hair, and pulled her to a standing position. With his other hand he clutched Jack by the neck.

"We need to take a ride," he said.

CHAPTER 47

Perlmutter and Duncan had just gotten off the Garden State Parkway at Interstate 287, no more than five miles from the house in Airmont, when the call was radioed in:

"They were here—Lawson's Saab is still in the driveway—but they're gone now."

"How about Beatrice Smith?"

"Nowhere in sight. We just got here. We're still checking the residence."

Perlmutter thought about it. "Wu would figure that Charlaine Swain would report seeing him. He'd know he had to get rid of the Saab. Do you know if Beatrice Smith had a car?"

"Not yet, no."

"Is there any other car in the driveway or garage?"

"Hold on." Perlmutter waited. Duncan looked at him. Ten seconds later: "No other car."

"Then they took hers. Find out the make and license plate. Get an APB out right away."

"Okay, got it. Wait. Hold on a second, Captain." He was gone again.

Scott Duncan said, "Your computer expert. She thought that Wu was maybe a serial killer."

"She thought it was a possibility."

"You don't believe it though."

Perlmutter shook his head. "He's a pro. He doesn't pick victims for jollies. Sykes lived alone. Beatrice Smith is a widow. Wu needs a place to stay and operate. This is how he finds those places."

"So he's a gun for hire."

"Something like that."

"Any thoughts on who he's working for?"

Perlmutter held the wheel. He took the Airmont exit. They were only about a mile away now. "I was hoping you or your client might have an idea."

The radio crackled. "Captain? You still there?"

"I am."

"One car registered to Mrs. Beatrice Smith. A tan Land Rover. License plate 472-JXY."

"Get an APB out on it. They can't be far."

CHAPTER 48

The tan Land Rover stayed on side roads. Grace had no idea where they were headed. Jack was lying on the floor of the backseat. He had passed out. His legs were duct-taped together. His hands were cuffed behind him. Grace's hands were still bound in front of her. Her captor, she figured, had seen no reason to make her put them back.

In the backseat Jack groaned like a wounded animal. Grace looked at their captor, his placid face, one hand on the wheel like a father taking the family out for a Sunday drive. She ached. Every breath was a reminder of what he'd done to her ribs. Her knee felt as if it'd been ripped apart by shrapnel.

"What did you do to him?" she asked.

She tensed, awaiting the blow. She almost didn't care. She was beyond that. But the man did not lash out. He did not stay silent either. He pointed with his thumb toward Jack.

"Not as much," he said, "as he did to you."

She stiffened. "What the hell is that supposed to mean?"

Now, for the first time, she saw a genuine smile. "I think you know."

"I don't have the slightest idea," she said.

He still smiled, and maybe, somewhere deep inside of her, the gnawing started to grow. She tried to cast it off, tried to concentrate on getting out of this, on saving Jack. She asked, "Where are you taking us?"

He did not reply.

"I said—"

"You're brave," he interrupted.

She said nothing.

"Your husband loves you. You love him. It makes this easier."

"Makes what easier?"

He glanced toward her. "You both may be willing to risk pain. But are you willing to let me hurt your husband?"

She did not reply.

"The same thing I said to him: If you talk again, I won't hurt you. I'll hurt him."

The man was right. It worked. She kept silent. She gazed out the window and let the trees blur. They veered onto a two-lane highway. Grace had no idea where. The area was rural. She could see that. They took two more roads and now Grace knew where they were—the Palisades Parkway heading south, back down toward New Jersey.

The Glock was still in the ankle holster.

The feel of it was constant now. The weapon seemed to be calling to her, mocking her, so close and yet out of reach.

Grace would have to figure a way to get to it. There was no other choice. This man was going to kill them. She was sure of that. He wanted some information first—the origin of that photograph, for one thing—but once he had it, once he realized that she was telling the truth on that score, he would kill them both.

She had to go for the gun.

The man kept sneaking glances at her. There was no opening. She thought about it. Wait until he stopped the car? She had tried that before—it hadn't worked. Just go for it? Just pull it out and take her chances? A possibility but she really did not think she'd be fast enough.

Pulling up the leg cuff, unsnapping that safety strap, getting her hand around the gun, withdrawing it . . . all before he reacted?

No way.

She debated the slow approach. Lower her hands a little to the side. Try to work her cuff up a bit at a time. Pretend like she had an itch.

Grace shifted in her seat and looked down at her leg. And that was when she felt her heart slam into her throat. . . .

Her cuff had ridden up.

The ankle holster. It was visible now.

Panic spread through her. She cut a glance at her captor, hoping that he hadn't seen it. But he had. His eyes suddenly widened. He was looking right at her leg.

Now or never.

But even as she reached, Grace could see that she had no chance. There was simply no way to get there in time. Her captor put his hand on her knee again and squeezed. Pain blasted violently through her, nearly knocking her unconscious. She screamed. Her body went rigid. Her hands dropped, useless now.

He had her.

She turned toward him, looked into his eyes, saw nothing. Then, without warning, there was movement coming from behind him. Grace gasped.

It was Jack.

Somehow he had risen up from the backseat like an apparition. The man turned, more curious than concerned. After all, Jack's hands and legs were bound. He was totally spent. What harm could he do?

Wild-eyed and looking something like an animal, Jack reared back his head and whipped it forward. The surprise caught the man off guard. Jack's forehead connected with the man's right cheek. The sound was a deep, hollow clunk. The car shrieked to a stop. The man let go of Grace's knee.

"Run, Grace!"

It was Jack's voice. Grace fumbled for the gun. She unsnapped the safety strap. But the man was back up again. He used one hand to grab Jack's neck. With the other he went after her knee again. She pulled away. He tried again.

Grace knew that there was no time to get the gun. Jack could no longer help. He had used up everything, sacrificed himself, for that one blow.

It would all be for nothing.

The man punched Grace in the ribs again. Hot knives blasted through her. Nausea swam through her stomach and head. She felt consciousness start ebbing away.

She couldn't hang on. . . .

Jack tried to thrash away, but he was little more than a nuisance. The man squeezed Jack's neck. Jack made a sound and went still.

The man reached for her again. Grace grabbed the door handle.

His hand clasped her arm.

She could not move.

Jack's head slid down the man's shoulder. It stopped on the forearm. And there, with his eyes closed, Jack opened his mouth and bit down hard.

The man howled and released his grip. He started shaking his arm, trying to get Jack off. Jack clenched his jaw and hung on like a bulldog. The man slammed his free palm into Jack's head. Jack slumped off.

Grace pulled the door handle, leaned her body against it.

She fell out of the car and landed on the pavement. She rolled away, anything to get farther away from her captor. She actually rolled into the other lane of the highway. A car swerved past her.

Get the gun!

She reached down again. The safety strap was off. She turned toward the car. The man was getting out. He pulled up his shirt. Grace saw his gun. She saw him reaching for it. Grace's own gun came loose.

There was no question now. There was no ethical dilemma. There was no thought about maybe yelling out a warning, telling him to freeze, asking him to put his hands on his head. There was no moral outrage. There was no culture, no humanity, no years of civilization or breeding.

Grace pulled the trigger. The gun went off. She pulled it again. And again. The man staggered. She pulled it again. The sound of sirens grew. And Grace fired again.

CHAPTER 49

Two ambulances arrived. One whisked Jack away before Grace could even see him. Two paramedics worked on her. They were in constant motion, asking questions as they worked, but their words did not register. She was strapped to a stretcher and wheeled toward the ambulance. Perlmutter was there now.

"Where are Emma and Max?" she asked.

"At the station. They're safe."

An hour later Jack was in surgery. That was all they would tell her. He was in surgery.

The young doctor ran a battery of tests on Grace. The ribs were indeed cracked, but there was nothing you could really do for cracked ribs. The doctor wrapped them with an Ace bandage and gave her a shot. The pain began to subside. An orthopedic surgeon checked out her knee and just shook his head.

Perlmutter came into her room and asked a lot of questions. For the most part Grace answered. On some subjects she was intentionally vague. It wasn't that she wanted to keep anything from the police. Or maybe, well, maybe she did.

Perlmutter was pretty vague too. Her dead captor's name was Eric Wu. He had been in prison. In Walden. That did not surprise Grace. Wade Larue had been in Walden too. It was all linked. That old photograph. Jack's group, Allaw. The Jimmy X Band. Wade Larue. And yes, even Eric Wu.

Perlmutter deflected most of her questions. She did not push it. Scott Duncan was in the room too. He stayed in the corner and did not speak.

Grace asked, "How did you know I was with this Eric Wu?"

Perlmutter clearly did not mind answering this one. "Do you know Charlaine Swain?"

"No."

"Her son, Clay, goes to Willard."

"Okay, right. I've met her."

Perlmutter filled her in on Charlaine Swain's own ordeal at the hands of Eric Wu. He was expansive on the subject, purposefully, Grace thought, so that he could keep mum about the rest of it. Perlmutter's cell phone rang. He excused himself and headed into the corridor. Grace was alone with Scott Duncan.

"What are they thinking?" she asked.

Scott came closer. "The popular theory is that Eric Wu was working for Wade Larue."

"How do they figure?"

"They know you went to Larue's press conference today, so that's link one. Wu and Larue were not only in Walden at the same time, but they were cell mates for three months."

"Link two," she said. "So what do they think Larue was after?"

"Revenge."

"On?"

"On you, for starters. You testified against him."

"I testified at his trial, but not really against him. I don't even re-member the stampede."

"Still. There is a solid link between Eric Wu and Wade Larue—we checked the prison phone records; they've been in touch—and there is a solid link between Larue and you."

"But even if Wade Larue was out for vengeance, why not take me? Why take Jack?"

"They think maybe Larue was trying to hurt you by hurting your family. Make you suffer."

She shook her head. "And that weird photograph arriving? How do they figure that into the mix? Or your sister's murder? Or Shane Alworth or Sheila Lambert? Or Bob Dodd getting killed in New Hampshire?"

"It is a theory," Duncan said, "with lots of holes. But remember—and this plugs most of them—they don't see all these connections the way we do. My sister may have been murdered fifteen years ago, but that doesn't have anything to do with now. Neither does Bob Dodd, a reporter who was shot gangland style. For now they're keeping it simple: Wu gets out of jail. He grabs your husband. Maybe he would have grabbed others—who knows?"

"And the reason he didn't just kill Jack?"

"Wu was holding him until Wade Larue is released."

"Which was today."

"Right, today. Then Wu grabs you both. He was taking you to Larue when you escaped."

"So Larue could, what, kill us himself?"

Duncan shrugged.

"That doesn't make sense, Scott. Eric Wu broke my ribs because he wanted to know how I got that photograph. He stopped because he got an unexpected call. Then he suddenly packed us in that car. None of that was planned."

"Perlmutter just learned all that. They may now alter their theory."

"And where is Wade Larue anyway?"

"No one seems to know. They're searching for him."

Grace dropped back on her pillow. Her bones felt so damned heavy. The tears started flooding her eyes. "How bad is Jack?"

"Bad."

"Is he going to live?"

"They don't know."

"Don't let them lie to me."

"I won't, Grace. But try to get some sleep, okay?"

In the corridor Perlmutter spoke to the captain of the Airmont Police Department, Anthony Dellapelle. They were still combing through the home of Beatrice Smith.

"We just checked the basement," Dellapelle said. "Someone was kept locked up down there."

"Jack Lawson. We know that."

Dellapelle paused and said, "Maybe."

"What's that supposed to mean?"

"There's still a set of handcuffs against a pipe."

"Wu unlocked him. He probably left them there."

"That could be. There's also blood down there—not much of it, but it's fairly fresh."

"Lawson had some cuts on him."

There was a pause.

"What's going on?" Perlmutter asked.

"Where are you right now, Stu?"

"Valley Hospital."

"How long would it take you to get here?"

"Fifteen minutes with the sirens," Perlmutter said. "Why?"

"There's something else down here," Dellapelle said. "Something you might want to see for yourself."

At midnight Grace pulled herself out of bed and started down the corridor. Her children had visited briefly. Grace insisted that they let her get out of bed for that. Scott Duncan bought her some regular clothes—an Adidas sweat suit—because she did not want to greet her children in a hospital gown. She took a major pain injection to quiet the screaming in her ribs. Grace wanted the children to see that she was all right, that she was safe, that they were safe. She put on a brave face that lasted right up until the moment she saw that Emma had brought her poetry journal. Then she started crying.

You can only be strong for so long.

The children were spending the night in their own beds. Cora would stay in the master bedroom. Cora's daughter, Vickie, would sleep in the bed next to Emma. Perlmutter had assigned a female cop to stay the night too. Grace was grateful.

The hospital was dark now. Grace managed to stand upright. It took her forever. The hot scream was back in her ribs. Her knee felt more like shards of shattered glass than a joint.

The corridor was quiet. Grace had a specific destination in mind. Someone would try to stop her, she was sure, but that didn't really concern her. She was determined.

"Grace?"

She turned toward the female voice, readying to do battle. But that wouldn't be the case here. Grace recognized the woman from the playground. "You're Charlaine Swain."

The woman nodded. They moved toward each other, eyes locked, sharing something neither one of them could really articulate.

"I guess I owe you a thanks," Grace said.

"Vice versa," Charlaine said. "You killed him. The nightmare is over for us."

"How is your husband?" Grace asked.

"He's going to be fine."

Grace nodded.

Charlaine said, "I hear yours isn't doing well." They were both beyond phony platitudes. Grace appreciated the honesty.

"He's in a coma."

"Have you seen him?"

"I'm going there now."

"Sneaking in?"

"Yes."

Charlaine nodded. "Let me help you."

Grace leaned on Charlaine Swain. The woman was strong. The corridor was empty. In the distance they heard the sharp clack of heels on tile. The lights were low. They passed an empty nurses' station and got into the elevator. Jack was on the third floor, in intensive care. Having Charlaine Swain with her felt oddly right to Grace. She could not say why.

This particular section of the intensive care unit had four rooms with glass walls. A nurse sat in the middle, thus able to monitor them all at once, but right now, only one room had a patient in it.

They both pulled up. Jack was in the bed. The first thing Grace noticed was that her powerful husband, the gruff six-two hunk who'd always made her feel safe, looked so small and fragile in that bed. She knew that it was her imagination. It had only been two days. He had lost some weight. He had been totally dehydrated. But that wasn't what this was.

Jack's eyes were closed. He had a tube coming out of his throat. There was another tube in his mouth. Both were taped with white adhesive. Yet another tube was in his nose. Still another in his right arm. There was an IV. There were machines surrounding him, straight out of some futuristic nightmare.

Grace felt herself starting to fall. Charlaine held her up. Grace steadied herself and moved toward the door.

The nurse said, "You can't go in there."

"She just wants to sit with him," Charlaine said. "Please."

The nurse glanced around, then back at Grace. "Two minutes."

Grace let go of Charlaine. Charlaine pushed open the door for her. Grace went in alone. There were beeps and dings and a hellish sound like drops of water being sucked up a straw. Grace sat down next to the bed. She did not reach for Jack's hand. She did not kiss Jack's cheek.

"You're going to love the last verse," Grace said.

She opened Emma's journal and started reading:

> "Baseball, baseball,
> Who's your best friend?
> Is it the bat,
> Who hits your rear end?"

Grace laughed and turned the page, but the next page—in fact, the rest of the journal—was blank.

CHAPTER 50

A few minutes before Wade Larue died, he thought he had finally found true peace.

He had let vengeance go. He no longer needed to know the full truth. He knew enough. He knew where he was to blame and where he was not. It was time to put it behind him.

Carl Vespa had no choice. He would never be able to recover. The same was true for that awful swirl of faces—that blur of grief—he had been forced to see in the courtroom and again today at the press conference. Wade had lost time. But time is relative. Death is not.

He had told Vespa all he knew. Vespa was a bad man, no doubt about it. The man was capable of unspeakable cruelty. Over the past fifteen years Wade Larue had met a lot of people like that, but few were that simple. With the exception of full-blown psychopaths, most people, even our most evil, have the ability to love someone, to care about them, to make connections. That was not inconsistent. That was simply human.

Larue spoke. Vespa listened. Sometime in the middle of his explanation, Cram appeared with a towel and ice. He handed it to Larue. Larue thanked him. He took the towel—the ice would be too bulky—and dabbed the blood off his face. Vespa's blows no longer hurt. Larue had dealt with much worse over the years. When you've had enough beatings, you go one way or the other—you fear them so much that you will do anything to avoid them, or you just ride them out and realize that this too shall pass. Somewhere during his incarceration Larue had joined that second camp.

Carl Vespa did not say a word. He did not interrupt or ask for clarification. When Larue finished Vespa stood there, his face unchanged, waiting for more. There was nothing. Without a word Vespa turned and left. He nodded at Cram. Cram started toward Larue, who lifted his head. He would not run. He was through with running.

"Come on, let's go," Cram said.

Cram dropped him off in the center of Manhattan. Larue debated calling Eric Wu, but he knew that would be pointless at this stage. He started toward the Port Authority Bus Terminal. He was ready now for the rest of his life to begin. He was going to head to Portland, Oregon. He wasn't sure why. He had read about Portland in prison and it seemed to fit the bill. He wanted a big city with a liberal feel. From what he'd read, Portland sounded like a hippie commune that had turned into a major metropolis. He might get a fair shake out there.

He would have to change his name. Grow a beard. Dye his hair. He didn't think it would take that much to change him, to help him escape the past fifteen years. Naïve to think it, yes, but Wade Larue still thought that an acting career was a possibility. He still had the chops. He still had the supernatural charisma. So why not give it a go? If not, he'd get a regular job. He wasn't afraid of a little hard work. He'd be in a big city again. He'd be free.

But Wade Larue didn't go to the Port Authority bus station.

The past still had too strong a pull. He couldn't go quite yet. He stopped a block away. He saw the buses churning out to the viaduct. He watched for a moment and then turned to the row of pay phones.

He had to make one last phone call. He had to know one last truth.

Now, an hour later, the barrel of a gun was pressed against that soft hollow under his ear. It was funny what you thought of a moment before death. The soft hollow—that was one of Eric Wu's favorite pressure-point spots. Wu had explained to him that knowing the location was fairly meaningless. You could not just stick your finger in there and push. That might hurt, but it would never incapacitate an opponent.

That was it. That pitiful thought, beyond pitiful, was Wade Larue's last before the bullet entered his brain and ended his life.

CHAPTER 51

Dellapelle led Perlmutter into the basement. There was enough light, but Dellapelle still used the flashlight. He pointed it at the floor. "There."

Perlmutter stared down at the concrete and felt a fresh chill.

"You thinking what I'm thinking?" Dellapelle asked him.

"That maybe"—Perlmutter stopped, trying to figure this into the equation—"that maybe Jack Lawson wasn't the only one being held down here."

Dellapelle nodded. "So where is the other guy?"

Perlmutter did not say anything. He just stared at the floor. Someone had indeed been held down. Someone who found a pebble and scratched two words into the floor, all in caps. A name actually, another person from that strange photograph, a name he'd just heard from Grace Lawson:

SHANE ALWORTH

Charlaine Swain stayed to help Grace back to her room. Their silence was comfortable. Grace wondered about that. She wondered about a lot of things. She wondered why Jack had run away all those years ago. She wondered why he'd never touched that trust fund, why he let his sister and father control his percentage. She wondered why he'd run away not long after the Boston Massacre. She wondered about Geri Duncan and why she ended up dead two months later. And she wondered, perhaps most of all, if meeting Jack in France that day, if falling in love with him, had been more than just a coincidence.

She no longer wondered if it was all connected. She knew that it was. When they reached Grace's room, Charlaine helped her get back into bed. She turned to go.

"Do you want to stay a few minutes?" Grace asked.

Charlaine nodded. "I'd like that."

They talked. They started with what they had in common— children—but it was clear neither one of them wanted to stay on the subject long. An hour passed in a moment. Grace was not sure what they'd even discussed exactly. Just that she was grateful.

At nearly two in the morning the hospital phone next to Grace rang. For a moment they both just stared at it. Then Grace reached over and picked it up.

"Hello?"

"I got your message. About Allaw and Still Night."

She recognized the voice. It was Jimmy X.

"Where are you?"

"In the hospital. I'm downstairs. They won't let me up."

"I'll be down in a minute."

The hospital lobby was quiet.

Grace was not sure how to handle this. Jimmy X sat with his fore-arms resting against his thighs. He didn't look up as she hobbled toward him. The receptionist read a magazine. The security guard whistled softly. Grace wondered if the guard would be able to protect her. She suddenly missed that gun.

She stopped in front of Jimmy X, stood over him, and waited. He looked up. Their eyes met and Grace knew. She didn't know the details. She barely knew the outline. But she knew.

His voice was almost a plea. "How did you learn about Allaw?"

"My husband."

Jimmy looked confused.

"My husband is Jack Lawson."

His jaw dropped. "John?"

"That's what he went by back then, I guess. He's upstairs right now. He may very well die."

"Oh God." Jimmy buried his face in his hands.

Grace said, "You know what always bothered me?"

He did not reply.

"Your running away. It doesn't happen very much—a rock star just giving up like that. There are rumors about Elvis or Jim Morrison, but that's because they're dead. There was that movie *Eddie and the Cruisers,* but that was a movie. In reality, well, like I said before, the Who didn't run away after Cincinnati. The Stones didn't after Altamont Speedway. So why, Jimmy? Why did you run?"

He kept his head low.

"I know about the Allaw connection. It's just a matter of time before someone puts it together."

She waited. He dropped his hands away from his face and rubbed them together. He looked toward the security guard. Grace almost took a step back, but she held her ground.

"Do you know why rock concerts used to always start so late?" Jimmy asked.

The question threw her. "What?"

"I said . . ."

"I heard what you said. No, I don't know why."

"It's because we're so wasted—drunk, stoned, whatever—that our handlers need time to get us sobered up enough to perform."

"Your point being?"

"That night I nearly passed out from cocaine and alcohol." His gaze drifted off then, his eyes red. "That's why there was such a long delay. That was why the crowd got so impatient. If I had been sober, if I had taken the stage on time . . ." He let his voice drift off with a "who knows" shrug.

She didn't want excuses anymore. "Tell me about Allaw."

"I can't believe it." He shook his head. "John Lawson is your husband? How the hell did that happen?"

She didn't have an answer. She wondered if she ever would. The heart, she knew, was strange terrain. Could that have been part of the initial attraction, something subconscious, a knowing that they had both survived that terrible night? She flashed back to meeting Jack on that beach. Had it been fate, preordained—or planned? Did Jack want to meet the woman who had come to embody the Boston Massacre?

"Was my husband at the concert that night?" she asked.

"What, you don't know?"

"We can play this two ways, Jimmy. One, I can pretend I know everything and just want confirmation. But I don't. I may never know the truth, if you don't tell me. You may be able to keep your secret. But I'll keep looking. So will Carl Vespa and the Garrisons and the Reeds and the Weiders."

He looked up, his face so like a child's.

"But two—and I think this is more important—you can't live with yourself anymore. You came to my house needing absolution. You know it's time."

He lowered his head. Grace heard the sobs. They racked his body. Grace did not say a word. She did not put a hand on his shoulder. The security guard glanced over. The receptionist looked up from her magazine. But that was all. This was a hospital. Adults weeping were hardly foreign in this environment. They both looked away. A minute later Jimmy's sobs started to quiet. His shoulders no longer shook.

"We met at a gig in Manchester," Jimmy said, wiping his nose with his sleeve. "I was with a group called Still Night. There were four bands on the roster. One of them was Allaw. That's how I met your husband. We hung out backstage, getting stoned. He was charming and all, but you have to understand. For me the music was everything. I wanted to make *Born to Run*, you know. I wanted to change the landscape of music. I ate, slept, dreamed, shat music. Lawson didn't take it too seriously. The band was fun, that's all. They had some decent songs, but the vocals and arrangements were totally amateur. Lawson didn't have any grand illusions about making it big or anything."

The security guard was whistling again. The receptionist had her nose back in the magazine. A car drove up to the entrance. The guard headed outside and pointed toward the ER.

"Allaw broke up a few months later, I think. So did Still Night. But Lawson and I stayed in touch. When I started up the Jimmy X Band, I almost thought of asking him to join."

"Why didn't you?"

"I didn't think he was that good a musician."

Jimmy stood so suddenly that he startled Grace. She took a step back. She kept her eyes on him, still searching to make eye contact, as if that alone could keep him in place.

"Yeah, your husband was at the concert that night. I got him five tickets in the front pit. He brought some of his old band members with him. He even brought a couple backstage."

He stopped then. They stood there. He looked off and for a moment Grace feared that she was losing him.

"Do you remember who they were?" she asked.

"The old band members?"

"Yes."

"Two girls. One had this bright red hair."

Sheila Lambert. "Was the other girl Geri Duncan?"

"I never knew her name."

"How about Shane Alworth? Was he there?"

"Was that the guy on guitar?"

"Yes."

"Not backstage. I only saw Lawson and the two girls."

He shut his eyes.

"What happened, Jimmy?"

His face sagged and he suddenly looked older. "I was pretty wasted. I could hear the crowd. Twenty thousand strong. They would chant my name. They would clap. Anything to get the concert started. But I could barely move. My manager came in. I told him I'd need more time. He left. I was alone. And then Lawson and those two chicks came into the room."

Jimmy blinked and looked at Grace. "Is there a cafeteria in this place?"

"It's closed."

"I could use a cup of coffee."

"Tough."

Jimmy started pacing.

Grace asked, "What happened after they came in the room?"

"I don't know how they got backstage. I never gave them passes. But all of a sudden Lawson comes up to me and is all 'hey, how's it going?' I was happy to see him, I guess. But then, I don't know, something went really wrong."

"What?"

"Lawson. He went crazy. I don't know. He must have been higher than I was. He started pushing me, making threats. He shouted that I was a thief."

"A thief?"

Jimmy nodded. "It was all nonsense. He said . . ." He finally stayed still and met her eyes. "He said I stole his song."

"What song?"

" 'Pale Ink.' "

Grace could not move. The tremor started moving down her left side. There was a flutter in her chest.

"Lawson and that other guy, Alworth, wrote this song for Allaw called 'Invisible Ink.' That was pretty much the only similarity between the songs. That part of the title. You know the lyrics to 'Pale Ink,' right?"

She nodded. She didn't even try to speak.

" 'Invisible Ink' had a similar theme, I guess. Both about how fragile memory can be. But that was it. I told John that. But he was just out of his mind. Whatever I said just pissed him off more. He kept pushing me. One of the girls, she had this really dark hair, was egging him on too. She started saying they'd break my legs or something. I called for help. Lawson punched me. You remember the reports that I was injured in the melee?"

She nodded again.

"I wasn't. It was your husband. He hit my jaw, and then he jumped me. I tried to push him off. He started shouting how he was going to kill me. It was, I don't know, the whole thing was surreal. He said he was going to cut me up."

The flutter expanded and grew cold. Grace was holding her breath. This couldn't be. Please, this just couldn't be.

"By now it was just so out of hand, one of the girls, the redhead, told him to calm down. It's not worth it, she said. She pleaded with him to forget it. But he wasn't listening. He just smiled at me and then . . . then he took out a knife."

Grace shook her head.

"He said he was going to stab me in the heart. You remember how I said I was stoned out of my mind? Well, that sobered me up. You want to sober someone up? Threaten to stick a knife in their chest." He went quiet again.

"What did you do?"

Had she spoken? Grace wasn't sure. The voice sounded like hers, but it seemed as though it'd come from someplace else, someplace tinny and distant.

Jimmy's face, lost in the memory, went slack. "I wasn't going to just let him stab me. So I jumped him. He dropped the knife. We started wrestling. The girls were screaming now. They came over and tried to pull us apart. And then, when we were on the floor like that, I heard a gunshot."

Grace was still shaking her head. Not Jack. Jack wasn't there that night, no way, no chance at all. . . .

"It was so loud, you know? Like the gun was behind my ear or something. All hell broke loose then. There were screams. And then there were two, maybe three more shots. Not in the room. They were from far away. I heard more screams. Lawson stopped moving. There was blood on the floor. He'd been hit in the back. I pushed him off and then I saw that security guard, Gordon MacKenzie, still pointing his gun."

Grace closed her eyes. "Wait a second. Are you telling me Gordon MacKenzie fired the first shot?"

Jimmy nodded. "He heard the commotion, heard me calling for help and . . ." Again his voice trailed off. "We just stared at each other for a second. The girls were screaming, but by now they were being drowned out by the crowd. That sound, I don't know, people talk about the most terrible sound, like maybe it's a wounded animal, but I've never heard anything that comes close to the sound of fear and panic. But you know that."

She didn't. The head trauma had wiped out the memory. But she nodded so that he'd keep talking.

"Anyway, MacKenzie stood there for a second, stunned. And then he just ran. The two girls grabbed Lawson and started dragging him out." He shrugged. "You know the rest, Grace."

She tried to take it all in. She tried to understand the implications, tried to fit it into her own reality. She had been standing yards away from all this, the other side of the stage. Jack. Her husband. He'd been right there. How could that be?

"No," she said.

"No what?"

"No, I don't know the rest, Jimmy."

He said nothing.

"The story didn't end there. Allaw had four members. I've been checking out the time line. Two months after the stampede someone hired a hit man to kill one of the members, Geri Duncan. My husband, the one who you say attacked you, ran overseas, shaved his beard, and started going by Jack. According to Shane Alworth's mother, he's out of the country too, but I think she's lying about that. Sheila Lambert, the redhead, changed her name. Her husband was recently murdered and she disappeared again."

Jimmy shook his head. "I don't know anything about any of that."

"You think it's all just a big coincidence?"

"No, I guess not," Jimmy said. "Maybe they were scared of what would happen if the truth came out. You remember what it was like those first few months—everyone wanting blood. They could have gone to jail, maybe worse."

Grace shook her head. "And what about you, Jimmy?"

"What about me?"

"Why did you keep this secret all these years?"

He said nothing.

"If what you just told me is true, you didn't do anything wrong. You were the one attacked. Why didn't you just tell the police what happened?"

He opened his mouth, closed it, tried again. "This was bigger than me. Gordon MacKenzie was part of it, too. He came out the hero, remember? If the world ever learned that he fired that first shot, what do you think would have happened to him?"

"Are you saying you lied all these years to protect Gordon MacKenzie?"

He didn't reply.

"Why, Jimmy? Why didn't you say anything? Why did you run away?"

His eyes started shifting. "Look, I told you everything I know. I'm going home now."

Grace moved closer. "You did steal that song, didn't you?"

"What? No."

But she saw it now. "That was why you felt responsible. You stole that song. If you hadn't, none of this would have happened."

He just kept shaking his head. "That's not it."

"That's why you ran away. It wasn't just that you were stoned. You stole the song that made you. That was where it all started. You heard Allaw play in Manchester. You liked their song. You stole it."

He shook his head, but there was nothing behind it. "There were similarities. . . ."

And another thought struck her with a deep, hard pang: "How far would you go to keep your secret, Jimmy?"

He looked at her.

" 'Pale Ink' became even bigger after the stampede. That album ended up selling millions. Who has that money?"

He shook his head. "You're wrong, Grace."

"Did you already know I was married to Jack Lawson?"

"What? Of course not."

"Is that why you came by my house that night? Were you trying to figure out what I knew?"

He kept shaking his head, tears on his cheeks. "That's not true. I never meant to hurt anyone."

"Who killed Geri Duncan?"

"I don't know anything about that."

"Was she going to talk? Is that what happened? And then, fifteen years later, someone goes after Sheila Lambert aka Jillian Dodd, but her husband gets in the way. Was she going to talk, Jimmy? Did she know you were back?"

"I have to go."

She stepped in his path. "You can't run away again. There's been too much of that."

"I know," he said, his voice a plea. "I know that better than anyone."

He pushed past her and ran outside. Grace was tempted to yell, "Stop! Grab him!" but she doubted the whistling guard would be able to do much. Jimmy was already outside, almost out of sight. She limped after him.

Gunshots—three of them—shattered the night. There was the squeal of tires. The receptionist dropped her magazine and picked up the phone. The security guard stopped whistling and sprinted toward the door. Grace hurried behind him.

When Grace got outside, she saw a car shoot down the exit ramp and disappear into the night. Grace had not seen who was in the car. But she thought she knew. The security guard bent down over the body. Two doctors ran out, nearly knocking Grace down. But it was too late.

Fifteen years after the stampede began, the Boston Massacre claimed its most elusive victim.

CHAPTER 52

Maybe, Grace thought, we are not supposed to know the entire truth. And maybe the truth does not matter.

There were plenty of questions in the end. Grace thought that she would never know all the answers. Too many of the players were dead now.

Jimmy X, real name James Xavier Farmington, died from three gunshot wounds to the chest.

Wade Larue's body was found near the Port Authority Bus Terminal in New York City less than twenty-four hours after his release. He'd been shot in the head at point-blank range. There was only one significant clue: A reporter for the *New York Daily News* managed to follow Wade Larue after he left the press conference at the Crowne Plaza. According to the reporter, Larue got into a black sedan with a man fitting Cram's description. That was the last time anyone saw Larue alive.

No arrests had been made, but the answer seemed clear.

Grace tried to understand what Carl Vespa had done. Fifteen years had passed, and his son was still dead. Weird to put it that way, but maybe it was apropos. For Vespa, nothing had changed. Time had not been enough.

Captain Perlmutter would try to make a case against him. But Vespa was pretty good about covering his tracks.

Both Perlmutter and Duncan came to the hospital after Jimmy was killed. Grace told them everything. There was nothing to hide anymore. Perlmutter mentioned almost in passing that the words *Shane Alworth* had been scratched into the concrete floor.

"So what does that mean?" Grace asked.

"We're checking the physical evidence, but maybe your husband wasn't alone in that basement."

It made sense, Grace guessed. Fifteen years later they were all coming back. Everyone in that photograph.

At four in the morning Grace was back in her hospital bed. Her room was dark when the door opened. A silhouette slid in quietly. He thought that she was asleep. For a moment Grace didn't say anything. She waited until he was in the chair again, just like fifteen years ago, before she said, "Hello, Carl."

"How are you feeling?" Vespa asked.

"Did you kill Jimmy X?"

There was a long pause. The shadow did not move. "What happened that night," he said at last, "it was his fault."

"It's hard to know."

Vespa's face was no more than a shadow. "You see too many shades of gray."

Grace tried to sit up, but her rib cage would not cooperate. "How did you find out about Jimmy?"

"From Wade Larue," he said.

"You killed him too."

"Do you want to make accusations, Grace, or do you want to know the truth?"

She wanted to ask if that was all he wanted, the truth, but she knew the answer. The truth would never be enough. Vengeance and justice would never be enough.

"Wade Larue reached out to me the day before he was released," Vespa said. "He asked if we could talk."

"Talk about what?"

"He wouldn't say. I had Cram pick him up in the city. He came out to my house. He started in with some touchy-feely crap about understanding my pain. He said he was suddenly all at peace with himself, that he didn't want vengeance anymore. I didn't want to hear any of that. I wanted him to get to the point."

"Did he?"

"Yes." The shadow was still again. Grace debated reaching for the light switch and decided against it. "He told me that Gordon MacKenzie had visited him in prison three months ago. Do you know why?"

Grace nodded, seeing it now. "MacKenzie had terminal cancer."

"Right. He was still hoping to buy a last-minute ticket to the Promised Land. All of a sudden he can't live with what he's done." Vespa cocked his head and smiled. "Amazing how that happens right before you're going to die anyway, isn't it? Ironic timing when you think about it. He confesses when there is no personal cost, and hey, if you buy into that confess-and-forgive nonsense, there could be a big upside."

Grace knew not to comment. She stayed still.

"Anyway, Gordon MacKenzie took the blame. He was working the backstage entrance. He let some pretty young thing distract him. He said that Lawson and two girls sneaked past him. You know all this, don't you?"

"Some of it."

"You know that MacKenzie shot your husband?"

"Yes."

"And that's what started the riot. MacKenzie met up with Jimmy X after the whole thing went down. They both agreed to keep it quiet. They worried a little about Jack's injury or if those girls were going to come forward, but hey, those three had plenty to lose too."

"So everyone just kept quiet."

"Pretty much. MacKenzie became a hero. He got a job with the Boston police from that. He rose to captain. All off his heroics from that night."

"So what did Larue do after MacKenzie confessed all this?"

"What do you think? He wanted the truth to come out. He wanted vengeance and exoneration."

"So why didn't Larue tell anyone?"

"Oh, he did." Vespa smiled. "Three guesses who."

Grace saw it. "He told his lawyer."

Vespa spread his hands. "Give the lady a Kewpie doll."

"But how did Sandra Koval convince him to keep quiet?"

"Oh, this part is brilliant. Somehow—and let's give the lady credit—she did what was best for her client *and* her brother."

"How?"

"She told Larue that he'd have a better chance of getting out on parole if he didn't tell the truth."

"I don't understand."

"You don't know much about parole, do you?"

She shrugged.

"You see, the parole board doesn't want to hear that you're innocent. They want to hear your mea culpas. If you want to get out, you have to hang your head in shame. You did wrong, you tell them. You've accepted blame—that's the first step toward rehabilitation. If you keep insisting you're innocent, you're not going to get better."

"Couldn't MacKenzie testify?"

"He was too ill by then. You see, Larue's innocence wasn't the parole board's concern. If Larue wanted to take that route, he'd have to request a new trial. It would take months, maybe years. According to Sandra Koval—and she was telling the truth here—Larue's best chance of getting out was to admit his guilt."

"And she was right," Grace said.

"Yes."

"And Larue never knew that Sandra and Jack were brother and sister?"

Again Vespa spread his hands. "How would he?"

Grace shook her head.

"But, you see, it's not over for Wade Larue. He still wants vengeance and exoneration. He just knows he'll have to wait until he's out of jail. The question is, how? He knows the truth, but how will he prove it? Who will, pardon the expression, feel his wrath? Who is really to blame for what happened that night?"

Grace nodded as something else fell into place. "So he went after Jack."

"The one who pulled the knife, yep. So Larue got his old prison buddy Eric Wu to grab your husband. Larue's plan was to hook up with Wu the moment he got released. He'd make Jack tell the truth, film it, and then, he wasn't sure, but probably kill him."

"Find exoneration and then commit murder?"

Vespa shrugged. "He was angry, Grace. He might have ended up just beating him up or breaking his legs. Who knows?"

"So what happened?"

"Wade Larue had a change of heart."

Grace frowned.

"You should have heard him talk about it. His eyes were so clear. I'd just punched him in the face. I'd kicked him and threatened his life. But the peace on his face . . . it just stayed there. The moment Larue was free, he realized that he would be able to get past it."

"What do you mean, past it?"

"Exactly that. His punishment was in the past. He could never really be exonerated because he wasn't blameless. He fired shots in the middle of the crowd. That raised the hysteria level. But more than that, it was like he told me: He was truly free. Nothing was left to tie him to the past. He was no longer in prison, but my son would always be dead. You see?"

"I think so."

"Larue just wanted to live his life. He was also afraid of what I'd do to him. So he wanted to trade. He told me the truth. He gave me Wu's number. And in exchange, I'd leave him alone."

"So it was you who called Wu?"

"Actually Larue made the call. But yes, I spoke to him."

"And you told Wu to bring us to you?"

"I didn't realize you were there. I thought it was just Jack."

"What was your plan, Carl?"

He said nothing.

"Would you have killed Jack too?"

"Does it matter anymore?"

"And what would you have done with me?"

He took his time. "There were things that made me wonder," he said.

"About?"

"About you."

Seconds passed. There were footsteps in the corridor. A stretcher with a squeaky wheel rolled past the door. Grace listened to the sound recede. She tried to slow her breath.

"Here you were nearly killed in the Boston Massacre—yet you end up marrying the man responsible for it all. I also know that Jimmy X came to visit your house after we saw him at that rehearsal. You never told me about that. And then there's the fact that you remember so little of what happened. Not just that night, but for almost a week before."

She tried to keep her breaths even. "You thought—"

"I didn't know what to think. But now maybe I do. I think your husband is a good man who made a terrible mistake. I think he ran away after the stampede. I think he felt guilty. That was why he wanted to meet you. He saw the press reports and wanted to know you were okay. Maybe he even planned on apologizing. So he found you on the beach in France. And then he fell in love with you."

She closed her eyes and leaned back.

"It's over now, Grace."

They sat in silence. There was nothing else to say. A few minutes later Vespa stole out, silent as the night.

CHAPTER 53

But it wasn't over.

Four days passed. Grace got better. She went home that first afternoon. Cora and Vickie stayed with her and the children. Cram came by that first day too, but Grace asked him to leave. He nodded and complied.

The media went crazy, of course. They only knew bits and pieces, but the fact that the notorious Jimmy X had resurfaced only to be murdered had been enough to send them into a state of total derangement. Perlmutter set up a patrol car in front of Grace's house. Emma and Max still went to school. Grace spent most of her days in the hospital with Jack. Charlaine Swain kept her company a lot.

Grace thought about the photograph that started it all. She now figured that one of the four members of Allaw had found a way to get it in her packet. Why? That was harder to answer. Perhaps one of them realized that the eighteen ghosts would never sleep.

But then there was the question of timing: Why now? Why after fifteen years?

There was no shortage of possibilities. It could have been the release of Wade Larue. It could have been the death of Gordon MacKenzie. It could have been all the anniversary coverage. But most likely, what made the most sense, was that the return of Jimmy X set everything in motion.

Who really was to blame for what happened that tragic night? Was it Jimmy for stealing the song? Jack for attacking him? Gordon Mac-Kenzie for firing a weapon under those circumstances? Wade Larue for illegally carrying a gun, panicking, and firing more shots into an already frenzied crowd? Grace did not know. Small ripples. All of this carnage had not started with some big conspiracy. It had started with two small-time bands playing some dive in Manchester.

There were still holes, of course. Lots of them. But they would have to wait.

There are some things more important than the truth.

Now, right now, Grace stared at Jack. He lay still in his hospital bed. His doctor, a man named Stan Walker, sat next to her. Dr. Walker folded his hands and used his gravest voice. Grace listened. Emma and Max waited in the corridor. They wanted to be there. Grace didn't know what to do. What was the call on this one?

She wished that she could ask Jack.

She did not want to ask him why he had lied to her for so long. She did not want an explanation for what he had done that terrible night. She did not want to ask him how he'd happened by her on the beach that day, if he had been intentionally seeking her out, if that was why they fell in love. She didn't want to ask Jack any of that.

She only wanted to ask him one last question: Did he want his children by his bedside when he died?

In the end Grace let them stay. The four of them gathered as a family for the last time. Emma cried. Max sat there, his eyes trained on the tile floor. And then, with a gentle tug at her heart, Grace felt Jack leave for good.

CHAPTER 54

The funeral was a major blur. Grace usually wore contact lenses. She took them out that day and did not wear her glasses. Everything seemed a little easier to handle in the blur. She sat in the front pew and thought about Jack. She did not picture him in the vineyards or on the beach anymore. The sight she remembered best, the sight she would always carry with her, was Jack holding Emma after she was born, the way his big hands held the little wonder, carrying her as if afraid she'd break, scared he might hurt her, the way he turned to Grace and looked at her in pure awe. That was what she saw.

The rest, all she now knew about his past, was white noise.

Sandra Koval came to the funeral. She stayed in the back. She apologized that their father could not come. He was elderly and ill. Grace said that she understood. The two women did not embrace. Scott Duncan was there. So were Stu Perlmutter and Cora. Grace had no idea how many people showed up. She didn't much care either. She held her two children and fought her way through it.

Two weeks later the children went back to school. There were issues, of course. Both Emma and Max were suffering separation anxieties. That was normal, she knew. Grace walked them to school. She was there before the bell rang to pick them up. They were hurting. That, Grace knew, was the price you paid for having a kind and loving father. The hurt never goes away.

But now it was time to end this.

Jack's autopsy.

Some would say that the autopsy, when she read and understood it, was what sent Grace's world off-kilter again. But that really wasn't it. The autopsy was merely independent confirmation of what she already knew. Jack had been her husband. She had loved him. They had been together for thirteen years. They had two children together. And while he had clearly kept secrets, there were some things a man cannot hide.

Some things must truly remain on the surface.

So Grace knew.

She knew his body. She knew his skin. She knew every muscle on his back. So she really did not need the autopsy. She did not need to see the results of the full-exterior examination to tell her what she already knew.

Jack had no major scars.

And that meant that—despite what Jimmy had said, despite what Gordon MacKenzie had told Wade Larue—Jack had never been shot.

First Grace visited the Fotomat and found Fuzz Pellet Josh. Then she drove back down to Bedminster, to the condominium development where Shane Alworth's mother resided. After that, she plowed through the legal work on Jack's family trust. Grace knew a lawyer from Livingston who now worked as a sports agent in Manhattan. He set up plenty of trusts for his wealthy athletes. He went through the paperwork and explained enough for her to understand.

And then, when she had all the facts pretty much down, she visited Sandra Koval, her dear sister-in-law, at the offices of Burton and Crimstein in New York City.

Sandra Koval did not meet her in the reception are. was inspecting the photo gallery, stopping again at the tler, Little Pocahontas, when a peasant-bloused woman t   ome this way. She led Grace down the corridor and into the exact same conference room where she and Sandra had first talked a lifetime ago.

"Ms. Koval will be with you shortly."

"Great."

She left her alone. The room was set up exactly the same as last time, except now there was a yellow legal pad and a Bic pen in front of each seat. Grace did not want to sit. She did her own version of a pace, more a limp-pace, and ran it over in her head again. Her cell phone buzzed. She spoke briefly and then snapped it off. She kept it close. Just in case.

"Hi, Grace."

Sandra Koval swept into the room like a turbulent weather front. She headed straight for the little refrigerator, opened it and peered inside.

"Can I get you something to drink?"

"No."

With her head still in the minifridge, she asked, "How are the children?"

Grace did not reply. Sandra Koval dug out a Perrier. She twisted the top off and sat.

"So what's up?"

Should she test the temperature with her toe or just jump in? Grace chose the latter. "You didn't take on Wade Larue as a client because of me," she began without preamble. "You took him on because you wanted to stay close to him."

Sandra Koval poured the Perrier into a glass. "That might— hypothetically—be true."

..1ypothetically?"

"Yes. I may, in a hypothetical world, have represented Wade Larue to protect a certain family member. But if I had, I would have still made sure that I represented my client to the best of my ability."

"Two birds with one stone?"

"Perhaps."

"And the certain family member. That would be your brother?"

"It would be possible."

"Possible," Grace said. "But that wasn't what happened here. You weren't out to protect your brother."

Their eyes met.

"I know," Grace said.

"Oh?" Sandra took a sip. "Then why don't you clue me in."

"You were, what, twenty-seven years old? Fresh out of law school and working as a criminal lawyer?"

"Yes."

"You were married. Your daughter was two years old. You were on your way to a promising career. And then your brother messed it all up for you. You were there that night, Sandra. At the Boston Garden. You were the other woman backstage, not Geri Duncan."

"I see," she said without a trace of worry. "And you know this how?"

"Jimmy X said one woman was a redhead—that's Sheila Lambert—and the other, the one who was egging him on, had dark hair. Geri Duncan was a blonde. You, Sandra, had dark hair."

She laughed. "And that's supposed to be proof of something?"

"No, not in and of itself. I'm not even sure it's relevant. Geri Duncan was probably there too. She might have been the one who distracted Gordon MacKenzie so you three could sneak backstage."

Sandra Koval gave her a vague wave of the hand. "Go on, this is interesting."

"Shall I just get to the heart of the matter?"

"Please do."

"According to both Jimmy X and Gordon MacKenzie, your brother was shot that night."

"He was," Sandra said. "He was in the hospital for three weeks."

"Which hospital?"

There was no hesitation, no eye twitch, no give at all. "Mass General."

Grace shook her head.

Sandra made a face. "Are you telling me you checked every hospital in the Boston area?"

"No need," Grace said. "There was no scar."

Silence.

"You see, the bullet wound would have left a scar, Sandra. It's simple logic. Your brother was shot. My husband had no scar. There's only one way that can be so." Grace put her hands on the table. They were quaking.

"I was never married to your brother."

Sandra Koval said nothing.

"Your brother, John Lawson, was shot that day. You and Sheila Lambert helped drag him out during the melee. But his wounds were lethal. At least I hope they were, because the alternative is that you killed him."

"And why would I do that?"

"Because if you took him to a hospital, they would have had to report the shooting. If you showed up with a dead body—or even if you just dumped him on the street—someone would investigate and realize where and how he was shot. You, the promising lawyer, were terrified. I bet Sheila Lambert was too. The world went crazy when this happened. The Boston DA—hell, Carl Vespa—was on television demanding blood. So were all the families. If you got caught up in that, you'd be arrested or worse."

Sandra Koval stayed quiet.

"Did you call your father? Did you ask him what to do? Did you contact one of your old criminal clients to help you? Or did you just get rid of the body on your own?"

She chuckled. "You have some imagination, Grace. Can I ask you something now?"

"Sure."

"If John Lawson died fifteen years ago, who did you marry?"

"I married *Jack* Lawson," Grace said, "who used to be known as Shane Alworth."

Eric Wu hadn't held two men in the basement, Grace now realized. Just one. One who had sacrificed himself to save her. One who probably knew that he was going to die and wanted to scratch out some last truth in the only way left to him.

Sandra Koval almost smiled. "That's a hell of a theory."

"One that will be easy to prove."

Sandra leaned back and folded her arms. "I don't understand something about your scenario. Why didn't I just hide my brother's body and pretend he ran away?"

"Too many people would ask questions," Grace said.

"But that's what happened to Shane Alworth and Sheila Lambert. They just disappeared."

"True enough," Grace admitted. "And maybe the answer has to do with your family trust."

That made Sandra's face freeze. "The trust?"

"I found the papers on the trust in Jack's desk. I took them to a friend who's a lawyer. It seems your grandfather set up six trusts. He had two children and four grandchildren. Forget the money for a second. Let's talk about voting power. All of you got equal voting shares, divided six ways, with your father getting the extra four percent. That way your side of the family kept control of the business, fifty-two percent to forty-eight. But—and I'm not good with this stuff so bear with me—Grandpa wanted to keep it all in the family. If any of you died before the age of twenty-five, the voting power would be divided equally among the five survivors. If your brother died the night of the concert, for example, that would mean that your side of the family, you and your father, would no longer hold a majority position."

"You're out of your mind."

"Could be," Grace said. "But tell me, Sandra. What drove you? Was it fear of being caught—or were you worried about losing control of the family business? Probably a combination of both. Either way, I know you got Shane Alworth to take your brother's place. It'll be easy to prove. We'll dig up old pictures. We can run a DNA test. I mean, it's over."

Sandra started drumming the table with her fingertips. "If that's true," she said, "the man you loved lied to you all these years."

"That's true no matter what," Grace said. "How did you get him to cooperate anyway?"

"That question is supposed to be rhetorical, right?"

Grace shrugged. "Mrs. Alworth tells me that they were dirt poor. His brother, Paul, couldn't afford college. She was living in a dump. But my guess is, you made a threat. If one member of Allaw went down for this, they all would. He probably thought he had no choice."

"Come on, Grace. Do you really think a poor kid like Shane Alworth could pull off being my brother?"

"How hard would it be? You and your father helped, I'm sure. Getting an ID would be no problem. You had your brother's birth certificate and the pertinent paperwork. You just say he had his wallet stolen. Screening was easier back then. He'd have gotten a new driver's license, new passport, whatever. You found a new trust lawyer in Boston—my friend noticed the change from the one in Los Angeles—someone who wouldn't know what John Lawson looked like. You, your dad, and Shane go in to his office together, all with proper ID—who would question that? Your brother had already graduated from Vermont University, so it wasn't like he'd have to show up there with a new face. Shane could go overseas now. If someone bumped into him, well, he'd go by Jack and just say he was another John Lawson. It's not an uncommon name."

Grace waited.

Sandra folded her arms. "Is this the part where I'm supposed to crack and confess everything?"

"You? No, I don't think so. But come on, you know it's over. It won't be any problem to prove that my husband wasn't your brother."

Sandra Koval took her time. "That may well be," she said, her words coming out more measured now. "But I'm not sure I see any crime here."

"How's that?"

"Let's say—again hypothetically—that you're right. Let's say I did get your husband to pretend to be my brother. That was fifteen years ago. There's a statute of limitations. My cousins might try to fight me on the trust issue, but they wouldn't want the scandal. We'd work it out. And even if what you said is true, my crime was hardly a big one. If I was at the concert that night, well, in the early days of that rabid frenzy, who could blame me for being scared?"

Grace's voice was soft. "I wouldn't blame you for that."

"Right. So there you go."

"And at first you didn't really do anything that terrible. You went to that concert seeking justice for your brother. You confronted a man who stole a song your brother and his friend wrote. That's not a crime. Things went wrong. Your brother died. There was nothing you could do to bring him back. So you did what you thought best. You played the terrible hand you were dealt."

Sandra Koval opened her arms. "Then what do you want here, Grace?"

"Answers, I guess."

"It seems as if you already got some of those." Then she raised her index finger and added, "Hypothetically speaking."

"And maybe I want justice."

"What justice? You just said yourself that what happened was understandable."

"That part," Grace said, her voice still soft. "If it ended there, yeah, I'd probably just walk away. But it didn't."

Sandra Koval sat back and waited.

"Sheila Lambert was scared too. She knew that her best move would be to change her name and disappear. You all agreed to disperse and stay silent. Geri Duncan, she stayed where she was. That was okay, at first. But then Geri found out she was pregnant."

Sandra just shut her eyes.

"When he agreed to be John Lawson, Shane, my Jack, had to cut all ties and go overseas. Geri Duncan couldn't find him. A month later she learns that she's pregnant. She's desperate to find the father. So she came to see you. She probably wanted to start anew. She wanted to tell the truth and have her baby with a clean slate. You knew my husband. He would never turn his back on her if she insisted on having a child. Maybe he'd want to wipe the slate clean too. And then what would happen to you, Sandra?"

Grace looked down at her hands. They were still shaking.

"So you had to silence Geri. You're a criminal defense attorney. You repped criminals. And one of them helped you find a hit man named Monte Scanlon."

Sandra said, "You can't prove any of this."

"The years pass," Grace went on. "My husband is now Jack Lawson." Grace stopped and remembered what Carl Vespa had said about Jack Lawson seeking her out. Something there still didn't mesh. "We have children now. I tell Jack I want to go back stateside. He doesn't want to. I push him on it. We have kids. I want to be back in the United States. That's my fault, I guess. I wish he had just told me the truth—"

"And how would you have reacted, Grace?"

She thought about it. "I don't know."

Sandra Koval smiled. "Neither, I guess, did he."

It was, Grace knew, a fair point, but this was not the time for that sort of contemplation. She pressed on. "We ended up moving to New

York. But I don't know what happened next, Sandra, so you're going to have to help me with this part. I think what with the anniversary and with Wade Larue coming free, Sheila Lambert—or maybe even Jack—decided it was time to tell the truth. Jack never slept well. Maybe they both needed to ease their guilt. I don't know. You couldn't go along with that, of course. They might be granted forgiveness but not you. You had Geri Duncan killed."

"And again I ask: The proof of that is . . . ?"

"We'll get to that," Grace said. "You've lied to me from the start, but you did tell the truth about one thing."

"Oh goodie." The sarcasm was thick now. "What was that?"

"When Jack saw that old picture in the kitchen, he did look up Geri Duncan on the computer. He found out she'd died in a fire, but he suspected it was no accident. So he called you. That was the nine-minute phone call. You were afraid he was about to crack, so you knew that you had to strike fast. You told Jack that you'd explain everything but not over the phone. You set up a meeting off the New York Thruway. Then you called Larue and told him that this would be a perfect time to get his revenge. You figured Larue would have Wu kill Jack, not hold him like that. You ended up, in fact, having to kill Larue to keep him quiet."

"I don't have to listen to this."

But Grace did not stop. "My big mistake was showing you the photograph that first day. Jack didn't know I'd made a copy. There it was, a photograph of your dead brother and the man who had claimed his identity for all the world to see. You needed to keep me quiet too. So you sent that guy, the one with my daughter's lunchbox, to scare me off. But I didn't listen. So you used Wu. He was supposed to find out what I knew and then kill me."

"Okay, I've had enough." Sandra Koval stood. "Get out of my office."

"Nothing to add?"

"I'm still waiting for proof."

"I don't really have any," Grace said. "But maybe you'll confess."

Sandra laughed at that one. "What, you don't think I know you're wired? I haven't said or done one thing that'll incriminate me."

"Look out the window, Sandra."

"What?"

"The window. Look down at the sidewalk. Come on, I'll show you."

Grace limped toward the huge picture window and pointed down. Sandra Koval moved warily, as if she expected that Grace would push her through it. But that wasn't it. That wasn't it at all.

When Sandra Koval looked down, a small gasp escaped her lips. On the sidewalk below them, pacing like two lions, were Carl Vespa and Cram. Grace turned away and started for the door.

"Where are you going?" Sandra asked.

"Oh," Grace said. She wrote something down on a piece of paper. "This is Captain Perlmutter's phone number. You have your choice. You can call and leave with him. Or you can take your chances with the sidewalk."

She put the piece of paper on the conference table. And then, without looking back, Grace left the room.

EPILOGUE

$\int$ andra Koval chose to call Captain Stuart Perlmutter. She then law-
yered up. Hester Crimstein, the legend herself, was going to represent her. It would be a tough case to make, but the DA thought, because
of certain developments, that he could do it.

One of those developments was the return of Allaw's redheaded
member, Sheila Lambert. When Sheila read about the arrest—and the
media appeal for her help—she came forward. The man who shot her
husband fit the description of the man who threatened Grace at the supermarket. His name was Martin Brayboy. He'd been caught and had
agreed to testify for the prosecution.

Sheila Lambert also told prosecutors that Shane Alworth had been
at the concert that night but that he had decided at the last minute not
to go backstage and confront Jimmy X. Sheila Lambert wasn't sure why
he'd changed his mind, but she speculated that Shane realized John
Lawson was too high, too wired, too willing to snap.

Grace was supposed to find comfort in that, but she was not sure she
did.

Captain Stuart Perlmutter had hooked up with Scott Duncan's old
boss, Linda Morgan, the U.S. attorney. They managed to turn one of the
men from Carl Vespa's inner circle. Rumor had it they'd be arresting
him soon, though it would be hard to nail him on Jimmy X's murder.

Cram called Grace one afternoon. He told her Vespa wasn't fighting back. He stayed in bed a lot. "It's like watching a slow death," he told her. She didn't really want to hear it.

Charlaine Swain brought Mike home from the hospital. They returned to their regularly scheduled lives. Mike is back at work. They watch TV together now instead of in separate rooms. Mike still falls asleep early. They've upped their lovemaking somewhat, but it's all too self-conscious. Charlaine and Grace have become close friends. Charlaine never complains but Grace can see the desperation. Something, Grace knows, will soon give.

Freddy Sykes is still recuperating. He put his house up for sale and is buying a condo in Fair Lawn, New Jersey.

Cora remained Cora. Enough said on that subject.

Evelyn and Paul Alworth, Jack's—or in this case, she should say, Shane's—mother and brother, have also come forward. Over the years Jack had used the trust money to pay for Paul's schooling. When he started working with Pentocol Pharmaceuticals, Jack moved his mother into that condominium development so they could be closer. They had lunch together at the condo at least once a week. Both Evelyn and Paul wanted very much to be a part of the children's lives—they were, after all, Emma and Max's grandmother and uncle—but they understood that it would be best to take it slow.

As for Emma and Max, they handled the tragedy in very different ways.

Max likes to talk about his father. He wants to know where Daddy is, what heaven is like, if Daddy really sees them. He wants to be assured that his father can still observe the key events of his young life. Grace tries to answer him the best she can—tries to sell it, as it were—but her words have the stilted hollow of the dubious. Max wants Grace to make up "Jenny Jenkins" rhymes with him in the tub, like Jack used to do, and when she does, Max laughs and he sounds so much like his father that Grace thinks her heart might explode right then and there.

Emma, her father's princess, never talks about Jack. She does not ask questions. She does not look at photographs or reminisce. Grace tries to facilitate her daughter's needs, but she is never sure what approach to take. Psychiatrists talk about opening up. Grace, who has suffered her share of tragedies, is not so sure. There is, she's learned, something to be said for denial, for severing and compartmentalizing.

Strangely enough, Emma seems happy. She's doing well in school. She has lots of friends. But Grace knows better. Emma never writes poetry anymore. She won't even look at her journal. She insists now on sleeping with her door shut. Grace stands outside her daughter's bedroom at night, often very late, and sometimes she thinks she hears soft sobs. In the morning, after Emma goes to school, Grace checks her daughter's room.

Her pillow is always wet.

People naturally assume that if Jack were still alive, Grace would have a lot of questions for him. That's true, but she no longer cares about the details of what a stoned, scared kid of twenty did in the face of that devastation and aftermath. In hindsight he should have told her. But then again suppose he had? Suppose Jack had told her right in the beginning? Or a month into their relationship? A year? How would she have reacted? Would she have stayed? She thinks about Emma and Max, about the simple fact that they are here, and the road untraveled brings a shiver.

So, late at night, when Grace lies alone in their too-large bed and talks to Jack, feeling very strange because, really, she doesn't believe he's listening, her questions are more basic: Max wants to sign up for the Kasselton traveling soccer team, but isn't he too young for that kind of commitment? The school wants to put Emma in an accelerated English program, but will that put too much pressure on her? Should we still go to Disney World in February, without you, or will that be too painful a reminder? And what, Jack, should I do about those damn tears on Emma's pillow?

Questions like that.

Scott Duncan came by a week after Sandra's arrest. When she opened the door, he said, "I found something."

"What?"

"This was in Geri's stuff," Duncan said.

He handed her a beat-up cassette. There was no label on it but faintly, in black ink, someone had written: ALLAW.

They moved silently into the den. Grace stuck the cassette in her player and pressed the PLAY button.

"Invisible Ink" was the third song.

There were similarities to "Pale Ink." Would a court of law have found Jimmy guilty of plagiarism? It would be a close call, but Grace figured that the answer, after all these years, was probably no. There were plenty of songs that sounded alike. There was also a fine line between influence and plagiarism. "Pale Ink," it seemed to her, probably straddled that blurry line.

So much that went wrong did—straddled a blurry line, that is.

"Scott?"

He did not turn toward her.

"Don't you think it's time we cleared the air?"

He nodded slowly.

She was not sure how to put this. "When you found out your sister was murdered, you investigated with a passion. You left your job. You went all out."

"Yes."

"It wouldn't have been hard to find out she had an old boyfriend."

"Not hard at all," Duncan agreed.

"And you would have found out that his name was Shane Alworth."

"I knew about Shane before all this. They dated for six months. But I thought Geri had died in a fire. There was no reason to follow up with him."

"Right. But recently, after you talked to Monte Scanlon, you did."

"Yes," he said. "It was the first thing I did."

"You learned that he'd disappeared right around the time of your sister's murder."

382 · HARLAN COBEN

"Right."

"And that made you suspicious."

"To put it mildly."

"You probably, I don't know, checked his old college records, his old high school records even. You talked to his mom. It wouldn't have taken much. Not when you're looking for it."

Scott Duncan nodded.

"So you knew, before we even met, that Jack was Shane Alworth."

"Yes," he said. "I knew."

"You suspected him of killing your sister?"

Duncan smiled, but there was no joy in it. "A man is dating your sister. He breaks up with her. She's murdered. He changes identity and disappears for fifteen years." He shrugged. "What would you think?"

Grace nodded. "You told me you like to shake the cages. That was the way to make progress in a case."

"Right."

"And you knew that you couldn't just ask Jack about your sister. You had nothing on him."

"Right again."

"So," she said, "you shook the cage."

Silence.

"I checked with Josh at the Fotomat," Grace said.

"Ah. How much did you pay him? A thousand dollars?"

Duncan snorted. "I only paid him five hundred."

"To put that picture in my envelope."

"Yes."

The song changed. Allaw was now singing a song about voices and wind. Their sound was raw, but there was potential there too.

"You cast suspicion on Cora to distract me from pressuring Josh."

"Yes."

"You insisted I go with you to see Mrs. Alworth. You wanted to see her reaction when she saw her grandchildren."

"More cage shaking," he agreed. "Did you see the look in her eyes when she saw Emma and Max?"

She had. She just hadn't known what it meant or why she'd ended up living in a condo right on Jack's route to work. Now, of course, she did. "And because you were forced to take a leave, you couldn't use the FBI for surveillance. So you hired a private detective, the one who used Rocky Conwell. And you put that camera in our house. If you were going to shake the cage, you'd need to see how your suspect would react."

"All true."

She thought of the end result. "A lot of people died because of what you did."

"I was investigating my sister's murder. You can't expect me to apologize for that."

Blame, she thought again. So much of it to go around. "You could have told me."

"No. No, Grace, I could never trust you."

"You said our alliance was temporary."

He looked at her. There was something dark there now. "That," he said, "was a lie. We never had an alliance."

She sat up and turned the music down.

"You don't remember the massacre, do you, Grace?"

"That's not uncommon," she said. "It's not amnesia or anything like that. I was hit so hard in the head I was in a coma."

"Head trauma," he said with a nod. "I know all about it. I've seen it in lots of cases. The Central Park jogger, for one. Most cases, like yours, you don't even remember the days before it."

"So?"

"So how did you get into the front pit that night?"

The question, coming out of nowhere like that, made her sit up. She searched his face for a clue. There was none. "What?"

"Ryan Vespa, well, his father scalped the ticket for four hundred bucks. The members of Allaw got them from Jimmy himself. The only

384 · HARLAN COBEN

way to get up there was to shell out a ton of dough or know someone."
He leaned forward. "How did you get into that front pit, Grace?"

"My boyfriend got tickets."

"That would be Todd Woodcroft? The one who never visited you at the hospital?"

"Yes."

"You sure about that? Because before you said you don't remember."
She opened her mouth and then closed it. He leaned closer.

"Grace, I talked to Todd Woodcroft. He didn't go to the concert."
Something inside her chest lurched to the side. Her body went cold.

"Todd didn't visit you because you'd broken up with him two days before the show. He thought it'd be weird. And you know what, Grace? Shane Alworth broke up with my sister on that same day. Geri never went to the concert. So who do you think Shane took instead?"

Grace shivered and felt the tremor spread. "I don't understand."

He pulled out the photograph. "This is the original Polaroid I had blown up and put into your envelope. My sister wrote the date on the back. The picture was taken the day before the concert."

She shook her head.

"That mystery woman on the far right, the one we can barely see? You thought it was Sandra Koval. Well, maybe, Grace—just maybe—that's you."

"No . . ."

"And maybe, while we're looking for more people to blame, maybe we should wonder about the pretty girl who distracted Gordon Mac-Kenzie so the others could get to Jimmy X. We know it wasn't my sister or Sheila Lambert or Sandra Koval."

Grace kept shaking her head, but then she flashed back to that day at the beach, the first time she laid eyes on Jack, that feeling, that instant grab of the gut. Where had that come from? It was the kind of thing you feel . . .

. . . when you've met someone before.

The strangest sort of déjà vu. The kind where you've already connected with someone, gotten that first head rush of infatuation. You hold hands, and when the turmoil begins, there's that stomach-dropping feeling of his hand slipping from yours. . . .

"No," Grace said, more firmly now. "You got it wrong. It can't be. I'd have remembered that."

Scott Duncan nodded. "You're probably right."

He stood and popped the cassette out of the machine. He handed it to her. "This is all just crazy conjecture. I mean, for all we know, maybe that mystery woman was the reason Shane didn't go backstage. Maybe she talked him out of it. Or maybe he realized that there was something more important right there, in that front pit, than anything he could find in a song. Maybe, even three years later, he made sure he found it again."

Scott Duncan left then. Grace stood and headed into her studio. She had not painted since Jack's death. She put the cassette into her portable player and pressed the PLAY button.

She picked up a brush and tried to paint. She wanted to paint him. She wanted to paint Jack—not John, not Shane. Jack. She thought it would come out muddled and confused, but that wasn't what happened at all. The brush soared and danced across the canvas. She started thinking again about how we can never know everything about our loved ones. And maybe, if you think about it hard, we don't even know everything about ourselves.

The cassette ended. She rewound it and started it again. She worked in a delirious and delightful frenzy. Tears ran down her cheeks. She did not brush them away. At some point she glanced at a clock. Soon it would be time to stop. School would be letting out. She had to get the kids. Emma had piano today. Max had traveling-team soccer practice.

Grace grabbed her purse and locked the door behind her.

Photo by Béatrice le Grand

Harlan Coben is the bestselling author of numerous novels, including the #1 *New York Times* bestsellers *Caught*, *Long Lost*, and *Hold Tight*. Winner of the Edgar Award®, the Shamus Award, and the Anthony Award, Coben lives in New Jersey with his family. Visit his Web site at www.harlancoben.com.